Mission Code
Revival

Mission Code Revival

Death Bringer
Book II
Zodiac Universum Series

Adrianna Biełowiec

MISSION CODE REVIVAL
BY ADRIANNA BIEŁOWIEC

***

ALL MATERIAL CONTAINED HEREIN IS COPYRIGHT
COPYRIGHT © ADRIANNA BIEŁOWIEC, 2022

***

ORIGINALLY PUBLISHED IN POLISH AS MISJA ODRODZENIE
TRANSLATED AND PUBLISHED IN ENGLISH WITH PERMISSION.

***

PAPERBACK ISBN: 979-8-9869299-6-5
EPUB ISBN: 979-8-2016949-1-3

***

WRITTEN BY ADRIANNA BIEŁOWIEC
PUBLISHED BY ROYAL HAWAIIAN PRESS
COVER ART BY TYRONE ROSHANTHA
TRANSLATED BY SZYMON NOWAK
PUBLISHING ASSISTANCE BY DOROTA RESZKE

***

FOR MORE WORKS BY THIS AUTHOR, PLEASE VISIT:
WWW.ROYALHAWAIIANPRESS.COM

***

You're going to fight
With that pathetic body
Brittle biometal
Which won't stop a shot
Better become our servant
Before you finally run foul of the better

Diarduk over the tissue
Moss over the organics
What is broken you can fix it
What is lost - you will regain it soon
Kunhikar means eternity
Time won't cut our hearts
We are kings among species
Executioners and gentlemen for centuries
Connected by the upper collectivity.

Kandrok War Song

Table of Contents

The year 2955

During the first days in K'otz'ib'aja, Alejandro Cortez was most afraid of losing his job in a team of qualified geneticists. The causes of anxiety were typical of most young people starting their serious careers: that despite his best effort, he would trip up and bungle the job, or become a victim of the intrigue of a colleague who disliked him. There was also an immortal like the Kiritians, though unwritten, Murphy's law, assuming that when a man finally succeeds in something and it revives a glimmer of hope in them, it will immediately take a nosedive. For Cortez, it would mean a return to unemployment, or so he believed. In the Kiritian nation, it was said that every citizen was needed and worked in a profession suited to their psychophysical characteristics, but for Cortez, originally from the low social class of the planet Calvary (known as the Land of the Gangsters), it was hard to believe at first. He remembered all too well the words of the Oderses, persons who weren't Kiritians, who had said a lot of negative things about them.

From the University of Genetics and Bioengineering on Mars, Andro graduated with honors. He even received a scholarship, but as a graduate, for many years he couldn't find a job related to the field of study. He took regrettable jobs just to have a handful of uinals to live on. He didn't understand why this was happening. He met all the recruitment requirements for the positions he applied for. However, the attempt to start a career always followed a fixed pattern: Andro wasted time and funds on interplanetary travels and live talks, then waited weeks for the promised contact with the employer, which never happened. "Thank you for the conversation, we will contact you after we interview the rest of the candidates, no matter we want to hire you or not." Apparently, recruitment processes had been the same for millennia - they lacked logic and respect for job seekers.

In the end, however, there had to be a mathematical counterbalance in the form of due success. And a great one! For the position offered to Cortez, any Oder was secretly ready to kill, but only the chosen ones with certain qualities were honored with a complete change in their lives.

And Andro had these qualities.

He couldn't snap out of shock for a long time after he learned that he had been admitted to the medical sector in the capital of the Immortals itself. It was like getting to the summit of Olympus Mons when you have walked your whole life over the hills the height of a house. You have climbed low peaks only to stumble and shamefully roll off the slope every time. And suddenly you got something like this! Applying for a job with the Kiritians, Andro found getting it less likely than seeing a frozen star. He even laughed at himself for having a good sense of humor trying to get into such a league. And here you are - life can surprise you. Forkis himself hired him on the top science team at the Zodiac Universum, while mediocre eggheads from mediocre planets had refused his candidacy. There could be no mistake. The First Galactic Dignitary was familiar with humans because, as a telepath, he could read minds. Some believed that his gaze pierced the soul. Otherwise, he wouldn't have created the homogeneous society and raised the Kiritian to the pinnacle of power. Forkis, in the course of group or individual recruitment, accepted people who were utterly devoted and loyal, and sent away anyone who raised even a shadow of doubts in him. The latter sometimes didn't return home, but in unexplained circumstances disappeared somewhere in the cold, empty depths of space. Therefore, a few decades after Forkis came to power, no spy or traitor applied for a position with the Immortals.

Like any new member of the Kiritian community, Alejandro had the right to choose when he wanted to become infected with the super virus. He didn't have to make a decision hastily; he could do it in a week or two decades. So his thoughts were completely absorbed by the aspect of acclimatization to the new environment.

Kiritians ...

He would be working among the Kiritians on the planet Morascrik!

And recently he had been worried about with what he would pay the bills. With a little embarrassment, he realized that the morality of the Immortals was irrelevant to him. Rather, they weren't monsters that rebels incapable of catching up with them militarily and socially, believed them to be. There was no tagging among Kiritians, an achij as an individual was as important as a battalion, because any unit could induce the butterfly effect. How differently they were presented by

Oderses, which had nothing to do with them, driven by the propaganda of beaten rebels.

Working in a new job exceeded all expectations of the young geneticist: the latest technology, no environmental factors harmful to health, convenient working hours, trouble-free breaks, meals tailored to the biological and cultural needs of the consumer, advanced healthcare, nice company. A private apartment.

The idyll couldn't, however, last forever.

One morning, Cortez was surprised to find out that damned Sariel Jelinek also worked in the same building. He hadn't seen him before, because Sariel had temporarily been in the other hemisphere. Before the colonization of the planets, one could have said, "it's a small world", but the aphorism could have been successfully applied to the Zodiac Universum. Fawn (as he nicknamed him) had become Cortez's number one enemy during his studies on Mars, and the igniting spark that had set fire to the electrified space between them was Marianna, the former object of their sighs, now Jelinek's wife. He had also hated Sariel for receiving a scholarship three times his own, not for honest work, but for ass-licking and cheating. The icing on the cake of humiliation was a fight in a bar on the orbital station, where Sariel had knocked out Alejandro. His pride had been hurt, his ego had deteriorated, but Cortez had consoled himself with the thought that after completing his studies, he most likely wouldn't see him again.

However, it came out as usual.

Cortez worked in the genetics department of K'otz'ib'aja, Sariel had had a first aid medicaments room under the auspices for several months. In practice, this meant that they could see each other in the corridor several times a day. They happened to exchange a few sentences with each other. The first conversation developed as a result of the mature people's surprise that their paths had crossed again, and there were no juvenile episodes. The second ended in an argument and it concerned Marianna. In the third, Sariel accused Andro of stealing a box of bionanites from a medical emergency room. Days passed and it wasn't found. Cortez became the prime suspect, because only him was seen near the container at the unlucky hour. The Kiritians didn't use monitoring or any other form of surveillance of their own citizens because of complete trust. The method worked, there were rarely minor incidents like that now with Andro, who couldn't prove his innocence, and so far, no one wanted to use the truth serum. Informing Forkis was completely out of the question.

"On the other hand, the lack of vision is conducive to revenge," Andro thought as he sipped his fourth beer in the canteen. He smiled at the heavenly liquid at the bottom of the mug. If he played everything out well, he would take Jelinek down for good.

Every Kiritian had access to tall first aid buildings. Andro knew one of these objects very well, connected with the research institution where he worked. More than once, he used it when he needed something for a hangover, bionanites or molecular glue to instantly close minor wounds. That is why he knew where, when and how many employees he could meet.

There should have been three people in the sector that night, each on a different level. After leaving the canteen at a slow pace and tweaking the plan, Cortez entered the science section building and walked down the maze of darkened corridors towards the room where Sariel worked during the day. The Kiritians hadn't fought any war in decades and were rarely sick, so there was a slim chance that someone would suddenly come in for help. A level warden, Andro didn't notice either. He supposed that, to pass the night, he had gone to the other floor to chat with his friend.

His idea was infantile, but in a state of intoxication, it seemed funny: he would swap around some medications, but within reason, so as not to harm anyone. That should have been enough for Sariel to be punished.

He entered the medical room when a transparent, automatically sliding door opened. The temperature difference between the warmer hallway and the cool office, coupled with the alcohol in his blood, the smells of drugs and chemicals made him dizzy. Leaning against the wall, he stared at trauma capsules, shelves full of specifics, egg-shaped refrigerators, vials immersed in tanks and cupboards marked with symbols.

"Hi, pretty girls." Having moved to the armored glass case, he grinned at dhurnsteel bottles shrouded in misty gas. He noticed that many preparations looked the same, and that their belonging to a given class was determined by an incomprehensible order, not by code or label.

He set to 'work'. He opened the door, emptied the containers and exchanged their contents. Having dealt with the cupboard, he crouched down and moved on to the next one. A burp took the sardonic smile off his face.

"You'll be in for it, Fawn. There is not enough space here for both of us."

He didn't notice an arm of a disabled robot and as he stood up, he slammed his shoulder against the gripper. He panicked, thinking he had collided with someone who had silently approached him from behind. He lost his balance and fell to the floor along with the machine, knocking over several cylindrical containers. Their contents covered him like a swarm of white worms. Cortez closed his eyes, grimaced, and curled up like an embryo, waiting out the metallic clamor as if the entire building had been collapsing on his head. When all fell silent, he tried to get up, but put his foot on a rolling object and chucked himself down.

He lay beside the robot for a moment, sprawled like a marionette with cut strings, and groaned, sore.

"Connor's ass ..." His head started throbbing exactly like it would in the morning due to hangover, unless he took something to remove the alcohol from his blood.

Finally, he got up. He froze as he listened.

Seconds full of tension passed. He exhaled the air accumulated in his lungs. He was very lucky that no one heard the noise - or someone was yet to come here. So, there was little time.

He looked at his handiwork and wrung his hands.

"Just lovely."

Having put the robot to its feet arduously, he knelt and began to anyhow load the capsules into the containers by handful, so as to quickly bring the room back to its - roughly - original state. Every now and then he looked nervously towards the door.

"Gne... um... orium B1, gneumorium B2, protoson F4, inhibi... spermato A2. Andro read the few markings on the containers. "What the hell is that? Not my level of initiation.

Spermato... is it sperm? In the first aid section? Hey, I don't think it's Fawn's office. Damn it ... shit ... all the cubbyholes around look the same ..."

Despite his numbness, he felt more and more nervous. He was a young geneticist, not a first aid doctor, had just started working with the Immortals, so he didn't know three-quarters of the medications in the room. What consequences would he experience if he had destroyed something expensive and rare? Kiritians were famous for good health due to immediate medical assistance and easy elimination of all cataloged diseases, but sometimes it might have meant that a patient constantly took a drug. What if he had just deprived someone of a drug that had taken a long time to produce?

Arranging the last containers with trembling hands, he heard the characteristic clatter of military boots down the corridor. Two people had a nervous dialogue, the meaning of the words was suppressed by still a considerable distance.

Going on all fours, Cortez climbed behind crates from the last shipment, set in the darkened corner. He could feel his heart beating loud and hard like an alarm siren; noises from his chest could have drawn the Kiritians straight to his makeshift hiding place. At least the office didn't look as if after a vial battle anymore.

The door opened with a soft clash. Someone walked heavily inside.

"I don't understand what these secrets are for, Fork," said a slightly irritated male voice.

Fork ...

Andro paled as if he had been about to pass out. Icy sweat appeared on his forehead and back, and heat overwhelmed the rest of his body, as if the blood had turned to boiling water, creating a sobering mixture. Only one person's name in K'otz'ibaja started with 'Fork'. Xajb'a Kej. Forkis. Emperor. First Galactic Dignitary. "You've gotten in big trouble, you drunk idiot," he thought in panic as he struggled with his breath to maintain a void silence.

His assumptions were confirmed when he heard an answer in a characteristic baritone:

"How many times do I have to say there's nothing to talk about, Necron?"

Forkis and Kiret 'Necron' Biffter. Kiritian Number One and Kiritian Number Two. The boss and his deputy. Usurper and lictor, but friends at the same time. It couldn't be worse! By a cough that didn't sound like Forkis' or Necron's, Cortez could tell that there was another person in the room, possibly a level medic.

"It's not a crime that predators are kept in the apartment," said Kiret wittily. Jokes weren't his forte, and if anyone laughed at them, it was just out of courtesy. "If you only knew, boss, what people can smuggle." He laughed to lighten the situation, and when that didn't work, he added seriously, "I just don't get it. You got scratched by the stupid furball, and you panic as if it was infected with some new virus that will wipe out all Morascrik overnight. There is currently no pathogen in the Zodiac Universum that the Kiritians couldn't deal with in an hour."

Forkis sighed nervously.

"I already told you I don't have any cat! Give me a break at last, man!"

"So where did this come from? Did you scratch yourself? Forgive me, but I've been alive for hundreds of years, and I think I can recognize claw wounds."

"Great, but why the heavy stars are you prompting?" Forkis snapped.

"Well, as you want, I'm shutting up now," Biffter said peaceably. His light armor clanked as he raised his arms, parodying a gesture of surrender.

"Someone's messed up quite a bit, nothing is evenly aligned," the medic muttered. "I will talk in the morning with an achij working on the last shift."

Andro heard a disturbing noise - rummaging in one of the ill-fated ampoule cylinders. Until now, he had been staring at the number of the nearest box, with his face pressed against it, and relying on his hearing, so he couldn't see a puronax cover to the right. As his aching neck forced him to turn his head, he saw the reflection of Biffter, Forkis, and the level medic injecting something into the Emperor's arm pulled out of the bracer.

"Last time when I was given gneumorium bionanites, it was prickling like injecting acid. Now I don't feel anything," commented Forkis.

"You have an exceptionally strong body," the medic pointed out. "I'm betting on cellular memory. I have already had cases where people who have been given regenerative nanites several times have finally stopped feeling the effects of letting them into the bloodstream. In any case, the wound will heal faster than with molecular glue. Personally, I prefer nanobots to stem cell modifier slime.

"Thank you." Forkis stood up and rubbed the slightly stinging injection site. He put on the bracer and turned to Kiret,

"Satisfied? Let's go to your questioning before Gareth torments the prisoner to death."

The men exchanged a few more sentences and left soon. Motionless, Andro felt as if he hadn't been breathing the entire time they had been in the room. His lungs stung, his skull hummed, but at least a blissful silence returned. He realized with concern how lucky he was. If he had been discovered, the emperor would have read his thoughts; the finale of the idiot idea would have been obvious.

He waited a moment to be sure he was indeed alone upstairs, then hurried out of the apartment.

Returning to his dwelling, he prayed that his prank wouldn't endanger Forkis' health.

I. Surprising request from Necron

The year 2957

The fragrant tropical air of the planet Chulimal, renamed H14 by humans, had always soothed Q'ualel's nostrils. He associated it with the home, bright past and beneficial influence of forgotten gods. Now, also with stability, although almost everything he loved had been taken by the hands of the first colonists soaked in the blood of the Onkalots. Although his only friend Forkis had died in a terrorist attack many months earlier, in Q'ualel's life returned peace; similar blissfulness covered the entire Zodiac Universum. Aggro didn't wish Forkis death. He wanted him to withdraw from the century-long vengeance, and not to be killed by the bomb by the rebel Beliar Drunkenstein. "At least Forkis has experienced eternal rest," he thought, savoring the rays of the K'ajolom star approaching the zenith, stroking his jaguar fur through the thick tree crowns.

He waited patiently for a cowak with the bow ready to shoot; his paw didn't quiver even on the string. Resembling a cross between an okapi and a farmed cow, the animal had extremely sensitive hearing. John Schindler, to whom Aggro returned after Forkis' death, might have given him a... Kalashnikov, but he preferred to hunt like his ancestors: using primitive tools and neurotoxins, sometimes the body itself. These were methods that were ritualistic in a way, and more exciting than killing with a human weapon shot with 100% accuracy.

A fat, horned animal with striped limbs walked lazily into a small clearing near the pool. It stopped, raised the head, perked up its ears, then bent down to drink the water. Hidden on the windward side, the humanoid jaguar moved its bow noiselessly, the point now aimed under the animal's shoulder, where the heart was beating.

Before Aggro could release the arrow, a machine's monumental silhouette emerged from its stealth mode. Anti-gravity thrust drives put forward shook the entire jungle. Blown away fragments of plants fell on the hunter and his would-be prey.

"By all the gods," commented the Onkalot.

The cowak started to run away surprisingly quickly considering its weight and short paws. Soon it disappeared from view, sinking into the green thicket. The Kiritian ship that significantly decelerated, was headed towards Schindler's farm.

Concerned, Q'ualel was several kilometers away from the jungle, dropped his bow and began racing towards the farm.

***

Aggro reached the hill at the edge of the forest that overlooked several hectares of Schindler lands. Leaning on a tree fern to catch his breath, he looked at the underbelly of the corvette black like obsidian. Undoubtedly, the ship was Kiritian - only the hulls of the Immortal units weren't marked, which was supposed to make it difficult for enemies to define the hierarchy of the machines during battles.

The corvette settled down, causing severe swirls of heavy hot air. Many of the trees were turned into splinters because, at a hundred meters in length, it didn't fit in the area John used for the agricultural transporter landing site.

By the time Aggro made his way to the nose, the crew had time to step out from the opposite side of the corvette. Several Kiritians stood near the open airlock. One of them had a fragmentary helmet slid down above his neck - the man's baldness at once struck the eye - and he was talking to Schindler, holding an energy rifle with the barrel lowered to the ground. It looked comical. Like any sane farmer in the wilderness, John did not go out to strangers with his bare hands, but the weapon with the power of a hoe directed against the star was unlikely to impress the Immortals. Behind the host's back, his son Darius was wandering as barefoot over hot coals; Eredal and his mother stood on the terrace and anxiously waited for the further course of events. Previous concerns left the Kiritian. The behavior of the Kiritians showed no ill intentions, but it was still hard to guess why they had come here.

"Aggro!" Eredal started heading towards the humanoid jaguar. Her exclamation attracted everyone's attention. She cuddled in his fur. Q'ualel could feel the intense pounding of her heart clearly, and even more strongly the magnolia scent of her hair washed with homemade shampoo.

"What's happening?" He asked.

The girl withdrew her hands.

"I thought you would tell me this. The First Galactic Dignitary has come to you. He's the bald guy," she added with pious fear. There was indeed Kiret 'Necron' Biffter by the corvette's ramp, which Aggro hadn't associated before, too confused to pay attention to the details of the newcomers' appearance. In addition, he didn't remember well the face of the new emperor, wearing unmarked armor like everyone else. It was undoubtedly weird that the highest head of the Immortals had taken the trouble and flown to Chulimal. Apparently, Necron, just like Xajb'a Kej, preferred to settle some matters personally, rather than send his subordinates. It also reflected well on him that he had no hesitation in dealing with the lower social strata, as now talking freely with the Schindlers.

"Q'ualel," said Kiret, smiling slightly. They greeted each other, squeezing each other's forearms as Aggro approached. "Good to see you again."

"Same to you, First Galactic Dignitary. Although I must admit that you have surprised me with this visit, not to say - you've terrified me."

Kiret grew serious.

"I'd like to talk privately."

If the Schindlers had been visited by someone with less prerogatives, Aggro would have insisted on talking in front of the foster, apolitical family, because he had no secrets from them. However, the highest head in the universes was at stake, and the serious expression on the man's face made it clear that he would have rather argued without witnesses. The Onkalot looked back at John. The latter shrugged and headed for the house.

"Kids, come on. Let the gentlemen talk," he called.

Eredal executed her father's command, but only when Aggro nodded his head reassuringly. Worse was the case with twelve-year-old Darius, who, apart from a few commercial forays to orbital bazaars, had spent his whole life on the farm and its surroundings.

"You promised me I would see the ship!" He protested, looking longingly at the magnificent machine and the awesome achijes' armors.

"To be precise, this is a naval craft, not a ship," Kiret corrected brightly. "It has a combat character, but I understand that it is difficult for Oderses to distinguish one from the other, because many of our ships also have combat equipment, just like combat transporters."

"I didn't promise anything like that," the farmer growled. "Stir your stumps, Darius, and run along home! Don't get involved in matters that defeat us, ordinary people."

"It won't be a problem," replied the Emperor. "Let the young one take a look, since he had an opportunity."

"Can I really?" Darius' eyes almost fell out of his skull, he goggled them so much.

"No!" The father growled.

"Sure," Biffter chuckled.

"Sweetheart?" John tried to find support from his wife standing on the terrace. "If it is safe and it really doesn't cause a problem, then why not," she dotted the i's and crossed the t's. "Mr. Biffter is right: this may be the only chance for Darius to see a Kiritian corvette from inside."

Eredal smiled, seeing her brother's simulated dance of joy and her father's expression full of amazement; the corner of Aggroteh's lips moved up as well.

"I knew, darling, I could count on you," John ground out. "Go, snot." He wanted to push his son, but didn't manage to touch him, because the rapturous boy rushed like fired from a cannon.

"I'll accompany the turd, sir," said at Biffter's ear, grinning Corporal Tsar Seymour, one of achijes traveling with him. He soon disappeared into the hangar with the boy.

"Let's go that way," Aggro suggested to Kiret. "Unless I'm also supposed to board the ship."

"After all these hours of travel, I'm eager to breathe fresh Chulimal air," replied Necron. "My legs will get a little rest with your weaker gravity. The engine-room operator had created too much mass for the corvette from atoplaxal particles."

"So, I invite you to the vantage point, it's not far away." They walked slowly down a hard-packed road between the rectangles of the fields, then followed a path meandering through the tropical vegetation. Kiret looked up at the darkening sky to see the partial eclipse of K'ajolom, called the Parent in Onkalotian; the small rocky planet was just flowing between Chulimal and the life-giving star. The barely visible sickle of one of H14's two moons appeared to the east. The air was filled with the pleasant scent of fresh peat and purple flowers, with names unknown to Biffter, blooming in the fringes of the jungle. He inhaled too deeply and felt dizzy, took a sharp step.

"All right, sir?" Aggro grabbed his arm.

"Don't 'sir' me, you were Forkis' friend," Kiret said with a smile. "You have a different gravity than we do on Morascrik, more oxygen as well. In our place, you can still feel sulfur due to seismic activity and volcanoes. I'm used to such air and now I have to switch to H14 conditions. However, they are not so drastic for my body that I have to wear a breathing mask. Besides, we won't stay here for long."

"Can we talk more informally?"

"That's what I'm counting on. Ask what you want, Aggro."

"How are you doing after assuming power? How is Anna Sandstorm?" It didn't escape his notice that there was a fleeting confusion in Kiret's face and eyes. The Emperor thought before he replied:

"I'm coping somehow. Sandstorm is healthy, still on the Council of Five. She wanted to come here instead of me, I persuaded her for a long time to stay in K'otz'ib'aja, because the task must be approached ... less emotionally. I'll explain everything to you in a moment. Tell me, are you interested in the political situation at the Zodiac Universum, or you have decided to return to the calm life in ignorance?"

"I'm interested in politics only so much to know if Chulimal is in any danger. Unlike Forkis, I'm the type of Onkalot who appreciates peace. Why are you asking me about these things? I noticed your consternation when I asked about the widow Sandstorm."

They came to a stone gazebo entwined with vegetation, raised in front of a cliff's edge. The resting was protected from the heat of K'ajolom by a shed with an octagonal roof. An additional shadow was provided by a cluster of slanted palm trees. Behind a railing there was a view of the jungle carpet, bounded on the east by a wall of high rocks, and on the west by a river of turquoise color.

Kiret tapped his gloved fingers on lanterns that were inactive during the day, then turned his back to Aggroteh and leaned against the railing. He stared for a moment at the canopy of distant trees and listened to the screams of the birds before speaking:

"Kiritians are known for their truthfulness, so I will tell you clearly and simply what the case looks like. You are a politically and socially neutral person, so you won't do anything with the information you are about to hear, and you must hear it if you want to understand the meaning of our intentions. It's bad." Necron turned around and directed his worried face towards the interlocutor. "The Kiritian army is falling apart before my eyes. Forkis had big possibilities, carrying a living artifact of the Ancient Onkalots, or whatever they were called, whose technology is still incomprehensible to us. He also had telepathy familiar to you. Thanks to this, for centuries there were no traitors among the Immortals, and each of our achijes was one hundred percent honest, fearing rejection and even the death penalty. However, it wasn't fear that held society together, but more the cult and splendor of the individual. The Kiritians are humans, however, and every human has insubordination in their genes that comes to the fore when not controlled enough." He crumbled a piece of bark. "Sometimes it is enough to loosen the noose around the neck and even the most perfect system starts to fall apart like a dry sandcastle. Heavy star, I'm starting to talk like a dictator." He began to walk from left to right; the dry leaves that covered the basalt floor creaked. "When I relinquished my post of governor under succession to the First Galactic Dignitary, I thought I could follow in Forkis' footsteps and continue his policy." He stopped in front of the humanoid jaguar, shook his head, looking into his hazel red eyes. "But I'm not Forkis, Aggro. I'm a poor epigone. I have different ideas, different weaknesses, a different personality. It was he who became an icon, got overgrown by legend, not me. I was just his right hand, a lictor, a sidekick, as some people said secretly. I don't have his charisma or anything to keep the Kiritian unchanged. Traitors break into our ranks, it can be anyone newly incorporated into the army. The infiltration systems don't work as smoothly as Forkis' innate ability. Even after scanning the candidate's brains, we wouldn't be 100% certain that we don't deal with an infiltrator or a second Beliar Drunkenstein. But there's more to it than unsure achijes. Recently, there has been a rupture between those who want to see me on the K'otz'ib'aja throne and opponents who believe that I'm a shallow leader of the nation. One planet has already detached itself from the alliance and it is possible that others will follow suit. The old Kiritian power politics is no longer being used, so I won't crack down bloodily on those who want to live by their own rules. Many resent me for that, with General Warfighter at the helm. After Forkis' death, the councilors began to argue with each other about everything that happened at the meetings. Every hearing is a mess now. Coming back to Anna Sandstorm. She has kept her position only because of me, as who is on the Council depends on me, and I've had no reason to remove the former oppositionist from it. She is smart and energetic, but her past has become a problem. The rest of the councilors consider her a traitor who has abandoned her people, and believe that she can do the same to the Kiritians at any time. Forkis was in full control of Anna. He gave her power not because she was his toy, but he had calculated everything while on the planet Aj. The Nephrid rebels have officially ceased to exist, laid down their arms and are now under the auspices of the Kiritians, but when they see that their overseer suffers from the internal disease, they may organize themselves and drive an extra nail into our coffin."

"Indeed, it doesn't sound positive and I feel very sorry for you. But what can I have to do with the collapse of the human empire?"

"Do you remember the golden mouse? That living artifact recreated for you by our former scientist, Maksimus Figam, currently living on planet B9 in the Pisces Universe?"

"Pisces?" Aggro blinked in surprise.

"Yes. But what one ..."

"Now focus, my friend." Kiret spoke more slowly. "Was it exactly the same mouse Forkis had killed in 2511, after he had already used it for his purposes?"

The Onkalot thought for a moment.

"No, just a maple made of remains with the faithfully reproduced properties of the original. You just said it yourself."

"Could you, or any living member of your species, create the same mouse? That is, to resurrect it so that it has the properties of the original, if you had the remains? Ah, that archaic terminology ..."

Aggroteh felt dizzy, which wasn't related to the high oxygenation of the atmosphere. He walked over to a gazebo post and leaned against it. He outthrusted his claws and ran them with a clank over a stone.

"Biffter, you don't want to usurp the powers of the Ancient Onkalots, do you?"

"I'm far from there. Maybe I will put it ... more brutally. Yes, you could say it will sound brutal given the Onkalots' respect for the dead, so you'd better hold on to this pole." The Kiritian managed a short smile, but Aggro didn't share it. "Do you have any knowledge of necromedicine? Speaking in your language, can you raise the dead? By asking for the mouse, I just wanted to direct you to the problem. This was an example."

"What problem? Speak more sensibly."

Kiret clasped his hands behind his back, looked at the ceiling consisting of eight marble triangles, then at the shoe over which went a fur caterpillar, to again fix his eyes on the Onkalot.

"I want to resurrect Forkis. I still have his DNA that you found on Aj, including the DNA we got in K'otz'ib'aja. Recreating a body that matches the original perfectly is not be a problem for Kiritians, but it will be a human body."

The Onkalot didn't listen Necron and walked away from the pole earlier, which he regretted because he almost fell over.

"Most Holy Tonatiuh."

***

Darius had occasionally flown with his father to the orbital station to help him sell and watch him haggle over prices, so he was familiar with the civil transporter. However, as he boarded the Kiritian corvette, he felt as if he had been transferred to another reality. The temperature was much lower than on the planet, so the boy rubbed his shoulders at first, before speechless, he began to move briskly on the board, with Tsar behind his back. The air turned out to be odorless, though it can be said that metal was sensed. It was almost everywhere, from dhurnsteel that made the ship's skeleton to transparent elements but harder than meteorite crystalline coal. Minimalist lamps in rooms and corridors created a composition of lights, giving a dreamlike impression, although some had been turned off after landing. Sterility and cleanliness emanated from every angle. Darius examined every installation or device with undisguised fascination, he was especially amazed at the sight of the engine room, which he entered without permission, having outwalked briefly the corporal.

"Your ship is insane!"

"How is it going? Have you seen enough?" Tsar stopped next to Darius, who was now looking at arsenal cupboards with devout admiration.

The boy raised his hand to touch the cover of a miglight-powered pulse rifle.

Amused, Seymour smiled.

"That bastard would destroy your shack along with the field in a second."

A broken leaf fell out of Darius' pocket. Tsar frowned, leaned over, and picked it up. He sighed with no less enthusiasm than young Schindler at the sight of technological marvels.

"Devil's herb ... Damn, real devil's herb!" He looked at Darius in amazement. "Where did you get this stuff?" The confused boy yanked the remains of the leaf out of his hand and put it in his pocket.

"I've found it. Flatspine is good for wounds."

"For wounds?! Do you know how rare crap it is in the Zodiac Universum, resistant to cultivating? Do you know how much is a gram?! And it has a slightly ... better application than a compress on a cut."

Darius smiled slightly. He took out the dried leaf again and closed it in his fist.

"Do you want it?"

"Sure, come on!" Seymour extended his hand, but the boy withdrew his.

"Not for free."

"Look at that turd. I just showed you the corvette!"

"Because Kiret told you to."

"And he's also foul-mouthed." Tsar put his hands on the hips. "For you, it's Mr. Emperor Biffter, the First Galactic Dignitary. Alright, if you grudge me the devil, show me where it grows, I'll collect it myself."

"It's gone. I collected everything, and I found only one such plant in my life."

"What do you want in return?"

"Hmmm ..." Darius ostentatiously began to look around the room, pretending to think. "This." He pointed to the previously admired pulse rifle.

Tsar spat, waved his hands as if the board had been full of carbon monoxide.

"You must be crazy, sonny. This is a weapon for men, not for crybabies, and you don't need it for anything on the planet."

"There may always be a threat, then I will be prepared. I will help my father defend the family."

"At least you're talking sensibly. But I won't give you this weapon because you don't know how to use it. It's too big to be smuggled out of the corvette and costs a lot of money."

"I guess the Kiritians make it in series, so it's not that expensive."

"It's good that you're familiar with economics. However, we don't produce it in series, because there is no war. Unfortunately, kid, you won't get the rifle."

Darius shrugged.

"No gun, no flatspine. Thanks for the tour." He moved toward the hangar ramp.

"You ... Wait a minute." Seymour caught him in the corridor, looked for other Kiritians nearby. "Maybe you want a bracer?" He pointed to the part of an armor. "You will break any aggressor's jaw if you hit him with it. Moreover, it has such a gadget." Darius flinched and squinted as the dhurnsteel blades slid out of the bracer and loomed right in front of him. "Nice, huh? A little training and stamina, and you will take out any opponent without a ranged weapon. I have also a locator of small organisms underground, it will be useful for growing crops."

"Boredom. I want the gun."

"I'm not gonna convince you to something else?"

"No."

"Goddamn market trader's son."

"Don't insult me, or I'll tell Kiret that you smoke the forbidden herb."

"Gee, careful, I might be fired!" Tsar was starting to like the boy, so he smiled instead of scolding him again for not using the emperor title. He leaned over him. "I will tell you in secret that I'm irreplaceable."

Darius smiled too.

"Then give me the gun."

The Kiritian exhaled long and loudly as he looked at the ceiling.

"I can see that I won't win this fight. Okay. But don't tell anyone, and I know you'll be tempted to show off."

"I won't tell anyone, I swear."

Tsar pushed Darius in the back. They returned to the arsenal.

"We must, however, compromise. I can give you this." He pointed to an X17A4, a self-renewing light ammo gun that was the primary weapon of any achij. "And no negotiations. I can't explain later how the pulse rifle has disappeared. The missing X17A4, however, won't be noticed. We have a fu ... shitload of it."

Darius winced for a moment.

"Well, let it be."

"Do you have a lot of this devil's herb?"

"About fifty grams - my father sometimes makes me measure out that amount of the insecticide to be diluted in water - but I can give only half. It really comes in handy for any cuts."

"Because it's a god, not a plant. Here is your payment." Tsar took the weapon from behind a cover and handed it to Darius, whose eyes almost popped out of his sockets. "Just hide it neatly. And I hope you won't use it to act tough and scare your friends."

"And how does it work?"

"You move the fuse, aim and press the actuator. And that's it. The X17A4 is made of dhursteel, which means you can throw it into an abyss on rocks, and it won't even get scratched. It will also not break down under water. However, you need to keep an eye on the energy bar, because when it reaches zero, you have to put your weapon aside for a few minutes. Therefore, the X17A4 is suitable for basic equipment and emergencies that don't require a longer fire. Do you get it?"

"Yeah. For several years I have been able to use a weapon, my father taught me." Darius hid the pistol under his baggy shirt, tucking it behind his pants belt. "Thanks, Corporal Seymour. When we get out, I'll bring you flatspine leaves in no time."

"Let's agree that you will leave them for me somewhere. I don't want anybody to see you giving me anything. I will say that I'm going to pee or something, and take the hidden package." The Kiritian winked at him.

They agreed that Darius would leave the wrapped dried leaves next to the circle of boulders near the farm where John Schindler burned weeds.

Shortly before the departure of Tsar's corvette, having made sure that no one was paying attention to him, he went to the appointed place. He found the stuff quickly. He looked into a sand-covered linen bag and the satisfaction crawled off his face.

"Let me get that brat ..."

There were only four leaves stuffed inside. He looked around, but as he expected, Darius was nowhere to be found. It amazed him that the turd wasn't afraid to trick the Kiritian.

"Tsar, where have you gotten lost? We're leaving soon," said Sergeant Victor Shane over the communicator.

Sour-faced Seymour had no choice but to go to the naval craft.

***

Aggroteh mentally was grateful to Eredal for bringing them refreshingly cool drinks on a tray right after Kiret's words. The girl was worried to find him concerned, leaning against the railing. She gave Kiret the look of a scared animal, because she was unable to send a different one to the First Galactic Dignitary, for whom she felt awe and whom she feared. She said nothing, dismayed by the closeness of the man wielding such mighty power. Her heart was pounding as if after a run - she wasn't used to guests like this, as well as strangers in general. John would have rather taken Aggro and Darius to the trading stations than her.

"Thank you." Seeing her consternation, Necron managed a warm smile. He took a glass filled with juice squeezed from local fruit. "You don't have to worry about anything, child. We just talk and it'll stop there." He tasted the drink. "Very good. It has a natural taste. Did you do it yourself?"

"With my mom." Eredal calmed down a bit, looked searchingly at Aggroteh.

"Mr. Biffter told the truth, we're just talking." The humanoid jaguar took the tray from her and set it on the table.

"The Rafens have just come," the girl said reluctantly. "The father and sons were scared of the corvette. They wanted to see for themselves what was going on, even though we had sent them a holographic message earlier."

"At least you can talk to Anton."

Eredal gave Q'ualel a dry look and asked very officially:

"Do you gentlemen wish for anything else?"

"There's no such a need. Thanks, sunshine," said Biffter.

"She's an adult woman," Aggro announced as Eredal moved away. "She's twenty-one Terrenic years old. She doesn't like being spoken to as to a child."

Biffter emptied his glass halfway. The girl's arrival allowed him to catch his breath and temporarily postponed the probably embarrassing conversation. He expected that the Onkalot being a traditionalist might have reacted nervously to the mention of breaking the natural order.

"I don't think he likes your neighbors."

Aggro sighed, and also reached for the vessel, which he grabbed with his paws. He played with it, twirling it with his fingers.

"The Rafens' older son, Anton, is seeking her hand, but Eredal has been infatuated with me for several years and I cannot talk her out of these senseless feelings."

"It's rather good. In the sense that Eredal likes you. You're special. Anyway, all girls love furballs." The Kiritian chuckled.

Q'ualel looked at him as at a pitiful person.

"Sorry, I have a rather bad sense of humor." Necron gulped down the rest of the juice and put the glass back. "I don't remember when I lastly drank something fully natural. Months ago, I think, while Forkis was still alive. He went for similar drinks from Chulimal."

"I can provide her with care, company, but we can't ... you know. The genetic distance between Onkalots and humans is over sixty percent, which means, according to human scientists, that our species were once related on a planetary level, but that's still not enough ... that it won't even come to..."

Biffter helped without hesitation:

"Fertilization."

Q'ualel's blush was completely hidden by the cat's fur, which couldn't be said about the embarrassed gaze. Biffter, though he was in supreme authority and had hundreds of years to gain all kinds of experience, still lacked tact and timing. "And it will probably never change," Aggro realized.

"I regret a bit that I went back to the Schindlers," he announced. "But there is my home on Chulimal, I was born here, I didn't want to wander around the forests alone again and live like an animal. Maybe I should be more ruthless and hard-faced, I'd hurt Eredal then, but at least she would start talking to that Anton. I guess."

"You know that hybrid offspring is no problem for Kiritian technology, even with zero genes in common. We could take your reproductive cells and artificially create a little man, an Onkalot, or even the aforementioned hybrid."

"You do have a specific sense of humor, Mr. Biffter. I'm a supporter of the traditions of my ancestors and I don't like to reach for what is divine," Aggro said the last sentence more sharply than he intended. With a loud click, he put the glass back intact, while Necron finished the third, having emptied most of the jug.

The Kiritian frowned.

"I've comprehended the hint. So, I understand that your position regarding the case I asked about earlier is the same?"

"You can't give Forkis his life back."

"Figam can recreate his human body. However, the clone will be soulless."

"In our language it is called atole. The driving force of every living being, like energy in a machine. Atole enters the body before birth when the nervous system is formed, and escapes after the host dies. It is the energy that circulates in the universe like water in the Chulimal lands. Immortal, changeable, multiform." Aggro stared at a palm tree's crown.

"We have many beautiful myths about it."

"And you've just gotten to the bottom of it. We Kiritians are able to keep this atole of yours in a body forever. Although we don't know how it works, as no one has ever understood what consciousness ultimately is, but the biological mechanism works, it is enough to physically immortalize the body. Thanks to this, we have discovered that atole preserved in the body also doesn't age, although it was once believed that at the moment of immortalization of a shell there would be a dissonance between it and the soul, which should have left this shell within a certain unit of time. However, we don't know what happens to the soul after death. No science has discovered this yet, and the answers provided by religions, para-scientists, and philosophers can be put between fairy tales. No offense."

"If I were you, I wouldn't take faith lightly, Necron. Each one contains a piece of truth. Sometimes a huge part."

"I don't take it lightly." Instinctively, he reached for a silver cross around his neck and twisted it with his fingers. "I was a Christian myself and in a sense I'm still it, although my faith has weakened due to many events. However, I don't want to talk to you about theology because firstly, that's not what I'm here for, secondly - we have different views and we will not get along. I just want to know how to recover atole lost from my body. Atols ... Atol. Is this word neuter?"

Suddenly, Aggroteh exploded with anger, pointing with his claw with an extended finger to an unspecified place above the cliff.

"Why do you want to do this?! Forkis is gone. Understood? Dead. What had been supposed to happen, happened. Why play gods and change the course of history?"

Biffter sighed. The matter would be more difficult than he had imagined, and he thought what he was trying to do seemed almost impossible. While making the impossibly crazy plan, he hadn't taken into account his innate passivity and respect for the tradition of the Onkalot. He decided not to owe him and, despite his position, also raised his voice:

"You are so annoyed by this conversation? I'm human, it is in our nature to break all kinds of laws! But I'm not ashamed of it and I don't renounce it. Were it not for the tendency to turn the rules inside out, humanity would still be stuck, if you'll pardon the expression, on your level. Well below the number one on the Kardashov scale. We wouldn't have flown to the stars. We wouldn't have colonized new worlds. We wouldn't have discovered the secret to immortality. If something can be improved, why would a man sit on their hands?"

The Onkalot waved his paw and tail nervously.

"Because you break God's laws! Because you don't improve anything, you only implement your subjective plans! The universe has been perfect!"

"What can someone who would rather stay hidden for most of their life than act, know about breaking the law?"

"If you were one of the last of your kind, you would have done the same. You don't even know how hard it was for me, how lonely I felt. Were it not for the help of god Tonatiuh, I would still be stuck like a savage in the Chulimal forests, sleeping, eating and hunting like my four-legged ancestor." Aggro lowered his voice. "I don't think we will come to an agreement on this matter, because you come from the winners, and I - from the defeated."

Necron brought his hand to his forehead, shook his head in frustration as if he had been arguing with an extremely stubborn child.

"You will probably also tell me that this is not your business with which I come to you, but people's. But it is not so at all. If the current order collapses, the fate of the few remaining Onkalots will also be uncertain." After taking a deep breath, the

Emperor calmed down and continued softly and gently: "After thousands of years of human civilization existence, Forkis was the first to create the perfect and durable system. It was an empire controlled by an army, which in turn was controlled by an admirable unit. I would love to preserve Xajb'a Kej's legacy. You found out for yourself, Q'ualel, that you had wrongly judged your friend, believing that he had been guided only by revenge on the people for the murder of the Onkalots. If only you could help me rebuild his empire ..."

"I have no idea what happened to Forkis' atole," Aggro said tactfully as well, staring at the horizon above the jungle. "Only primeval gods and Ancient Onkalots called Nimja, or the Great House or the Dynasty, knew about things not available to mortals. According to the Nimja myths, they were so powerful and educated that they could control the elements and raise the dead. Only they could help you, but they are gone. We are talking about the ancestors of the Onkalots who disappeared thousands of years ago."

"Became extinct?" Necron brushed off an insect humming at his ear.

"According to myths, they walked away forever, leaving the Chulimal lands for a new generation of Onkalots."

Kiret stood next to Aggroteh, put his hands on the hips, and looked where he did.

"Despite the cooling systems, I'm about to boil in this armor. It's a pity you don't have some local air temperature regulators here."

"They are unnecessary with a small population of Chulimal. Nobody installs them because of the cost. In addition, generations of inhabitants, mainly landowners, have become accustomed to the conditions prevailing on the planet."

Kiret pulled off his protective armor above his waist, remaining in his shirt, and put the elements on a bench. He breathed a sigh of relief.

"I could have done it sooner, since we have the whole area under control. So, you can't help me? Wouldn't you like to get your lost friend back if you could?"

"Admirable game of emotions, Emperor. At most, I could search through known and preserved temples and ancestral libraries, perhaps I could find a manuscript that didn't turn to dust. Either a stone plaque or a relief containing ancient knowledge."

"That would be a beginning already." Kiret smiled. "A terrenic year ago, being a staunch realist and skeptic, I would have laughed at my own request and subjected myself to psychiatric treatment. However, after the adventure with Xajb'a Kej and the living artifact, I became more open to phenomena unexplained by science. I realized that I know little about the universe despite hundreds of years of life, and according to Figam, there are infinitely many of them. My vision of the universe as being governed by the same laws as a microsystem like a planet, turned out to be false. The hermetic principle works, simple microsystems function much like complex, elaborate macrosystems, but they don't explain many phenomena. Thanks anyway, Q'ualel."

"I didn't promise anything. I just said what I could do."

"I respect your views and ... indolence, to put it so ugly. However, I don't want anything from you other than tools that I will use myself. Just give me a fishing rod and I will take care of a catch. So, you will uphold the tradition you respect, and in no way break the laws close to your heart. Maybe let's make an agreement. Soon I will fly to inspect Nephrida, where our beloved rebels live, since I'm already in the Lion Universe. I'll leave a small transporter at the Schindlers' landing field. So, if you decide to cooperate, send me a message from the cockpit in the meantime, according to the code that will be given to you later by the corvette's communications officer. Calmly consider everything I have told you. If you refuse to cooperate, we will come and search the temples anyway, but the help of the guide would be invaluable, otherwise we will surely be straying." Kiret collected the pieces of his armor.

"I agree. I will think about it."

Aggro finished his drink, took the tray, then they both turned back to the farm.

***

Biffter decided to stay on H14 until dusk, he allowed his subordinates to relax in a beautiful, peaceful area. Taking advantage of the opportunity, he bought from delighted John Schindler several tons of food grown using traditional, natural methods, especially famous multi-purpose bulbous onions. Since the Kiritians were not in conflict with the inhabitants of the planet, and the heat turned out to be more severe than on the warmest days on Morascrik, the emperor suggested the achijes that they could get rid of the armor.

To get some exercise, instead of using machines, the Kiritians brought food packed in canvas sacks into the hold. Darius volunteered and worked with them, only dragging weights instead of carrying them on his shoulders. He couldn't see Tsar nearby, but he was ready to bolt silently if he appeared in sight."

"I will join you in a few years," he said with a smile.

"Oh, look! The turd has gone completely mad," grumbled John standing nearby. "The fields will cultivate themselves, when your father grows old?"

Darius shrugged and said to him:

"You can buy farm machinery and androids and laze all day in the glow of the K'ajolom. I would like to travel around the Milky Way and Andromeda, have a powerful weapon and be immortal."

"Powerfully, I'm going to get the nonsense out of that cabbage head right now!" Father raised his hand, but Darius quickly fled out of its reach. Kiret, standing by the hold, laughed.

After the achijes dealt with the goods, Biffter ordered one of the corporals to bring a transporter called the Drunkenstein sphere from the hangar. He remembered the moment when he had seen for the first time on H14 the prototype of the then unknown to Immortals, the opposition's flying machine. Young Anna Sandstorm and her friends had stolen it from Carlos Drunkenstein and by accident they had ended up near the Onkalotian ruins of Ajb'atenaja, where the Kiritians had set up camp. After the Immortals had defeated the rebels in a short, uneven battle for Nephrida, they had gotten the spherical scout design and, after their own modifications, had released a series of inconspicuous transporters, round like billiard balls, but covered with dhurnsteel armor with the appearance of human tissue.

The first stars twinkled in the darkening patch of orange-pink sky as Biffter sat down in the cockpit seat behind the pilots' stations. One of the two lieutenants informed the security squadron stationed in an astro-aircraft carrier in orbit that the corvette was getting ready for flight, then the officers awoke its powerful propulsion. Relaxed, Kiret leaned against the headrest and stared at the puronax canopy that looked like thick glass but was as hard as the solid core of a planet. Plunging into a cloud of sand and dust, the corvette began to take off, but fell to the ground.

"He's crazy," Biffter heard the biting word from the pilot to the left.

"Is something wrong with the engines, Lieutenant Aurelius?"

"No, sir. All is normal. Please have a look." Aurelius zoomed in on an image of one of the cellulas monitoring the hull.

Kiret saw Aggroteh waving his paws before the machine nose.

"It looks like I won't have to wait too long for an answer."

II. The unexpected discovery of Tsar

Kiret returned to H14 a week later. Because of his prerogatives, he could send a search party to Aggroteh, but he was very curious about the ancient Onkalotian temples. That's why he personally appeared on the planet, along with a team of achijes and researchers-oderses. Due to rebel riots during the reign of Forkis, the exploration of Chulimal had been postponed indefinitely, but now that the defeated opposition was under Kiritians' control, they could calmly take a look at the Onkalots' culture destroyed by the colonists.

Several small ships landed on a terrain free from vegetation, where natural disasters or human activity had led to a strong acidification of the soil in an area of many hectares. Before they left the machines, the search party had gathered in the briefing room on Biffter's corvette, where Aggroteh was given the floor.

"Even though I grew up on this planet, I don't know many temples," he said as he wandered around a presentation table, watched by the achijes and three scientists. "Just like an inhabitant of a huge city doesn't know all its streets. Several objects of interest to you were destroyed during Chulimal terraforming, others were consumed by time. So, we will limit our search to five sanctuaries that are the treasury of Nimja's knowledge, where we can come across the information we need." Projections of selected objects began to appear above the table. The images came from the earlier mapping of the indicated areas by drones.

"This is Tukumb'akam, the Temple of the Monster which, at the behest of the gods, destroyed the first, weak and ungrateful generation of Onkalots ..."

"Forgive me for interrupting," said an Indian archeologist who specialized in an ancient Mesoamerican culture similar to the Onkalotian one. "Isn't it about Tukumb'alam, or the Tugging Jaguar?"

The long time spent with people contributed to Aggro's having a good command of many of their languages, as well as knowing very well aspects of human knowledge. Therefore, he had no problem answering the question regarding the related but different cultures:

"In our language, jaguar is b'akam, in this case the word is used figuratively and refers to a Beast or Monster. A jaguar itself as an animal is a predator coming from stars, related to Onkalots, just as humans are related to apes. We also use the language of Quiché, which is divided into regionalisms. It's obvious: tribal migration and the creation of new societies in city-states. Thus, the speech which my ancestors were taught by Nimja which came from the stars was tribally deformed."

"Thanks for the clarification. As far as I know from the Onkalotian myths, Nimja members were travelers. They mastered the ability to travel between star systems thanks to a web of technolithic porters or devices of this kind - for lack of terminology, let me call them that. They conducted experiments on organisms encountered on inhabited globes, transferred animals from planet to planet. They also visited Earth and taught certain Central American populations the Quiché language that they themselves spoke. The same language was used by the later classical Onkalots, as we have defined you. Thus, the linguistic differences also result from the fact that the peoples of Mesoamerica and Onkalots were formed on other planets, but the two languages are still very similar to each other."

"It matches my knowledge," Aggro replied. "Coming back to the point. Another target temple will be Toniatuh's Sanctuary, where there is a nonfunctional porter of the ancients. Then we have the Q'ijik astronomical observatory, the House of the Sovereign Feather Serpent Yolcuat and the House of Ojer tzij, the Ancient Word, which is the place of most interest to us - the library. Its former janitors have mastered the methods of preserving the written word and stone, therefore, if the object hasn't collapsed, we have a good chance of finding reliefs, glyphs and hieroglyphs there that can provide us with," he looked at Necron sitting next to him with his hands clasped on his chest, "the sought knowledge."

"I have a suggestion: let's call these rubble 'Temple 1', 'Temple 2' and so on. Nobody will remember those idiot names anyway." The members of the expedition glanced at Corporal Tsar Seymour, but no one commented on his words.

"Do you know the language of the Ancient Oncalots?" the humanoid jaguar was asked by a linguist, the second of the scientists, an older, almost bald, but energetic man.

"Their signs and symbols are similar to ours, that is the classical epoch Onkalots', as you put it, but more crude, with more angles per letter. The grammar is completely different, but I suppose it will be understandable to me."

"Nice to hear it. At least we'll have less work deciphering the ancient records," said an architect-Egyptologist, also an older man, albeit with a storm of grizzled curls.

"I hope to be of some use," replied the humanoid jaguar.

Then he described the vicinity of the sanctuaries and the dangers of treasure looters traps that the expedition might have encountered while exploring the halls and corridors.

After the meeting, when scientists prepared the equipment, and the achijes reluctantly donned biometal armors instead of summer uniforms (Necron believed that armors would be better in a cool temple interior, where it was easy to injure yourself or knock something over your head), the machines took off and headed for the Tukumb'akam Temple, the first site on the list.

The gray, dilapidated pyramid and the surrounding remnants of columns and buildings, which in its heyday had had religious and social functions, were completely absorbed by the jungle. Had it not been for topographic surface scanners, the expedition wouldn't have seen much through the portholes, the area was overgrown and obscured by treetops.

After scanning the substrate near the temple, a combat orb was released, which used a wide solar beam to burn the jungle rectangle to ashes. The machines hanging in the air soon extended their undercarriages and settled on the solid ground.

The expedition went outside over the gangplanks. Necron breathed in the heavy, sweetish air of the jungle, much wetter than in the vicinity of the Schindlers' farm. He intended to reach the cool underground of the building as soon as possible, to give some respite to his subordinates.

"Then have fun, gentlemen," he said shortly. He waved his hand. "We're going."

Orbs flew in front of the achijes to remove huge leaves and branches of the dense jungle with the rays of light. The group made their way quickly to a path that led near a stream, where insects buzzed loudly and fire-bellied toads croaked.

"Is it possible someone lives here?" Corporal technician Rasmus Darkoris turned to the humanoid jaguar, pointing his barrel at the path. The man was easy to remember due to a few strands of trimmed red hair on the top of his head, though now obscured by a helmet. Contrary to the name associated with the dark, his freckled skin was very pale, almost anemic.

"I don't know." Aggro looked around the area. "These lands hundreds of years ago belonged to the cruel people of the cannibals Jun Kame, One Death. I come from the Place of Fire, Chiq'aq '. Jun Kame lived far from our city, we saw each other only during long trips through the jungle, and when our warriors went to rescue the captured from their paws. However, the One Death people have long since vanished, so neither of them has trodden the path."

"The scanners of the ships found no one weighing more than twenty kilograms within a radius of many kilometers," said Corporal Tsar Seymour in his signature nonchalant tone. "Probably the path has been trampled by some animals, which we will quickly fry if they start throwing. So, either someone is hiding in the basement of Tukutakam ..."

"Tukumb'akam," corrected Aggro.

"Whatever. Or the path has been made recently, but whoever made it has already gone. In any case - no one is threatening us here."

"The only danger here is us," Darkoris said firmly, which sounded like boastfulness. "We'll kill anyone who gets in our way."

Q'ualel glanced at him surreptitiously. He wondered if it was right to agree to help the people who had wreaked violence and domination in the past, even if time and the new emperor had softened their mores.

"Enough, we're going." Necron waved his hand at the squad leader Sergeant Victor Shane. The black-haired man of medium height, with skin pale as snow and a calm face, nodded.

Soon the expedition went out into an area that in the heyday of the Jun Kame people had been an open space, and now overgrown and covered with leaves. The largest ones were the length of a multi-story house, and the members of the expedition walking below them felt like insects. A plaza in front of the square pyramid - which Seymour had determined with the help of an erdoscope[1] to be one hundred and forty meters at the base and seventy meters high - was covered with stone objects integrated into ubiquitous vegetation. There were glyph steles, remnants of rectangular buildings, an empty pool filled with ant mounds, columns leaning or lying on the ground, statues and stone idols knocking around, depicting Onkalots in the form of monsters, demons, and skeletons. The five-level

---

[1] A device for mapping an area and converting its size into units specified by the operator. It can be in the form of a drone, a fire crest or a bracer, or it can be part of a ship's or naval craft's instrument console.

pyramid itself was far from a technolytic masterpiece, for which the classic Onkalots were famous, because the warlike people of Jun Kame hadn't belonged to the masters of architecture. It had been erected using dried bricks and earth, the structure was casually reinforced with slabs of black basalt, just to keep the whole thing as a giant pyramid, which made the building look stark and inconsistent. Decorations had been missing. A temple at the top, to which led broken stairs, had collapsed.

"Complete ruin." Necron shifted his gaze from the pyramid to the people walking around it, then to the humanoid jaguar. "Are you sure we'll find Nimja's knowledge in something like this? You said Jun Kame members are barbarians and cavemen."

"These lands are foreign to me due to the reasons I mentioned at the briefing," said Aggro. "I'm also not sure whether the people of One Death built this pyramid, or they moved to the surrounding area after displacing its indigenous people. It is also possible that they took over the abandoned city."

"I don't know much about old civilizations, but savages wouldn't have made something like this, would have they?" Tsar Seymour suddenly grew up next to Necron.

"Nevertheless, the facility must be checked. You shouldn't judge a book by its cover," summed up the humanoid jaguar. On Kiret's face bloomed a slight smile as he heard the old human saying, now virtually unused.

Sergeant Shane approached Necron.

"Sir, Corporal Darkoris' probes found tunnels and chambers under the pyramid. We are just finishing mapping the area." He turned to the corporal, "Tsar, go to the technician and help him with the lighting."

Seymour walked away, humming a song about picking up women. Biffter and Aggro followed the sergeant, joined the scientists standing by an entrance at the base of the building, obscured by roots like by a drape. From the dark tunnel emerged the last probes, stylized as fast-running trilobites, able to travel across ceilings and walls. They rolled into balls and grouped themselves together. Corporal Darkoris, in charge of the technical part of the expedition, put them in a box and placed them beside the rest of the equipment.

"There's one more probe left in the tunnels," he said, sliding his helmet open for a moment. "Its bioctovisor and thermoindicator are looking for living creatures. Initial plans are these."

They gathered around the displayed holographic map of the pyramid's interior. After a short analysis and reaching into the recesses of memory, Aggro began pointing his claw at individual elements of the map.

"The rectangle in the center is probably a sacrificial altar, so here will be a ceremonial chamber. These three rooms are empty, I don't know their purpose, but rather they are not tombs, because you cannot see sarcophagi. "Is the map detailed?" He asked Darkoris.

"Yes, the probes took into account every geometry that is important to us." Tsar approached them with a stuffed military bag.

"Look how many traps are here." He smiled as he waved the barrel at the holograph. He enlarged several areas of interest to him. He ran a hand over the dark blond hair which, in the beam of sunlight breaking through the canopy, was almost red like Darkoris'. "The spiked pits are my favorite. A very old school. The blocks crushing a delinquent into mush are good too. Haha, look, some dickhead was pressed!"

"All the traps look dilapidated," the archeologist took the floor.

"Is the facility safe?" Necron turned his gaze to the Egyptologist architect who was fanning himself with his hat. "Are we in danger of collapsing?"

"According to the readings of the probes, the inside of the pyramid is stable. So is to my eye. It's an old building, but is still in very good condition. The construction of bricks, slabs and mud only seems to be not very solid."

"Here is our latecomer." The last trilobite emerged from the tunnel, Darkoris picked it up and studied the notes. Soon he said, "It found only bones inside. No biological hazards whatsoever."

"All right then, gentlemen." Biffter turned off the map, focused the group's attention on himself. "We're looking for anything that has traces of handwriting and glyphs, and Aggroteh will translate for us."

They entered the tunnel stretching behind the dilapidated gate. Seymour, who had packed dozens of small generators, walked close to the wall and hurled the devices against a stone, whistling. Lamps clung to the hard surface, outthrusted electrowicks, and soon the darkness was dissipated by the famous multicolored Kiritian fire. Additionally, Viktor activated a blue flare and walked with it being the spearhead.

The tunnel ran straight at the level of the pyramid base until it forked. One of the three embranchements (the others turned out to be blindly ended) began to descend, leading to the nether regions. The temperature was lower, more pleasant than in the square, but because of the cramped conditions, it was harder for a few claustrophobics to breathe. The walls were gray stone slabs devoid of decoration.

The expedition encountered the first trap, previously commented on by Tsar - the open trapdoor in the floor, where there was grimly stuck a headless human skeleton impaled on sharpened rock. Dressed in cobwebs and rags, the unfortunate man was bent into a sharp arc, as if he had weights attached to his limbs.

"The bones don't look particularly old," Seymour noted. "Like the guy impaled himself on the spike forty years ago."

"And where's the skull?" The linguist looked expectantly at Aggroteh, who quickly guessed that he meant his skill. As a psychometrician, he was able, by touching an object, to recreate its history in his mind, seeing images from the past.

"Let me focus."

He lay down on his belly and leaned over the hole, extended his paw far. He managed to reach with his claw the closest ribs. He closed his eyes, made his breathing shallow and decreased its frequency, focusing on his own mind and the object being touched. Kiritians and scientists responded to his request, because no one was talking or clanking the equipment, even Tsar, known for his stupid comments, fell silent. Pictures from the life of the skeleton owner appeared relatively quickly. Many of them were not related to the Kiritian case and were from the distant past of the dead man, so Aggro had to work hard with his mind to reveal essential details. More minutes passed. The man turned out to be a looter, he had flown to Chulimal to plunder the pyramids and earn some money from the treasures found in them. Shortly before his death, he had panicked, he had run down the corridor, had been chased by some animals making sounds like wolves - Q'ualel, just like the thief, didn't see the pursuers. The man's attention had been fully absorbed by the attackers, and thus he hadn't thought about the potential pitfalls that had usually existed in the key structures of Oncalots worshiping the gods of darkness. Maybe he hadn't even realized they had existed. He had rushed at breakneck speed to escape from the nether regions as soon as possible. Aggro winced as the stone flaps collapsed under the thief, who impaled himself on a stalagmite. The next image was not about the living being, but about his head - something snarling like an animal took it, but it was impossible to recognize the details because the view was as if from the perspective of a kicked ball.

Onkalot, breathing heavily, returned to reality, stood on all fours and looked up. He saw focused, serious faces around him.

"And?" Biffter helped him up. Aggro told about what he had seen.

"Sounds cute." Tsar raised an eyebrow. "But who was chasing him?"

"I guess people. However, they growled like wolves."

"Lycans. Damn transhumanists." Viktor spat, staring glumly into the corridor. He noticed that the linguist unfamiliar with the H14 population looked at him curiously. "This is a group of adventurers, a fraction of psychopathic Satanists who worship animal deities, mainly werewolves. Completely backward freaks. They took a liking to forests and other wildernesses of different planets, so they are difficult to spot. They especially like H14. You can recognize them by implants integrated with the body or genomes turned upside down, but it costs money, so most of them run in rags or half-naked."

"Lycans once killed Anna Sandstorm's mother," commented Necron glumly. "Admittedly none of Hanako's searchers saw it, but evidence was found."

They avoided the trap and moved on. The tunnel descended to the basement, where it turned into a larger complex - a maze of corridors and chambers. It was Seymour who first noticed that in the dust on the floor were visible numerous human footprints, even trails, as if something heavy had been dragged. They found another used trap: boulders knocking around to crush uninvited guests, spears scattered under loopholes, spikes soaked in a deadly neurotoxin stuck in the sallow walls, cavernous wells. This time, the remains of their victims were not found. Necron ordered Tsar to refrain from disposing the mini-generators to save them for places worth more attention. The immortals turned on night vision or infravision in their helmets, the scientists settled for flashlights, while the Onkalot didn't need electronic aids to see in the dark.

In the searched rooms, before their eyes appeared reliefs and paintings, but everything concerned the prayers, mythology and everyday life of Onkalots. Aggroteh explained that the secret knowledge of the Ancients wouldn't be publicly available, but so far, they hadn't found a library. Instead, they found more headless skeletons, all gathered in the extension of the corridor, which might have been taken for a small underground square.

The skulls were found in the next room - a vast columned chamber with a stone grid in the center of the floor. Fragments, mainly of people, also of Onkalots, formed an additional wall reaching the ceiling. The free spaces were stuffed tightly with crossbones so that the nightmarish structure didn't collapse in the absence of traditional mortar.

"Oh, shit." Seymour stared at the ghostly skulls in the glow of Viktor's blue flare and the scientists' flashlights. He tapped a few. "What a sick mind did something like that?"

"Perfidious hypocrite," Darkoris said both sharply and jokingly. He slid his helmet open, as did a few achijes. "And what do you do with the heads of the killed enemies?"

Tsar glanced instinctively at the uppers of high boots, with which he had integrated covers for two machetes.

"So what? But I don't build a shack out of them. A well-deserved trophy doesn't count."

"You're screwed up."

"We call it tzompantli," said Aggro. "Such walls were erected by the most primitive tribes of Onkalots, which built them from the skulls of war victims or those sacrificed to gods."

The archaeologist looked closely at the structure with his keen eye.

"The bones are complete and prepared, showing no signs of damage caused by time. At least when it comes to the human skulls. The skulls of the Onkalots are old, possibly drawn from the tombs."

"So, somebody has built the damn thing recently?" Necron asked.

Nobody replied.

Aggro was the first to hear a soft scratching noise, as if a heavy boulder had been moved on the ground a few chambers away. Viktor nodded at him to indicate that he had picked up the sound, too; in the flare, his face was whiter than a skull.

Scratching multiplied and ceased to be discreet. Everyone looked around the room, trying to find the source of the sounds that seemed to come from everywhere.

"I think your toys to detect life are broken," Tsar said to Darkoris.

"They are operational. It's more likely that something is wrong with this pyramid, as if it was causing equipment interference."

The achijes put on their helmets, switched to bioctovision, to see living creatures in bright colors against the dark background of the lifeless environment. They raised the barrels of their weapons; Aggro outthrusted an obsidian dagger from its case by maxtlatl[2]. The scientists stood behind the Kiritians, shining their flashlights nervously in all directions. The scratching noise intensified, the echo disturbed the identification of now not a few, but several dozen sources of noise.

Something huge jumped out of the darkness, yelping. It fell to the ground and rose quickly. It was a dirty man with greasy, tousled hair, dressed like a slum tatterdemalion. He bared his teeth, displaying long metal implants in his upper jaw, his eyes glowed red like Onkalotian ones, his wrists were armed with knuckle dusters with protruding claws. More tatterdemalions leaped from different parts of the room, screaming like furious animals, each carried some close-range weapon, even as primitive as an ax or a sword.

One of the savages jumped onto the linguist's back, knocking him off his feet, and drove a blade up to the haft in his shoulder. The older man screamed.

---

[2] A piece of fabric covering the hips, tied with a belt or rope.

A maddened squeaking woman attacked Q'ualel with a club, intending to crush his skull. The humanoid jaguar deftly dodged the blow, tripped up the woman, who lost her balance and fell to the ground along with a stele, raising a cloud of dust. However, she quickly got up and attacked with even more fury, albeit she didn't reach the Onkalot. She stared in amazement at her torso with four dimples; a trickle of blood flowed out of her mouth. Necron yanked out of her body metal blades exsertile from a glove's metacarpus. For the Kiritians, hidden spikes, as part of their permanent equipment, were the same as bayonets to foreign infantry, and despite having firearms, they often used them in a clash.

Q'ualel was accosted by another transhumanist - a man with wolf ears instead of human ears, and a tail, also longer tusks in place of canines. He roared at the Onkalot, but he didn't owe him and discouraged the daredevil with the wilder power of his voice.

"Shoot!" Shane ordered. "They are lycans! Spare no one!"

The man who knocked the linguist down got a kick in the face with Seymour's armored boot, so strongly that he was thrown backwards with his jaw broken. He stood up, with blood trickling from his mouth and nose. He grinned madly at Tsar, screamed.

"Seriously?" The corporal raised his arm. A brief flash of hot combat gas from a plasma gun blew off the ragged man's head.[3]

---

[3] Battle plasma is not ionized matter with the properties of a gas, but the colloquial name of melting thermal energy, usually of orange color. It is formed when molecules packed under high pressure react to each other in a generator. The dhurnsteel weapon casing is resistant to internal reactions.

The fervor of the lycans faded quickly. The men and a few women clustered together, looking at the achijes, first with surprise, but after a moment with fear, as more companions were lost.

"It's not them!" The gang leader growled in lopsided Kiritian, with a half of a skull on his head and tiny bones attached to a laced kapok.

The brutal fight was turning into slaughter. More lycans, unfamiliar with the enemy's identity, burst into the chamber, as those who had already known it, either tried to flee, or seeing their own death in the bright eyes of the Kiritians, tried to hurt one. However, they didn't stand a chance in the fight of cold steel against firearms, the armor of the Immortals itself was almost complete protection.

Only one lycan managed to reach the enemy and stab him with a knife in a weak point of armor - the neck, where there were thinner, moving parts. Attacked, Viktor managed to throw the madman sitting on his back over his shoulder and shot him when he hit the ground. The wound wasn't fatal, but it was bleeding heavily as it soaked clothes under the breastplate. The sergeant felt faint and dropped to his knee.

The Kiritians immediately cordoned him around. Seymour inspected the wound and confirmed that Shane's life wasn't in danger.

Subsequent lycans who decided to fight were shot dead before they caught the enemy. The escapees were hit in the back.

"No running for the hills from battlefield, you dirty bastards!" Seymour's long not fought battle heated his blood, his adrenaline level jumped.

A half-naked lycan rushed towards him, waving his hands armed with spiked brass knuckles. Tsar made a cheeky face, threw the plasma rifle aside, and outthrusted the metal spikes from his gloves. The opponent stopped.

"You're not supposed to shoot him! Come on!" Seymour encouraged the lycan, who made a point of granting his request and attacked in a flash. Confident Tsar even let himself to be hit in his torso. The bone blades broke after hitting the armored biometal. The armor of the Immortals was relatively tough, so well-adjusted to current standards that it was often easier to blow up an achij with it than to pierce a carapace with a bullet.

Surprised, the lycan stared in amazement at the brass knuckles made in a garage, then outthrusted a club-spear from a bag on his back.

The corporal disregarded his opponent, which made him lose his balance from the impact, and they both flew against the wall of skulls which overwhelmed them like infernal soccer balls.

Seymour tried to dig himself out of the pile of bones, but caught his foot on the opponent's weapon and fell over, in addition was hit by a stone falling from the ceiling. The blow to the helmet didn't hurt, but it stunned him briefly.

The lycan straddled him, aimed the point at the neck. He pushed with both hands and all his might, but Seymour grasped the shaft in a flash and pushed it aside. He knocked the man off himself and jumped on him. He swung his left hand and plowed his face with metal claws, then the other hand. He repeated the action many times, over his face, neck and chest, even when the lycan was already dead.

Panting, Tsar wiped the blades on the defeated lycan's tunic and slipped them into his gloves. He got up, stepped on the corpse's chest, looked at him for a moment. Then grasped the dirty hair of the transhumanist and lifted the dead head slightly, and with his other hand outthrusted the machete from the high upper. He was unhurriedly cutting the skull off the neck until it hung on the shag, sprinkling the blood on Tsar's decapitated body and boots.

"What a wimp." Puffing, he spat at the corpse. He saw that the skirmish was over. All the lycans lay dead or dying.

Darkoris, gasping for breath, walked over to him. He looked at Tsar, who removed his helmet, then at the blood-dripping trophy in his hand. He made an arc with his eyes and shook his head.

"You could have picked something from the tzompantli collection you just smashed."

Seymour took a step toward the achij - and sank into the ground. He fell painfully a few meters below, groaning, with his wrists tried to free his eyes from the risen dust. The trophy rolled into the darkness, and the corporal was showered with shards from the broken wall.

"Are you alive?" Darkoris kicked off deeper into the room a few skulls balancing on the edge of the hole.

"If I'm moving, it means I'm definitely dead." Seymour sat up, dusted himself off. He looked up and saw several faces poorly visible in the blinding light of the flashlights.

"Get the linguist and Sergeant Shane to the corvette and take care of them." Biffter gave the order to the three closest Kiritians, and to the next three he said, "Tidy up this mess, finish off the wounded lycans, then secure the chamber. The rest is to come here to me. Corporal Darkoris, map new terrain. Tsar, you're not to go anywhere."

Seymour waved his hand carelessly, as if he had wanted everyone to leave him alone.

Rasmus took out the trilobite probe, turned it on, and put it into the opening. The artificial crustacean went swiftly down the wall, passed Tsar following him, the severed head, and disappeared into the darkness of the corridor. Darkoris placed the controller on the ground, and gradually a detailed holographic map of the discovered passage began to appear there.

"This is some sort of hemispherical room," he announced soon, when the map was ready, and the trilobite returned and went onto his clasped hands. A deep corridor led to it, but it was completely collapsed. It can be entered only through a vestibule with a short tunnel, discovered by Tsar."

"Hey, maybe you'll kindly get me out?" Seymour shouted from below, surrounded by skulls.

"Nobody's going to drag you out," said Biffter, "you'll have your bag of lamps in a moment." He looked at Darkoris. "Get some rope or a folding ladder. You will replace Sergeant Shane until they patch him up with molecular glue."

"Yes, sir."

Kiret tapped a finger on his chin, whispered more to himself than to Rasmus:

"We seem to have destroyed a nest of lycans who lived in the chambers below the pyramid, catched and murdered anyone they found in the area. Therefore, they didn't run away from us, taking us out of habit for a harmless group of civilians heading straight for the trap. Now let's check what our unruly Tsar has discovered."

"Catch it and get to work." Darkoris tossed the corporal a package containing the remaining mini-generators.

Seymour pulled his helmet on, chose the night vision mode, then walked first down the vestibule corridor, then around the newly mapped room, throwing lamps against the walls.

As the last activated Kiritian fire flashed, the corporal heard a muffled blow: Aggroteh cushioned the jump with four legs, having leapt into the vestibule through the hole. Soon the Kiritians and two scientists still touched by the attack descended the ladder. Seymour smiled crookedly. From the beginning of the expedition, he had known that there would be a problem with the civilian Oderses without combat training. However, Biffter had insisted on taking them as unique experts on H14 and Earth twin cultures.

In the discovered chamber, the only thing worth paying attention to was a map precisely carved in a stone slab, inscribed in a circle in the center of the floor. The dyes of blood, rocks and plants used to create the ornaments had faded almost completely. Darkoris, holding the flare, knelt down and illuminated the emblems. The others began to gather around the map.

Seymour spat.

"And that's all? I almost broke my neck to see some patterns as a reward?"

"Shut up, Seymour, okay?" The technician corporal hissed.

"This is a map of the Chulimal sanctuaries," said Aggro. He turned to Darkoris, "May I have the projection turn on, with the temples I indicated marked?"

Rasmus crouched down and placed on the ground the cube which generated a three-dimensional map of H14. He chose with his thumb the area with all the temples marked, and transformed it into a simple, schematic, two-dimensional object that could be manipulated with the fingers as desired. Aggroteh compared the plan preserved in the stone slab with that of the Kiritians.

"What do the skulls above some of the pyramids mean?" The archeologist pointed to the floor.

"Enemies. The head of the jaguar is allies," explained Q'ualel, focused on studying the holograph.

"These Jun Kame probably didn't have too many friends," Seymour said.

The humanoid jaguar quickly noticed that the Kiritian map lacked the temple present on the floor slab. Biffter noted the same:

"All the temples we're supposed to search are as if on a circular plan. However, our electronic map doesn't have the largest object, this one." He pointed to a temple with a skull symbol in the center of a circle.

"It's my fault." Aggro crouched down, started to move his fingertips with deliberation along the lines forming the temple symbol. His smile widened more and more. "I've thought it doesn't exist. These areas were inhabited by hostile Chiq'aq tribes, so we have never had the opportunity to learn the truth. We've thought it was a legend. When the Onkalots became extinct, I had no need to venture into the areas of our enemies."

"No brachylogy please," Seymour said. Aggro looked at him.

"This is the sanctuary of Tz'aqol, the Highest Gods of Light. Uk'ux cho, Uk'ux palo, Uk'ux kaj, Uk'ux ulew ..."

"We don't understand Onkalotian," Necron admonished.

Q'ualel felt more and more excitement, was unconsciously moving the tip of his tail sideways.

"Heart of the Lake, Heart of the Sea, Heart of the Earth, Heart of Heaven, Creator, Maker, Holder, Hurricane, Newborn Lightning ..."

"And what about that?" Darkoris asked quickly.

Aggro got up, looked at the emperor with a smile.

Most likely we will find there what you are looking for. Perhaps even an artifact similar to the one that made Forkis human and let him conquer all mankind."

Biffter patted surprised Seymour on the shoulder.

"Well done, Corporal." He added, seeing that the Kiritian made a foolish face, "You found the map and perhaps you saved us a lot of time and work during raking all the selected temples." He walked over to the wall and pulled down the turquoise fire mini-generator.

"Corporal Darkoris, mark a new object on the map and convert alien distances into ours."

"Yes, sir."

III. The Guardian of the Heart of Heaven

The members of the expedition spent the night in the open, chatting and joking by a big fire. They took off in the ships at dawn and flew to Toniatuh's temple, more than eight hundred kilometers from Tukumb'akam's sanctuary. Necron was eager to first see the object with the porter that, according to the Onkalotian myths, had served Nimja thousands of years earlier for travel between terrestrial planets, thanks to which they had spread knowledge across the cosmos among primitive species. For henotheistic Aggroteh, the temple was of special importance. Firstly, because thanks to the porter, he and Forkis had accidentally survived the Onkalots' pogrom, secondly - the sanctuary was dedicated to Tonatiuh, his most important god. The chambers and corridors had been created inside the mountain. In many places, the walls hadn't survived the test of time or construction errors and had collapsed. The only surviving tunnel leading inside was so narrow that only Q'ualel, having more flexible joints than humans, could pass through it.

Therefore, Necron had a mining mole brought from the corvette, with which a tunnel had been drilled three meters in diameter. The Kiritians made their way through the mountain slope to the ceremonial hall with the altar and porter.

They spent two days exploring the sanctuary, but the search didn't advance even a step. The porter lay in ruins, its design and operation were closely tied to the technolytic technology that Nimja had mastered, and forces that at best Aggro could have understood. He didn't know, however, how the device worked, in the past he and Forkis had turned it on by accident. It didn't matter, anyway, as the conveyor had long since turned into a ruin.

Tz'aqol's Temple, dedicated to the Highest Gods of Light, was third on the updated list. As Aggro flew on the corvette over the surface of Chulimal and watched it through the porthole, he understood why the sanctuary had once been considered mythical: it was in a jungle enclave protected by canyons, cavernous seismic cracks, steep mountains and sucking swamps, and string bridges were guarded by wardens of the hidden people. Even if a daredevil had overcome the first and second obstacle, he could have died by crossing the next one. It took the Kiritians a few minutes' flight to achieve what many humanoid jaguars had achieved drudgingly in weeks. "No wonder," Q'ualel thought grimly, "those humans had ousted Onkalots with the anti-psionic technology and simple mechanical weapons at their disposal." Much earlier, a wise man had told him that no civilization lasted forever, for eventually a stronger one would emerge to supersede the predecessor. Q'ualel looked at the profile of Necron, who, with his arms folded over his chest, was sitting nearby and, with melancholy understandable only to him, watched the surroundings through the cockpit cover. Did he have a grievance about what the humans had done to the Onkalots, even if the colonists who had come to Chulimal had had nothing to do with the Kiritians? Aggro had felt in the past a regret that had faded with time, perhaps because he had been focused on current affairs. Forkis, on the other hand, has been able to feed on hatred for centuries like a star on hydrogen.

"We are there. We're landing in a moment." Viktor Shane roused him from his meditations. Thanks to the molecular glue, which instantly recreated damaged tissues, the sergeant had fully recovered.

Aggro had time to inspect the pyramid before it was obscured by monumental trees as the corvette descended. Tz'aqol was the largest he had ever seen. It was in perfect condition as if it had been abandoned twenty years earlier, not five centuries. It seemed to be iridescent with shades of gold in the rays of K'ajolom, according to legends, the metal desired by the gods. In any case, the fact that it was sacred to the highest gods was adequate to the majesty of the nine-story structure. The only thing that was needed for its full perfection was a well-kept area - uncontrolled vegetation, especially ivy and lichens, had taken over the courtyard and the objects arranged on it.

The landing took place in a similar way as before: a fragment of the surface was cut down, and the obtained biomass was turned to dust and blown away. The vital jungle, however, would regenerate quickly and fill the devastated niche. Corporal Darkoris scanned the area for the presence of larger living creatures and tracked down only a variety of pangolins that escaped into the burrows anyway.

After walking a short stretch of the jungle, the expedition emerged into the square at the foot of the steps leading to the chapel at the top of the pyramid. The neighborhood looked peaceful, the gentle chirping of birds and the lazy buzzing of insects didn't herald trouble. The vegetation was barely being brushed by a faint gust of wind. Lizards basked on the steles and the ground. A tiny monkey was swinging on the branch, watching the newcomers with its bulging eyes. The full effect of bliss was spoiled only by the bones of people and Onkalots, scattered as if a supporter of Beliar Drunkenstein's methods of extermination had blown himself up at some local assembly in the past.

"Bones." Darkoris tapped a tibia with the toe of his boot. "Why do there always have to be damn skeletons in run-down ruins?"

"Tz'aqol is not ruined." Aggroteh thought he saw movement beyond the distant stele. He looked in that direction for a moment, but the effect didn't repeat.

Seymour, with a conspirator's smile, placed a human skull on his hand, approached Darkoris from behind, and 'kissed' his cheek with the teeth.

"You frigging idiot!" Rasmus instinctively punched the skull, at the same time hitting amused Seymour in the face. The skull fell apart. The technician corporal took the forehead bone and hurled it angrily at Tsar.

"You would kill yourself if you jumped from your stupidity to your IQ level! Forkis must have been drunk when he accepted you to the Immortals."

"Enough, you both," growled Necron. "Take a look around here a bit." He turned to the humanoid jaguar when they were gone, "Aggro, you know this planet best. Do you have any idea what the broken skeletons of both species are doing in the square?"

"They're lying, sir!" Seymour called from a distance.

Biffter sighed and shook his head.

"Forgive me if I evoke memories painful for you, but I have to ask about this: did during the colonial massacre, the Onkalots fiercely resist, which resulted in numerous victims on both sides?"

"It was a pogrom," whispered the humanoid jaguar, as if he hadn't wanted to defile the sanctity of this place by noise. "Massacre. Our fighters didn't stand a chance. Few of the colonists were killed then."

"These bones appear to differ in age by several hundred years." The archeologist pointed to the closest remains of an Onkalot, then of a man. "Note, Mr. Biffter, the signs of erosion on the former, the dryness of the tissue and the faded color of the skeleton." He crouched down, took out the analyzer with the attached knife and started scraping the samples, which he poured into the containers. Soon he read the results of the study, "Four hundred and forty-seven Terrenic years the bones of this Onkalot are old, while the bones of the human are thirty-two. Estimating roughly, it will be the same for the rest. However, the weirdest thing, Mr. Biffter, is that the remains of humanoid jaguars, as I mentioned earlier, are slightly destroyed by time, but not as much as they should look after centuries of lying alternately in sun and rain, in high temperatures."

Necron ran his glove over his shaved head.

"What are you suggesting, doctor?"

"Probably they have been moved from somewhere, from a closed room or cave, such as tombs."

"Why would someone take the remains out of the pyramid and spread them across the square?" Shane walked over to the group with some achijes. "I'm reporting, sir, that the area is clear. We found nothing that could have affected these unfortunates like this." He made an arc with his arm, pointing to the ground.

"So, lycans again?" Seymour also finished his brief reconnaissance. "They took cat bones out of the graves, performed rituals, and then killed themselves by swallowing the drill bullets that had torn them apart? Actually, it suits these sickies."

Aggroteh sniffed for a moment.

"Apart from you, I don't sense other people's scent."

While a conversation developed between the Kiritians and the scientists, he walked away a bit and looked at the fifth level of the pyramid. He thought he saw a huddled figure going quickly round the corner.

He felt peculiarly as if an undefined psychotropic agent had been starting to work in his body, or he had inhaled something from the air. The wind blew stronger. The clatter of Kiritian boots on the stone floor became clearer, the words were stretched, and their sound distorted, which was like catching the sounds of the surface from under the water. The world began to slow down. K'ajolom rays, penetrating through the dignified crowns of rustling palm trees, flickered with a dreamlike glow. Added to this was an unknown presence, but clearly felt. And then the whispers, at first not much different from the murmur of the wind, similar to the voices of spirits eager to convey something to one of the last living descendants.

Aggroteh began to recognize the words. His eyes got moist, his heart was beating faster, for he had not heard the indigenous speech for a long time, the accent of which he had lost due to being among people:

Juraqan, ch'ipi kaqulja
raxa kaqulja
uk'ux kaj, uk'ux ulew
tz'aqol b'itol
alom k'ajolom.[4]

The rest also realized that something strange was happening. They stopped talking and began to look around, mostly glancing towards the chapel at the top of the pyramid. The achijes put on their helmets to help themselves with electronics, raised their weapons to a combat position, ready for all kinds of threat. All but one - a psionic activity known only to Onkalots. The words of the ancient speech continued to flow in. The bones began to rise as if they had been made of metal, and attracted by a gigantic, invisible magnet hanging above the square. To the disbelief of the viewers, they merged into their original shapes, creating full or incomplete skeletons.

"What the hell?!" Seymour fired a plasma gun at the nearest skeleton. War gas melted some of the bones, and the rest

---

[4] (Quiché) Hurricane, Newborn Lightning, Sudden Lightning, Heaven's Heart, Earth's Heart, Creator, Maker, Holder Parent.

scattered within a few meters. However, they rose and reunited into the macabre creature of an Onkalot, though less complete than before.

"What's happening?" Necron asked Q'ualel nervously.

"I don't know. This is the first time I see something like this."

"How do you not know, cat?!" Tsar shouted at him. "Skeletons are very dead, lie on the ground or in caskets, not walk on the ground! Look!"

The achijes formed a cordon around the scientists Q'ualel and Necron, surrounded by skeletons moving slowly towards them. The First Galactic Dignitary also slipped his helmet over his face, in thermovision mode he couldn't see any warm colors at the remains of the processed energy, which clearly indicated that they were dealing with dead matter. He took a three-barreled plasma launcher from the hands of the nearest subordinate, set it on semi-automatic fire, and stepped out of the circle, jostling Darkoris away with his shoulder. He watched with a fierce expression on his face at the infernal show unfolding around: bodiless limbs shuffling on the ground, crookedly twisted arms flailing about with phalanges and claws, wobbly rib cages, chattering skulls eager to sink their teeth into the flesh of intruders.

He shot. His hands twitched in delightful recoil.

The partly melted skeleton flew a few meters and crumbled upon hitting a boulder, but as in Seymour's action, it merged again and continued its danse macabre march.

Shane understood the emperor's unspoken command and waved his arm.

"Fire!"

The square flashed the blue and orange cannonade of the energy weapons. The dead opponents posed no threat to the armored Kiritians, but there was no way to stop them. The broken bones rose steadily and assumed their earlier forms, less and less complete with time, but they didn't lose their feisty steadfastness. The Onkalots' skanks were jumping on the achijes' backs and trying to tear up their helmet covers with their claws, to get to their throats with their teeth; the human skeletons waved their fists limply.

"Get that shit off me!" Seymour was moving in circles, hitting his back with the gun barrel, trying to knock down the attached skeleton. Q'ualel rushed to his aid, yanked the dead man hard by the ribs and knocked him off clattering to the ground. Swearing, Seymour began jumping on the bones, crushing them like dry sticks, but the disjointed pieces were still moving. "I don't think they like us on this planet."

"It's pointless, we're just wasting the energy of the weapons." Victor Shane kicked his opponent where he had once had his stomach and sent him to an empty reservoir. "We would have to hover in the ship over this and incinerate it all to hell."

Aggro realized that skeletons, for some reason, attacked only humans. He caught the words coming out of nowhere, spoken faster and faster, with greater emphasis. The declaimer raised his voice in ecstasy, like an ancient priest who, thanks to patient incantation, felt within himself the activity of some god from the Onkalotian, polytheistic pantheon. That's why Aggro recognized it as a kind of prayer:

K'a katz'ininoq!
K'a kachamamoq!

Katz'inonik!
K'a kasilanik!
K'a kalolinik!
Katlona puch![5]

A hunch turned his gaze again to the pyramid. Indeed, where he had previously thought he had seen something, a black silhouette against the background of K'ajolom appeared, raising their arms high. Q'ualel ran out of the breaking circle of the achijes who, busy with the pointless shooting, didn't even notice him, and headed for the stairs. Climbing on all limbs, he quickly reached the fifth level. He jumped down from the steps onto multi-ton rock blocks and moved towards the corner of the building. The suspicions that there might have been a source of trouble turned out to be correct: he saw a completely material figure on the landing. To his great surprise, it belonged to a representative of his kind. It was a female dressed in an off-kilter poncho, with a leather purse hung on a belt slung over her chest. The Onkalotian female was kneeling, chanting, and twitching her front paws as if she had been holding rattles in them. Her eyes were closed, she was so absorbed in the ritual that she didn't catch with her senses the intruder standing next to her.

Q'ualel leapt at her with a roar, pinned her thin shoulders to a stone with his paws.

The female opened her green eyes, her mouth expressed extreme terror, which quickly turned into surprise and finally

---

[5] (Quiché) Everything is still waving! Now is purring! Trembling! It's still sighing! It's still humming! And it's stretching with emptiness!

anger. She made a sound bordering on screaming and huffing, then hit Q'ualel in the belly with her hind limbs and knocked him off herself.

Aggro lost his balance, fell painfully two levels below, groaning with each hit against a stone block. The fall stunned him.

The female leaped at him quickly like an arrow, grasped his exposed throat with her fangs, but clenched her jaws painfully instead of deadly. As Aggro tried to twist backward, he saw that the bones in the square were motionless again and lying in disarray, and the members of the expedition shouted something and ran towards the stairs.

"Traitor!" Growled the Onkalotian female in the beautiful speech that Q'ualel hadn't heard for a long time. She got up and began to scratch his torso with her claws throwing fur tufts in the air, then to punch him. "Traitor, traitor, traitor! Allied with the metal demons!"

Her eagerness faded; despair broke into her words. Aggro slipped her off himself, knelt beside her, not afraid of any more scratches. All the anger disappeared from the Onkalotian female, being replaced by despondency. She rested her head against surprised Q'ualel's chest and broke down.

"It's been so long since I saw our companions. And Hurricane must have sent me the traitor. I am still alone! I've had enough ..."

Having known the female's ambivalent tendencies, Aggro hesitated, then carefully raised his arms and embraced her reassuringly. She didn't break away, she didn't react at all.

"You were controlling those bones. You are a telekinetic. And skillful one. You've called the entire necropolis out of the graves!"

The she-cat didn't answer, she rubbed her nose with her fist.

"What's your name?" Aggro withdrew his paws.

"Chimalmat." She looked at him sadly in the eyes. "I'm the Shield-Net, the last guardian of Tz'aqol. Why are your words the words of demons?"

"You mean my grammar? What am I talking about ... You don't know this notion anyway. My name is Minister, Q'ualel. And I speak quite strangely, because I have been with people for a long time."

"Traitor!" Chimalmat got angry again, jumped away from him like from a poisonous snake. "You walk with metal demons! The bodies of other enemies were soft and torn by bones as they desecrated the holy lands. These demons cannot be destroyed! Stone, claws and teeth are helpless!"

Aggro tried to speak as simply as to a child:

"Calm down, they're not demons, they're Kiritians. They are wearing biometal armor, indestructible with our traditional weapons. They are people, but they are on our side."

"They killed us!"

"No, it wasn't the Kiritians who killed us, but colonists, other people who were looking for planets ... territories for themselves."

"What's going on here?" Darkoris grew up behind Q'ualel's back. Fear twinkled in the female's eyes as she looked at the blackness of the barrel pointed at her.

"Everything is okay, Rasmus," Aggro reassured him. "The incident with the bones was a perfect form of telekinesis. This is Chimalmat."

Surprised by the presence of the second Onkalot, the corporal immediately understood the meaning of these words. Experiences with Forkis' telepathy and Aggro's psychometry had sensitized the Immortals that each humanoid jaguar developed a certain psionic skill which, upon recognition, could be improved. Nevertheless, these abilities had remained incomprehensible to Kiritians dealing with advanced technology to that day. Too few Onkalots had survived to be able to conduct research on their brains that required the participation of a larger population.

"Chimalmat?" The corporal didn't know if it was a name or some social status.

Q'ualel switched to Onkalotian and made soothing gestures.

"You don't have to be afraid, he's our friend. I'm with these people and you are safe."

"What do you want?" Chimalmat looked at Rasmus as if he had been going to hit her with a whip.

Aggro saw no reason not to tell a part of the truth, especially since it would have paid off with her trust.

"We came here to find a way to revive my friend Xajb'a Kej. He's an Onkalot like us. But you probably don't know him because he came from the Chiq'aq people living far away."

"I don't. I'm from Ik'ib'akam, the Dark Jaguar. Why would metal people care about a descendant of the Great House?"

"Because he is a very important Onkalot, both for me and for them."

Aggro grabbed Chimalmat gently by the arm. She was breaking away, imagining that he wanted to hand her over to the Kiritian talking via the communicator, but let herself be humored when the Onkalot patted her shoulder, whispering soothing words:

"Now we will go down. Don't be afraid of these people. They have terrible weapons, but designed for enemies. You, however, are not one of them. Trust me. Come on."

The rest of the expedition waited in the square in front of the pyramid, peering suspiciously at the remains scattered everywhere. Those descending the stairs joined the group. Aggro could feel the taut muscles of the female under her fingers as she rolled her gaze nervously over the mass of armed aliens.

Necron ordered to holster the weapons and walked over to the humanoid jaguar. The female took a step back, clenched her claws painfully on Aggro's arm.

"The wild Onkalot, well, well," muttered the Emperor. "Who would have expected. So this telekinetic show is your doing? Where did you come from?"

"She doesn't understand Kiritian." Q'ualel switched to his native language, turning to Chimalmat: "The chief is very curious about you. Will you tell us about yourself? What are you doing here?"

The female looked him in the eye, stepped back, tightened her fingers on the poncho.

"I don't know what to think. I've never seen any of the people walking with the demons. I can't tell if you are a traitor or a friend."

"These people are called Kiritians. They come ..." Aggro was looking for a simple, understandable word on the tribal culture level, "from the stars."

There was a shadow of interest on her part as well as pious fear.

"They are gods?"

"No. They have machines that make them travel between worlds, just like once the Great Family. The Kiritians are friendly to us, otherwise I wouldn't fall in with them. Xajb'a Kej himself was their leader, but he lost his life, being killed by an evil man who wasn't a Kiritian. We need Nimja's knowledge to bring Xajb'a Kej back to life. Can you help us? Are you guarding the great knowledge of Nimja?"

She didn't answer right away. She looked at one achij after another, she was frightened by Seymour, who grinned sardonically and waved to her.

"No," she finally replied sharply, firmly. "I have no evidence that you are telling the truth. You can be thieves like the rest." She pointed her claw at the nearest remnants. "And I will continue to guard these holy lands."

Q'ualel translated the words to his comrades. Necron sighed.

"We are going to waste too much time this way. Maybe we'd be better off if I could talk to her personally." The Emperor summoned Darkoris with a nod and whispered a command to him. The corporal looked at the Onkalot, nodded, and moved toward the jungle. "Equipment will be arranged soon, we will enter the pyramid."

Aggroteh looked at the Kiritians, he thought they had everything they needed to explore.

The technician returned a quarter of an hour later, during that time Q'ualel was unable to get anything concrete out of stubborn Chimalmat. She positioned herself on a low branch and watched the intruders suspiciously.

Darkoris walked over to Kiret and conspiratorially handed him something small.

Aggroteh's breath got stuck in his lungs as Biffter picked up a small pistol and aimed it at the dumbfounded Onkalot female.

"Sorry, Aggro. I have no choice," he said. And he fired.

The female squealed shortly after she had jumped off the tree. Q'ualel ran up to her and caught her in his arms.

"What are you doing?!" He growled at Biffter. Seymour put his hand on the butt of the gun.

Holding her shoulder, Chimalmat gave Aggroteh the hateful and despairing look of someone who had just been betrayed by a person to whom they were taking to. She sank limp in his paws, and her eyes moved into her skull.

***

Dusk was approaching, and Chimalmat had still not regained consciousness. The achijes and scientists sat down by the fire on the square in front of the pyramid, preferring to spend the night in the open air rather than in the ship orlops, just like the previous time. Aggro paced the area nervously, still angry with Necron for making the decision himself to put the female down without looking for a more humane alternative. With frustration, he remembered that the Immortals at the

Zodiac Universum were still law and established law, so they didn't have to ask anyone for permission.

"How much longer?" He asked the emperor sitting on a boulder and drinking a cup of soup.

"It takes longer for Onkalots to accept the entraser than for humans, but the female should wake up by now."

Aggro crouched down next to Chimalmat on a blanket. He checked the site on her left shoulder where she had been given an anesthetic with a plunger, then a hollow under the back of her head, where she had been later implanted with an entraser.

"What if something had happened to her? We are a dying species, and you must have put in danger perhaps the last female alive!"

"Calm down. She's just asleep. Her vital functions are normal. You saw how we examined her. Sleep is often the body's natural reaction after an entraser injection, when the brain absorbs a huge amount of knowledge being processed, initially sent from a chip as electrical impulses. Onkalotian physiology is similar to human one, so the data acceptance process is similar."

"Kiritian in five minutes," chuckled Seymour, listening to the conversation. His medically modified irises were perfectly red in the light of a burning fire.

"You meant five hours," muttered Aggro grimly.

The corporal lay down on the ground, clasped his hands behind his head, and returned to observing the swarm of small meteorites that burned spectacularly in the atmosphere. He breathed deeply.

"It's nice here. We should go out into the wild more often."

"Forgive me, Aggro, for acting without warning," Necron said to the Onkalot, who sat down by the fire, still offended. The Emperor put the empty cup back and folded his hands between his knees. "But I knew you would be against it."

"Typical Kiritians. Forkis trained you perfectly. You do what you want. I thought you were different. I thought of you as a man who respects the needs of the weak."

Biffter smiled soothingly. Aggro, staring at the flames, didn't notice that he got moody right after.

Taking advantage of the warmth and calm sounds of the night, the expedition began to spread across the tents. Many achijes liked the prospect of resting under the stars.

Chimalmat recovered two hours later and woke everyone up. Biffter was lured out of the tent by screeching sounds and screams. When he came out in the hastily donned pants, bracers and breastplate, he saw the growling Onkalotian female flattened to the ground by two achijes, similar to the skin of an animal decorating living rooms. Beside her sat nervous Q'ualel with his muzzle cut.

"The cntraser is up and running, sir," Seymour, one of those holding the female, announced cheerfully. He raised his hand to head height and twirled his fingers. "She's a complete nut."

"What did you do to me? By gods, what did you do to me?!" The she-cat spat. "I understand the speech of demons!"

"Hello, Chimalmat." Necron crouched down next to her, not making sudden movements. "My name is Kiret, I am ... the leader of these people. We are not your enemies. We put a special device in your head, completely harmless, so that we can talk to each other. I'm sorry for my warriors, but they were afraid you would run away or hurt yourself. Now I will order them to let you go, but promise them you won't run away." He didn't add that in such a case she would have been quickly captured, because it certainly wouldn't have built friendly relations.

She didn't answer, just looked at him with hostility. Kiret stood up, nodded, and the two achijes retreated. Chimalmat grunted, then rushed like a missile to leap at him with her claws. As a trained, tall, and powerfully built Kiritian, he easily grabbed her by the forearms and twisted her so that he found himself beyond the reach of her claws and fangs. He saw that she was surprisingly fragile, much more delicate than Aggro, and had poorer musculature, but she didn't lack strength.

Q'ualel caught her with his arm across her chest and pulled her toward him. Biffter peacefully raised his hands, hoping the cat would understand this universal gesture.

"You're safe, nothing endangers you. If we wanted to kill you or hurt you, we would have done it sooner."

Chimalmat's rapid breathing slowly began to normalize, she retracted her claws. Aggro felt his heart pounding under his arm slow down gradually. He withdrew his paw. Only now did he notice that Seymour had a gun at the ready, and onlookers' heads were sticking out of the tents. Some people had dressed hastily and gone out for some entertainment.

"So, you don't want to kill me?" The female now asked calmly, directing her gaze and words towards the Kiritian 'chief'. "You're not demanding, like the rest, the treasures of the Hurricane?"

"I swear we are not here to steal the treasures," replied the Emperor. At his beck and call, Seymour lowered his gun. "Only to gain the knowledge of your wise ancestors, important to us, which will allow our friend to come back to life. Besides, Q'ualel has already mentioned it to you."

Chimalmat tilted her head comically. Biffter indicated the structure.

"In the morning I want to enter the pyramid with the warriors and three priests." He pretended to think. "A guide would be useful to us. And the gods of light sent you to us."

Q'ualel smiled.

Chimalmat took a long time to reply, thinking. Having tilted her whiskers on the right side of her mouth so heavily that her tusk flashed, she looked first at the pyramid, then at Aggro and every man nearby. Eventually she looked at Necron.

"Okay, I'll help. Each of you," she pointed her claw at the people one by one, "who will smoke *xulu* with me."

"I'm for!" Tsar said enthusiastically.

Necron didn't have time to ask what Chimalmat meant, for she had already reached into a leather case and took out a handful of dried leaves. The weed tested during her sleep didn't contain harmful substances known to science, but the species couldn't be determined either, despite the fact that the H14 vegetation was derived from terraforming. The Kiritian supposed it was a new hybrid of local species, or a plant brought to the planet consciously or accidentally by its inhabitants.

"It's a ritual of integration," Aggro explained. "Kind of like a pipe of peace among human tribes."

"All right, then we'll smoke xulu with you," said the Emperor. The Onkalotian female began to move away.

"Where are you going?"

"Don't worry, I'm not running away. I need a large leaf. You can come with me if you want."

The archeologist volunteered.

"I'll go with her."

Seymour put his hands on his hips and looked at the two scientists which accompanied their colleague with their sight.

"So? Are we smoking weed?" He clapped his hands and rubbed them.

"Why should we play rituals?" Muttered the linguist, unhappy that the screams interrupted his sleep.

"It costs us nothing," Necron folded his arms over his chest, "and in return the she-cat will lead us through the pyramid. "Maybe she knows hidden chambers that it would take us some time to find. And all this xulu is harmless, so don't worry. If it turns out that someone is allergic to substances contained in the plant, it will take a few minutes to detoxify the blood.

"Can't we just threaten her with a gun?" Darkoris remembered Chimalmat's reaction when he had stood over her with the rifle barrel. "We could have done that at once."

"Then she won't tell us anything." Aggro gave him a dry look. "You will only receive information from an Onkalot if you convince them to yourself. If you use force, you'll kill them sooner, but you won't get anything out of them."

The members of the expedition had gathered around a newly lit fire before the archeologist returned with the Onkalotian female, carrying - to Tsar's disappointment - a banana leaf. The female sat on the crossed hind legs, took the dried leaves out of her pouch and efficiently made a large joint which she lit. She gestured for the rest to sit in a circle next to her.

"Who fails the xulu test, will not come with us," she said, emphasizing the meaning of the explicitly pronounced words with a wave of her finger. She flitted with her gaze across the crowd. "Let the worthy unite."

She took a deep drag and released a puff of gray smoke from her lungs. She handed the joint to Necron. The man, as a soldier for several centuries, had extensive experience in smoking various psychoactive substances, so he passed the integration trial successfully without coughing or gagging, which for Chimalmat would have meant having a weak, cowardly heart. The Emperor felt as if he had sucked in acrid fumes from some acid, but felt only slightly dizzy. Aggroteh was an Onkalot, and had undergone many similar rituals among his people in the past, and the body's cellular memory didn't fail, so the way he dragged seemed satisfactory to the female as well. Seymour's reaction was a dismissive smile of an interstellar engine builder who was given the extremely difficult task of tightening a screw. A problem started only with the scientists. Biffter was unlucky enough to gather a group that had avoided volatile stimulants, moreover, the bodies of oderses were weaker than the Immortal organisms changed with the super virus, and the substances contained in xulu turned out to be irritating. Each of the scientists either coughed solidly or choked (the archeologist had used to smoke drugs, but stopped due to bronchial problems). The coughing linguist said that Kiret's idea was nonsensical, which amused the achij.

"The priests are not coming with us! Otherwise, Chimalmat won't help!" the she-cat issued the final verdict, amazed that the spiritual, according to her, part of the expedition turned out to be the weakest one.

Necron asked the protesting three to stay in the camp for the sake of peace. He assured that the achijes would be broadcasting the expedition from probes or preview of the equipment.

"You can go inside when we no longer need the help of Chimalmat," he humored the scientists eventually.

Three hours remained until dawn, which Necron instructed his subordinates to spend sleeping.

When he left the tent in the morning and went to answer the call of nature, he noticed Seymour curling up on the ground with laughter. Next to it were the remnants of *xulu* and flatspike leaves colloquially known as the devil's herb. Astonished, he sighed, shaking his head. Tsar was the only man he knew to get hysterics from doses of drugs that were lethal to other people.

"So, this one doesn't come with us either, there must be some punishment." He moved to other bushes. "My army is falling apart before my eyes."

***

There were four main entrances to Tz'aqol with ornate portals located on each side of the pyramid. In the past, all of them could be used only by the priests of Onkalots - the plebs had used only the passage leading to a prayer room. Once a priestess, Chimalmat knew perfectly well the sacred building, which at first glance seemed to have a simple structure: three corridors converging in a tomb chamber and one ending in the prayer one. Once it had been believed that the sanctuary had been the seat of the gods of light, so it had been ensured that the holy fire burned constantly inside. Although the Onkalotian female had been in the Kiritian camp from the previous day, logs were burning along the corridor she led them. Necron assumed that she had lit them before they met her, using wood slowly consumed by fire, and soaked with something else. The straight corridor was decorated with reliefs depicting scenes from myths about the gods worshiped here. Chimalmat and Aggro translated the hieroglyphs, but there was no mention of living Nimja artifacts or bringing the dead back to life.

The rectangular hall inside the pyramid, also rich in reliefs, was divided by walls into burial chambers with catafalques. Almost all of them were open and empty - Chimalmat, through telekinesis, had dragged old priest-guards outside, so that even after their death they could punish those eager for Tz'aqol riches. Kiret was disappointed to think that there were only corridors and resting places of the ancient Onkalots in the sky-high pyramid, until Chimalmat shifted the lid of one of the sarcophagi with a masked lever.

"You have to take the light." She pointed to the hidden stairs leading to the nether regions. She jumped on them and walked down a bit, her eyes switched to infravision vision. She smiled smugly. "Unless you can see in the dark."

"Can we trust her?" Viktor whispered to Q'ualel, scratching his lower jaw. The molecular glue had left no trace of damage on the injured neck. "We have no guarantee that she will not lead us to death."

"That's true, we don't," replied the Onkalot. "But I believe she got convinced to us. She is crazy but not stupid. She knows she will die in no time at our hands if she makes a false move."

"Where are you taking us?" Echo repeated Necron's question three times.

"Come and see." The she-cat laughed eerily. Only a pair of red eyes were visible in the gloom apart from the circle of fire.

Biffter slipped his helmet on, switched to thermal vision and, to the consternation of Sergeant Shane, who wanted to go at the front, was the first to descend the steps. Viktor had never shared with him that his attempts to stylize himself as Forkis, literally and figuratively the head of achijes, were almost daring. He signaled the Kiritians on the team to follow him in the column, and two of them stayed on watch in the tomb chamber.

The steps led to a claustrophobic corridor that descended more and more. Many minutes passed before the team reached the landing, there its members turned and began to descend again endlessly down another sloping corridor, as if to the very core of the planet, deeper and deeper into the darkness, seeing only thanks to the helmet boosters. Although no one was claustrophobic, it was a discomfort for everyone to walk through the cramped tunnel, reeking of antiquity. Some, like Corporal Darkoris, imagined that Chimalmat would lead them to perdition, that they would be buried alive under thousands of tons of earth, flooded with water, or covered with sand as they were walking towards a trap created by ancient builders.

The journey was soon over. The team stopped in a recess with double door, in which there were engraved deep in the stone two several meters long anthropomorphs facing each other, similar to Onkalots, but more dog-headed than cat-headed. Dressed in flowing, aristocratic robes, they wielded in their right paws staffs as tall as their silhouettes themselves. Darkoris illuminated the space with generators of artificial fire, attaching them to the walls, and examined the air for the presence of pathogens and harmful particles - nothing exceeded the planetary norm. Next to the gate, under a drift sealed with clay were lying broken stone structures and ropes. When Necron touched the closest one, it crumbled to dust. He looked up.

"Once an elevator must have operated here, and the corridors we came through might have been emergency exits. Our doctors would probably know it better.

"The corridors could also act as shafts or ventilation," commented immediately the archeologist who listened from the ship.

"The gods don't like the weak or the indecisive in their habitats," Chimalmat said. "That's why I ordered the false priests to stay. Only the worthy pass the *xulu* test."

Aggro, staring at the gate, smiled broadly.

"These are images of Nimja. We are there."

The female raised her paw and closed her eyes, summoning her telekinetic abilities in focus. Unnecessarily, and only for the sake of greater ecstasy, she helped herself with the words spoken in Kiritian:

Heaven's heart
The Earth's heart
Creator Maker
Holder Parent
By my blood and bones
Leave ajar the ancient gate before us!

The multi-tonne gate did begin open slowly with a creak, creating arches on the sandy ground. The ever-wider space of clearance was being stolen by darkness.

"I'll go first." Viktor stepped forward, not wanting to let the Emperor take the initiative again and become the number one target for possible threats. He activated a yellow flare.

Kiritian's attention focused on the resulting space; the female's smile deepened; Aggro stared at the door with a hint of pious reverie. For a few moments there was silence, as if the living hadn't disturbed the peace of the underworld. Sergeant Shane ended it:

"Oh ... shit ..."

They stood in front of the entrance to a gigantic room, which originally had been a vaulted basalt cave, inlaid with iridescent minerals, until transformed at the behest of the Ancient Onkalots. The hall was divided into unequal sectors with stone blocks, and each had recesses filled with manuscripts and books. Fractal in cross-section, decorated columns supported the ceiling. Between four statues in the center of the room, there was a platform covered with old tools, a large part of it was occupied by a stone block with the appearance of a screw. Glyphs, hieroglyphs, and kabbalistic characters covered every wall. In the yellow light of the flare, the room looked as if completely made of gold.

Necron noticed paw prints on the dusty floor.

"Chimalmat, have you been here before?"

"Yes. I know this place. It is it that I guard against the world. I don't know what it was for, but since it was hidden, it had to be important. I'm not worthy to know old secrets."

"Is it safe?"

"It is, chief of the stars. It is a place of wisdom, only the high priests had access here, high enough to look into the splendor of the all-powerful Hurricane. They had weak bodies but strong heads, they said that I have a weak head, but a good body, so I became the last guardian before the extermination."

"Check the room," Necron ordered.

While the achijes were investigating whether the chamber was really safe, Aggro, fascinated, studied the wall. An expression of enchantment began to crawl off his muzzle as his fingers touched successive stretches of dusty facet, furrowy with hieroglyphs and glyphs. He ran his claw along the tangled grooves.

"I don't know this language. It's very old." He looked sadly at Necron.

"I know it perfectly well. I know the language of the Ancients," said the Onkalotian female with an enigmatic smile.

"So, we were lucky that our paths met," replied the emperor, admiring the architectural precision of the ancient builders who, by means unknown to modern science, had been able to move huge blocks of rock so deep underground.

He ordered the achijes to illuminate the cave so that it could be viewed without the use of vision enhancers, thus catch more important details. Necron had already visited a few ruins left by Onkalots, he had stayed the longest in Ajb'atenaja, thanks to which he had remembered the form of the humanoid jaguars' writing. Each one outside of Tz'aqol had a more primitive character, while the signs and pictures around them were complicated and difficult to recreate by hand. If he had been to redraw them, he would have had to look at them often and stare at them for a long time, and he would copy only the simplest symbols anyway. Though he didn't understand anything about what was preserved on the walls, he knew from the easier-to-interpret glyphs that they had nothing to do with mythology, but rather with scientific knowledge. He recognized star systems, as if bacterial cells, flying machines, and tools, some of which rested in the center of the cave. It was enough for him to find the Great Family of Nimja - if they had indeed found their legacy - as an intellectually developed nation, although using a technology other than those based on electronics and radio waves. He went to the shelves, but he didn't stay there long, because the manuscripts made of pressed sheets of plants would have fallen apart when touched, and of the stone plaques and books, he understood nothing.

He returned to the center of the cave, climbed short steps to a circular platform. Above him, he noticed a drift in the ceiling that extended to the top of the pyramid. It was associated with a ventilation shaft, a sky observatory or an outlet for smaller aircraft, alternatively an elevator.

Shane, Aggro, and Darkoris joined him as he looked at the symbols between the boots. The technician had finished placing the lighting.

"Demotic writing," Biffter noted.

"This is the first time I see something like this," said Q'ualel. "In Chiq'aq, the Place of Fire, we only used glyphs and hieroglyphs as warriors and civilians, while the priests knew the hieratic writing."

Viktor frowned. Among the repeating letters that reflected the modern Kiritian alphabet, he noticed a multitude of faded drawings that looked like sketches. They depicted the constellations of stars and planetary systems. One was particularly eye-catching.

Necron, Darkoris, and Shane looked at each other in amazement, reaching the same conclusions.

"This is Earth. And the entire solar system!" The corporal crouched down and was pointing at the elements with his finger. "Sun. Planets. Eris tilted at forty-four degrees to the plane of the System. Sedna. Oort Cloud Sphere ... Nemesis."

"And this is the constellation of Orion." Biffter recognized the other system he had seen during his space travel from different angles.

"There is also Mezzo. Nephrid. H14 and K'ajolom. Also ..." Darkoris felt cold sweat flooding his back and neck. "Morascrik! Nearby stars, planetary systems, and asteroid belts are identical!"

"Exactly. The sketches show quite a few terrestrial planets, the same that were terraformed and inhabited by the Earth's population." Necron looked blankly at Chimalmat, who approached uncertainly. "Did Nimja know them also in the past?"

"But I don't know these." Shane pointed to successive drawings, in which stars, their planets and satellites could be recognized. He crouched like a corporal and rested his hands on the floor. "What the hell is that supposed to mean?"

"We need to catalog everything carefully," announced Necron. "Then we will compare it with our maps of the cosmos. It is possible that these are planets where life may have developed and which we don't know yet."

"As long as it's not a slick shit and trolololo."

Necron turned and saw Seymour who had recovered and followed them into the underworld. Eventually, no one had given him any order. The corporal's doubts were justified. Among the true celestial bodies there may have been nonexistent, for example, destroyed for some reason, or the probabilities related to myths rather than facts had been established. Necron, however, preferred to take the most optimistic version - that they were planets as real as the ones they recognized.

"Aggro, are you able to translate something of these notes?" He asked. Q'ualel nodded negatively, staring helplessly at the demotic writing.

"I don't understand any of this. Sorry."

Chimalmat crouched down, ran her fingers over a circled fragment of dusty text that ended with a drawing. She brushed the dirt away with her paw and blew.

"We have nothing more to do here," she began to slowly translate, according to her own line of reasoning. "We're leaving. Me and my immortal brothers. The land of Tamasul in the Jaguar Galaxy will be our new home. The era of the Dynasty is over, it is time to leave the world to our heirs. They were endowed with reason, so also with free will. We won't be needed anymore, because our time on this earth has passed ..."

"If a goat hadn't been jumping, the snail wouldn't show your horns," Seymour mocked the female.

"Tsar, damn it!" Necron growled.

The amusement didn't disappear from the corporal's face.

"What? Those Nimja members or whatever they are called had poor weed on the town. What's wrong with you guys? You are not taking the gibberish from some shitty pebbles seriously, do you?"

The achijes embraced the corporal with reluctant glances, though they gave him his due in spirit. The words could have been engraved by someone like an intoxicated shaman or religious fanatic.

"Go on, Chimalmat," Kiret encouraged. "You're translating well, because we understand everything. And you, Seymour, shut your trap. At least for five frigging minutes."

The Onkalotian female looked uncertainly at the achijes before she began to translate further:

"What path the descendants will follow doesn't matter to us anymore. We will never come back. The Off-kilter Fang, you will be the last to travel, make no mistake and destroy the porter. I took the notes about its operation with me. So, check the solar weapon carefully, then activate it. I don't know if I will ever have the opportunity to do this, so I'll tell you it at the end: thank you for giving me back my life after fifty tunas[6] of lying in the tomb. At the time of my execution, I lost all hope of survival when I was wrongly accused of murder, then dismembered. Fortunately, truth and knowledge won, but I will have to hide again. So goodbye and good luck. Seventh Minister, The Bone Crusher." Chimalmat breathed again. "My head has gotten tired." She tapped her forehead. "Q'ualel doesn't understand the letters, and I don't understand their meaning. I will not help the Kiritians with this."

---

[6] Year in the Mayan calendar.

"And you, sir, do you understand any of this?" Shane turned to Kiret. He noticed that everyone was already standing on the platform.

"Land of Tamasul in the Jaguar Galaxy. Earth probably as land, because rather not our Earth. What planet can it be?"

Kiret looked glumly at the porter's rubble lying in the center, which might have been a screw-like colossus. He was silent for a moment.

"If it is really not the cheap bilge that our highly respected corporal sometimes tells us,"He glared at Seymour, "perhaps we made two of the greatest discoveries in human history: we found ancient 'gods' present in all myths, and a way to restore life to the dead. However, we need to thoroughly investigate the Tz'aqol finds to learn more. It is really a strange coincidence that we now met the Onkalotian female who knows Nimja's writing, and she accidentally read the fragment that may refer to our case."

"It was circled, that's why Chimalmat began to translate it," Q'ualel said, pointing to the obvious scratches on the stone. "Thanks to it, the Off-kilter Fang was to notice the note thousands of years ago. I suppose he was someone who was ordered to seal the chamber and cover the tracks."

"It may be a deception, sir." Shane watched Chimalmat suspiciously. "She has known our plans."

"Vaguely," corrected Biffter. "Yes, it might be a deception, but why would she make things up? Show 'demons' where Nimja went?"

"Or a place where certain doom awaits us. But okay. Let's suppose this is true. What are we going to do with such knowledge? How are you going to use it, sir?"

Necron stared at the constellation drawing below the Bone Smasher's note for a long time before answering:

"What a Kiritian endowed with such knowledge would do." He gave the subordinate a beaming look. "We'll use it wisely."

Everyone, except Chimalmat drawing patterns in the dust, looked at the destroyed object in the center. Viktor guessed what was on the Emperor's mind.

"This is crazy," he said aloud what the others were thinking.

IV. Skelver and the Council of Five Dignitaries

After carefully photographing Tz'aqol and sending the information to the database, the Kiritians spent another week exploring the other temples. Kiret managed to take Chimalmat on a journey, although he had long persuaded her that the ship was not a metal monster that devoured the living.

The Q'ijik astronomical observatory hid more maps of the sky, the Immortals found nothing of importance in Yolcuat's house, and the looters had long since gotten to the Ojer tzij library. Chimalmat described another H14 metropolises, unknown to Q'ualel, where Nimja's knowledge could be gathered, but Kiret decided to end the search, claiming that the temple of Tz'aqol provided him with the necessary data. His decision was mainly influenced by a disturbing news he received on the corvette's bridge that the planet Mezzo, the former headquarters of the opposition, which had been in the hands of the Kiritians until a week earlier, rebelled and riots took place there. Apparently, a faction of Kiritian radicals, who considered

Kiret to be too gentle and ineffective a leader, turned to the side of the rebels. In addition, the Council of Dignitaries, also known as the Council of Five, was preparing deliberations in Morascrik, at which Necron wanted to be present.

Q'ualel felt sorry for Chimalmat that they had to leave her alone at Tz'aqol's Temple again, but the Kiritians hadn't figured out what they could do with the Onkalotian female fearing technology and the vastness of space. On Morascrik, she would have been tired of the volcanic air itself, and to the Schindlers, Aggro didn't want to take her because she would have probably been at loggerheads with Eredal. So, he went there alone. Chimalmat announced that she would return to the jungle to further protect the temple, but she looked resigned. Q'ualel decided to visit her from time to time.

Thanks to hyperspace leaps, the Kiritians' journey to the capital on Morascrik took a Terrenic week. During it, scientists translated cataloged notes from temples using capripods, and attempts were made to synchronize the military map of the cosmos with that created by Nimja. To Necron, his own idea of finding a solution to the problem of power among stones and myths seemed absurd, but he made a point of checking all the possibilities that could have helped bring Forkis back to life. He certainly didn't lack money for it. He had an open mind to unknown and inexplicable phenomena, which the traditionalist part of the Kiritians didn't like. Examples of Forkis' living artifact or the psionic abilities of Onkalots proved to him that he couldn't base his knowledge solely on the fact that the truth was provided by hard facts and conventional science.

***

Kiret was very fond of the city of K'otz'ib'aja, peculiarly named by Forkis in his native language. The new First Galactic Dignitary could change the Onkalotian name to a different one, but he chose to keep the original version. He wasn't going to get involved in what everyone was used to and what didn't bother anyone. He liked the slightly sulfur air, cones of inactive volcanoes on the horizon, looking like the jaws of a giant reptile, the sky of an ever-reddish color, architecture reminiscent of ancient Mayan cities, but stuffed with electronics, sky-high collectors accumulating cosmic energy from above strands of clouds. Although the place plumed itself on a dark charm, you always wanted to come back to it. However, this time, when the corvette's chassis touched a landing pad near the famous Utza'm Achij cave, which was the place of collective and small Kiritians' meetings, assailing thoughts of the impending trouble returned to Necron. They appeared to be the most serious since the Immortals had come to power in 2570, when the Earth's New Order Army had fallen, and with it the remnants of a global government. No good news came during the trip to the capital. Signals about Forkis' disintegrating empire grew clearer.

The case of mysterious refugees from an unknown galaxy where allegedly war had broken out and local inhabitants had salvaged themselves flying into unknown corners of space, turned out to be particularly disturbing. Apart from the fact that with the arrival of the migrants, the Zodiac Universum learned that somewhere in space a similar civilization had developed, Kiret wondered why the refugees flew blindly, not knowing if they would find habitable planets along their route.

While still on board the corvette, he had learned from the preliminary report of scientists that the alien people had developed in far seclusions of the universe on the basis of biological convergence and visually didn't differ from the inhabitants of the Zodiac Universum, although the two species didn't share even a single gene. The case of the mysterious journey was also clarified in subsequent reports, now flowing in rapidly. It turned out that the migrants followed a mathematical formula, thanks to which it was possible to determine, having in the database trillions of cataloged celestial bodies, where the next habitable planets were. It assumed the repeatability of macrosystems in space; an equation based on this formula had been developed by the Kiritian mathematician and astronomer Wiliam Baks, using the files created after the testimony of refugees interviewed in K'otz'ib'aja. Hence this equation was called using the author's surname. The discovery seemed groundbreaking for the Immortals - if alien knowledge didn't turn out to be false, it would mean accelerated space colonization and billions of uinals saved. It would be enough to fly straight to the destination instead of looking for it, as had been done so far.

Biffter had slept in the corvette shortly before landing, so he wasn't tired of the journey and decided to convene a council meeting that same day. Having the mentality of a simple soldier, he hated to sit for hours on a diorite throne in the Utza'm Ahiji cave and listen to five dignitaries arguing, only to say 'yes' or 'no' after presenting all the arguments on a given case, thereby approving or rejecting a decree in question. However, he had to face it as a politician and ruler. On his decisions depended further steps in the procedure of accepting refugees at the Zodiac Universum. No matter how stormy the meetings were, it usually took a day to settle an issue. Therefore, another was to be devoted to internal problems, including revolts in certain sectors and increased activity of the rebels who had taken advantage of Necron's mild policy after taking power.

After setting the time of the meeting, Kiret went to his office in the building that had once belonged to Forkis, which also housed an apartment of Sandstorm, a member of the Council. After refreshing himself, he went to visit her. Having reached the room in which Anna had locked him a few months earlier, which had saved his life from the terrorist attack by Beliar, he pressed a console plaque by the door and announced his arrival. After a while the entrance was opened. Sandstorm stood by the window, staring out at the city skyline. She was wearing a green and black gown, wide as her dark auburn hair flowing down her shoulders. As she turned, Kiret noticed she was holding a month-old baby in her arms and was rocking it gently. He smiled gently; there was a worry on Sandstorm's face.

"Hello, Anna. It's nice to see you again. Having approached her, he brushed the black hairs on the baby's head who waved its arms and stared at him curiously with its squinty hazel eyes. "And you too, little Jenny," he said to Anna in a joking tone. "I thought you would be more pleased to see me."

She managed a forced smile.

"How was your trip? Something interesting happened? You sent only superficial information to the Council."

Kiret thought about killing the lycans and shooting the walking skeletons.

"Let's say the expedition was interesting. We found an Onkalotian female in the ruins, and together with Aggro she helped us translate the writing of the elders of their people."

"That's not what I'm asking about, sir."

The man scratched his head in embarrassment. He had grown up in the world of science and technology, and despite witnessing the unexplained phenomena associated with Onkalots, it was difficult for him to squeeze absurd-sounding words down his throat, "We have found records dating back thousands of years according to which the race that prayed to the sun and the gods, or perhaps even considered itself gods, knew a way to bring the dead back to life." So, he replied evasively:

"We have a lot of data and new information we are currently analyzing it. You should find out everything tomorrow. And how was it during my absence?"

He frowned as he saw that the girl was looking for something on the walls and ceiling.

"Wait a minute, I'll go lay her down."

She walked away to the next room, whispering soothing words to Jenny as she fell asleep. She returned a quarter of an hour later. She sat down heavily on a blanket-covered bed, looking more distressed than before. Necron sat down next to her, as there was no furniture nearby apart from the bed - Sandstorm had moved chairs and table to Jenny's room so that she could place more things on them. He reassuringly put his hand on her shoulder.

"What's going on? Did something happen?"

"Yes, it did. Yesterday someone let a fist-sized poisonous spider into my daughter's room."

He had expected various news, but certainly not such information. He took into account the fact that since Anna had become a mother, she had been more emotional and able to exaggerate unimportant things.

"Are you sure it was poisonous?" He put his foot in the mouth, which he regretted immediately.

"Do you think I'm stupid?!" She reacted with an anger, with which she had used to solve almost all problems. The events on the planet Aj, the subsequent attack in the capital and the death of both partners added seriousness to her, but with the advent of motherhood, indispensable had become nervousness and concern for Jenny's safety.

The man withdrew his hand.

"Relax. Just asking. How did it come about?"

"I was away from my apartment all evening. You understand, the duties of a councilor should be shared with private life. When I got back and dismissed the babysitter, I noticed the spider on the wall by the crib. I was terrified, I knocked it off with my clothes thrown, and crushed it with the headboard of a chair. Lured by the noise, the babysitter came back, I shouted at her and told her to get out. When I cooled down, I took Jenny in my arms and went to talk quietly with the girl. She had nothing on her conscience, had never caused any problems, nevertheless agreed to testify with a lie detector. I agreed to it since she insisted, although I believed in her Kiritian truthfulness anyway. She claimed that she didn't know where this spider came from, which turned out to be true. The windows to Jenny's room were closed the whole time yesterday, the gaps in the door are too small for such a large maggot to pass through. I took the remains to the laboratory and it turned out that the spider was so venomous that the poison from one bite could have killed thirty people. The strangest thing is that the species doesn't exist in the database. It has not been seen on any planet, as if it hadn't been discovered yet, or was artificially created or brought from a biotic world we don't know yet. No genetic similarities were found." Sandstorm was moved when she thought what the incident might have ended with. She rested her forehead on the chest of the surprised Kiritian. "Kiret, hug me."

He hesitated before granting that request, and regardless, he hugged Sandstorm stiffly like a first-generation android. He had liked her from the moment he first saw her during landing on Aj. So beautiful, young, petite and confused, but also with a fiery temperament. However, aside from professional matters, he had always stayed away from her because of Sandstorm's relationship with Forkis and his rules about monogamous Kiritian relationships. After his murder, Kiret hadn't wanted to impose on Annie, lest she hadn't interpreted his behavior as an attempt to use her in moments of weakness. In addition, Anna's low prestige would have deteriorated even more if she had started going around with Biffter right after Forkis's death, especially since she had recently been in a relationship with the rebel Drunkenstein. So Kiret chose to abnegate. The youngest member of the Council of Dignitaries had changed a lot since she lost Forkis and then gave birth to the child. She had become more vulnerable, often fell into apathy, and then exploded unexpectedly with anger. However, she indulged herself only in contacts with her relatives, and publicly tried to pass as a reasonable person, usually flaunting with an indifferent face. The destabilization of the nation made her fear for her daughter, although a political attack on Jenny's life would have been pointless. Forkis had only followers among the Immortals, and Biffter was chosen to succeed him. As far as Anna knew, Kiret didn't get under the skin of anyone, so those around him couldn't be terrorized for his decisions. She herself, although a councilor, was too petty for someone unfavorable to want to harm her or her daughter.

Jenny herself was the fruit of Anna and Forkis' romance on Aj. Before they left the planet, they had had intercourse many times. Forkis was as sure of his sterility as any Immortal from the moment of kiritianization. This process, initiated by Dr. Figam's super virus, altered the program of action of all cells in the body, which began to regenerate on average every five Terrenic years, so that the biologically regressed host didn't age. A medically stimulated side effect was infertility as a fair price to pay for immortality, according to Forkis, necessary and in accordance with the norms of nature. For achijes it became the highest law and it was obeyed. However, even before the skirmish with the rebels, when the emperor had been in the capital, he had injured himself and instead of regenerative nanites he had been unknowingly given a reproductive restorative, used on rare occasions. To blame, was the drunken geneticist Alejandro Cortez, who had wanted to get back at his friend, but had overdone it and made a mess in his office bigger than he had intended. The supervirus didn't pass to Jenny in maternal blood as it was single host-linked, tuned to its protein sequences, and therefore the disease wasn't inherited. Forkis had died before finding about the offspring.

Kiret was afraid that the little one would inherit from Forkis the features of an Onkalot, fortunately he hadn't noticed anything suspicious so far. Apparently, the inheritance of traits after transmutation - the quintessence of which no one had yet understood - took place in a biological way. So only the proper organism mattered, not the previous one.

"You don't have to worry about anything, I'm with you," he said. "In my opinion, you isolate yourself too much from everyone. Ever since you got Jenny, you have spent time only with her and the nanny, and all the rest you see out of necessity. Isolation is not healthy, with time you get freaked out. You look for irregularities in yourself and your environment. Get out to the people. You've been alone since Forkis left. Tense and nervous all the time. Maybe you should really ... find someone."

The girl smiled in a vague way, looked with her green eyes in Kiret's hazel ones. Forkis had had eyes similar to his, only the infravision after dark had revealed his origins.

"You old bastard. I know you have the hots for me."

"Me, old? I'm only thirty-four."

"I think four hundred and thirty-four. But you look forty."

"Alright, so let's count it. I was born in 2483, and it's 2957, you almost guessed it - I'm four hundred and seventy-four. You know how the super virus works. It begins to change the cellular action program on average every five years, restoring cells to the state they were in when the person got infected. That's why I look older now."

Anna sighed as she rested her temple against his armored chest.

"I'm so sorry for that 'bastard'. Ever since Jenny was born, I've snarled at everyone.

"It's normal. You're afraid for your daughter, you want to protect her. Every woman becomes oversensitive after childbirth." He added quickly, lest it looked like an insult: "In the sense of being sensitive to external stimuli." He stumbled. That line was even worse.

"What about you?"

"And what's supposed to be?"

"Do you have someone? We've never had a chance to talk about it. It has become an undetermined taboo subject."

"With such a multitude of duties, I don't have time ..."

Necron didn't finish, his eyes widened in surprise as Anna moved, clasped her hands around his neck and kissed him on the lips. He lightly brushed her lips, grabbed her waist. She gently pushed him with his back to the sheets. Kiret turned so that Anna found herself between his arms leaning against the bed.

"Stop it," he said firmly, looking to the side. "What exactly was that supposed to be?"

"You said a moment ago ... I thought that you too ..."

He got up, took a few nervous steps, and turned to face her.

"The collapsed star, that's not what I meant. I meant company. An interlocutor. A person who is on the same wavelength and is not an emperor who has to be out all the time."

Sandstorm sat up, hid her face in her hands, felt ashamed.

"Sorry. The empire falling apart, spider, less and less friendly people around. Now some refugees. I'm not good at dealing with stress, I will not hide it from you. Playing in front of the Kiritians, that everything is fine and that I have a great grasp of the new reality, tires me a lot. I have no strength. I thought ... that in this way I would somehow ease the tension. I really apologize to you, Kiret, for my selfishness. I still love Forkis and I believe he will come back. That you will find a way ..." She lowered her voice. "I do fit perfectly with the definition of a traitor, as they whisper behind my back. And I don't mean what I did now."

"How you can jump from one subject to another." Kiret smiled briefly. "Yes, you walked unexpectedly from one yard to another, but when you look closely at their structures, you will notice that the opposition and Kiritians are very similar to each other. It all depends on a point of view, that's what Forkis taught me. There is no bad side or good side, just a different story, ideology and motivations." He sat back on the bed, moved aside Annie's hair that covered her eye. "Nothing happened. I'm not angry. Everyone has the right to a moment of weakness revealed ... to their friends. The most important thing is that we are honest with ourselves."

"You have more sense than me."

"Old beggars are like that." Necron grinned.

"Thank you for stopping me."

This time Kiret felt ashamed of his own thoughts. He could use her so easily, young, recently kiritianized and still very naive, even though the events of recent months had left a mark on Anna. Admittedly, she had been infected with the super virus, but had not yet received a fertility inhibitor due to her past pregnancy and motherhood. Such a biochemical shock would have amounted to an endocrine disruption. Therefore,

Anna was guided by both biological and mental needs, while Kiret approached other women solely for entertainment, although he had ceased to enjoy it for a long time. He did it practically only at the urging of achijes, who wanted him to stop being such a wet blanket and melancholic, and get a bit distracted. As the centuries passed, he still remembered how he had feared at the beginning of his new Kiritian existence that he would become a cripple unable to fertilize, which derogated manhood. Fortunately, he quickly accepted the changes, he coped with them quite well. The immortalized body made up for its inability to procreate with the fact that the achij felt greater ecstasy during an intercourse than an ordinary human. Pregnancy didn't exist in the nation, unless a Kiritian was given a drug called inhibispermato A2, which restored the ability of reproductive cells to fertilize. The permission to have a child was sometimes given by the emperor, the law softened in times of war or other conflict in which there were casualties, but this rarely happened in Kiritian history. Forkis was dead, but there was a little chance that he could be recreated with body, soul and mind. Therefore, Kiret preferred not to come near Anna. Although for the brief moment when she had kissed him, he had indeed wanted her.

"I'll do everything possible to get him back," he said. Anna got up and went to the window, rubbing her shoulders.

"Did you find out something specific on H14, or you are just comforting me?"

"Tomorrow I will know for sure, as I said. Now I don't want to mislead you." Biffter stood beside her.

"What happened a moment ago ... Forgive me for my selfishness."

"And you're going to apologize so until tonight? At the Council meeting too?" He smiled. "At least it will be interesting." He shook her shoulder. "A simple communication error, no big deal really." He turned to the door. "Get ready slowly."

"I fear for Jenny."

"Unfortunately, you cannot take her to the deliberations. But relax, I'll get the baby the best care in the capital."

***

Before Necron left the building, he heard a rumble like from a hundred zurnas. There was a terrible bang, followed immediately by a shuddering earth. Like a couple of people nearby, he ran outside, at first associating the noise with the collapsing edifice or the awakening of the inactive volcano, which would have contradicted seismograph readings.

Almost immediately, he ran back to the gate, as a shock wave passed through the district, carrying fragments of the road and buildings.

As the tumult died down, Kiret noticed through the wall of fluttering dust that one of the giant collectors reaching above the clouds was missing.

Michael Avadar, the captain with white short-cut hair, ran up to him.

"Sir, you'd better go to Utza'm Achij Cave to be safe. We don't know what happened yet. Sir?"

Biffter wasn't listening. Chased by the confused officer, he headed for the place where to the ground, had fallen the collector with a diameter of twenty-five meters, looking like a kilometer-long dead caterpillar. As it collapsed in an empty area on the edge of town, it didn't cause any damage other than shattering the ground and blocking the way Kiret intended to go for deliberation.

"What's that supposed to mean?" he asked an encountered technical repairman.

"Emperor, the bond at the base broke. However, I guarantee that none of the employees abandoned their duties. The collector was routinely inspected and the strobili' condition was exemplary. Everything was regularly scanned by technical drones. We don't know how the collapse happened. Rather than sabotage, it was just a coincidence, as only trusted employees were around. Nevertheless, we will investigate the matter. Fortunately, no one was killed or injured."

"All right. Thank you," Kiret said politely, seeing that the man was nervous. He took a roundabout route to the Council annex.

"Shall I call the team to escort you, sir?" Suggested Avadar, who was near Biffter all the time. "The repairman could be wrong, he's a civilian, after all. Maybe someone tried to cause the cancelation of the Council meeting?"

"Dropping the pipes from above?" Necron sneered. "No equipment or building can last forever, and many of them in K'otz'ibaja are hundreds of years old. Thank you for your concern and the offer, but the last thing an Emperor needs is an escort in his own capital. It's against our rules. Nobody has to worry about anything here and can go almost anywhere they want, especially the leaders. This is Morascrik, not some shabby Oderses' planet. If it was indeed sabotage," he immediately thought of the poisonous spider in Jenny's room, and it flashed through his mind that, unless Anna had exaggerated her assumptions, the two incidents could indeed have been related, "by changing the security status, we would only give satisfaction to those wishing to perturbate in the capital city. Get back to your duties, Captain."

"Of course, sir."

Biffter turned and walked across a parade ground to a side alley that led between buildings to be demolished.

After a few minutes, he heard raised voices, the shuffling of shoes, and a thump. As he reached a blind alley darkened by the silhouettes of empty warehouses, he spotted Kiritians and a refugee - one of the few who had been brought to the capital for examination and questioning, then set free into the city and secretly watched. The emaciated man in his thirties was of medium height, fair skinned, and had short straw-colored hair. He was being hold painfully from behind by a half-heavier achij, characterized by two little finger-length blonde braids on his chin. The other one, short-haired, tall, pale and beefy, stood beside him, with his arms folded across his chest and a smile of satisfaction, watching the show. The black Kiritian with dreadlocks raised his glove and outthrusted metal blades; he was clearly planning to kill the defenseless refugee, already bleeding from wounds on his face.

Amazed Kiret not for the first time that day thought that the installation of monitoring in K'otz'ib'aja wouldn't have been a bad move. Though it would have reflected fatefully on the wielder.

"Enough!" Immortals got confused. The last thing they had expected was to see the emperor himself in an unused alley.

"Since when are guests in my capital tortured? The degree and superior!"

The beefy Kiritian who had been passively watching the refugee being beaten was the first to regain his speech ability.

"I'm Private Kazuo Shimizu."

"Private Nexon Walker," said the one with the braids.

"Private First Class Tau Bradshaw. We're on the fourth team, third platoon, company ..."

"Who commands you?"

"Corporal Rasmus Darkoris, sir."

"Then it's not good. Mr. Darkoris had just returned from his trip and was counting on a day off. He's gonna be lumbered with the three of you now. Explain, Bradshaw, what happened here. And I advise you to let him go."

Tau slid the spikes deep into the bracer while Nexon released the detainee who took a drunken step forward, gave the three an angry glare, and began massaging his twisted wrists.

"This punk was messing with the strange transmitter." Bradshaw pointed to the trampled device lying by the wall of a building. "We were just passing by. At the sight of us he was acting like a caught thief, he sauced when we wanted to talk politely, he started to thrash. It's the saboteur who blew up the collector!"

"What's your version?" Necron turned to the refugee, having glared at Brandshaw. The stranger, however, even though he had acquired the Kiritian language thanks to the entraser, looked at Biffter indifferently and remained silent. "Suspicion is no reason to mutilate or kill someone. Although self-judgment is allowed here, as long as the guilt turns out to be a fact and not an assumption."

The judiciary among Kiritians was practically non-existent, the only legal code was the one with the ten commandments. Crimes were rare, because each achij always got what they needed, no one was missing anything. The mere gifts of immortality and power in the cosmos were enough to faithfully follow the ideals of the nation which citizens joined voluntarily. In addition, the new ones were indoctrinated that each individual was equally important and that only together they created a harmonious, invincible nation, which they adhered to. Nobody wanted to lose wealth, freedom and existence full of emotions, especially immortality in the case of the death penalty, which was practically a thing of the past in Kiret's time. Conflicts were solved individually and usually in private, so that both sides were satisfied, or at least a compromise was reached. It was believed that every case of dispute was different, and that it would have been a great evil and foolishness to attribute it to legal patterns. The best solution was simplicity, everything was within the Kiritian decalogue. Therefore, Necron used common sense and wisdom, not procedures, when witnessing the would-be crime.

He turned to the senior private again:

"I don't have time for a lark. Besides, this is not a matter for the Emperor to deal with. Mr. Bradshaw, please take this device from the ground and show it to Corporal Darkoris, as well as report with your comrades to him and talk about the incident. Mr. refugee, who didn't deign to present himself, should be temporarily arrested until the matter is resolved. If he has nothing on his conscience, he will be released."

"I will gladly escort the larva to its place." Bradshaw smiled like a wolf at a hare, grabbing the stranger. "Could I briefly express my opinion on the recent events, Mr. Emperor?"

"Of course, everyone has a right to do so. But make it quick."

"I believe we should close the boundaries of both our galaxies to aliens and shoot anyone who crosses them. Something smells wrong here to me in this fairy tale about the war. I feel this will turn out to be a big deal. Maybe I'm a simple achij, and I have a short internship among Kiritians, but I'm interested in the history of mankind, and this is full of similar situations. First poor refugees," the private first class made a pitying, ironic face at the stranger, yanking him back, "and then economic instability and the invasion of the enemy leading them. And bang! Shit thrown at a fan."

"We are sorry for the whole incident, Mr. Biffter," Shimizu said hurriedly, seeing that Bradshaw overshot the mark. "We're going."

Before they left the alley, the immigrant being held by the arm said, looking at Necron:

"Thank you for saving me. I'm Skelver."

Kiret looked for a time at the place where the Kiritians and the man being taken not very gently disappeared. The private first class' words disturbed him a little, but he supposed that these weren't his thoughts. The achijes must have overheard General Warfighter's opinion about refugees, who didn't hide his dislike of them. Opinions about the newcomers were divided, but most Kiritians didn't want them within their borders. Necron didn't realize, however, that the lowest-ranking achijes, indoctrinated by commanders or not, felt such a repugnance towards strangers, blaming them for any perturbations in the empire. He hoped that the problem would be resolved at the Council meeting.

The day was clearly full of strange events.

***

A quarter of an hour later, Biffter walked through the vast Utza'm Achij cave, enjoying its coolness, pleasant filtered air, the reigning silence, decorations made mainly of dripstones, and lighting in the form of real and artificial fire. He would have preferred to organize meetings there, but it would have meant that the facility would have had to be closed for the duration of the meeting, moreover, the sounds of conversations (as well as arguments) would have reflected off the distant walls and the ceiling bathed in the shade, which would have distracted the participants' attention. Therefore, the meetings were held in the annexe connected to Utzah Achij; until Forkis died, they had been held in his throne room.

The council building also looked like a cave. The blue-gray walls, ceiling and columns were scarcely illuminated by the artificial flames, keeping the object in the twilight that Kiritians liked. At the front there were five stone armchairs lined with artificial leather, stiff and without bristles, to remind the Immortals that they were a military and tough nation that didn't indulge itself too much. Therefore, although the meeting was political, light armors were required, as if during a briefing.

As Necron sat down on a porphyry throne set on the landing, five members of the Council took their seats. The Emperor moved his look over the people of different characters and views. This was a fundamental element in the Council - for pluralism to exist. On his right, settled down a sixty-year-old general Velkee Warfighter, a traditionalist, supporter of quick action and brutal solutions. In his youth, he had changed his surname from Warfighter to the one appropriate to his explosive character and love of war. At the time of joining the Immortals three centuries earlier, the new name had sounded infantile, but not wanting to be considered a humorless stiff, the general had kept it. Despite his age, which was considered average by people who didn't use the achievements of the most modern medicine, Velkee had the body of a forty-year-old soldier and as much energy as an adolescent. He wore his cropped mustache and hair gray, however, but he liked it that way. Likewise, he decided not to medically correct the milky white left eye, a birth defect, but only improved his vision with it. He also left a scar running across that eye as a souvenir, adding to his face dreadfulness.

Next was Vitani Kinsey, a former politician from the home planet TRAPPIST-1d, one of the first to be colonized by humanity. The woman was the opposite of the general in views, so at the meetings there were often quarrels between them.

Calm Roger Larsen came from the street, his mind was impartial, as clear as a tabula rasa, which is why Kiret especially appreciated the opinion of this middle-aged man who, thanks to the Kiritians, had turned the corner.

A cyberneticist by education, Richard Durand was responsible for collecting information and presenting it to the Council.

There was also Captain Anna Sandstorm, who had been kiritianized at twenty-four. For her whole life she had had little to do with the Immortals, and therefore she represented a different point of view than the rest of the Council. The Kiritians found the objective view of an outsider useful, even if they looked at biologically and calendar young Anna with a grain of salt.

Necron glanced surreptitiously at his armored wrist, where he had discreetly written a number.

"Hello everyone. I'm opening one thousand seven hundred and fourteenth meeting of the Council. Today's conference will be about refugees seeking asylum in a part of space taken over by Kiritians." Pretending to adjust the bracer, he blurred the numbers with his right thumb. Velkee looked up at the ceiling; Anna lowered her head and, looking at her shoes, tried to keep her countenance. It was a tradition that you had to know the number of the meeting, so it was not displayed in the room.

It could be said that the Emperor's participation in the meeting ended with the introductory words. From now to the end, he would listen to the debate and intervene only to add a necessary comment or to cut off a fierce argument.

"Let me, ladies and gentlemen, begin." Cybernetic Richard Durand walked a few meters and activated a holographic board with the information prepared. "Currently in the capital there are five refugees under surveillance, inoculated with entrasers, whose accounts from the interrogation allowed me to create this report. I think it is worth starting with astro geography and numbers." The holograph showed a star system with five small rocky planets and six gas giants. "According to the accounts, the immigrants come from the RC Galaxy unknown to the Kiritians - this is a working name, with time it will probably be changed to another - located twenty-two billion light-years from the center of the Milky Way. It's a converted distance, we can't see this RC. Physically, it can be up to twice as far." The star system shrank to the size of a luminous grain of sand, and the overall view changed to the described galaxy. "It could make sense and confirm the multi-verse theory, which we still cannot take for granted, because even with our Alcubierre drive, it would take tens of thousands of years to fly from Morascrik to the edge of our universe. Simply put: the refugees claim to live in a different universe, twin similar to ours."

No one was shocked by this information, because with the theory of the multiverse - that there were countless A-universes, like their native ones, and other, with different properties and characters, denoted as B, C, and so on - the Kiritians had long been familiar. Perhaps they now received the proof of it.

Warfighter whistled.

"And I am to believe the story that random fugitives flew from somewhere all the damn way to the Zodiac Universum on a junker similar to what Earthlings had used in the twenty-second century to colonize the Moon? As long as they came from that RC, and not from a Milky Way planet, which someone had colonized without our knowledge."

"And how would they have zero percent of their genes in common with us then?" Vitani Kinsey interjected. "After all, we examined them. How to explain it?" Velkee had no answer to that question, just glanced indifferently at the woman.

"Is this information confirmed, Mr. Durand?"

"Yes, General, this is confirmed information. Incredible but true. The inconsistency with our genetic material is proof that the refugees have nothing to do with the Earth from which we spread throughout the Zodiac University. And about the way they travel, you will learn in a moment, which I also included in the report. Coming back to the RC Galaxy. For comparison and illustration, the diameter of the Milky Way is approximately one hundred thousand light-years, so if it were to be defined as one section of the cosmos, the RC Galaxy would be two hundred and twenty thousand units away. Unlike Earthlings, who in the past began to terraform and occupy terrestrial planets scattered throughout the Milky Way, and then the Kiritians did the same with several Andromeda globes, immigrants focused only on five adjacent star systems whose planets, apart from the gas giants, they transformed into habitable ones. The displayed RC Galaxy changed to the previous star and the planets orbiting it. "This is one of those systems in which battles are being fought currently. According to the interviewees, the war is being played out in four out of five systems, as the fifth has been destroyed. In the sense its components ceased to be habitable, because it physically exists."

"It's unheard of that somewhere in space, developed people like us that we had no idea about," Kinsey commented. "The more we know, we learn that we don't really know anything."

"What guarantee do we have that these immigrants are not lying?" The general asked dryly. "If they really live twenty-two billion light-years from Morascrik ..."

"Strictly speaking from the center of the Milky Way," Richard Durand corrected.

"... clustered in adjacent star systems, what sense did it make for them to build long-range spacecraft, ideal for space explorers, not people colonizing a planet next to a planet? How long did it take them to reach us?"

"An equation known to the refugees come into the picture, which was worked out and defined by our mathematician

Wiliam Baks. Thanks to the calculations, the refugees found habitable planets, the ones that we had transformed using the terraforming method. The closest were those in the Milky Way, so they headed to us in civilian ships, without weapons, certain that the new globes would be empty. This is proof that a powerful war may indeed be fought in the RC Galaxy and that the desperate refugees decided to travel such a colossal distance to avoid destruction. Moreover, fly blindly, without discernment." Richard changed the image of the star system to a ship that looked like a cigar. "We got to see their machines, seemingly primitive, as Mr. Warfighter put it before. Scientists and soldiers were quite surprised to learn that the drive had already been tested in the engine room of the laboratory. They call it an elevator drive, it is similar to our Alcubierre drive, but the difference is that the Kiritians constantly cover pulsely the same defined jump distance calculated for the flight. So, from A to B, B to C, C to D and so on where the distances between the points are equal. The elevator drive finds in space the sources of energy unknown to Kiritian scientists, which were the places where refugees jumped. Approximating. Please imagine a chamois wanting to descend from the top of a rocky mountain to the ground. Extremely tough chamois, indestructible." Durand smiled briefly, but the others' expressions remained serious or suspicious, like the General's. "The chamois jumps from the top to the lower ledge, covering three meters. Then she bounces off it and jumps onto another rock, covering ten meters. Then she jumps again to the next ledge, this time going fifteen meters. The same thing is repeated many times, the distances are greater or lesser, and eventually our goat lands on the ground at the foot of the mountain. In the case of refugee machines, rocks and ledges are randomly found sources of energy that the ship 'senses'. They were called nodes. What we know for now is that these are unstable regions, comparable to wandering islands in an ocean, it is not known where and when they will appear, but hundreds of them are said to be active every second in the universe. When the closest node to a ship with the elevator drive is located, the machine flies to it and ports[7] through it to another node in a fraction of an instant. For example, it travels a thousand light years. Other times, four nodes should be used for the same distance traveled, for the reasons I discussed earlier. However, a journey with this technology can take five minutes instead of a hundred years. It is in general, the known details of the porting process will be available for review."

Kiret flinched as his head leaned against his hand moved too low. The eyelids had been covering the eyes for, it's not known, how long. It was hard for him to tell if he was tired of the trip from Chulimal, the boring speech filled with numbers, or Durand's soporific voice. Anna gave him a peculiar look, for he smiled goofily the moment she accidentally looked at him. He felt ashamed of himself, immediately took a posture worthy of the head of an eight-million nation and tried to sit proudly on the throne, like his predecessor.

For the next hour, Richard Durand talked about everything that had been collected about the Erceses, as refugees from the RC Galaxy were called. The disquisition was interrupted by questions. Necron tried to remember the most important

---

[7] Lat. portare - 'to bear'. Here, a sudden transfer from place to place, but without the continuity of the object's existence in space.

information. According to the report, about seven thousand refugees had broken through to the Zodiac Universum and had been interned on the recently developed moon of U1, Eos Endymion, apart from a few brought to K'otz'ib'aja. These people had developed in an environment similar to that of the inhabitants of the Earth, where the same chemical elements prevailed in circulation, and the structure of the atmosphere was almost identical. Erceses, before they had left their home planet and colonized the cosmos around it, just like Earthlings had lived in countries that had had their own laws, economies, troops, religions and languages. The difference between the populations of the RC Galaxy and the Zodiac Universum, however, was that, according to biological convergence, the bodies were composed of different proteins but physically looked the same. Richard gave the example of a fish and a dolphin that looks like a fish but is not it. Therefore, the truth sera didn't work on the immigrants taken to K'otz'ib'aja, but unexpectedly did the entraser, which allowed them to speak Kiritian. The interrogation was therefore made by referring to psychological methods and monitoring the activity of the brain. It was recognized on the basis of consistent accounts and body language that Erceses didn't lie, and a war had really broken out in their homeland, which had already taken millions of victims with it. The enemy, they described anonymously.

Necron perked up when he heard the general's angry voice. After listening to the report, it was time to give their opinions. Durand deactivated the holograph and returned to his place.

"We are Kiritians!" Warfighter walked in front of the rest, sometimes making a sweeping gesture. "We should remember what our methods were like before we became soft." He sent a cold look at Vitani looking at him reluctantly. "We debate for hours, orbiting around problems, instead of making quick and accurate decisions. On Mezzo, they sensed our weakness, which sparked a riot. Mysterious accidents take place in the capital, but the culprits are missing. By a strange coincidence, the events began to happen exactly when we brought to the capital these parasites living off our money!"

"I would like to remind you that they are refugees from war zones," Roger Larsen interjected calmly. "In addition, people with a different culture from another world, so it will take some time for them to get to know our habits and become able to do jobs required on our market."

"But they don't want to work," the general continued, refraining from an ironic smile. He tapped theatrically his chin with a slight stubble. "Apparently they fled the war, and they behave like aristocrats who returned to their property after years of travel. I was born on Mars in 2597 and was an active soldier from an early age. I saw many conquered worlds and I know perfectly well how refugees from areas of bloody fighting behave. They are jaded, intimidated, cry over and over again, or stare blankly ahead. They would give anything for a quiet corner, a warm cover, a slice of bread, and a cup of water. On the other hand, the refugees from the RC Galaxy - surprisingly, almost all men of draft age - are rident, lively and want to get out of the safe U1 moon that we offered them. They talk shit about the only right religion they profess, and that everyone should adopt it. About semi-autonomy, electronic mind control, and some Lightbringer who is a god of a nation much more powerful than theirs, as if it was about their own enemies. Supposedly Erceses are highly developed, because cavemen can't cover such a big section of space, and they behave like a herd of monkeys. They destroy the housing centers on U1 intended for them, provoke riots, and clash with the local order service. Do you know why? Because the truth is," the man wagged his finger as if to a naughty child, "that they are not poor immigrants. It's a Trojan horse with better technology than ours. It is a future invasion preceded by the spies pretending to be victims of the war. They discovered our civilization by accident, they want to know it as best as possible ... to attack at the right moment, knowing about the parasite that is devouring the Kiritians from within. My decision is as follows." The general rolled a serious look over the audience, wanting to make sure everyone was listening carefully. Kiret nodded. "Send back all those who have crossed the Zodiac Universum border. Close it to strangers by deploying warships in strategic locations. Announce ostentatiously that no one wants them here. And shoot every newcomer. I have no respect for men who leave their endangered homeland and want to go where everything is ready. As long as the endangered homeland exists at all. And if it exists, we will surely got lumbered with the enemy who chased the Erceses out of their homes."

"That's exactly the opinion I've expected from you, Mr. Warfighter," Kinsey said with a mocking smile as the general sat down and clasped his hands into the basket. She got up, drawing the attention of the rest of them to herself. "Bans, terror and dead bodies. Yes, it may be a ruse, but more likely they are real fugitives looking to break free from the clutches of the cruelty of war, and you want to send them back to hell. Thus, take away their freedom and the right to a happy life."

Velkee snorted.

"We have no way," she continued, "to verify their testimony, and here I agree that we should exercise caution. But without exaggeration. Right, we are Kiritians, but we are no longer murderers as in the times when Forkis' power was rising. We were a young nation, unappeased, yearning for adventure and attention, also blindly following our leader, whose goal was to kill as many people as possible. Thanks to the war, we rapidly developed various technologies. But we finally matured. We found out who Forkis was. We became the rulers of the Milky Way and part of Andromeda. Now we are responsible for everything we gained. The age of destruction should always give way to the age of enlightenment. I believe that we should give these people a chance and a good start on the U1. Then let's separate them into different worlds, see if they adapt. These are just a handful that we have full control over. If there is a problem, we will surely find a solution. That's all from me." Vitani sat up, sighed, closed her eyes.

It was Roger Larsen's turn. The statement of the man, who had been silent for some time after getting up, composing a monologue in his mind, surprised everyone. Especially Necron, who had expected a pacifist solution to the problem from the man from the street stricken by fate. But Roger gave up his speech and simply said:

"I fully support the statement of the general." He nodded approvingly to the Warfighter. "So, I don't see any point in soliloquizing. The too loose behavior of the runagates is suspected, I have never encountered such in a refugee. In addition, the propulsion of their ships is better than ours, so we can expect equally interesting inventions in the star systems from which Erceses are said to come from. It is crucial if it turns out that we will come into conflict with these people."

"We'll come into anyway if we get them out of the Milky Way," said Richard Durand.

"Kiritian immigration law is clear," the general said flatly, droning the words. " We are under no obligation to help anyone who asks us for asylum. It is only our good will. In turn in the defense of the nation, we have the right to throw out strangers, and even kill them, if we had the slightest doubt as to their intentions."

Kinsey quickly took the floor:

"It's our right, not theirs. Since the refugees come," the Warfighter stroked his short mustache, "from civilized star systems, they should be aware that another intelligent nation also has its own rights, which may not necessarily coincide with their own. It is the guest who conforms to the host's standards."

"You already know my opinion. So, I'm in favor of sending immigrants back to the RC, preferably in their own ships." Clanking his armor, Roger Larsen sat back in the chair.

"I will also refer to the previous statement, as did Mr. Larsen." Cyberneticist Richard Durand approached Kiret, intending to address the Emperor directly, but changed his mind as he turned his face to the Council members staring at him. "I, in turn, agree with Mrs. Kinsey. I would also like to add that after centuries of conquest, we have accumulated a huge amount of money and resources, so financially, we will not feel at all that we help strangers. Even if new ones start coming to us. We are building a new space station on the planet Eos Endymion. I propose to give them a job there, which any healthy Erces will have to accept under the threat of losing our help. The rest can be split between the Cargoo planets in the Lion Universe, which we retook from the rebels, and Calcaris. On both some hands for harder work would be useful, since we gave up full industrial automation a long time ago."

Anna Sandstorm held her breath for a moment, hearing the name of her birthday world. Vague memories about her childhood returned, during which she had lost her mother Hanako killed by lycans, and then Father Krystian had taken her to H14, where she had met Beliar, the Croft siblings, and late Jarret Nelson. She missed the moment when Durand finished his short speech and returned to his seat. She felt embarrassed to see that everyone was staring at her in silence. As the youngest by age and experience, she expressed her opinion at the end. She preferred cases where four or three people agreed on a point, then whatever her decision might have been, it had no bearing on the decree approved by Biffter. Kiret respected the decisions of the Council, and it was rare for him to decide differently from her, using the power of the imperial vote. Worse were the situations when on Anna depended the final decisions in two-on-two cases, like now. Velkee looked at her as if she had been the Council's mascot and she felt embarrassed; Vitani smiled slightly, with urgent gaze demanding haste; Larsen's flinty face expressed nothing, and Durand in turn admired a corner of the chair.

Not liking protracted sessions, Necron was clearly fed up, he changed his position on the throne again. He fought the urge to prop his head with his fist and yawn.

Sandstorm stood up, exhaled too loudly.

"In my opinion, we should give the immigrants a chance at the Zodiac Universum."

The general covered his face with his hand. Kinsey nodded gratefully to the girl, while the rest listened and waited.

"It's incredible," Sandstorm continued, "that we discovered the different civilization, in addition the people who are almost the same as us. It's a pity, however, that it happened in such unfortunate circumstances. By helping them, we will have a chance to get to know them better and get closer to their worlds. Maybe we will be able to avert the conflict in the RC Galaxy and form an alliance. We could learn a lot from each other. So, let's admit these people to us, naturally maintaining all safety measures."

Sharper discussions began, conducted in an official tone, as well as personal attacks lasting the next thirty minutes.

When they were over, Necron struggled to get up, went to the podium situated in front of the throne. Then activated the holographic panel.

"Anyone else have anything to add?" The council denied. Biffter stared at the decree for a moment before he placed his signature on it. "By the decision of the emperor and the council, I announce to everyone that the issue of immigrants has been considered positively. At the next meeting appointed by me, we will arrange the details."

The General Warfighter stood up abruptly, began to stride towards the door. His heavy boots clinked against the firm ground as he stepped off the carpet. Before leaving, he turned to Kiret.

"When it comes to fighting, you will be able to count on my divisions," he announced and left the room. Kinsey raised her eyebrows and shook her head with a sigh. Anna settled in an armchair, tilted her head slightly back, as if trying to relax after a hard day's work. Mentally, it really was so. Necron had a resigned expression on his face, he wanted to get back to his dwelling as soon as possible and lie down in bed.

As the rest of the Council began to diverge, Kiret received a message from an astronomical observatory. Sergeant Victor Shane spoke excitedly through the communicator:

"Sir, we used Baks' equation and we determined the location of the Jaguar Galaxy and the earth Tamasul itself! We carefully examined the prizes from Tz'aqol's Temple and it turned out that a certain area of alien celestial bodies from the maps there is a planetary system around the planet. It really exists! Would you like to see the research report from astronomers and capripods right away or talk in person?"

Kiret rubbed his forehead. Even such great news didn't rouse him from weariness that overwhelmed him every time he had to listen to a protracted debate. Not for the first time in this room, he thought he was a terrible emperor. He definitely preferred to travel in space or be in the field like an ordinary achij.

"I'll come tomorrow morning. Thanks for the info, Sergeant Shane."

***

As announced, Kiret went to the astronomical observatory at dawn, whose shape and size was similar to that of Onkalotian pyramids, except that at the top the sky was indicated by measuring instruments. Sergeant Shane was on the H14 mission, so Necron continued to work with him on Forkis' case, instead of involving more people in private searches. He decided that when everything was certain and the Onkalotian myths were fairly separate from the facts, he would officially inform the Council of Five that he intended to bring Xajb'a Kej back to life. Of the dignitaries, about his crazy idea knew only Anna, and she guaranteed silence. Kiret hoped to receive at the observatory good news, whose foretaste he had gotten after the end of the deliberations, but he sensed that the matter wouldn't be easy.

He was right.

Only the two of them remained in the vaulted room. Viktor presented to the emperor, fascinated as much as he was, a new, multidimensional map of the cosmos, extended by several dozen universes, the average size of each of which was two hundred billion light-years in diameter. The knowledge brought by refugees allowed to confirm the assumptions of Kiritian scientists that the cosmos may have had no limits, and the universe with the Zodiac Universum was a tiny macrosystem in its structure. Astronomers wondered whether to create in theory another unit thanks to Baks' equation - a super universe made up of universes, because the concept of multiverses seemed archaic after the calculations made.

When Shane showed Necron the earth Tamasul, the sergeant's face fell.

"The planet exists, but is unattainable," he said. "We calculated before your arrival, sir, that if we used the fastest Kiritian machine, it would take us hundreds of thousands of years to travel in subspace jumps."

"It doesn't really sound appealing." Kiret looked at a few slowly spinning, because in unreal time, galaxies from Shane's map.

"There is, however, something worth trying." At Viktor's touch, the space model changed its place with a ship that looked like a cigar. "The technicians and mechanics examined the refugee machine down to the smallest atom and fully understood its principle of operation. However, we still don't know what the mysterious energy source called a node that the ship uses as a port station is."

Keeping his hands clasped over his chest, Necron grunted and nodded. He thought Richard Durand had apparently contacted Shane while gathering information for the Council at yesterday's meeting.

"Go on."

"So far some facts have been established. I admit that I was very interested in it, I spent half a day and a whole night to encompass it all."

"Unfortunately, my friend, we have to deal with it in this way for now, without involving more professionals. If I admitted publicly that I'm organizing a long journey because I saw the lines and dots on the floor of the pyramid," the emperor smiled, "you know what the Kiritians would think of their new ruler."

"I understand it perfectly well, sir." Shane went back to explaining. "Thanks to the accounts of the interviewed Erceses, the scientists involved in the project were able to use the capripods with the best computing power to make simulations, using Baks' equation, and created the models we needed. We know that nodes are materiophobic, that is, they arise away from celestial bodies, but it is difficult to determine when and where they will appear, because they are ephemeral creations and decay quickly. Quickly in a cosmic concept, but not in a human, although it can be different. A 'station' may exist for 24 hours, but also for many Terrenic years. Erceses know several dozen of such places, currently existing, but it was enough for the simulation based on Baks' equation to work." The sergeant brought up the space map hanging overhead again, more specifically the schematic section from the planet Morascrik to the land of Tamasul. "Assuming that nodes occur in space in a repetitive manner, knowing the characteristics of the places where they can activate, we would currently have one thousand and forty-five such 'stations' on our route, unexplored but existing jump sources for a ship with an elevator drive. Do you understand what I've said so far, sir?"

Necron waved his hand, crooking his mouth.

"More or less, I'll learn more later. So, we don't know what a node is, and if our ships were to appear at a 'station', we would be destroyed. Since nodes are unstable and fall apart, they can vanish exactly in the moment of the jump. If you were to find yourself in an unfortunate place at the time of disintegration, it could be accompanied by a huge burst of energy or a collapse."

"I wish to remind you, sir, that the refugees traveled along this route and reached the Milky Way, safe and sound. Erceses' bodies don't consist of the same proteins as ours, but they have identical properties, having developed in the Earth-type environment.

"I think I know what you're getting at, achij." Kiret smiled.

The sergeant replied with the same.

"If we were to build a ship based on the technology of the Erceses' ship and send it to the planet Tamasul," he paused for a moment, "the journey would take five or nine years one way."

Necron staggered.

"What?! It is physically impossible to travel through dozens of universes in five years!"

"So, I would prefer to watch out for our visitors from the RC Galaxy, Mr. Emperor," Shane replied grimly, reminding Biffter of the Council meeting. The sergeant was even more daring: "And remember that we shouldn't be arrogant and think that we Kiritians are the strongest and wisest in the entire universe. Although now I should say - in an infinite number of universes."

Kiret remembered the incident with inconspicuous-looking Skelver, who had nearly died at the hands of Senior Private Bradshaw. He realized how little they know about aliens. If it turned out that Velkee was right, the Kiritians who had ruled this part of space for several centuries may have a serious problem.

"Great job, Shane. You showed your mettle during the H14 expedition, then suppressing the opposition's rebellion in recent months and now, with your knowledge and eloquence, not very common in an ordinary achij. You're getting the promotion personally from me. You're a second lieutenant from now on. The rank will be officially bestowed upon you at the next celebration."

Surprised Shane, who had just jumped two steps higher, didn't quite know what to do, especially if he should have saluted. He had never received a promotion from a person with such high prerogatives.

"Thank you, sir," he said finally. Biffter nodded to him with a smile, not wanting to make the man more perplexed, and it ended there. He switched off the holograph and opened the room's drapes with a switch as the mortuary darkness inside the observatory's dome became unnecessary. He stared at the puronax shield, above which stretched a pale orange tilt of sky with a red Betelgeuse supergiant. The star was light years away from Morascrik, but it was still the main supplier of light and energy to the planet which, being the last in its planetary system, was almost cut off from the influence of the yellow dwarf it orbited around.

"Lieutenant, arrange a flight on H14, we're going back for Q'ualel. And as we agreed, please don't tell yet anyone outside the insiders about this conversation and my plans."

"Of course, I will be discreet, sir."

***

Necron returned to his apartment, thinking intensely about the pros and cons of the trip to Tamasul he planned to organize. His mind was troubled also by the disturbing reports that had been flowing in since the morning. According to them, strange accidents happened in various parts of Morascrik, like last day the case of the collector in the capital: a bridge collapsed, a stable tunnel of a mine that had already been closed caved in, there was a serious accident at an android factory. All the events had common features - the functional objects were destroyed, no perpetrators were found, and no one was killed, although the third one might have been a big break.

Betelgeuse's hellish eye reached its zenith as it struggled with layers of gray clouds floating against the amber sky. Kiret almost got to the gate to the building when a terrible rumble sounded above. Instinctively, he fell to the ground, covering his head with his hands; shards of the edifice fell around.

After waiting a moment, he rose sharply and appraised the area. He noticed a hole yawning on the floor occupied by Anna Sandstorm. Achijes' feet patter mingled with the woman's scream.

Necron pulled an X17A4 energy pistol out of his cuisse and, despite the warnings of Batab Gareth, the leader of the guard group, ran into the building. Covering three steps at a time, he quickly reached the right level and made his way to the Sandstorm door. It was open. Scared, but safe and sound, Anna was standing against the wall, far from the window, shaking reassuringly the crying child. Several achijes with weapons in their hands were walking around the apartment, others, like a pack of hunting wolves, had already scattered, running down the alleys around the building, scanning the area and looking for the perpetrator. The explosion under the window in Jenny's room was not the result of a malfunction, as there was no installation in the area.

Angry, Kiret approached Gareth, whom he had assigned to watch over Anna and Jenny.

"And you what, were you sleeping?!"

The batab replied with coolness:

"It had to come from outside, Mr. Biffter. Maybe it was a small drone with a payload or a flying mini bomb. My men are already searching the entire sector meticulously. I swear there was no stranger in the building. We also didn't find any wiretaps."

As Gareth, called out, left the room, Kiret slammed his fist against the wall. He took a deep breath to calm himself, then walked over to Sandstorm.

"Are you alright?"

"I can't take it anymore," she replied. Jenny stopped crying and was falling asleep.

Necron glanced discreetly at the guards. The nearest one was a few paces away, standing with his back turned, talking through the communicator.

"Anna, pack your bags, I'm taking you from this planet. You will remain in a safe place until the matter is cleared, we catch and shoot the saboteurs."

Anna narrowed her eyes, her face hardened. She resembled the aggressive lieutenant of the 78th Rebel Squadron again, whose only overt emotion had been anger.

"No, Kiret," she replied firmly. "Take only Jenny. I'm a Council member, captain, ex-pilot, and I'm not going to run into a hole like some peasant girl whose settlement is raided by soldiers. Thanks to holovision, I can watch Jenny whenever I want. I'd been thinking about it for some time, weighed the pros and cons, and made my final decision at the moment of the explosion by the window. This is for the best. If I quit now, I will lose everything in the eyes of the Kiritians."

"I don't want anything to happen to you, especially since we don't know the bastards who are putting on this goddamn show in Morascrik. In our own backyard! But we'll catch everyone soon and they'll be dead. However, now your's and Jenny's safety is paramount."

"Give it up and don't convince me anymore, because you won't achieve anything. I've already made my decision, irrevocable. I won't leave the capital."

Necron left her alone for a moment. He exchanged a few words with Gareth, who came again and disrupted their conversation. He returned to Anna as new orders were given and the guards fell out. For the next minutes he failed to convince the girl to leave.

"Alright," he capitulated, "but from now on you'll walk with an escort. All the Council members will get it."

"I don't like it, but I will endure it. Regarding Jenny's spot, how about planet Calcaris? My father lives there with his second wife, I cannot imagine better care for the little one. Especially since after suppressing the opposition, Krystian completely abandoned his military service and opened a private shipping company."

"Doesn't he hate you after you went over to the Kiritian side?" The man glanced at Sandstorm scoldingly as he saw her biting her lip. "Anna, why does it seem to me that you want to use Jenny to improve your relationship with Krystian? It's a terrible idea. Especially because of who her father is. It will be awkward for both Krystian and his wife. It's not the right way."

"But he won't refuse knowing who I'm siding with, which is why Jenny will be duly taken care of by him. After all, she is his guilty of nothing granddaughter."

"It smells of burning in here, let's go to the corridor. Can I hold?"

"Of course." Anna lifted the corners of her mouth and handed Necron the sleeping daughter wrapped in a blanket. He took her into his powerful arms. An involuntary smile flowed out onto his face as he stared at such a defenseless, pretty little creature.

"Aren't you sorry sometimes?"

He didn't understand.

"What?"

The girl nodded towards Jenny.

"You know ... that you can't have one."

Kiret stroked her little head, Jenny grunted in her sleep and wrinkled her nose in a funny way.

"A bit. But something for something. Dura lex, sed lex. Immortality in exchange for some humanity is a low price anyway. Forkis told me exactly what awaited me before he infected me with the super virus. He was hiding nothing."

"I suppose that's where your nickname 'Necron' came from?"

"Yes. I am the only Kiritian to be reborn from the dead. The supervirus works for a short time after a person's murder, when the blood is still warm, and a certain group of genes activate only posthumously in an attempt to bring the body back to life. The combination of one and the other acted as a powerful stimulator, in the sense of injecting a neutral form of the super virus. I heard achijes quipping that supposedly the process changed something in my brain," he joked. "Some even believe that thanks to my unusual kiritianization, Forkis couldn't read my mind, although personally I think it was a matter of training. You would have to ask Dr. Maksimus Figam about the details of the trial, what happened at all, because I'm green in these matters. But I know that nature would never accept such excess and alteration of the evolutionary agenda if one wanted to use the super virus to revive long dead whose bodies are preserved." Biffter immediately thought of what he was going to do with the former Emperor, and felt like a hypocrite.

Anna took up the subject, wanting to distract from the shock she had experienced. Nevertheless, she glanced nervously at the window anyway.

"You can always restore your reproductive capacity. Forkis didn't forbid Kiritians from reproducing, but limited it very much. As the new Galactic First Dignitary, you can change the law. Within reason, of course."

Kiret became serious, for a moment he looked like a middle-aged man, devastated by his hard life. He looked down the long hall.

"Honestly, I don't want to be like before the infection or change anything. I wouldn't be able to live like a normal man anymore. You see, dear Anna, an unnaturally long life turns a person partially into a machine, even completely if you put it under deeper scrutiny. A lot of achijes suffers from anhedonia, they wouldn't be able to provide an appropriate emotional palette for their partners or offspring. Sometimes it is necessary to medically interfere with the body and psyche in order for a Kiritian to live a normal life, but hardly anyone agrees to it. Nature has designed few creatures to be immortal or long-lived, only the simplest ones, such as the small jellyfish *Turritopsis nutricula* or the shellfish ocean quahog. The dark side of Kiritians is that despite strict selection in recruiting, half of the population doesn't stand the test of time and wishes, on average, after two Terrenic centuries, to be mortal again." The man parted a hem of the blanket and smiled. "You're reminiscent of your daddy, blob." He looked at Anna. "Returning to the merits, I consider the idea of sending Jenny to Calcaris fatal, moreover, we don't know what kind of enemy we are dealing with and how much they know. I wonder whether the attack was aimed at your daughter, because if so, and the saboteur discovers that she has disappeared from Morascrik, they will first start looking for her from your relatives, and Krystian's place of residence is not shrouded in mystery."

The girl sighed sadly.

"So, what are you suggesting?"

"Atla in the Pisces Universe comes to mind. I have a residence and friends there. The most brutal accident that can happen on this boring planet is when a cesspool is poured out or a well-padded woman is stuck on a swimming pool slide. Jenny will have first-class care; I'll get it done."

Anna took her daughter from Necron.

"I associate Atla. Seems like a good choice. So, I will defer to your judgment."

"When can I get her? I'm ready at any moment."

"The sooner the better. Thank you, Necron."

Anna stood on her tiptoes and kissed his cheek.

***

Skelver was a preventative terrorist, exactly such as he was trained to be. The explosives received from a person in command were small, and he carried dummies with him to divert the Kiritians' attention to other tracks. If he had aroused suspicion, he would have allowed himself to be deprived of the fakes and had gone to jail, from where he would have been released soon, because no one punished for carrying primitive devices for private use, such as garage music players. This is what happened, anyway, after the incident with Bradshaw and his henchpersons. He had been checked before arriving at

Morascrik, so he didn't mind another search. The real charge that could be stored in the body was impossible to detect, as the technology given to Skelver was alien to him as well as to the Immortals. The commander had only taught him to use it. In the case of this assignment, however, Skelver didn't have to take such desperate steps and hide the bomb within himself, because only a few looked suspiciously at the poor Erces, who had escaped from the war.

It was not the first time that he had managed to deceive Kiritians with his false innocence, although in the case of Shimizu, Walker and Bradshaw, meeting them almost cost him his life. The Emperor unknowingly saved his own enemy.

He waited some time so that after meeting three achijes and a brief stay in jail, wasn't associated with the attack in Sandstorm's apartment, then released the mini-drone with the payload. He was commissioned to murder Jenny. After that, the entire Council of Five and the Emperor were to die, but the commander explicitly demanded that the child be killed first. Skelver didn't go into detail, he was afraid for his own life, so he did as he was told. The mini-drone and the bomb planted consisted of a metal that could change from a solid to a liquid and vice versa. In the first case, the particles reached nanometer sizes, which allowed them to penetrate the pores in windows and walls, and regain the form of ordinary metal after overcoming the obstacle. In turn the detonated bomb itself didn't leave any traces - it turned into an ultra-light gas and flew towards the sky. Skelver didn't understand this process of manipulating matter either, but he had received training and had to follow orders under pain of death.

Hidden a few kilometers from the blast site, he heard footsteps, unluckily as the mini drone was about to penetrate the wall, then drop the payload and escape the remote detonation safely. The man didn't have time to turn the machine around, so he blew everything out in front of the window.

Frightened and irritated, he managed to escape from Victor Shane before the second lieutenant emerged from around the corner, heading for the hangar.

V. Journey to Tamasul

Due to the accidents in the capital, Kiret was unable to fly to H14 for Aggroteh, so he selected Viktor to take care of the case. The Lieutenant with the Onkalot were to later meet him at one of the space stations orbiting Chulimal, where John Schindler sold the field crops.

Shane selected a few achijes and immediately set off.

They landed where they'd last been - not far from the farmhouse darkened by storm clouds. Shane stepped onto the gangway in front of the open airlock and saw John, curious, slightly embarrassed, wiping his hands with a rag.

"Good morning, Sergeant Shane." Schindler remembered the achij from the previous meeting. "What brings you to our humble abode this time?"

"Good morning, good morning. Now it's second lieutenant, Mr. Schindler."

"Forgive me. I'm an ordinary man, and I cannot distinguish the decorations and grades on your armor. Anyway, I would be lying if I said that I see anything there."

Three more people came out of the ship. Shane stood by the host, smiled brightly, and shook his hand.

"Never mind, almost everyone gets lost in it. As for the purpose of the visit, I will be brief because I don't have much time. I flew for Q'ualel."

The worry on John's face deepened.

"And what happened? What do you need our kitty for?"

"The emperor himself wants to talk to him, he will need his help in some matter. I can't say any more."

"Where do you want to take him?"

"To the station where you trade, Mr. Schindler."

"What's going on here?" The landing ship had caught the attention of the humanoid jaguar man who had been checking a fence at the edge of the jungle. He walked over to the people talking. Viktor noticed by the expression on his face and the way he moved that he was nervous. "Hello, Mr. Shane."

"So, I'm going back to work, because it will be raining soon, and you guys talk." John turned and minced toward the field. He spotted Darius and was surprised to find that the boy was hiding among the leaves of young banana trees, since the last time he had been drawn with such enthusiasm to the Kiritian ship.

The gray rug of clouds glowed blinding white for a fraction of a second. It thundered immediately. The treetops flapped as if the ship had been still hanging over the ground. Aggro and the second lieutenant looked up to feel the first drops of the coming downpour on them.

"Why did you come this time?" Brushing the mud off his tail, the Onkalot looked reluctantly at the Kiritian.

"The First Galactic Dignitary is calling you. He couldn't come himself, so he sent me because we already know each other. He wants to see you urgently on the M2 space station in the H14 orbit as he returns from the Pisces Universe. There were twelve Terrenic hours left until the scheduled meeting. It's about Tamasul in the Jaguar Galaxy, Aggro." A slight excitement burst into the words of the second lieutenant. "We've found it. The planet does exist. Mr. Biffter needs the Onkalotian knowledge and wants you to join the expedition that is being organized."

The attention of those talking was caught by a rustle in the corn area. Shane noticed Eredal getting up from her crouch, holding a crop basket with her arm. The girl glanced coldly at Aggroteh, then turned and, with her chin tilted up ostentatiously, marched towards the house.

Aggro sighed nervously.

"These women. Look." He pointed at the circle of boulders at the edge of the forest. Chimalmat was sitting there, crouching down and carving something in the wood with an obsidian dagger. The tip of her tail moved briskly like a stepped caterpillar.

"What is she doing here?" Viktor asked. "As far as I remember, she was supposed to come back to guard her pyramid."

"It turned out that she had known the Schindlers' farm for a long time. She didn't harass it, since its inhabitants didn't care about the treasures of the ancient Onkalots. She associated me too, but never revealed herself because I was with people. However, after our visit to Tz'aqol's Temple, she stated that we had stolen valuable scrolls from the hall of knowledge and some statues. So, she came to me and said that she wouldn't leave until I returned the stolen things. You know it's a spoof. Eredal, on the other hand, got it into her head that Chimalmat was my partner. They both took offense. I really have had enough. Get me to that Necron as soon as possible, Sergeant Shane," Q'ualel grunted softly.

"Lieutenant Shane. I've gotten a promotion." The man smiled. "I'm glad that we at once came to an agreement."

Aggro gave the Kiritian a look full of frustration, then headed home to inform John of the immediate departure.

Viktor was climbing the gangplank to the hangar when the world was attacked by a furious downpour.

***

Aggro knew very well a four-kilometer-long multi-level M2 space station with a base two meters wide, so the flight towards it didn't make the slightest impression on him. The station staff wouldn't have paid any attention to the frequent visitor either, if not for the fact that he had come in the Kiritian ship. It was rare to see the Immortals on M2, where primarily the sellers and merchants of the Lion Universe congregated. The Kiritians continued to sort out those who resisted them or might have posed a threat in the future, and though no one on the station belonged to one group or the other, the sight of the new arrivals was still disturbing. Tensions eased only when it became known that from the ship were leaving the four Kiritians, accompanied by freely behaving Q'ualel. They were walking towards a recreation center for moneybags.

After receiving the code for an apartment booked on the top floor, overlooking a large part of the beautifully lit station, Shane suggested they get some entertainment. So, they went to a bowling alley connected to a bar and visional room, where matches were broadcast.

Fully armored, so unrecognizable, Necron (security procedures didn't apply to fearless Kiritians, but sometimes they didn't want to be conspicuous) showed up ahead of time. Having left the rest of the achijes in the arcade, he went with Aggro and Viktor to the reserved suite. Kiret, who had just left Jenny on Atla, hadn't mentioned to Q'ualel about the offspring of Anna and Forkis. He wasn't very familiar with the Onkalots' customs, but he had heard the mention that they looked after their friends' half-orphans, and he didn't want to have any additional problems with Aggro if he had thought Jenny was due to him. He decided to tell him about it another time, but not before the mission that required concentration. So when Shane 'asked' Kiret with his eyes about the flight to Atla, he merely nodded to him.

They settled down in armchairs. Having slid open the helmet strobilus, the Emperor instructed Shane to tell Aggro clearly what he had told him at the Astronomical Observatory, which the Second Lieutenant did very well.

"So, we want to use the known refugee technology and Baks' equation to organize a trip to Tamasul," the emperor completed. "Within a month[8], an innovative vessel with an

---

To facilitate the conversion of time, a main, conventional Terrenic calendar was in use in outer space. Watches were synchronized only on individual planets or moons. But usually the main calendar was used on them, with

elevator drive will be built on Eos Endymion, and will fly to the Jaguar Galaxy." He rested his arms on the table and looked at Aggro seriously. "I thought a lot about this trip. I don't hide that if we manage to get to the zero point, we may not find anything there. It is possible that our data on the distant cosmos is incomplete, for example, the actual number of pulsars or black holes in a given sector is missing, which can result in a wrong calculation. Or the equation doesn't apply to all of outer space, but to a patch of the cosmos, and we misunderstood the explanations of the interrogated Erceses. We shouldn't exclude the possibility that strangers misled us deliberately during the interview. As you can see, dear Onkalot, there are too many 'maybes'. The trip is not safe and there is no guarantee of return. However, if you manage to find Tamasul and the mysterious Bone Smasher is actually there, it will be your chance to get to know your ancestors. As long as they survived."

The humanoid jaguar shook his head in disbelief and stood up. He pointed at his chest with his thumb.

"Me?"

"Yes, Q'ualel. I did my lesson on Onkalots. I analyzed everything we found in the temples and your accounts, and I know that the Ancient Onkalots were very wise but - with all due respect - also proud and self-centered. They may react badly if they discover that to their records, which no one had a right to know except the high priest caste, have gotten people who moreover, have decided to visit Tamasul. Especially if these people ask Nimja to share its knowledge." Kiret rose. He clasped

---

diurnal cycles similar to Earth's.

his hands behind his back and stood next to Aggro. "But if they see you, a distant descendant, they might want to talk."

"You don't understand anything." The Onkalot jumped back. Viktor raised his eyebrows. "They are like gods! Who am I to disturb their peace, if I find someone there at all?!" He rubbed his muzzle nervously, walked to the window that occupied the entire wall, and looked out into space.

"I'm not worthy of meeting the Ancients."

"I see that you glorify them a lot." Kiret found himself next to him, put his hands on the hips. "Wouldn't you like to meet your ancestors? Those who gave you such a wonderful civilization?"

"Of course, I would. But I'm scared. Not of death in space, of course, but of what I could find there. If the Ancients still exist and live on Tamasul, they may be furious when they realize they have been found by those they left. It was no accident that Nimja members left our changing world to us, because they didn't belong here anymore. Who would go with me?"

"I will not hide that it is a test and risky flight. So, as a Kiritian, I will tell the truth. The more people would fly, the greater the losses would be in the event of a machine failure or other tragic setback. Additionally, I don't know how Nimja would react to the presence of people, assuming all the time that they existed at all. Therefore, I would like to minimize the losses in case the expedition fails. I think you understand. So, I thought you would go with a couple of great mercenaries I know: the android Paul and his partner, female android Kate Gessner."

"So only me with the machines." On Q'ualel's face appeared ambivalent feelings.

"Yes. But that doesn't mean I don't value your life. Don't even think like that. It is quite the opposite. However, I believe that only you can fly there of the living, as you are best suited to it because of your bond with Nimja. If you agree, we'll run the necessary tests on you, take your generative cells in case you die, and prepare a ship for your needs, including a cryogenic chamber. It's necessary. You will sleep throughout the trip because you would have nothing on board to do or to talk to, except for Paul and Kate, of course. And the flight will be long. I know from experience that if a crewman is not put into anabiosis for such a space trip, they will contract an unpleasant mental illness. It can be worse with you because you come from a different culture than humans and you rarely travel like us."

"Mr. Emperor is right," Viktor confirmed.

"I apologize for my earlier reaction," said the Onkalot, "but in this case ... You understand yourself. I'm a believer, attached to tradition and respect for it. It is as if someone offered you a meeting with a god."

"I may not understand your faith, but I respect it," replied Necron.

They returned to the table where Shane tasted a drink the female android had just served.

"You don't have to make a decision right away," suggested Kiret, sitting down. He raised the liquor to his mouth and tasted it. "Huh, it tastes like piss," he said thoughtlessly.

"Sorry, Mr. Biffter, human urine tastes more acidic and smells more intense," said the female android leaving the room, having turned around.

Shane choked, put the glass back too quickly, and poured half of the contents onto the table and himself.

"Oh, shit ... Who entered into you the data on this subject?

"I can talk about all the compounds and substances known to science, even though I only serve guests. And now, if you gentlemen excuse me, I have to go to work."

"Here is the Liquid 2 model, annoying and primitive." Kiret waved his hand towards the door behind which the waitress had disappeared. "But don't worry, Aggro, you'll fly with a Liquid 5 model that's more human than a man. So intelligent and independent that its production was discontinued a long time ago. You understand: a machine is always supposed to be stupider than a human, so that it doesn't allow itself too much. There is only one Liquid 5 in the universe, and that is Paul, the most advanced AI ever produced by human hands. So perfect that Kate fell in love with Paul while she was still an organic woman, thinking that he was an ordinary man because he could express emotions like a real human being."

"And the other android?" The Onkalot looked at a green palque drink but hadn't tasted it yet. Meanwhile, the cheered second lieutenant was finishing another drink.

"The second one is an androlak, that is human consciousness irreversibly transferred to a machine. Kate Gessner was fatally wounded and dying. Making her an androlak was the last resort for the woman." The Emperor stared at the frothy liquid in his vessel. "It can extend life indefinitely, as long as being a machine can be called life. It used to be thought that the method would be adopted and popularized, and that humanity would gain an alternative immortality to the Kiritian one. It was the pinnacle of dreams, but with time it turned out that few people were able to bear eternal existence on their shoulders. Forkis carefully selected the people he wanted to join his nation, and an androlak, could become anyone with money. After kiritianization, an immortal remains themselves, keeps the body, and only becomes the carrier of the super virus. But let's return to the topic of the expedition. The story of Kate and Paul is quite interesting, maybe they'll want to tell you it themselves. Think, Q'ualel, if you want to go. I can give you time to think like the last time, but the flight will take place anyway. If not you, I will have to prepare Chimalmat for the trip. I know by sight a few Onkalots on Nephrida who were freed after the planet was taken from the opposition, but I doubt they will cooperate. The presence of a humanoid jaguar aboard would be most advantageous, I told you the reason earlier. So, it would be best if you agreed."

"I don't want to have anything in common with the cannibals Jun Kame, One Death, from Nephrida," Aggro said sharply, having caught the obvious hint of gentle blackmail in the emperor's speech. "Don't involve Chimalmat in it as well, Kiret. I will fly."

The First Galactic Dignitary raised his eyebrows slightly as well as the corners of his mouth.

"You made up your mind so quickly? You had doubts a moment ago."

"I still have them," Q'ualel paused for a while, with his eyes closed, "but the urge to see living ancestors makes my blood boil. After that, I would really regret not taking this chance. Curiosity smothers my fear."

"I will do as much as I can to make the journey safe." Necron raised the glass, Aggro and Shane did the same with their vessels. They got up. "To Forkis, the successful trip and Nimja."

Glass rattled, everyone drank up, whereby Viktor finished first, as he had little drink at the time of the toast.

***

Departure day was fast approaching, but the prototype vessel Perfarius had been completed two nights before the planned date. Aggroteh brought to Eos Endymion - a small, gray-blue planet in the Scorpio Universe where the rebels and Kiritians once fought - had some time to familiarize himself with the machine and its two-man crew. The ship, forty meters long, resembled a stingray. It was covered with a thick, matte, resistant to cosmic rays and most mechanical factors armor, made of brown-black dhurnsteel, so that without external lighting switched on, it was to be invisible in space. It was equipped with a stealth screen, which also causes scanner invisibility. Also, a multi-drive was mounted in it: anti-gravity one, used for the earth-orbit take-off and when moving in the planet's atmosphere, impulse drive, allowing to move by leaps and bounds through space on the principle of jet force and inertial flight, another was plasma drive with a continuous stream and subspace drive. Added to the Immortal technology collection, the most important, elevator drive was mounted separately as it was not compatible with the rest. Perfarius was supposed to fly as a standalone unit, so it was armed for a variety of events, from destroying space rocks to fighting a not numerous enemies.

The man walked across the board, visited the hold with the cryogenic chamber, an orlop and a small galley, and glanced at the three-seat captain's bridge. There he met the crew: the tall, slim, brown-haired man Paul with metallic blue, cool eyes, and his partner Kate Gessner, a nice-looking blonde with a fair complexion. If Kiret hadn't told Aggro that one was an android and the other an androlak, he would have mistaken the couple for ordinary people, and would have only known the truth if one of the machines had been injured or he had realized that they didn't eat, sleep or drink. Admittedly, they could simulate human metabolic needs, it didn't involve obtaining or processing energy, as Paul and Kate got it from helion batteries[9]. Q'ualel's fears after meeting the android waitress were slightly alleviated. The Emperor seemed sincere: Paul was incredibly advanced and passed on many of his skills to Kate, who had been a geologist before she died and herself was transferred to the machine.

Thanks to Paul's kindness, Q'ualel listened to their tragic story. The girl grew up without parents on the streets of Calvary and by chance she met a scientist who adopted her, and many years later set her up with the entrepreneur Sirua Kalderash, as it turned out later - an influential gang boss from the Capricorn Universe. Kate escaped from his residence to the research facility on the planet B9. There she met Paul and fell in love with him, believing that the hated by the all workers, introverted and haughty bachelor was human. The android reciprocated her feelings. Disgraced, Sirua found Kate, kidnapped her to a dead space station, where she got fatally wounded. In the conflict were involved Kiritians, including

---

A high performance rechargeable battery, successor to a nuclear battery. Created thanks to the understanding of the energy processes taking place in stars. Mostly used to power androids.

Forkis himself, who, together with Paul, killed members of the mafia and helped transport the dying girl to the research facility, where she became an androlak.

A few hours before departure, while Q'ualel was putting in order in his mind information about the mission passed on to him, a tamed smilodon was brought from Morascrik to the underground assembly hall. In fact, it came from the planet Aj, where fauna similar to that of the Earth's Quaternary lived. The thick-haired cat was almost two meters at the withers, and the upper tusks were the length of an adult's forearm. Nature gave it a brown-ginger coloration of the back and a whitish one of underbelly and paw area. Aggro, gently uttering words in his native language, quickly calmed down his distant relative, nervous about the journey, and made it feel comfortable with him. He had come to the idea of bringing the animal in when Kiret had told him about a skulak, an anti-gravity vehicle looking like a wheelless motorcycle, which was used to patrol a small area of land. As Aggro didn't like human vehicles, he saw the best alternative in the smilodon as transportation, if it turned out that Tamasul was not machine-accessible. The animal was moved to an isolated room in the Perfarius' hold, where it was put into anabiosis, then its digestive system was rinsed and an enema was done. Aggro looked at it reluctantly - soon it would be his turn.

Although he remembered all the procedures well, he listened to another batch of the same from Necron, who appeared shortly before take-off on the spaceport's underground pad. When finished, the emperor put his hands on the hips.

"How are you, Aggro?"

"I'm more and more nervous, as if I was going to be executed."

Necron lifted the corners of his mouth in a warm smile.

"Is it so bad? If everything goes according to our expectations, you will meet Nimja. And it might tell us how to bring Forkis back to life."

"I admire your optimism, Kiret. Let us not forget, however, that if Xajb'a Kej ever gets revived, he will remain human forever."

"Do you think a body swap would be any problem for such advanced aliens? Anyway, it would rather depend on Forkis what form he would like to take, as long as Nimja give him the choice."

"Speaking of which, what about his body?"

"Dr. Maksimus Figam recreated it at my request, using human DNA, which was not difficult to obtain, since Forkis had functioned as a human for hundreds of years. His Onkalotian remains were completely destroyed in the blast."

"When you came to Chulimal, you mentioned that the doctor left you."

"Yes, he hasn't been Immortal anymore for some time, he gave himself the serum for the super virus. Forkis ordered to erase some of the scientist's memory so that the known Kiritian technologies didn't accidentally fall into the wrong hands, but Figam continues to work with us. A few years ago, he moved to B9, to the former cradle of scientists." Kiret paused for a longer breath. "After the departure of Perfarius, I have to return to the capital. The council is organizing an investigation into subversive activities."

"Does the Council know about the mission?"

"Not yet, I just told Anna informally, but she can keep a secret. As Galactic First Dignitary, I'm an autocrat, have unlimited power, and don't have to confess my actions to anyone. The council is below me; I will tell it after your take-off. If someone cared about perturbations in K'otz'ib'aja, including killing people associated with the government, it is possible that they would try to disrupt the Tamasul expedition if they found out that its end might be the revival of the former emperor. That is why I involved a small group of people in the idea."

"Do you suspect someone on the Council of Dignitaries of these perturbations?"

"Rather I don't. But I cannot rule out that the Council is being watched. If it's true, I'll find out about it."

The Onkalot heard footsteps, turned and his ears drooped - the medical team was coming.

Biffter laughed, seeing his resigned but hilarious expression.

"Relax, my friend, an enema is not the end of the universe. Before the Kiritians built the Alcubierre drive, the colonists of the new worlds went through the same thing every time they flew dormant for many decades. If you were traveling within the Milky Way, this wouldn't be necessary. Unfortunately, this Nimja was blown far away, so the flight, although with the Erceses drive, will last even a decade."

"I hate doctors."

"Hardly any patient likes them. Usually, it's a childhood trauma when your parents tell you that you are going for ice cream and you are given an injection instead. In any case, this is such a maxim about human society."

Soon the medics asked Aggroteh to go aboard the ship, but instead of doing him an enema, they gave him plenty of laxative to drink, and then he went to a bathroom.

To his great relief, medics were not needed to put him into hibernation. An apparatus under a carapace of a 'casket' worked automatically and anyone could handle it - it was enough to press touch points one by one, from left to right. Q'ualel decided to go to a long rest in the later stage of the flight, because he wanted to see the space through portholes from the board of the fastest ship constructed at the Zodiac Universum. He had heard stories that people sent dogs, cats or rodents on the first space flights, now he himself, in a way resembling those furry unfortunates, was the tester of the new machine. He tried not to think about whether he was really on board as the best candidate to meet Nimja, or the Kiritians considered him someone mediocre whom it wouldn't have been a pity to sacrifice. Necron assured him of the first intention, but could Aggro still believe the Kiritians famous for truthfulness after the death of Forkis, who had been able to infiltrate anyone telepathically?

There were a few minutes left to the take-off. Technical personnel were leaving the landing site; the rotors inside the spacious, egg-shaped room heralded the crack opening of the under-ceiling airlock with sound and flickering. Having put on an anti-g suit, Aggro sat in a chair behind Paul and Kate's seats, who were testing the devices while communicating with the control room. Over a personal communicator, the humanoid jaguar heard Kiret's voice, who was standing behind a balustrade surrounding Perfarius:

"Good luck. May you succeed and your journey will be safe. Remember my words well: I will wait for your return and be the first to contact you. If I fail for some reason, it will be either Second Lieutenant Victor Shane or someone on the Council, to which I will report shortly. It is important, it's a safety procedure. See you later."

Eight sections of the bulkhead of the ceiling slid apart. The bright white lighting of the hangar turned deep blue, mingled with the yellow glow of the cyclically spinning rotors. The anti-gravity drive started to work, quickly, smoothly and quietly tearing Perfarius away from the pad.

The mission to Tamasul began.

After reaching dense night clouds, the first propulsion was replaced with the impulse propulsion, the massive jet force of which launched the ship into space like a slingshot a stone. Squeezed into the armchair, Aggro couldn't satisfy his eyes with the views of the individual layers of the Eos Endymion artificial atmosphere.

The noise of the underground hall contrasted with the reassuring silence in the cabin, as if everything turbulent and traumatic had remained behind the Perfarius drives. Sitting motionless, Aggro closed his eyelids for a moment. Paul and Kate discussed the fast-moving ship being driven by the force of inertia. Q'ualel turned his head to the left, saw the small white moon U1 behind the armored canopy and the Kiritian mining ships stationed in its rock-filled orbit. Soon the satellite was far behind the Perfarius nozzles, it seemed larger than Eos Endymion which looked like a large steel-colored star. In front of the nose there was infinite blackness, flecked with millions of bright spots.

"Mr. Aggro," the android secured with belts barely turned in his seat, "now is the best time to go to rest. What impresses you at present will soon begin to cause trauma. Onkalots are not used to distant space wanderings like Kiritians."

"Call me Aggro or Q'ualel. On the contrary, Paul. This sight is one of the most calming things I have experienced in my life. The vacuum affects me like this every time I leave my planet."

Paul smiled gently.

"Apparently, you have seen few things in your life apart from Chulimal. For now, there is nothing to watch anyway. If you go into hibernation now, you'll make my job easier. At the border with the Scorpio Universe, I intend to use a new elevator drive. It is not known how your fully functional body will react then."

The android could be wrong. Q'ualel thought of his ancestor, the Bone Crusher, who had taken notes in the basement of Tz'aqol's Temple, then moved with his countrymen to far-flung corners of space. The journey considered innovative by the Immortals had already taken place thousands of years earlier, and it is possible that the Nimja had taken a few humanoid jaguars with them. The myths portrayed the Ancient Onkalots visiting the worlds through a network of porters - Q'ualel and Xajb'a Kej had even used one to escape to Aj - but it couldn't be ruled out that they had moved in a manner similar to that of Erceses.

Aggro agreed to Paul's request as they reached the edge of the Scorpio Universe, the main sector of the Kiritian. After unfastening the seat belts, he floated away and hit the ceiling. If he hadn't hooked his claws on the cover of the lamp, he would have done another inert somersault.

"Are you alright?" Kate asked with concern.

Paul was amused to see Aggro struggling against the lack of gravity. He also unfastened his seat belts and smoothly left the position, catching the cabin elements along the way, thanks to which he easily reached the cockpit door.

"The ship is too small and light to be able to produce with machinery the equivalent of the appropriate mass and create illusory gravity, especially since the elevator drive takes up a lot of space, which meant that unnecessary components had to be reduced. For this reason, the technicians didn't use the mass of atopaxial particles either. But I think the next versions of the drive will be minimized. Besides, the board wasn't intended to be used for walks. Kate's and mine's job is to bring you to Tamasul and then safely transport to the Scorpio Universe."

The girl also left her post and surrendered to the state of weightlessness. She flew to the Onkalot and grabbed his arm.

"You've never experienced anything like this before, have you?" She smiled. "It's much easier than swimming. You bounce lightly off the floor, walls, or ceiling, then grab something steady, and again. Look." She demonstrated her instructions in practice, reaching Paul, whom she kissed on the cheek. "Let's go to the cryochamber."

Q'ualel quickly mastered the quite pleasant art of moving around the ship's corridors. 'Walking' on the ceiling like a huge spider, he followed the guides to an orange-lit room with the chamber. Instead of one, he saw two.

Kate answered his would-be question:

"As you already know, I have human consciousness, such a long journey in the small space would be traumatic for me. Therefore, we will go to sleep together."

"And you?" Aggro asked Paul, who put his arm around Gessner's waist.

"I can handle it. I'm a 100% machine, although I feel many things the same as people, including I'm aware of my existence. I often react emotionally, but it doesn't affect my job in any way. Permanent patience, inability to go crazy and lack of boredom are my strengths, very useful during long journeys. I also have to keep an eye on flight parameters and look for nodes so that Perfarius can port from one to the other."

He kissed Kate, they talked for a moment, then Paul placed her in the chamber similar in shape and size to the next one, though both had different equipment. Specifically, in the solid of the androlak there was only a cage put on the head, which, combined with a capripod, was to "reset the activity of consciousness", as the android put it, defending itself against the use of the phrase 'switch off'.

When the girl appeared to be in REM sleep a few minutes later, Paul moved away from the chamber, onto which a teardrop-shaped carapace slid with a soft hiss.

"Good night, Kate." He held his hand on the transparent surface for a moment. "Now it's your turn, Aggro."

The second sarcophagus waited open to receive the crewman. Q'ualel stared at the plum-colored geometric interior, but matched to his proportions, some nourishing liniment and equipment protruding like lampreys' snouts. He turned and was about to float away, but Paul grabbed the fold of his neck.

"Where are you?" Aggro sighed nervously.

"I can't."

"You can. It just looks terrible. Among people, there are only four deaths in a thousand during hibernation, and this is only because someone ignored the safety procedure or badly performed medical tests, sending people with cardiovascular or respiratory system defects to sarcophagi."

"You can console."

"But we have examined you very carefully, you are healthy. You don't have to worry about anything, you can fully trust me and this chamber. Otherwise, I wouldn't pack someone I care about inside." Paul nodded towards Kate.

"But she is ..." Q'ualel was unfamiliar with the sensitivity of androids and didn't want to offend his companion, so he refrained from speaking about robots. Paul, however, resolved his dilemma. He smiled soothingly.

"A machine. Yes, I know. But awareness is the most precious thing she has, and she could lose it really easily. However, these are not matters that I can explain to you."

"Okay, got it." Aggro took a deep breath. "Then let it be so. After all, I'm doing it for Xajb'a Kej and my ancestors."

After a short prayer to Tonatiuh, he allowed himself to be placed in the cryogenic chamber and connected to the 'snouts of lampreys'.

"Any tips?" He asked Paul, who floated to the capripode controlling the sarcophagus.

"None. The system is fully automatic and works continuously as long as the ship itself has power. And even if it lost them, the aggregate will support the vital functions for six months. The apparatus will take care of everything. Even if something broke, I could fix it. I have been thoroughly trained in the possible shortcomings of 'Perfarius'."

"And how will I feel when I wake up? If I wake up at all."

"Stop blubbering finally," the android said in a tone of joke. "I've heard you were a priest-warrior in the tribe. I don't understand why the toughest guys are always afraid of syringes, doctors and everything related to medicine in general. Now, thanks to you, I know this is true for probably all intelligent species."

"It's easy for you to sneer. It is not you who will be killed for quite a few years. If you understand what I'm talking about at all."

"I'm used to such comments and it doesn't bother me at all," Paul replied sincerely, fumbling with the capripod. "I lack practice, yes, because I don't live in the biological sense, but the theory itself is enough for me."

"Will you answer the earlier question?"

"The result of long sleep will surely be pain in the whole body, stiffening of bones and joints, muscle weakness, slight amyotrophy. The grippers sticking out above you will turn you from time to time to prevent pressure ulcers, which, anyway, would be partially eliminated by the organic fluid and semi-organic substrate. You will experience headache, vision problems, discomfort in your empty stomach. You won't vomit, because you were thoroughly cleaned. The crew must not be put to sleep with food, because it would be killed by flatulence and the decay process. The entire cabin and chambers have been designed so to be able to protect the sleeping from gravity loads during a flight. Thanks to your cellular memory, all physiological faults will go away when you start to function normally again. The post-anabiosis state will pass within a few to several hours." The android grabbed a lever, turned to Q'ualel. "Are you ready?"

Aggro, lying rigidly in the chamber, nodded. He felt no emotion as he undressed and lay down, and slime lining the soft interior moistened half of the fur. However, he panicked when the carapace began to slide to hermetically seal the sarcophagus. He associated the process with a funeral, he was afraid he would suffocate. He clenched his fingers tightly on his tail like a drowning man on a lifebuoy, the outthrusted claws pierced the skin; blood appeared. He missed the moment when, in panic, he grabbed it with his paws.

He quickly found that he could breathe freely in the cool, odorless air as soon as a respirator stuck to his mouth. He supposed that a sedative was sprayed into the gas mixture, for he was immediately overwhelmed by tiredness, strong enough to make him incapable of reflexively opposing it. The pounding heart was beating slower and weaker. The initial throbbing in the skull stopped. The breath lengthened, became deep and regular. The body went numb. Paul appeared to be standing on a rocky shore of the ocean with a vertical wall, while Aggro descended into the deep water which turned out to be pleasant.

The dreams came almost immediately, lucid at first, mingled with a torrent of thoughts. He saw his homeland in them, the city of Chiq'aq known as the Place of Fire in the era of its prime, before the human race plunged everything into death and ruin. Xajb'a Kej from the time before he was changed by the golden artifact of the Ancients, because Nimja idolized gold. He saw the colonists to whom he was a slave after the loss of his homeland. Eredal, the farm of the Schindlers.

He climbed the steps to a very high pyramid, the lower levels were engulfed in darkness merged with mist, while the sanctuary at the top loomed against the blood-red setting sun. Q'ualel stumbled and slid down the step, loose stones like the severed heads of Jun Kame victims rolled down. A shudder shook his body, but he didn't wake up.

He couldn't remember how he found himself at the top of the pyramid — stretched out over a rudely dressed sacrificial boulder. He was held by all of his limbs by Onkalotian priests wearing gaudy, colorful costumes depicting demons. The fifth was standing over Q'ualel, with an obsidian dagger in his paws, ready to strike him between the ribs. The sky darkened rapidly as the K'ajolom shield was obscured by one of the two Chulimal moons, as long as the ritual was taking place on that planet. Sweaty, Aggro tried to break free, he twisted, arched himself, but in vain, the humanoid jaguars with their muzzles crooked in poisonous smiles held him tightly. The priest with a dagger began to pronounce the words of the incantation, mumbled at first, but the last sentence, he shouted in ecstasy. The blade rose even higher - and dropped abruptly. Aggro screamed in pain; blood trickled from his mouth.

Everything suddenly disappeared and he began to fall into darkness. He fell painfully on the flat, ashen earth illuminated by a circle of white light of unknown source. Then there was only blackness. Grimacing in pain, he got to all fours, then knelt. He checked the ribs. He had no cut and his heart was still beating.

His attention was caught by snarling and scuffling, as if something heavy had been lazily approaching him. Soon he saw in front of him the silhouette of a smilodon with glowing pink eyes. He recognized that it was an animal they had taken on their journey to Tamasul. The creeping cat, however, turned out to be much larger than in reality, and the tensed muscles of its open mouth with glistening fangs didn't herald anything good.

Aggro sprang to his feet, surprisingly not feeling any pain after the fall, he reached for the cover, but there was no weapon, which he had always carried with him. He was condemned to the mercy of the irritated predator, having at his disposal his own teeth and claws, many times shorter than those of the approaching smilodon.

The giant cat entered the circle of light and attacked immediately. So fast that Aggro didn't have time to jump back. Pain was inflicted to him again, but this time it was worse than the last, when huge jaws clenched at his sides, capable of shattering bones at best and halving a victim at worst.

The smilodon disappeared unexpectedly, along with the neurotic scenery.

This time Q'ualel was lying on the hot sand, it could have been a desert or a beach, matter was hovering over the wasteland, ruled by a strong gale. When he opened his eyes slightly to at least partly protect the dry conjunctiva from the particles, he thought he found himself in the heart of a sandstorm. The wind carried the smell of burning and charred bodies. A yellow flame danced at the edge of his field of vision, illuminating the rubble. Aggro got up, took a few steps, and stopped abruptly, having noticed human remains on the ground. They were freshly torn off limbs, and then there were bloody ribs, broken bones, fragments of soldiers' armor, empty rifles and scraps of clothing. More macabre fragments appeared as the distance was covered. He thought he saw a glimpse of a pale cyborg with a drone accompanying it.

He was among the casualties on the battlefield. He felt a peculiar sense of terror that the scenery was more than a psychedelic dream.

He found a head lying on the sand. He shuddered, felt like throwing up. He quickly recognized who it belonged to: Beliar Drunkenstein. Aggro found himself in the arena in Morascrik, where Xajb'a Kej had been killed, along with many Kiritians. The head opened the eyes, looked at the stranger, and smiled horribly, widening the bloody lips that let the words out:

"Die. It will be better for you. Why bother?"

"Go away! You are dead!" Growled the Onkalot, assuming the attitude of someone confident, although inside he was boiling.

The head chuckled brazenly. Aggro noted with horror that he was no longer talking to the skull wrapped in rotting skin and muscles, but to a bare one partially covered with sand. It uttered things he feared the most, the things he didn't share with anyone, not even Eredal or John:

"You're also dead. You fall lower and lower each day; you can't even laugh and joke anymore. You're being consumed by blues. You have a body, but you have long been dead. You lost everything: family, home, friends, gods. So, what is the point of your existence? Why are you still fighting? And it will get worse, you will lose even those who are kind to you."

"Shut your mouth!" Aggro couldn't stand it. Screaming, he kicked the laughing skull far away. He fell to his knees and cried. "Let this nightmare end ..."

He remained so for a few minutes until he felt a hard touch on his shoulder. He turned around and stood up, noticing that he was in the desert under a starry night sky. He decided that this time he wouldn't let himself to be hurt or pushed around. He outthrusted his claws from the fingers of his left paw. He swung, wanting to mutilate another enemy of this gloomy dreamland, for in a nightmare there is no chance of meeting someone good.

The blow was stopped with a mighty armored hand that grabbed Aggroteh's wrist. It was Xajb'a Kej in human form, clothed in Kiritian war armor. Streaks of windblown black hair protruded from between the slits in the helmet. The immortal had a serious expression on his face, and was staring discerningly at the humanoid jaguar whom he had released from his steel grip.

"I'm your target. Bring me back to life," Forkis said in his signature baritone. "I must kill all the enemies that will soon take over our sectors, or else we will be doomed to unimaginable losses. Maybe we'll even cease to exist."

"This is insane."

Xajb'a Kej swung and fetched him a blow to the face with strength reinforced by an exoskeleton, so great that Aggro made a semicircle and fell heavily on the sand.

"This is the future. Emerge from your malaise and complete the task."

"You think it's easy for me?" Q'ualel whispered to the grains of sand sprinkled with the blood from the nose.

He waited until the dizziness passed. Forkis was gone when he turned. He didn't bother to get up, just rolled over from his stomach to his back and rested so. He stared from under his closed lids at the stars swirling overhead, unsure if he still felt the impact of the blow.

A glimpse of reality cut off sharply from the nightmares experienced; even in a dream, Aggro could separate truth from fiction. He remembered that Paul had put him in an anabolic state, and that all was the reflection of an internal breakdown he had struggled with for hundreds of years. The dream couldn't be pleasant, because only the bad ones clear the mind, but he wanted it to end kindly by now. He wondered if humans hibernated the same way, that they had nightmares throughout a journey. It would have been more convenient for him to plunge into non-existence, as Beliar's skull suggested. After all, it's so easy and simple.

Another change of scenery, this time he was in a swamp covered with a foul-smelling mist, and above it was hanging broodily dark thunderclouds. Skeletons of thickets protruded in the distance, which could mean hibernation time or poisoning the plants with swamp vapors. He noticed that he was standing knee-deep in a thick slush, and his tail was covered with mud. He was thirty meters from the barely outlined shore. He immediately moved in that direction. Walking got harder and harder with each step, as if he had been fighting in a pitchy slurry, his paws were sunken more and more. The mud already reached his hips, and a moment later Aggro, worried, was stuck, submerged up to his waist. It was impossible to walk any further, the slush was too dense, the movement caused him to sink faster in the smacking liniment. To make matters worse, he was still far from the nearest branches. He stopped, having noticed on the shore ... Eredal? She was sitting crouched next to a fallen, mighty tree, her dress was tousled with mud and her dirty face showed despair and fear.

"Eredal!" Instinctively, the Onkalot made a step, so sharp that his hip ached and he sank even deeper. He raised his arms high, lifted his muzzle as the mud already reached his chest. He realized that he wouldn't make it to the shore unless someone helped him.

Hearing her own name, the girl jumped up abruptly and looked around, except at the place where the humanoid jaguar was stuck. From the depths of the dark forest came Anton Rafen, a boy living on a farm similar to that of the Schindlers. Having noticed Eredal, he ran to her, grabbed her and kissed, and she replied with the same as if they had been a couple for a long time. That sight hurt Aggroteh, and for a moment he forgot that he was drowning.

"Eredal, help me!" He exclaimed. Both, however, didn't hear him or didn't want to hear him. The couple walked away as if the humanoid jaguar hadn't existed.

Resigned, having lost the only thing he still cared about, he let the swamp swallow him up. He wasn't fighting as the slush reached his neck and it was about to pour into his nose.

Also, this time he wasn't supposed to die, for something strong and lithe floating in the smelly liniment grabbed him around the waist and easily dragged him ashore, as if Aggro had been standing in plain water. He was saved by Chimalmat who, begrimed with mud, looked like a black panther. Behind her, light brightened on the hill, white and intense as Beliar's bomb blast. For contrast, a figure standing on the hill and a large chest were bathed in darkness.

"That's enough," the man said emphatically. He moved the lever at the chest.

This caused Q'ualel to die. His heart stopped, breath froze in his lungs, the pupils narrowed. The last thing he remembered before going into the eternal embrace of death were the green glowing eyes of Chimalmat, fading into the widening blackness.

***

He remembered this man from his dream, as long as his dying brain hadn't given him false images, drawing patterns from Onkalot's rich memory. The blurry figure, backlit in blue, stood over him, making no noise and not moving. Who was he? Was he a guardian from Xibalba? A god of death personally welcoming the dead to the other world? A demon? The man finally shuddered, performed an undefined action at the chest, as a result of which the senses of the Onkalot were reached by a blaze of colors and noises. He could also breathe normally, felt his heartbeat again. Only the eyes saw everything as dimly as through a layer of gel. Is this what life after death looks like, as if you were still alive? Maybe Q'ualel existed in a different form, peculiar to the world of the dead, where all life processes had stopped, although the dead still thought that the body was functioning?

"Welcome to the world of the living, Aggro," the man said cheerfully. "Keep lying for some time more, you have short loss of memory. Just don't get up shar..."

The humanoid jaguar got up a little and would have screamed in pain if a pathetic crackling sound hadn't come out of his throat. Capillaries entwining him sank into the body as stiff as a log. He fell onto his back again.

The man sighed half irritated, half amused.

"Didn't I tell you so? You have been lying almost dead seven years, three months, thirteen days, two hours, a minute, and now seven seconds in Terrenic time. But you dreamed only twenty-three minutes, of which a quarter was at the time I was waking you up. Your heart is beating only three times a minute. Let your body return to physiological normality. Yes, you are alive and well," he added, guessing from Q'ualel's face the question impossible to utter at the moment. "But you need to lie down a bit until the vital functions normalize, then we'll deal with the musculoskeletal system."

Slowly, his memory began to come back to him, and the dreamy specters to go away. The name of the man flying in the air was Paul, he was an android, and had just awakened him after a very long hibernation. Fortunately, Aggro's eyesight didn't deteriorate - the carapace of the hibernation chamber covered the sarcophagus.

Half an hour passed before Paul removed the safeguards and stabilizers of the vital functions. The Onkalot rose weightless.

"It would be worse if gravity was working," said the android. "It would be more difficult to take the first steps. It's always more comfortable in the water and air. Move, bend and straighten your fingers, wave your paws, draw them to your chest and outstretch, twist your head, make movements as if you were swimming the breaststroke. You have weak bones, both from long sleep and being in space, you must keep moving. Then I'll give you a calcium/potassium injection as you won't be able to eat for a while. Breathe deeply now."

Aggro tried to obey all orders. At first he didn't do well due to the general stiffness and pain. However, as Paul announced, he gradually began to recover. The pain subsided, the fur became warm again and was getting dry after lying in the fluid, the joints bent more and more flexibly. An inexplicable joy overwhelmed him that he hadn't felt in a long time - he thought of awakening as a form of rebirth. He didn't inquire whether it happened spontaneously, or the android had administered some remedies to him while he had been still in the chamber.

"Hello, Paul. Are we there already?" He spoke the first words hoarsely after the years of silence. "Did I really sleep for over seven years? I didn't feel it ... It's like a day has passed."

"Because you were almost 'off'. Forgive me for that word, but it's easier for me to use it, considering who I am. In the state of anabiosis, you don't feel the passing time. Even if you had been lying down for a thousand years, it would have seemed to you after waking up that you had just gone to bed a day earlier. It always works that way."

Having pushed off the wall, Aggro did a slow somersault in the air. He noticed that Kate's chamber was empty, which meant that the androlak must have been awakened earlier.

"I had terrible nightmares. I was afraid it would never end."

"It happens, especially if a person going to the hibernation chamber is nervous about what awaits them. Some are afraid, especially those who are put to sleep for the first time. I was looking at your vital signs and you actually fidgeted in your sleep at first, then I injected you with extra sedatives and opiates, and it was all over."

"Where are we?"

"Can you move normally now? How are you?"

"Almost fine, but I'm terribly thirsty. Thank you for keeping me alive for so long. It is unbelievable that I slept so much."

Paul concluded the words with a quick nod of his head.

"I'll give you something to drink soon. Come with me." They moved from the orlop to the galley. Paul handed him an aluminum bag with a siphon for comfortable drinking under zero gravity, containing water enriched with vitamins and mineral salts. After taking the first portion of the liquid, Aggro vomited, and on the second attempt he also failed to hold anything in his stomach. Android considered hydrating him intravenously, but the Onkalot managed to drink a liter of water and not return it, although it took almost half an hour with small sips.

When they went to the cockpit, Kate was levitating at the control panel as if she had weighed as much as a helium balloon. She smiled warmly at the sight of the Onkalot, and was generally radiant.

"Nice to see you, Aggro. How are you feeling?"

"Hi, Kate. Now better. I felt terrible when I woke up, but Paul took care of me."

The android smiled half-arsed for a brief moment. He floated to Q'ualel, who had already stuck to the canopy and was eagerly watching the space.

"We're in a different universe, Aggro," whispered Gessner. "Can you imagine it?"

He already understood the reason why the androlak was pleased. He remembered the twisted cryogenic dream and Beliar's words about his anhedonia. Now, looking closely at the stars and planets of another universe inaccessible to the Zodiac

Universum's cognitive devices, he could definitely contradict them. Kate's mere information made him feel amazed and fascinated. He had missed it for a long time, he no longer had a sufficiently strong stimulus causing positive emotions in his life. And if something like that appeared, he must have spoiled it immediately, like the relationship with Eredal, which he had rejected due to numerous doubts.

"Amazing," he agreed. "It seems like ours, though I don't know any of these stars."

"It's physically like ours," Kate replied. "Type A universe. Assumptions turned out to be true. Until Erceses showed up at the Zodiac Universum, we just didn't have a way to investigate it."

"You travel a lot. Do you associate any pale cyborg with a drone?"

"What?" Paul looked at Kate, who shook her head.

"In fact, it's not important. I just dreamed about something strange."

"You have already recovered, so it's time for some information," the android announced. "We're there. The described star system, as well as the planet Tamasul itself, turned out to be true. It's an optically binary system. It has a main sequence star, there is another one nearby on a cosmic scale, but they both interact minimally, especially during a plasma ejection, but they are not forces that could destabilize the planets of one or the other system. Tamasul is the fourth planet from its star: it is preceded by a gas dwarf, a small rocky planet with no atmosphere, then there is an asteroid belt and another globe, also rocky, with mountains reaching forty kilometers and temperatures up to three hundred degrees

Celsius. Behind Tamasul, there are circling two gas giants and a series of small planets no larger than Pluto. Kate has turned off the drives so we're drifting temporarily. Before we woke you up, we had gathered information. We had to be sure we were there so you wouldn't get up unnecessarily. Aggro?"

The Onkalot got thoughtful observing two rather large, closest stars, his cherry eyes were shining almost like them. Paul suspected that most of what he said Aggro didn't hear.

"Sorry ... What about the trip? Did it go safely?"

"A stray rock from the meteoroids swarm damaged the ship's armor," Gessner now reported, "but minibots released into a vacuum successfully dealt with the problem. Two years ago, all power temporarily went down after reaching a node, and we strayed slightly off course. Besides, nothing else happened. The elevator drive passed muster. Paul and I have tried to define what a node is by analyzing the measurements obtained during the journey, but we don't have a satisfactory definition. Perhaps the essence of a node is understood by scientists from the RC Galaxy, because the immigrants from there can use only the ships in which they got to the Zodiac Universum, and the way they work, as well as the essence of nodes, they don't understand. Before the trip, we spoke to Mr. Biffter about it, he shared some information that he could afford. For now, we know only that at node-stations, enormous, undefined energy and trace amounts of matter are accumulated, which are important during portation. It is possible that it is a variation of black holes that don't absorb everything from the vacuum, but transport intact objects far away. They disintegrate when their critical mass is exceeded. So, in reality we know almost nothing, these nodes should be examined with a team of scientists.

Aggroteh floated away from the main cover, looked through the porthole to the right, and saw the neighboring star mentioned by the android. Without the optical instruments, it was possible to see clouds of yellowish-green dust surrounding it, which appeared as if a gas ball had been gradually disintegrating, releasing a thinned corona.

"Do you think the Great Family used nodes to travel through space? Have you seen it at all?" He asked, not hiding his nervousness.

"We didn't come across anything alive in the Jaguar Galaxy." Paul flew over to his chair and buckled up. "It is not even known if your ancestors are here, or if they ever were. We'll find out in seventeen hours, because that's how long a smooth flight to Tamasul will take. Buckle up, we'll set off in a moment."

Once they were seated, Perfarius rushed with the plasma drive, spewing blue jets of ionized matter from three nozzles. The journey began from the peripheral side of the star system towards the center, so the scanners showed first the small outer planets, invisible to the naked eye because they were too far from the light sources. They didn't find some of them at all, because they orbited closer to the star or on the other side of it.

Aggro detached himself and began to move again once they had reached a steady speed.

A few hours later, a large turquoise and navy-blue gas giant bloomed on the port side. Q'ualel counted four moons, but there may have been more beyond the planet. The active atmosphere was constantly shifting and swirling like thick paints being joggled in a vessel.

"It has a lot of clouds," the android announced, seeing the man's interest in the planet. "But they must be sulfides themselves or other toxic compounds analogous to those found on the gas giants we know. Gravity is too strong for life to develop there."

Another giant, this time visible on the starboard side, was even larger than its predecessor, had more satellites, and its atmosphere was arranged in dirty gray layers.

It turned out that Perfarius' instruments had made inaccurate initial measurements - or something from space had caused the disturbance - and there was another planet orbiting in front of Tamasul, about the size of it but on the other side of the star. The journey, during which the humanoid jaguar didn't stop admiring the views even for a moment, was therefore extended by two flight hours at a wrongly calculated distance. Eventually, the ship 'anchored' in Tamasul orbit, which was accompanied by silence and alertness of the crew. The planet visually resembled a miniature of the first gas giant, considering its turquoise-navy blue atmosphere and vigorously moving clouds. Paul fired several probes to examine it closely. That meant more hours of waiting for the ship to reach the surface, if Tamasul conditions allowed it at all. Upset, Aggro wasn't going to wait and create in his head darkest scenarios concerning the ancestors, so he accepted Kate's offer and went to sleep in his orlop. Before that, he had eaten a condensed meal, this time not feeling sick. Sleep was unable to silence his mind awoken by emotions, so Paul gave him an opiate, which worked instantly. A day later, the androlak woke him up nudging his arm.

"Come on. The probes are back. Paul has all the readings." Q'ualel stood up immediately, as if he had been ordered to put in an appearance to defend his hometown. He found the android in the cockpit; he hovered in front of the holographic image of the planet and didn't seem pleased.

"It looks bad," he said, rubbing his smooth chin. "The probes found numerous damages on the surface."

"Meteorites? Asteroids?" Aggro tried to find out, when the android fell silent for a moment.

"No. It doesn't come from nature. The area is swept as if after a nuclear detonation. However, the contamination is gone, which means that the undefined attack must have taken place a long time ago or the weapon used wasn't radioactive."

"What about the planet itself? How is it like?"

"The people of the Zodiac Universum prefer to be given parameters in relation to their home planet, the Earth. I understand that you probably would like a comparison to Chulimal."

"Yes please."

"Then I'll convert it. Are you familiar with fractions and percentages?"

"Yes. You probably know that I was with people for a long time."

"Alright." Android pointed to the holograph. "Tamasul is eleven percent larger than H14, and at its mass it also has three percent greater gravity. In terms of the types of elements, the components of the atmosphere are similar to those of Chulimal, most of them are: nitrogen, oxygen, argon, then we have carbon dioxide, methane, hydrogen, and helium. The probes found no sign of vegetation, yet oxygen makes up more than nineteen percent of the atmosphere, but much less than on H14. Of the poisonous gases, there is relatively much ammonia, but we have not been able to establish its origin either. Without a respiratory mask, you can stay on the surface of the planet for up to eight hours. One should also beware of caustic rains with sulfuric and nitric acid. The ocean makes up fifty-two percent of Tamasul's surface, the rest is one great supercontinent containing inland seas and rivers, linked into open water systems. The land is not diversified, the rocky-mountainous landscape dominates, and closer to the shores the terrain turns into highly salty deserts. In the present time of year, the daily temperature on the globe ranges from minus fifty-two degrees at night to plus seven during the day. It snows most of the year. The time to orbit the star is seven hundred two days, and a day lasts fifty-one hours. We found no pathogens known to science."

"And life?" The Onkalot asked. "Is the planet inhabited?"

The moment of silence was depressing. Paul looked at Kate seriously. He nodded and the girl replied:

"Sensitive probes found remnants of technolithic civilizations, but there is literally no stone left on the stone. As you heard, there must have been a major catastrophe on the planet. Of the preserved objects, we managed to see a kind of fortress stuck at the foot of the mountains. The spies, however, were unable to get in, not even close to it, as if something had been blocking them. We had to drop the search. We can try again ..."

"No, I'll check it myself," Aggro said flatly, staring defiantly at the planet's image. "I feel this is exactly what we are looking for," he added enigmatically.

"We have too little data for me to agree to a trip inland," the android turned off the holograph before his face, "and too many unknowns. Why are there no plants here but there is oxygen? What produces ammonia? What blocks our probes?"

The Onkalot persisted.

"Since you didn't manage to check it overnight, do you think you will get answers after sending the probes again? Is there any danger to us or the ship?"

"Generally not, but the devil is in the details." Paul smiled to ease the situation.

"I think Aggro is on the right track," Kate said gently, placing her hand on Paul's shoulder. "We didn't get achijes to help, there are only three of us, and the difficult task awaits us. We only have one chance and we cannot fail. If someone lives in this fortress, it is worth contacting them."

"They might be hostile. Surely, he or she was the one who stopped the probes they mistook for spies or a kind of weapon. Probably knows we're here, but doesn't want to communicate. Of someone who dealt so easily with technology from another universe we should especially be running scared.

"Why do you assume that the owner of this building thinks like us? It's probably natural for them to keep uninvited guests from bursting into their own property."

The android ignored the companion's comment and didn't point out that her second sentence contradicted the first.

"The damage of the planet is disturbing ..."

"But it occured thousands of years ago." The woman smiled.

"We don't know if thousands. You're teasing me, Kate. And you're challenging my authority," Paul growled.

"Paul, you're not risking anything, and neither is Kate. I will go there alone," suggested the Onkalot. "If something happens, you will pick me up with Perfarius and we will leave immediately. I don't understand your attitude. We didn't waste so much energy, time and money to give up at the destination."

"Nobody is talking about resignation," growled the android. "We have to think carefully and plan everything. Anyway, this is a scouting, not a research expedition focused on exploration, which Mr. Biffter will probably organize when we return."

"I know you can think surprisingly fast, and you probably haven't come up with anything better, because you'd have said it a long time ago. So, you agree with my suggestion?"

The android looked ironically at the humanoid jaguar. He floated to the porthole. He looked at Tamasul, analyzing the pros and cons once more.

"Okay, so be it," he said finally, turning partially toward his interlocutors. "To come only to encounter a few difficulties and hightail right away like a scared hare, it makes no sense at all. Here, I absolutely agree with you, Onkalot, and with the fact that too much time and energy was spent on this trip, because not the funds. Kiritians are rich. But I set the safety rules as the former security officer of the Terlendum III research facility on B9.

VI. Masters and slaves

Paul quickly tracked down a safe landing site. It was several kilometers from the fortress - as they christened the building, because the rocks and hills surrounding it prevented a closer approach - moreover, the android didn't intend to annoy any residents of the facility. This meant a short journey across the planet's surface for Aggroteh.

The ship broke through all layers of the atmosphere without any problems, it was only a few kilometers above the ground that it fell into turbulence due to bad weather and strong winds blowing from all directions at the same time. Clouds with an anemic, rotten green color turned out to be thick, constantly changed their position and shapes. Fine, dirty snow that resembled volcanic ash fell from them.

Perfarius extended its skids and landed gently on flat ground that was rare in a landscape. Wherever the GPR reached, lacoliths, cracks and other irregularities dominated. The second provisional landing pad found turned out to be too small for the ship's dimensions, and it was also stuck in a depression surrounded by perfectly vertical walls, not looking like a natural formation.

"It's like an open mine," commented Kate.

"Guys, finally the ground below us!" Paul said with evident relief. A smile appeared on his face, a slight at first, but it grew until it turned into a cheerful chuckle. He infected Kate and Aggro with it.

"Shit, we've found the un-terraformed Earth-like planet that could be inhabited!" He added a minute later. "This is an obvious proof that the cosmos still has a lot of similar houses for us."

"If it seems to be endless, then there will always be enough houses," the androlak corrected.

"It is not known if someone transformed the planet in the distant past," pointed out the Onkalot. "Do you remember the record content that Chimalmat translated to the Kiritians in the temple? The Bone Crusher had known exactly where he had been going. It is possible that Nimja had prepared Tamasul for their arrival in advance, or they simply had had a base here."

"Or they had come to a world they had known before without interfering with its structure at all," Paul suggested.

"I hope to find out more soon," Kate said, losing her previous optimism. The landscape after the raised dust fell didn't look inviting. The hue of the soil was grayer than brown, like a surface that has been digested agriculturally many times. The undulating terrain, cut by bumps, turned into steep mountains in the east. The mighty wind rolled looser matter on the ground, and in the sky, it made thick clouds fought against each other like oils heated in a vessel. Kate took the measurements, this time from the ground level. "Temperature: minus two degrees. Wind: one hundred and twenty-two kilometers per hour. No flora, fauna or any pathogens has been detected. Air that is breathable for humans or Onkalots for approximately eight hours, then you need to wear a mask because of the ammonia concentration and nineteen percent oxygen content. With the pressure prevailing here, too low percentage of oxygen absorption by the body will cause a rapid weakening of its physiological and mental functions after this time, eventually death. We also have to watch out for rainfall, because the air is polluted at the height of the clouds.

"Same thing as I said in space." The android rested his leg on the armchair, and his arms on it. He began to survey the landscape behind the cover. "If another study showed the same, it means that we are dealing with constant values, at least in the near future, and this will greatly facilitate the exit."

"I would like to go on a short reconnaissance," suggested the Onkalot. "I'm perfectly fine, I can leave immediately. I don't want any breathing mask."

"I know you're itching to see your supposed ancestor, but we should go there together," Paul said. "Kate would be guarding the ship."

The androlak nodded. The Onkalot thought the couple must have come to a consensus while he had been sleeping.

"Why couldn't I go alone? I thought everything was agreed," he added more sharply. "One can't change rules once established."

"Because you shouldn't walk around a newly discovered planet alone. These are common safety rules that I have taken under my auspices, remember? Anyway, I should go out first, because I'm immune to many factors that could harm you, Onkalot. Mr. Biffter, for fear of losing his people, did as he did and sent only three. All in all, it was reasonable except for the fact that he didn't appoint a commander of the expedition, so we have to get along somehow."

"Sure, but you, boss the show from the beginning." Aggro persisted. He kept from saying a biting remark about stubborn androids. "What would happen to me if you conducted the analyzes and said yourself that there was no danger?"

"It's impossible to determine everything exactly. What if there are bacteria in the soil or in the air with a specific cell structure that the probes didn't detect because there is no data about them in the central database?"

"I have heard from the Kiritians that pathogens that have developed on a given planet only harm organisms from the same planet."

"Or not. It is also possible that the alleged Nimja member distributed organisms around different worlds and they are related to each other. Anyway, I'm not going to bring up the problems of evolution and genetics right now. We also don't know what caused the disaster, which resulted in sulfuric and nitric acid in the rain. The most sensible thing to do would be to send probes to the fortress."

"Are you crazy?" The Onkalot wagged his tail vigorously to the sides. "You want to pack the probes to Nimja's headquarters? Don't you have enough analysis? It didn't work anyway."

Gessner tapped her hands on the edge of the control panel and stood up ostentatiously.

"Enough! We will draw lots if you can't get along." She took an old silver coin out of a cupboard, but with clearly visible emblems, and walked over to her companions. "Aggro, the image or obverse?"

"The image."

"So, for Paul, the obverse. The winner carries out his plan." Kate tossed the coin high enough to hit the ceiling, caught it smoothly as it dropped and placed it on the back of her hand. The picture showed a rusty bird holding a twig in its beak.

"The image. Aggro has won."

Paul sighed slightly.

"I'll go get the skulak from the hold."

"I'd prefer the smilodon," Aggro said to the android's back before he disappeared behind the cockpit door. When it clanged, he turned to Kate, "Thanks for solving the problem."

The androlak smiled.

"You're welcome. Some argue that there would be no war if women were in power. It's a pity also for me that Mr. Biffter didn't field a larger crew and set priorities. He probably counted on our prudence."

"Paul doesn't understand the important thing: if the Nimja is still living in the fortress, it might take it differently that I came with the android. In the past, they enriched our primitive culture with many customs, one of which assumed that the envoy would go to intertribal meetings alone, having gone before a line of comrades. It was a proof of courage, respect and consideration for tradition."

"I understand your worries. Paul doesn't know the customs of Nimja and Onkalots as well as you do. He would follow classical procedures in such a case, based on logic and training."

"This was what I was going to explain to him." Aggro wanted to wave his paw, but he raised it slightly and lowered it immediately. He gripped the back of the chair. "I didn't think there would be an argument between us. I had never dealt with androids, so I didn't know they were… so human."

"We should all be serious. This is an incredibly groundbreaking journey." Kate put a hand on his shoulder. "Go to him."

Aggroteh nodded to her. At least he could enjoy the fact that they were no longer in this terrible vacuum and he could move around normally. Although he felt a different gravity than on Chulimal, the difference was minimal, but sufficient to remind him with every step that they were unimaginably far from Kiritians' empire.

It turned out that in space the skulak had slipped out of the hangar's safeguards and gotten damaged. One of the four drives didn't work, so the machine, instead of hovering steadily, was spinning around its axis, scraping the ground. Paul went to wake the smilodon. Two hours after recovering from anabiosis, the big cat, fed and watered, was ready to go. The Onkalot reigned over his distant, primitive, but gentle cousin, who obeyed his commands.

"Here it is, I set the signalling device for eight hours." Paul attached the small device with a display to Aggro's left wrist. "When the counter is near zero, you absolutely must be on board. Otherwise, your body will start to fail, which you will feel anyway much earlier. And here you have real-time preview and messenger."

On the other forearm of the Onkalot, he placed a dhurnsteel bracer. "It's banally easy to use, so you can handle it. However, don't be nervous when perturbation occurs, as it was with the probes. Are you still of the opinion that you would like to go alone?"

"I can cope with it, don't worry about me."

Aggro tested the devices and when he determined that everything was working properly, he jumped on the smilodon's back. He scratched it behind the ears, causing the animal eager for further caresses to narrow its eyes with delight and tilt its head back.

"As you want. I will monitor your body condition with this device. If something bothers me or you don't come back ahead of time, we'll react. I'm even ready to use the ship's weapons. You can fully trust my reason and ability to assess a situation. I understand you have never worked with an android?"

Aggro wondered if Paul had somehow heard his conversation with Kate, which was likely on the board under his control. "That's right. This is new to me."

"The same for me - you are the first Onkalot that I have dealt with."

"Will smilodon be safe on the surface?"

"The planet Aj it comes from and Tamasul are similar to each other. In addition, the cat is tamed by the Kiritians, so it will be easier to control it in case of trouble."

"What trouble?" Aggro asked with a little anxiety. Previously, he had seen the plans to go outside abstractly, but as he reached the airlock, he felt fear of the alien planet and what might have been lurking behind the coarse, safe barrier. He could rely only on measurements of machines made by other machines. At least the presence of the smilodon, the only living thing in the vicinity, comforted him.

Paul shook his head.

"I don't know. I have informed you about everything Kate and I learned. Theoretically, you will be safe, but practice is different from theory, so I count on your creativity and imagination. The Emperor assured me that you were the right person in the right place. But enough talk. The day will end in nine hours and seven minutes, and then the temperature will drop sharply below freezing."

The android looked skeptically at his 'armament'. Aggro only took his inseparable obsidian dagger with him, refusing to take human weapons. Paul tried to convince him that it was unwise even if he visited an empty planet peacefully, but Q'ualel got his way, wanting to prepare himself to meet with his ancestor as with an important dignitary or priest. Going with stronger weapons to the Onkalots with higher prerogatives than the visitors was considered an insult, and humanoid jaguars adopted many Nimja's customs. The android stopped pushing, aware that he would have sooner persuaded a politician to tell only the truth than Aggro to bend the Onkalotian tradition.

They quarreled about putting on a hermetic suit, in which you didn't have to keep an eye on the counter. The Onkalot opposed this, arguing that the heavy, rigid protection would have restricted his movements, or even make it difficult to fight or flee in case of danger. The argument that this is how every human astronaut begins their journey on a foreign planet didn't convince him, moreover, Q'ualel had to return to Perfarius ahead of time anyway, because the smilodon, with a metabolism similar to him, didn't let him to put a respiratory mask on its muzzle.

The androlak had to intervene again. Paul finally gave it up. The only inconvenience for him was that if Aggro had died, he and Kate would have had to check the fortress all over again, and then somehow explain it to Biffter. However, the Onkalot's death was part of their contract.

The android connected to the cockpit.

"Kate, open the airlock. Do you have any questions, Aggro?"

"None."

Paul smiled slightly.

"Good luck then."

The huge, multi-toned gate was opening with a hiss for more than a minute before revealing the gray-brown rectangle of an alien world. The cool wind that burst into the hangar brought the scents of barren soil and dirty dust; no organic odors could be smelled in them. The smilodon snorted as it was hit in the nose with ashen snowflakes. Remembering from Paul's research that snow falling from clouds of this category wasn't harmful, Aggro tasted the flakes falling on his fur. He spat out saliva immediately. The snow turned out to be sour, and it stung slightly on the tongue.

The smilodon descended over the gangplank. Aggro directed it with leather cords extending from the sides of the collar. The massive paws of the big cat got slightly immersed in the snow mixed with ubiquitous dust and fine sand, a strong wind was ruffling the hair of both newcomers. The anxiety that had prevailed so far diminished when the Onkalot took his first breaths on the foreign globe and it turned out that the slightly sulfur air didn't blow his lungs apart. He was overwhelmed by a wave of enthusiasm as before after landing, once again recently he managed to chase away blues. Looking through narrowed eyes, he checked his surroundings. To the left, to the horizon stretched a cracked ice desert swept by a wind; hills and mountains rose on the opposite side, broken and jagged, as if they had been reached by a powerful explosion.

On command, the smilodon moved with slight leaps towards the mountains. Soon it switched to a fast run, as it was more comfortable for it to overcome with long jumps numerous cracks in the ground, deeply black, as if bottomless. With the passenger on the back, it easily jumped over successive obstacles, using its strong muscles and accelerating mass. It was climbing, then running down.

It stopped only before a precipice that ended the route. Aggro stepped off the back of the predator, which was sniffing the ground, and crouched over the edge.

The Onkalot was astonished by the unexpected sight. He stiffened as if the temperature had dropped a hundred degrees and his blood had been congealed.

"By all gods, can you see it?" He asked Paul and Kate on Perfarius.

"And very clearly," the android replied officially. "The probes failed to register this area."

"How is it possible?" Kate was disbelieved. "The objects known to us in the completely different universe?"

The valley turned out to be an artificial structure, its walls were perfectly vertical and layered - while the center was covered with mining tools frozen to the ground. It was possible to descend there over rocky ramps hugging walls, stretching in a wavy line. Aggro scanned the surroundings, watched the smilodon for a moment, and when he saw nothing disturbing about its behavior, he returned to his back and steered the animal towards the ramp.

At the bottom, contact with Perfarius was cut off. The image transfer from the cellula to the board also stopped working, but the counter, which wasn't transmitting signals, but operated only on the battery, was still working normally.

Aggro decided not to give up exploration, moreover, Paul foresaw that something like this could happen with the signal, and devices even break due to some unknown reason. The last images captured by 'Perfarius' didn't record anything bad happening with the humanoid jaguar, so both sides remained calm. Whatever was causing the disturbance, Aggro took into account that it might have been about devices and not biological organisms. He himself was feeling very well, the smilodon seemed to be behaving normally too.

The depleted mine in the valley left no doubt that the planet was or had been inhabited by intelligent creatures, even if abandoned, dilapidated tools turned out to be primitive. Similar ones were used by peasant families who couldn't afford to buy machines, so they made a lot of everyday items by hand. Overturned carts were missing wheels, even entire sides. Rails had bent and cracked, damaged by the hand of erosion and time. A similar fate had befallen pickaxes, buckets, shovels, saws, ropes, and each item was relatively small, as if the mining crew had been dwarfs. "But where are they?" wondered Aggro. "How long did they work here?" Despite the graveyard of equipment and the icy blasts falling into the valley like the waters of the sea into a cave-in, he felt a pleasant warmth on his heart. A broad smile appeared unconsciously. Someone had actually lived here! The notes from Tz'aqol's Temple didn't turn out to be a myth or a fiction! The discovery motivated him to search further.

Soon the smilodon was racing forward again, with Aggro clinging to its back.

The opencast mine was connected with another with a pass, also abandoned and littered with dilapidated equipment. After a quarter of an hour of searches, the humanoid jaguar found the entrance to a cave, covered with a ledge, perhaps another mine, this time arranged inside the mountain. His olfactory sense was of little use as he could only smell weathered rock. The whistle of the wind drowned out all sounds. Nothing was visible except the curving black throat of the cave, smooth as the wandering site of an extremely large earthworm. Q'ualel directed the smilodon there. Paul had built lights with automatic light intensity adjustment in the collar, but both travelers could see well in the dark, so Aggro didn't activate them.

The corridor initially curved to the left in a long, gentle arc to straighten itself in front of the entrance to a small grotto, where there was nothing but a roughly dressed entrance to another tunnel. Aggro concluded that whatever function it had served in the past, due to its small size, it had been unlikely to be suitable for transporting uncarved dimensions from the surface. The next corridor wasn't tall, the Onkalot had to lie on the back of the crawling smilodon so as not to scrub his head against the rock. As he went into the mountain, the temperature rose, he could smell the hydrogen sulphide scent of rot; the dryness gradually gave way to moisture. The wind, which in the grotto had seemed to whistle like condemned souls, also died down.

Instead, there was light.

At first, as a delicate bluish glow that could be easily confused with a figment of imagination and grew stronger as you traveled. Drops, glistening like diamonds, ran down the walls and dripped from the ceiling. Q'ualel outthrusted his claw and take a drop off the stalactite, then, cursing at his possible stupidity, touched with his tongue like before snow.

"Water," he whispered. "Plain water. As for Chulimal." The next cave turned out to be so monumental that you couldn't see the ceiling and walls, as if you had gone out to an empty, open space on a cloudy night. Aggro slid off the smilodon's back and began to walk as if hypnotized, looking around in amazement. The excess oxygen made him feel dizzy. The cave was full of bioluminescent light and its source - flora and fungi growing safely in the interior of the mountain. As a whole it resembled a rich coral reef, and Q'ualel even wondered if there were really plants around him. Some of the little stalks, though they resembled thick grass, moved like the limbs of Coelenterata waving in the ocean. Big quasi-leaves after being nudged, violently took the shape of, rolls, balls or curls. Abrus' colonies overgrowing a hill turned from blue and yellow to red when you got too close to them. A variety of mycelia protruded from the gigantic, twisted trunks branching high above, from wholly fanciful fractal structures to polypores, out of which glowing, flying spores fell. The Onkalot was sure that he had seen a similar phenomenon somewhere. His mind quickly showed him the location - the Chulimal equator. That's how he found further evidence that the two planets shared common characteristics, since someone intelligent could travel between them and transfer organisms.

Walking through the yard along a path lined with turquoise boulders, he reached the wall of the grotto, where he noticed a fragment of a sloped ceiling perforated by galleries. With his infravision and the bioluminescence light, he could clearly see forms of mesh-like filters mounted on the funnels, so fine that no sediment could pass through them, and probably also poisonous rain, and if so, the membranes trapped toxins. Soil irrigation was working though, Aggro could feel the wetness under his paws as he stepped onto springy skins of plants. Questions began to appear in his mind, "Was it one singularity for the entire planet, or there were more of them? If more, did it mean that the underground yards provided Tamasul with oxygen? If so, there would have to be a lot of them. But who made them?"

He froze hearing a rustle. At the same time, he registered the movement. Whatever it was, it must have stopped with it, for all he could see was plants and mushrooms. After some time, he thought that it had been a hallucination, which wasn't uncommon with such a blaze of colors and lights.

And yet it wasn't true.

As he kept standing still, a silvery figure flashed among the stalks. Even glistening, as if mercury light had been emanating from inside it. Many long hairs rose and fell on the fine back. The animal with ears reaching its rump resembled a cross between a rabbit and a weasel, but it was more like a predator: it had clawed limbs, eyes on the front of its skull, and several pairs of tusks. Certain that it was left alone, it trotted on two paws to a bare patch of earth. When it turned around, its eyes flashed black. It was the look of an intelligent being. The creature lifted its front paws and began swaying them over the ground. It moved its long fingers. The heads of bioluminescent earthworms came out of the ground, and more segments were quickly emerging. The fascinated humanoid jaguar realized that they were moving plants, growing at a surprisingly fast pace. He had already seen a similar phenomenon of incomprehensible biomatter control once - when Forkis had changed from a human to an Onkalot with the use of Nimja's artifact. The creature's role had to be to care for this peculiar oxygen-producing yard. Aggro stood dumbfounded, also this time not understanding the workings of the forces he had just witnessed.

His stupor was interrupted by a growling colossus that with a rumble started to rush through the yard like a speeding machine. The entity turned, stuck its ears to its back, and fled with a squeal. It turned out that there were more of them, hid in different parts of the cave, but all scattered like a flock of birds scared by a cat.

Aggro also broke into a run.

"Stop!" He yelled at the smilodon pursuing the creature and trampling the plants. The frightened animal was chased against the wall, where, thanks to its flexibility and lightness, it turned to the right. The heavy smilodon struck the rock hard, but quickly recovered and continued the pursuit. It found a hole in which the 'gardener' had disappeared and began to dig it up.

"Enough! Calm down." The Onkalot grabbed the leather harness, pulled it tightly, and began to pat the smilodon on the neck and stroke it alternately. "Now, take it easy. This is nothing for you. Enough, leave this hole."

The giant soon calmed down, began to squint its eyes and purr, mollified by stroking of his forehead.

A clatter of falling boulders caught the attention of the humanoid jaguar. A hole was made in the corner where the smilodon's body had crashed against the rock. It may have been there all the time, but Aggro hadn't noticed it before until it was widened. He tied the now calm cat to a thick branch, hoping that the plant would endure if the smilodon began to jerk. At any rate, he was hoping that when he returned from the reconnaissance - if the narrow tunnel beyond the breach turned out to be more than a short, dead end - the cat would remain where it was.

Having walked to the wall illuminated by the cold bioluminescence light, Aggro saw that it was covered with signs that looked more like patterns than letters. The combinations seemed complicated, although they consisted of simple geometric signs arranged in larger structures. He wondered about their meaning. Was it about some information? Warning? Maybe someone who had been previously in the cave had created meaningless scribbles? Aggro felt uneasy as his thoughts flowed in a free stream. He had no doubts anymore that the planet had been and most likely was inhabited, but he still didn't know by whom: enemy or friend. If he found the intelligent animals in the cave that did wonders with plants, who would he encounter next? Could he really meet someone from the Great Family?

Having pulled the obsidian dagger out of the case, he picked out a few sharp, interfering boulders and plunged down the aisle. Contrary to assumptions, he didn't have to go on all fours, it was enough to keep the leaning silhouette. The glow from the yard soon disappeared, but the Onkalot didn't use the night vision, for in the distance a dull light was seeping in, which intensified as he traveled the distance. The passage was different from the smooth tunnel that led to the yard: roughly dressed, dirty with dust, and claustrophobic. Also not used, because the ground covered with gravel and dirt had only paw prints of small animals, probably 'gardeners'.

The tunnel led upwards, curved in different directions, and gradually widened. On the walls, loomed yokes destroyed by time, for torches or forms of primitive lamps, stairs also appeared. In front of Aggroteh, orange light quivered, flowing into the corridor, which might have indicated the presence of a fire nearby, especially since smoke as if from a fire could me smelled in the dry air. There was another peculiarity: an irregular, suggestive rumble, as if jackhammers had been abusing a rock.

Biff, biff, biff.

Something swished. A very low-pitched voice groaned like a squirrel being stepped on.

Aggro was getting more and more nervous. His hair bristled on his back, the tip of his tail quivered. The heart seemed to beat to the mysterious, metallic blows to the rock.

Biff, biff, biff ...

He wondered if he had found another mine, this time under the mountain. If so, and it was still functioning, who worked in it? An answer came extremely quickly. Having lied down on the ground, Q'ualel began to crawl in the shadows until his eyes were irritated by the intense glow of the fire. He emerged from a mine shaft two meters above the ground, one of several excavated in the great grotto.

Small creatures guarded by larger ones worked below. A brief observation was enough to infer that they were slaves and hacks. The former were relatively short, slouching, their height was less than one meter. Aggro had once been a slave himself, he remembered that a pug had been kept in one of the houses where he had served. The short, flat muzzles of the mine creatures resembled the face of such a dog, but the rest of the body resembled a lion's silhouette, but emaciated, dressed in rags, and instead of a proud mane, two strands of spiky red hair stretched behind the ears. The humanoids were hitting the wall with pickaxes, and successive groups were dragging with ropes the raw boulders towards the adjacent cave, where another crew was carrying similarly dressed blocks of rock. Nobody took care to facilitate the work of the slaves with a cart or even a platform with wheels. Only the creatures by the tracks had carts, which they were filling, using levers or the strength of their own arms. The other kind of humanoid did nothing that required more effort than lashing the back of a subordinate from time to time with a whip. Taller than Aggroteh, they stood erect and presented themselves proudly, on their shining gray hair, they had figure-fitting leather garments reinforced with metal elements. The skirts-pants had openings for jackal tails reaching to the knees, because Onkalotian guards were most associated with this animal brought by humans to terraformed planets. Their dog heads were protected by helmets made so that sloping ears could move freely.

A hack standing closest to Q'ualel didn't like the slave's work pace at the cart, he shouted something in a harsh, rumbling language and hit him with a whip. The unfortunate man flinched, but didn't react in any other way, though the blow, even through the thick layers of rags, must have hurt.

Hidden, Aggro spent the next minutes observing from a shaded ventilation recess. He was afraid that in his crimson eyes would be visible reflections of torches and wall lamps, so he kept them squinting. He glanced at Paul's reader: there were five hours and forty-two minutes left before returning to the Perfarius. He began to count the kobolds - he didn't think of a better name for slaves, who he associated with creatures of human legends - as well as the guards. The former were numerous, the jackals only eleven, at least in plain sight. He supposed that the kobolds were either docile in nature, or had been mentally broken enough not to be able to stand up to the torturers armed only with the whips and bizarre lances. He looked at the latter held by a pair of guards wandering at the entrance to the cave complex, from where the screech of machines was coming. It resembled a simple planed staff, with a four-bladed mechanism attached to the top, probably for more than just decoration. Since there were slaves and guards, there had to be their masters as well. Q'ualel considered whether he should have just come out of hiding and reveal himself. If he had kept the rules of refinement universal for intelligent species, he would have had a chance to get to the pivot men of the hacks. Naturally, if he hadn't been killed on the spot, forced to work with the slaves, or thrown into a dungeon, probably somewhere in the basement of the fortress.

Biff ... Biff ...

The hack brutally kicked the kobold as he stopped mining the ore. The weakened creature squealed pitifully from beneath the rags, and fell to the ground like a sack of misfortune. However, he quickly got up on trembling legs, not wanting to get any more strokes.

Aggro would have liked to go back to the ship and discuss with Kate and Paul what to do next, but it all would have taken too long. He decided to take a risk and delve deeper into the complex.

A rock protruded beneath the ventilation inlet, and several stalagmites protended at it. Having put the dagger in the case, Aggro patiently waited for the moment when the kobolds were occupied only with their work and the guards were not looking towards the ventilation, then he left the opening and fell silently on the pads of his paws. He had made the right decision, though probably procedurally irresponsible, that he hadn't let himself to be persuaded to wear the rustling suit. Noisy crushers and machine tools nearby worked to his advantage. Cautiously, he leaned out of the hideout plunged in the twilight.

Leaning down, he passed the two guards standing dangerously close. The taller one, with the face of disdain preserved on the weary dog's face, turned casually, but then returned to his previous position. The Onkalot could smell the dusty, sweaty hair of the guards. They apparently had a weaker sense of smell than him or suppressed by a long experience in the mine, where there were many intense smells, because they didn't sense him.

He reached a side walkway to an underground square, full of slaves storing aggregate with carts, baskets, nets, and ropes. So, he withdrew and tried a different path. Soon he found a breach in the wall between the neighboring caves, through which, unnoticed, he got into the area of another guarded object. From what he had observed so far, he concluded that the creatures living on Tamasul weren't technologically advanced, otherwise they would have been detected much earlier by some surveillance device popular in the worlds of people. Only the guardian lances didn't fit the full picture of a primitive culture of slavery. But he had to bear in mind that he had seen little so far.

There were fewer dark alleys in the second cave, but the rumble and whistling of working machines, powered by the muscles of the slaves, compensated for this inconvenience by muffling other sounds. It was enough to run from one hiding place to another while no one was watching. And such moments didn't happen often - several dozen kobolds were working in the hall and five guards were hanging around. Aggro noticed a smoky woodcut map of the dungeon on a wall. If he had interpreted it correctly, the mine and the fortress should have been connected by an elevator, but the distance between the objects was unknown. Q'ualel was guided by relatively legible pictures, and not by writing and markings that could mean anything.

One of the passing slaves noticed him. He released wheelbarrow handles from his dirty long-fingered paws, surprise instantly turned to fear. Irritated, Aggro didn't move for a moment, having no idea how the kobold would react. He raised a finger to his mouth, hoping that he would understand the gesture from another universe.

He didn't understand.

The kobold mumbled something to himself, then louder and louder, repeating a phrase that sounded like, "Kane hira pam." The words turned to a high-pitched scream. Even though Aggro didn't move much, the slave was overwhelmed by panick, as if the intruder had been a lurking assassin.

"Be quiet ..." hissed Q'ualel in Onkalotian. "Or you'll draw the guards." He made a gesture simulating a whip, then put his paws to his head to make them look like protruding dogs' ears.

He achieved nothing. The slave's screams caught the attention of others, who stopped working, goggled, opened their mouths, some bolted, others, on the contrary, gathered next to mentally swearing Q'ualel.

The agitation quickly leaped up at the guards. They were arranged in such a way that they initially saw the kobolds gathering without permission. The hot air of the mine was lashed by a serpent whip, followed by a groan filled with pain, mingled with menace.

While the hack was beating the kobold, another one, with a lance, began to approach Aggroteh's poor hideout, by which the frightened slaves were still standing. There was no way he couldn't have noticed the lurking intruder. He spotted him when he was in the center of the group, intending to disperse it with a weapon gathering light energy between core protrusions.

"So, they have technology," it flashed through Aggro's mind.

Eye contact was made. The janitor had yellow eyes and tiny pupils.

Q'ualel straightened slowly. The surprised guard froze like a slave before, anger appeared on his jackal face half hidden under his helmet. He roared something, grabbed the lance with both hands and pointed it at the intruder's chest. The hot blades of the trident stopped centimeters from the heart of the humanoid jaguar.

The guard spoke in an insistent, commanding tone.

Aggro shook his head helplessly.

"I don't understand," he said, first in the language of Onkalots, then in Kiritian. He raised his hands, hoping that at least this time someone would interpret his gesture appropriately. "I have no bad intentions. I'm looking for the Seventh Minister, the Bone Crusher. Apparently, he came here a long time ago."

The jackal fell silent. Grinning, he tilted his head.

"Kombadi Nanawak!" He barked. The kobolds standing so far fled in panic. Blue light illuminated the top of the lance.

"Not good," thought Aggro. The guard must have misunderstood him.

The lance did turn out to be a form of energy weapon, but it was not a laser that the eye cannot register when it is fired. Undefined, accumulated energy cut through the air in a long stream at such a pace that the humanoid jaguar managed to spring. Stalagmites shattered into dozens of pieces, painfully hitting him lying on the ground and covering his head.

An anger he hadn't experienced in a long time, being jaded with life, grew in Aggroteh. He got upset that he was being shot when he wanted to talk quietly. That those wayward munchkins had betrayed him. That he had found himself on the god-forgotten, contaminated by some catastrophic planet where he could only count on machines and the smilodon, because the Kiritians hadn't wanted to risk their precious butts on the expedition that had had little chance of success from the very beginning. They wanted to kill him, so according to the Onkalotian custom, he had the right to retaliate.

The scent of the dog's hair irritated the nostrils, the brain sent signals to attack, but Aggro didn't move under the pile of boulders and stones. It was important to him that the guard came as close as possible wanting to see if he was still alive. He already knew that the lance needed recharging before another shot. He felt on his body a painful stab of the blades, but he endured it. He didn't move.

The guard stabbed him a few more times, then crouched down, leaning on the weapon like on a staff. He outstretched a clawed paw with a finger-like structure, typical of intelligent beings with manipulative abilities.

Q'ualel started up in a flash, reached for his dagger, and violently plunged the blade into a shoulder unprotected by a leather armor. An expression of utter disbelief bloomed on the jackal's face, then he cried out in pain. He yelled but didn't react otherwise, as if he hadn't known what to do. Aggro was surprised by this reaction. Either he was dealing with an old individual, or with someone who only acted tough, beating smaller and weaker ones in the warm, safe seclusion of a mine. Meanwhile, he was the priest-warrior. He had survived the fall of the Onkalots, human slavery, sometimes overwhelming and degrading, and the Kiritian-rebel war in which he had been involved. He had been in the capital of the Immortals, surrounded by thousands of achijes, having as a companion the living Trojan horse with the bomb hidden in his body. And finally, he had flown through unknown number of universes to see evolutionary decadence.

The guard dropped to his knee, released the lance, and gripped the hilt of the dagger with his hands.

The so far scared kobolds began to chatter with squeaky voices, and then threw themselves with their tools and fists at the fallen tormentor. They were beating him from all sides. Randomly pounding with stone and metal, inflicting deeper and deeper wounds, releasing more and more rusty blood from the huddled, trembling body. From the depths of the cave, a pair of guards came to the aid of his companion, wielding whips, their mouths twisted in fury expressed pure hostility. They lashed the nearest slaves, forming long red stripes on the thin rags.

There was a fuss in the cave. The meek slaves unexpectedly turned into insurgents, without fear, hitting their oppressors with everything at their hands. The guards with the whips quickly disappeared inside the advancing circles.

Aggro wanted the dagger back, but lost sight of it. The kobolds continued to torture the unconscious hack, perhaps even dead. He grabbed the only available weapon - the trident lying on the ground, which the slaves were not interested in. He took advantage of the confusion and ran along the cave, holding with both hands a lance as tall as he was. When he reached the exit gate, out of the corner of his eye he saw kobolds cheering and bloody bodies lying motionless.

Another cave, lit by fire lamps, was smaller than the next one. There was a hissing steam engine larded with metal pipes, cylindrical pistons were working under pressure at regular intervals. A kobold who was guarding it fled when he saw the humanoid jaguar running and swinging the stolen lance.

Reproducing the memorized plan of the complex in his mind, Q'ualel climbed a rock-hewn ramp and reached a sturdy door. The leaf was opened wide, it was supported by a boulder. Further, stretched the gorge of the corridor, flooded with smelly, green from algae water. Round beetles with bioluminescent carapaces crawled over the walls and ceiling. Above the slurry was protruding a bridge, crudely pulled together from crooked planks, creaking with every step.

Aggro had almost reached its end when his path was blocked by a guard running from the opposite direction, directed as a backup to suppress the rebellion. He didn't have a helmet, but was carrying a sword. He attacked the intruder with it, hitting him from above as if he had wanted to chop off a condemned man's head on a stump.

Aggro knelt down and parried the blow with his lance. It was so powerful, fitting the muscled stature of the tall janitor, that searing pain pierced his shoulders and an unpleasant nervous current tossed his whole body. Sparks were formed as the metal slammed against the metal.

The guard withdrew his sword, growled something in his language, and tried to stab him. Q'ualel managed to jump to the edge of the bridge, a piece of the rotten plank fell into the foul-smelling liquid. The humanoid jaguar assumed a defensive posture, directing the trident towards the enemy.

"I don't want to fight you!" He shouted. The ranger's reaction was the more furious expression on the dog's face, so Aggro could have as well been insulting him.

The hack attacked again. He extended his left paw, wanting to grab the base of the trident and thus block the defensive stab of the Onkalot, and with the other, hit flatly using the sword, so as to rip his belly open. Aggro outmaneuvered him, the jackal took a few wobbly steps, almost losing his balance from the strong swipe of his sword. He immediately lost it completely when he was tripped with the lance and collapsed on the boards.

Q'ualel tried to negotiate, if not with an incomprehensible word, then with a diplomatic tone, setting out his intentions. The man responded aggressively in his own way. Having pulled himself up from the ground, he charged with fierce fury, carelessly inflicting blows with his sword but putting a lot of strength into each one. Aggro parried some with the lance or bracer from Paul, and the rest he avoided by rolling, jumping and bending. He still hoped the hack would take the hint, seeing his defensive behavior. The man interpreted it differently: the intruder is weak.

Aggro made a mistake and failed to dodge in time. The blade hit as he shielded his head with his arm. Fragments of the transparent cover spattered; the mechanism was crushed. The humanoid jaguar cursed. And this is all what was left of Paul's counter, but the most important thing is that the casing had survived intact and his paw wasn't cut off. The Kiritians made durable equipment, but small devices were not designed to be struck by two-hundred-kilo anthropomorphs with their swords.

He would have liked to pay back with the lance's energy, but he had no idea how to release it. The perfectly smooth stick was devoid of switches, plates, or other activators common to human weapons.

Avoiding another blow with the sword that had nearly decapitated him, Q'ualel stepped on a rotten plank. It broke in the middle and trapped his leg up to the knee. The guard, breathless, kicked the lance further onto the pier. He crouched down and put the sword to the Onkalot's throat.

Lying down on the planks, with his limb still trapped, Aggro gripped the blade with his paws. He was pushing it in the direction opposite than his opponent. He hissed with the effort, kept pressuring, even though his fingers were already bleeding. In a duel, where strength mattered, Aggro didn't have the slightest chance, moreover he was in a worse position. He couldn't think of any ruse. Withdrawing the paws or easing the pressure meant immediate death, which he could delay anyway by at most a few greedy breaths.

The jackal suddenly stopped pushing. Amazed, he released his sword, which slid down beside the man's chest, and he himself hung over him, resting his hairy paws at his sides. Aggro felt a metallic taste of blood on his tongue, similar to the

Onkalotian one except that it was denser, sour, and more rust-colored. At least that was what it looked like in the glare of beetle carapaces. Even though the weary organism was demanding air, Aggro closed his mouth, not wanting to taste more of this grunge. He focused his attention on the guard's face, twisted in a grimace of surprise and pain. And such a mask got preserved as the dead body fell on Q'ualel's sword and chest, depriving him of his breath.

He slipped out from under the gigantic body with difficulty, freeing the limb at the same time. Accompanied by the creaking of boards, he kicked the carcass from the footbridge into the water, where it fell with a loud splash. Aggro's blurry eyes regained normal vision. He got up, put his paws on his lap and, gasping for breath, tried to understand what had happened. He glanced at the dead jackal, whose head was protruding above the shallow water. He noticed a piece of rock sticking out of the back of his head.

At the end of the footbridge was standing a frightened kobold, hiding his face behind his fingers like a child regretting a deed after the fait accompli. Aggro picked up the lance and approached him, he hid his paws behind his back and took two steps back.

The Onkalot pointed to the guard lying in the water, then grinned in a fleeting smile.

"Thanks. You don't have to be afraid of me. I'm on your side. You saw me fight." He carefully moved the lance forward. "Do you know how it works?"

The kobold frowned with his bushy eyebrows, closed his muzzle and tilted his head. He looked back nervously as the muted calls of guards and footsteps echoed in the warehouse to which the corridor with the footbridge led. He grabbed the Onkalot by his elbow and pointed to a shaded alley behind a row of crates. They both moved immediately in that direction.

They stopped in the corner, where they waited for the guards to run out of the room.

"Do you know how it works?" Aggro asked again in a whisper, pointing to the lance.

The kobold stared blankly at him for a moment, then timidly tapped his forehead with a finger dirty with grease.

The Onkalot sighed.

"I know, I'm crazy that I entered the mine without any discernment or plan, and alone ... I don't think we understand each other. What do you mean, kid?"

The slave tapped again, this time more sweepingly, wrinkling his muzzle as if irritated. He pointed to the lance and began drumming his finger on his temple again.

"Am I soft in the head?" Aggro pointed to his own forehead. "Am I supposed to think, strain my brain, tap my head with the lance, imagine something?"

The kobold squawked in frustration and yanked his lance away. He leaned it diagonally against the rock. A quick glance towards the exit, a moment of contemplation - and a blue beam was fired towards the wall, turning its fragment into a pile of boulders.

"Of course! The lance is controlled by thoughts!" The humanoid jaguar raised his weapon. The kobold fled immediately and disappeared between the crates. "Hey, hold on. You could get me out of here. Anyway, never mind."

Holding the stick in both hands like a cave ranger, Aggro saw the flaws in his reasoning. However, this energy weapon worked, it was certainly adjusted to the standards of jackals who spoke the particular language, and their thoughts operated in it as well. The kobolds knew the language of the guards. Perhaps because of his ignorance he had misunderstood the slave, who might have meant something like an entraser being implanted in the brain? Maybe the lance was also synchronized with the ranger's head like this? He couldn't know if the locals underwent some sort of chipping procedure. Is it possible that in such a primitive place an advanced nano-digital technology functioned? After all, the trident shooting energy stood out boldly from its surroundings and could be equipped with a mini-generator.

He aimed the lance at a boulder and imagined breaking it with the energy of the trident. Nothing happened. He kept on trying. He could fight with the lance like with a staff, which would have compensated him for the loss of the dagger, but he would have preferred to use its full potential.

Only a dozenth or so attempt resulted in success: a ball resembling combat plasma was generated between the projections and flew towards the boulder, turning it into burnt dust. Aggro also managed to release a few meters long, sizzling stream of energy, cutting anything in its path. And all this didn't cause the weapon to recoil.

Unfortunately, it produced noise and light.

One of the hacks entered the room and headed straight towards the Onkalot's hideout behind the crates. The fire creeping on the wall distorted his shadow, adding harshness to the guard's silhouette, length to his grinning teeth and a sword clutched in his hand.

"Come on..." Aggro hugged the lance, pressed his back against a rough crate.

By visualizing a shot, he successfully turned his thoughts into reality. The energy ball threw the screaming jackal that fell into the crates and drowned under their blizzard. Aggro waited a moment. There were no sounds from under the mound, nothing was moving. He had learned, by the way, that he could regulate the weapon's killing force form, sometimes melting rock with it, other times throwing the target.

Holding the lance with his right paw, he ran past the pyramid of crates and rushed towards an open metal gate. He found himself in a corridor lined with blood-red bricks that, according to the wall map, was outside the cave complex. He soon reached an elevator platform, happily on the lowest level. It was activated with a lever and the destination was selected by stopping a wedge at a specific notch of a sprocket wheel meaning the floor, as a cog lock.

Hearing noises in the warehouse, Q'ualel pushed the stubborn lever to the maximum, hitting it with the bottom of the lance. A shot at the transmission destroyed it completely and blocked the mechanism, preventing the elevator from being pulled down.

The square freight platform shuddered as he hopped onto it, it whistled, then began to float over the corner rails. It rumbled as it passed each span. It was going quite fast for its weight. It was passing more underground floors and so far, no one had had any idea how to stop it. Aggro soon went above the surface; the shaft here had the form of a rudely dressed tower huddled against a high vertical rock crowned with a fortress. The interior was evenly illuminated by barred window openings, letting in the whistling wind along with the snow. Leaning on the lance, the humanoid jaguar was high enough to be able to admire the landscapes of Tamasul. Snow-capped, pointed peaks seemed to tease the stormy sky that shimmered with gaudy colors like a scared tropical amphibian.

He almost fell as the elevator came to a halt with a screech of brakes scraping against the guides. He got stuck between the floors. He listened for a moment but caught nothing but the whistle of the wind and the creak of the platform. It was unlikely that the mechanism broke right now - rather someone managed to jam it and would pull the elevator down to the floor. Aggro looked around his little prison. There was a metal floor under his paws, the ceiling was twin-like, and the two parts were joined by corner pillars. The shaft was made of blocks of rock. He surveyed them and noticed that they had slits big enough to put fingers there or catch claws on them. He raised the weapon. Like with a torch lancet, he began to burn a circle in the ceiling. He hoped the floor would be nearby and he would be able to climb there, though that might have meant falling into the hands of the guards. However, he couldn't wait any longer in that cage.

The section of the ceiling yielded, fell and hit the floor, making the elevator vibrate. Q'ualel threw the lance through the opening, then jumped up and climbed onto the roof of the cabin. It turned out that he was stuck about thirty meters below the floor - at this height they were very far apart. The elevator was held by a thick rope attached to solid hoops. Aggro used it to climb instead of struggling with the wall. Despite the presence of seemingly comfortable protrusions on the metal splices, climbing turned out to be quite a torment: the mutilated paw pads burned with live fire, and the lance held in his mouth was heavy and strained the muscles of the neck, made it difficult to breathe. The enemy could only wait for the intruder to come to him himself. The elevator might have moved unexpectedly.

Tired, the Onkalot reached the edge of the floor, threw the lance, then rolled onto his back himself. He lay so until he calmed his breathing. It was hard to say anything specific about the place, for there was only a short rectangular hall in sight, with a smooth ceiling and walls made of matching gray rock tiles larger than sand tiles lining the floor. The darkness was dissipated by a pair of wall lamps placed opposite each other - metal tongs closing the flames.

His rest was interrupted by a guard who emerged from around the corner with a two-handed ax. He stopped, surprised by the presence of the Onkalot, but then he moved towards him, striding and with teeth bared in anger. Like the hacks from the nether regions, he was also an anthropomorph resembling a dog or a jackal, but he looked like a different race. The short, reddish hair seemed to burn in the glow cast by the fires creeping in a draft. His chest and limbs, especially his upper ones, were as muscular as of someone working hard. Little eyes of indeterminate color, reflecting the light, glanced out over the wide mouth through the helmet holes. The hooked claws looked like a weapon as dangerous as an ax. The fluffy brush reached the knees. The guard's clothing differed from that adapted to the warm environment, worn in the mine: it was cut from thin metal so that ergonomically adjusted elements didn't obstruct the movements. There was a golden symbol in the center of the chest, representing the front of the head of something like a dog. Everything, along with the owner of the armor, presented itself neatly. Aggro concluded that the guardian might have belonged to the elite protecting the fortress.

He started up from the floor and stood defensively, holding the lance.

However, he quickly realized how naively he had acted assuming a provocative posture. The colossus charging at him would surely crush him with the ax, as long as he didn't knock him down into the shaft with the momentum itself. The guard, however, didn't attack, he probably played a scene with a display of strength and contemptuous countenance to frighten the intruder. He stopped at Q'ualel, rested the head of the ax on the ground, and extended his paw as if to snatch the lance from him. He said something in a stertorous voice.

Aggro did the only thing he could think of: using his agility and smaller size, he swiftly bypassed the colossus to escape. The prelude of the meeting didn't herald a civilized conversation.

A tug on his tail knocked him to the ground - the ranger managed to catch him with a half-turn. Aggro landed on his stomach, rolled over, and aimed the lance at his chest. He wanted to fire a small amount of energy as a warning just to char his breastplate. Not only the appearance of the argus indicated that he was more than a simple mine hack, the lightning-fast reaction and paring of the attack proved that the humanoid jaguar was dealing with a better trained individual. Having noticed the moment of accumulation of light, the guard raised his arm and dispersed the energy with a bracelet over the bracer.

Q'ualel clenched his jaws and thrust the trident like a spear into the man's hand. The guard hissed in pain and loosened his grip on the tail, which was enough for Aggro to escape. Mindlessly and blindly, because he didn't know the plan of the fortress. As he ran, he glanced at a broken wrist display. He estimated that he had maybe three hours left.

Behind him he heard the pounding footsteps and screams of the guard. The noises faded as Aggro entered the maze of corridors.

He ran to the great hall, stopped to catch his breath. The room was decorated with a seemingly incompatible panache worthy of ancient kings and gloomy austerity. The floor was covered with light gray stone slabs of various shapes, tightly adjacent to each other and without mortar. Smaller and darker lumps covered the walls. The distant ceiling was swathed in a faint twilight, but patterns as intricate as galaxy components could be seen on it. The builders gave the windows the form of colorful stained glass, truly precise works of art. They depicted some canine deities or rulers in flowing, rich robes, holding in clawed hands objects like the lance of Aggroteh. Similar figures could be seen on gigantic reliefs made in several shades of gray. The room was lit by fire coming from various sources: from stands to wall lights and lamps hanging on chains by the walls. Statues of shimmering stone or metal, arranged in two rows, seemed as natural as if real anthropomorphic warriors and priests had been standing there. The Onkalot didn't notice the slightest flaw in the chamber. Everything kept matching proportions and symmetry. The hall repulsed with coldness, but at the same time attracted with its harsh, soulless splendor. If

Aggro had been tasked with finding a home for some god, he would have placed it in a similar place.

The guard chasing him ran out of the corridor. Three more, armed with a personal weapon, fell from an embranchement on the left. They shouted to each other, and then one pointed to the intruder. The Onkalot ran towards the stairs through the line of statues. Behind the landing, he burst into the corridor, almost into the arms of another Cerberus. It was small, so he managed to knock it over and escape.

Escaping through the meanders of a half-dark, monumental fortress, he glimpsed details on columns, door leaves and walls. He was horrified to find that he knew some elements of architecture. Ornaments stylized as tissues, bones and organs were characteristic of Kiritians, who placed them especially on the armor of ships and naval craft. In turn, some columns or walls consisted of skulls - fleeing, Aggro couldn't tell whether they were real or carved in stone - which was associated with the most primitive factions of Onkalots, fond of the cult of death and dark creatures, like Jun Kame. Elsewhere, bright stones that fully reflected the light had been pressed into the structures. The mixture of different architectural styles clearly meant that someone rich in intergalactic knowledge had come here, or that the fortress inhabitants had made long space trips. It is not known, however, whether as teachers, or they themselves had adopted foreign patterns, hybridized them and applied them in their place.

Stairs. Halls. Corridors. A constant escape. Running around. The horde of chasing hacks that would eventually get him. He had no choice and he killed one by stabbing him in the throat, or at least he injured him enough that the guard fell on the casing of the fountain with his bloody muzzle. Q'ualel felt as if for many minutes he had been chased like an animal into the trap of hunters who know the forest perfectly.

Unexpectedly, he lost his balance and took the rest of the stairs rolling painfully past the dropped lance. Having hit the floor with a groan, he noticed that his hind legs were held in place by a bola. A guard with a launcher jumped off the low railing. A cordon of pursuers swiftly surrounded him. Aggro didn't expect so many of them. He was laughed at because of his humiliation, they congratulated each other on the success, orders were given. He was thrown from the side to his belly and pressed with a knee to the ground, someone took the lance.

A hard blow to the head with something hard, which was surely to knock him unconscious, only stunned Aggroteh. Before realizing that he was still conscious and the blow was successfully corrected, he felt more than saw hairy hands grab his sides and lift him without finesse.

VII. Nanawak

Onkalots, just like humans, sometimes liked to undergo the action of intoxicating or psychotropic substances obtained by natural methods. First of all, this concerned priests and shamans who, in a state of elation, tried to communicate with supernatural beings. Q'ualel, as a warrior priest who had once looked after Tonatiuh's temple and defended Chiq'aq on Chulimal, was also delirious, though rarely due to the constantly required efficiency of body and mind. So, he knew a famous hangover perfectly well, which on the one hand he accepted because it soothingly distorted the difficult reality, and on the other he hated for what it did with the body. But now that he had regained consciousness, he would have preferred alcohol problems to the feeling that his head was a meld of glasses and his stomach was about to explode like Drunkenstein's chest. His hind and fore limbs, on which he had lain sideways, looked like boulders. In general, everything hurt him, as if he had been badly beaten, and not just hit in the head, which he remembered. Maybe that's what had happened: the guards had taken their frustration out on him as he had lain unconscious.

He saw several blurry sources of light vaguely, as if he had been looking out from under the lake's surface at an evening harbor. He was in a different room from the one in which he had been captured - it was darker, had more stained glass and ...

His hair bristled on his back as he sensed someone's presence. His eyes regaining visual acuity registered movement. He heard the rustle of cloth being run over a hard surface. The tall silhouette blocked out almost all the light. Something heavy fell on his forehead. He felt disgusting processes moving on his skin, reminiscent of thick larvae. The object tightened painfully. Whatever it was, it caused Aggroteh such a fulminant, intense pain that he roared at the top of his voice, and then he went limp and fell into the depths black like the inside of a tomb.

***

He woke up feeling the same as the last time, though his body ached less and the blood was circulating freely in his limbs. The deadly pincers were taken. He choked on air like a prisoner lying on the ground, off whose chest a guard took heavy boot. For a critical moment, Q'ualel was out of breath, which made him panick, but then everything returned to normal. At least when it comes to breathing. The time set by Paul hadn't yet passed since he was still alive, but there might have been little left of it.

He realized that he wasn't alone.

At first, he mistook the creature for another of the many statues in this damned fortress. Statues, however, don't move, although the person standing nearby didn't differ much from a stone figure. Only the chest was quivering to the rhythm of the slow breathing.

Aggro put his front paws on the floor and pulled himself up enough to be able to tilt his head freely and peer at the figure that wasn't a delusion. Amazed, he forgot to breathe for a moment. The strangest being he had ever seen stood before him. They certainly belonged to the same kind of anthropomorphs as the keepers of the fortress and mine, but their animal features were more reduced. At least as far as the head and hands are concerned, for the rest of the body was drowned in flowing robes worthy of ancient rulers. From above the short snout glanced heterochromatic eyes: green and yellow, with tiny pupils, as if exposed to intense light. Although highly intelligent, also marked by contempt and amusement was that look. From their head covered with a short nemes with a gold band protruded wolf ears. The body was covered with a short, soft, soot-colored fur. The clawed hands protruding from the wide sleeves looked human. The creature was more than a head taller than Q'ualel. With their right hand, the being was holding a staff leaning against the ground, tipped with something resembling a retro lantern, which could be a symbol of power, a weapon, or a fanciful ornament. Aggro surveyed the bottom of the golden and white flowing robes hiding the legs, possibly the tail. His lance, taken from the mine, was lying nearby.

The being waited patiently for him to gaze his fill, and only then did they speak:

"You don't have to explain anything to me, Q'ualel, known by the people as Aggroteh, because I know it all from your head. As well as I can use languages you know." She spoke Kiritian fluently and freely, albeit with archaic syntax. Their voice was not very pleasant: it was harsh, hissing, medium-toned. Suitable for the archetype of cruel ruler or mad scientist inconsiderate to living objects of research.

"How do you know what I know?" Aggro asked, stunned.

The creature raised a hand and looked at the claws touched together.

"I have many talents, including psychometrics and telepathy, like you and Forkis. You can't hide anything from me, especially since I'm the Observer."

"You ... are you the Seventh Minister, the Bone Crusher?!" Aggro was still in a reclining position, glancing at the interlocutor with wide eyes. If he hadn't lied, it was scary to think what other abilities he had and what he was capable of.

"My name is Nanawak, although I have already been given different names. This worm Bone Crusher has long been dead, died in a fratricidal war that completely destroyed the previous Tamasul civilization. He raised his arm like an agitator and bared in a malicious smile his teeth with no distinct fangs. He looked deeper into the room for a moment as if he had been speaking to the audience in darkened corners, then shifted his gaze to Q'ualel. He grasped the staff with his hands. "I'm the representative of Nimja, I belong to the Great Family."

Tied to tradition and cultivating ancestors, Aggroteh was shocked by this news. Ignoring the fact that he might have been dealing with a very dangerous creature, he sprang to his feet abruptly. He was wagging his tail nervously, his ears clung to his skull.

"It's a lie! You are not my ancestor, they were... they looked..."

"Oh," Nanawak assumed a sympathetic expression. "The egocentric kitten has gotten angry? The kitten doesn't allow himself to think that his alleged great-great-great-grandparents could have been different than he thinks?" He began to circle around the shaky Onkalot, tapping his staff against the ground to the rhythm of his unhurriedly taken steps. "We are not your genetic ancestors; we merely guided your evolution and taught thousands of years ago a fraction of what we ourselves knew back then. A little bit, a trifle." He brought his thumb close to his index finger. "So that you never developed to our level, besides, everything was coded in your genome, predetermined. You yourself are not able to achieve even a hundredth of our knowledge, miserable zero coma two of the Kardashov scale."

"I don't think it is I who deserve to be called a megalomaniac," Aggro grunted, barely controlling himself. He remembered Tz'aqol's Temple he had searched with the Kiritians. In the part accessible to all inhabitants, Nimja was presented as humanoid men, but on the gates of the secret chamber intended for high priests and perhaps in the past for the Great Family itself, there were images of anthropomorphic dogs ... Aggro hadn't paid much attention to it then, absorbed in the search itself. Only now this shocking detail emerged from the depths of his mind, under the influence of Nanawak's words, soaked in contempt.

The Nimja member ignored him, kept moving and continued his speech:

"These were the times when we reached the level of galactic culture, drawing energy from all the components of the galaxy. From billions of stars. Even then, we were already using a quadrillion more energy than the modern people you are friends with. We've been able to cover the distance from star to star in seconds, as the Kiritians are now trying to achieve something similar in subspace leaps ... in weeks. In days only in case of closely spaced stars." He stopped with his back to the interlocutor, made a semicircle with his arm towards stained glass depicting, what Aggro now saw, a bulky owner of the fortress, or one of his kind.

"I don't understand what you're trying to tell me. Can you clearer?"

"Why not, actually. We have time, right?" Nanawak smiled wryly. "I will try to tell you about civilizations using notions that you understand, but I don't guarantee that you will understand much at your level of knowledge."

"Then let's try."

The Nimja member turned. He continued the annoying itinerary, admiring the details of the hall echoing his voice.

"The level of civilization is related to the energy it consumes, which also translates into space exploration. The more advanced it is, the further interstellar journeys can be made by its representatives. They also know tricks such as undoing the causes and effects of entropy, bending space-time, and other forms of breaking the laws of physics. Among intelligent beings, the lowest is civilization of the zero type, or interglobal, which obtains most of the things necessary for life from the earth. It is generally associated with the land and nature. The declining phase of such a culture is the use of fossil fuels and their combustion in chemical reactions, which may result in a flight into orbit. Onkalots were an example of this culture, but you stopped developing because you felt good in your existence and didn't make an attempt to reach the stars." Nanawak gestured toward the ceiling with his hand. "That's why you were defeated by a stellar civilization. You fell in a battle with the colonists from Earth who came out of Phase One and traveled far into space. The third type of cosmic civilization was represented by Nimja at the time when we created you, humans or avors. At that time, we could exploit the entire galaxy, drawing energy from any of its resources. We used up billions of times more than Kiritians now." He raised his voice in mounting excitement. "Now we represent level five, the culture of the multiverse, we will soon be on the sixth level. We can move freely between universes. We have become gods; we have broken natural laws. But soon our bodies will change, maybe they will become redundant. Neither to drink nor eat nor sleep. We no longer reproduce today. We will become pure energy! Perfect form! Supergods!" The passion left Nanawak, he lowered his voice. He gripped the staff tighter and put his forehead to it. "Our technology has evolved differently from humans' or avors', it is based on the power of the mind and artifacts working analogously to the laws of the cosmos. It's probably the most powerful right now, and we won't share it with anyone! We are ready to kill everyone to prevent it from falling into the wrong hands!"

"Because someone can match you?" Aggro muttered, feeling immensely disappointed. He had known Nanawak for only a few minutes and was already fed up with his arrogance and gibberish. It is possible that living here alone, he had simply lost his mind.

"You think right, little brother." The Onkalot refrained from making an inappropriate comment about their relationship. Nanawak smiled slyly as he read everything in his thoughts. "My nation is derived from a form resembling Earth dogs, specifically an organism called in our language resib. We are the oldest of all intelligent species in space, at least the older one we have never met. We have existed in intelligent form for millions of years. For comparison, you and humans are tens of thousands of years old, not counting of course the lifetime of your ancestors jumping on trees and sleeping in the mud.

"Did you create us?" Aggro asked nervously. He hadn't felt such terror and confusion since the colonists attacked Chulimal. His whole reality could collapse like a broken mirror at any moment. Even if haughty Nanawak had been going to make up stories to amuse himself at his expense, he would still disturb the calmness of the humanoid jaguar who wouldn't be able to tell the lie from the truth.

Before he replied, the Nimja member looked at Q'ualel for a moment, satisfied with his emotional storm.

"Yes. You come from Earth, from an animal called a jaguar, hence people call you humanoid jaguars because you have a human-like body and a bipedal gait. Anyway, you already know that more than sixty percent of your genes are human. During our wanderings through space, we moved the jaguar to Chulimal, where it adapted to the conditions there. One and a half million years later, as the unified Nimja carried out their Convergence Project, we subjected the animal naturally evolving into an intelligent being to genetic modification and experimentation to direct its development to our liking. Your appearance and level of civilization, then, is not a complete work of convergence, which goes naturally, but partially conscious creative process. You see ... Evolution goes basically in the same way all over the cosmos. At least in part we know, because even gods like Nimja haven't researched everything. A planet with the right conditions for the development of advanced life, such as Earth, Chulimal or Karikon - the last world is a peculiar reserve known only to a few Kiritians - always spews out a dominant species that evolves geologically very quickly and soon rules the globe. It doesn't matter whether the species arose naturally, or in a primitive form was brought from somewhere, the space program is the same. Such a species exists for several thousand years, sometimes even several million, but it eventually becomes extinct, ousted by someone better or through self-destruction, when for a long time it doesn't meet a species with which it could compete." Gesturing, Nanawak again paid more attention to the surroundings than to the interlocutor. He spoke aloud, passion burst into the words again. "We come from resibs, educated without anyone's interference on our mother planet. We knew that in other worlds, by this natural path, could arise someone able to overthrow us. We couldn't let that happen. Taking advantage of the fact that we didn't meet anyone more powerful than us, we took out the cosmos and took care of the evolution of intelligent beings ourselves."

"But why?" Aggro said almost through tears. Sparks of amusement appeared in the Nimja member's eyes.

"So that they never reached our level, the emerging civilizations started fighting each other in due time. Like now Kandrok killing Kiritians at the Zodiac Universum. We did it because we just could."

Every message was like a stab in the heart with a dagger. Aggro felt his paws soften, he staggered and almost fell on Nanawak, but regained his balance in time.

"What are you raving about ... How do you know what's going on somewhere fucking miles away?" Being nervous, he unconsciously said the phrase he had heard accidentally from Tsar Seymour. "And who are the Kandroks?"

"They are called Kandrok. It is the unchanging name of a supercollective, all together, but also one organism. Individually, but never separately. I know everything that happens in the universes that I observe. Omniscience is my domain. I rarely miss something. That's why they call me the Observer. I have a great observatory in the basement."

"And do you have proof that you are not lying?"

"I'll show you it. You won't understand how the devices work there or anything you see in the laboratories, so I'll let you see it. Maybe you'll leave alive after that. We'll have to go down anyway, if I don't change my mind on that matter, of course. I know what you came here for, Q'ualel. You want your friend's atole back, and you were convinced you would learn something important on Tamasul. Congratulations, you achieved that particular goal."

Aggro found that nature had kept tails in Nimja members (though rather they had decided themselves that they wanted them) when the fabric on the back of his robe bent. He had no doubts anymore that Nanawak could read minds and assimilate the interlocutor's knowledge, or had some invisible neural device that could transfer information between brains. And at lightning speed. He remembered Nanawak putting something to his head before he had passed out, but he couldn't tell if it was a hand or a machine. Since the Nimja member had such powerful abilities and bragged about his power over and over again, why would have he lied about Kiritians?

"What happened at the Zodiac Universum?" He asked in a whisper, shaky.

"The Kandrok people from another universe raided the Immortals. They are more technologically advanced, so they dominated them. Let me refer again to Kardashov's scale that you know. Kiritians reached the second degree and are entering the third, Kandrok is level three and a half, they can travel between universes now. But they are vermin compared to Nimja anyway." There was no reaction on Nanawak's face, he shrugged. "That's it. Ordinary war. The indispensable driving force for the development of most intelligent species. War clears minds, burns out aggression, accelerates evolution, thanks to it the best inventions are made. It,s lack leads to laziness and dullness - degeneration in general. Weak children are born. It must have happened in the end, since Kiritians hadn't had any serious enemy for centuries."

The Onkalot failed to maintain self-assurance. Broken, he fell to his knees and lowered his head low. It was getting harder and harder for him to breathe. He would have liked to rest on a chair, but the enormous chamber was devoid of furniture. He thought about the safety of Eredal and the Schindlers. He still wanted to believe that the descendant of resibs was playing on him and lying to him in his degenerate nature. Not such 'gods' he had expected to see on Tamasul.

Nimja stood over him like an executioner, his voice was dripping with toxic gentleness:

"You lost Eredal. You couldn't have a relationship with her anyway, because she is human. Mixing pure blood is a distortion, it leads to chaos. Features that have been shaped over millions of years are lost in a few generations. This is the best example of destruction because creating is time consuming and difficult, and destroying is easy. Your disappearance is all to the good for the girl. When you come back you will understand that it made her happy. Of course, if the war doesn't destroy her."

"Anton," Aggro ground out the competitor's name and focused on it so as not to send profanity about Nanawak. In the last few hours his mind was torn by as many emotions as probably during centuries of his apathy. He doubted, however, that Nanawak, knowing about this indolence, was deliberately trying to make him angry and influence his nature to make him like Forkis. Aggro was and will be his opposite, he preferred to withdraw and worry rather than fight and murder in revenge. Centuries of despondency had blunted the warrior in him he had been trained to be.

"First, your family and the whole species were taken from you, then your freedom and purpose in life. Even when you tried to smile and joke, you did so with self-imposed compulsion, it was rarely the result of your emotions." Nanawak moved towards the stained-glass window. Something outside made him amused; From his position, Aggro could see only flakes of gray snow gliding diagonally and flashes of blue light. "Onkalots are truly extraordinary creatures. No matter how broken they can be, what a terrible burden they may bear in their souls and minds, no one will commit suicide. They will lie like dead bodies, wake up in the morning and not get up until dusk, but they will not take their own life. Maybe that's why Nacxit, known as the Bone Smasher, liked you so much, he had a nature quite similar to yours. It's different for weak people for whom love quandary or job loss is enough to make an attempt on their life." He started to laugh, at first under his breath, and soon in the whole hall echoed his hideous chuckle. "However, it was these weak people who destroyed the Onkalots. Isn't that a beautiful paradox?"

Aggro jumped up from the ground, raised his fist. He felt dizzy, he was breathing hard for a moment, but he didn't stagger.

"Why didn't you do anything about it?! You could! Especially this Nacxit! You constantly emphasize how omnipotent and wonderful you are!"

"Did you even listen to what I was saying?" Nanawak turned to him. "It's happening what is supposed to happen, everything was programmed a long time ago. As far as we are concerned, it is in our nature to live in hiding. We sometimes hate each other, which is why there are so few of us left, usually one ruler on one planet. We live very far from each other; we don't get in each other's way. It's still incredible that we once came together to continue the Convergence Project. We gave you tools, we taught you how to handle them. We showed the direction. You were given fishing rods, but not fish." He indicated the humanoid jaguar with his staff. "Why do you think that we should still be responsible for you after all this?"

"Why did you leave?!" The Nimja member also raised his voice.

"I told you! We start the machine, then we don't control it anymore, since it can control itself! That's how it works. This is Nimja's law - to create and leave. And for your spiritual support, you had those stupid, imaginary gods of yours, after all!"

"How dare you," Q'ualel growled, showing his fangs. "The gods did a lot for us after you left us. It was thanks to Tonatiuh that I woke up from apathy and went to help Forkis. The sun god gave me strength and restored my faith in life, he spoke to me in the temple. What is so funny for you?" He asked as Nanawak laughed. Another wave of weakness hit Q'ualel, he coughed, couldn't breathe for a moment. He leaned heavily on the lance until was better. He felt his lungs working worse and worse, pain was building up between his ribs. He had completely forgotten about the toxins in the air. How much time did he have left? Maybe it's had already passed? If so, had Paul already started looking for him?

"You're a fool. I am Toniatuh!" The Nimja member thundered. He laughed again as Aggro, gasping for breath, got shocked. "All your gods are us! Their appearance is an exteriorization of your tribal ego! When you heard the voices, you must have imagined them or be on drugs."

The Onkalot was boiling.

"You're lying like a dog that you are."

Something snapped inside him.

The seconds during which he ran to Nanawak, yelling, vanished from his mind. The emotions that had accumulated for a long time took control of him. He could keep his nerves in check when someone insulted him, but he wouldn't forgive anyone who spoke a bad word against his most important god. Tonatiuh was the only being he had left who had never let him down and who he could always rely on. Now Nanawak tried to tar also his faith.

He sincerely wanted to smash the head of amused Nanawak with the blows of the lance, but the Nimja member easily parried his attacks with his staff, like an adult blow of a child.

Slightly bored, Nanawak, with a mere telekinetic brush, threw Q'ualel many meters away, thereby implying that any attack on him was pointless. Aggro dropped painfully to the cold floor tiles.

A pair of ax-armed guards burst through the gate. Nanawak set them away with sharply spoken words in the local language.

Once again, Q'ualel had the feeling that he was about to suffocate, as if the air in the room had been running out. He got up weakly, leaning heavily on the lance. But he wasn't going to let go. He attacked again, though slower than the last time.

"Seriously, didn't you get the hint? Or is it already just desperation?" Nanawak asked rhetorically, knowing perfectly well what was going on in the head of the humanoid jaguar. Also, this time he easily threw him, to diversify the fun, using the energetic bracer barrage, which was also used by the elite of the fortress guards.

After the fourth attempt, the bloody and bruised Onkalot didn't rise from the ground. He could see the details of the chamber twice, his lungs had failed him, his respiratory rate had tripled, but there was still not enough air. The pressure was dropping. His head was wheezing more than his ears, and the sounds around him seemed to trail away.

He felt it would be over soon.

But pride, dignity, and aversion to Nimja didn't allow him to ask for help.

He chose to die.

Nanawak sighed and shook his head as if he had been looking not at the almost corpse but at a kitten playing up.

"You are not adapted to life on Tamasul. It is very unreasonable of you that you went to explore the alien planet without a spacesuit."

He raised his hand more for effect and to show the Onkalot that he had taken some action because he could use only his mind.

Aggro felt a tingling sensation and a pleasant warmth throughout his body, as if he had drunk a lot of hot herbs. Then, against his own body, he made two very deep exhalations, after which he vomited. He definitely felt better. Nanawak changed the impurities from solid to air with another careless wave of his hand.

"Telekinesis is a powerful force. If you can use it well, you can do literally anything, as long as the action is related to matter. I've just cleaned your blood of poisons. You're zeroed again, Onkalot, as if you just left 'Perfarius'. But you still need to lie down and rest a bit."

Aggro was sincerely impressed. Nanawak, without any concentration or effort, had just changed his body biochemically, casually saving his life. No matter how corrupt he was, he was unfortunately also powerful.

"Thank you," he said, because it befitted. The Nimja member left him alone and walked away, letting the recovering humanoid jaguar lie on his side. The gates opened again, guards' clumpy boots and armor were clinking. The noise grew, then receded, and the gate banged again. Soon Q'ualel's breathing became deeper and slower, the ringing in the skull stopped, sharp vision returned, the pain disappeared in the lungs which again were flexible and prone to pumping air. In the twilight, by the walls, Aggro noticed wandering small animals, species he knew well: turtles, rats, lizards, fist-sized beetles. All of golden color, the color of the gods.

"Artifacts..." He got up and knelt. He looked surprised at the Nimja member, who was standing a few paces away, watching him indifferently. "You have plenty of living artifacts! You can create them! Forkis once had a golden mouse."

Nanawak looked in the same direction.

"You are talking about q'umaraq. It was the only one, it was the most powerful artifact that has ever been created. Therefore, Forkis was able to control millions of minds, impose his will on people. He himself didn't know what power had fallen into his hands. If he had known, it could have ended in disaster for humans."

He smiled, amused at such a prospect. "Even Tepew himself was afraid of q'umaraq. It's good that you got rid of him. What you see are much weaker artifacts. I treat them as decorations. I don't need them for anything. They are relics of the past, I have long learned to influence reality without their participation. If you want, catch yourself one, though I doubt that you will make it."

Aggro had no idea who Tepew was, and he didn't really care. In turn, Nanawak's words about q'umaraq, which he said with deliberation untypical of him, sounded strange, as if Nimja had no control over the artifact. This could explain why an incredibly dangerous living artifact wandered around Chulimal. But Q'ualel didn't want to belabor this either. He had been through so much for just one day, anyway. His health quickly returned to normal, so he accepted the offer and headed towards the nearest group of animals. However, he achieved nothing, all the living artifacts disappeared from the chamber into nooks known only to them, even the turtles managed to escape.

"They make wishes come true. One of them could help us safely return to the Zodiac Universum, perhaps even regain the Forkis atole ..."

"Unfortunately, you are wrong," said Nanawak. "You interpret it naturally in your primitive way. Using your vocabulary: artifacts can be called psionic transmitters. They don't fulfill wishes, the user only benefits from a certain kind of energy transferred to their animal bodies, known only to Nimja. Therefore, through thought or words, the owner of the artifact can influence the surroundings, not necessarily three times, as is commonly thought among Onkalots. If the tasks are of low priority, such as draining a well, the artifact can be used multiple times. At the time of the colonization of space by the people of the Old Zone, when your cultures clashed, Onkalots linked the human fairy tale of the goldfish with Nimja's artifacts fulfilling supposed wishes. Meanwhile, it is pure, high technology, giving the possibility of bending cosmic laws at someone's will through the mind."

Aggro approached Nanawak, all his anger was gone. He wondered if his calm, like detoxification, was related to a psychological force influencing his psyche this time.

"One of the ex-Kiritian scientists, Maksimus Figam, recreated the artifact from the bone that Forkis carried with him," he said.

"It happened so because an entire animal that has been turned into an artifact becomes a psionic transmitter, even the tiniest part of it, such as hair, fur, or a piece of skin. By cloning the artifact, this scientist restored its properties, but only as much power as was preserved in the bone."

"Could any Onkalot still use it? Did I waste the entire resource of the artifact? Is it possible to satiate it with power again?"

Nanawak laughed.

"Anyone can use artifacts, not just Onkalots. What would be the point of creating them only for one species?"

"I don't know, maybe one to give us a chance against the stronger, such as people?"

"Don't be too interested in it, because you won't understand any of it, anyway," the Nimja member dryly cut off the topic.

"Is it true what you said about my god?" The humanoid jaguar asked hesitantly.

"Every intelligent species of subglobal culture we visited took us for gods or great ancestors. We were included in the local mythology, giving us the appearance of believers themselves, local animals, monsters or demons. After many generations, no one could tell myth from truth anymore. We were the Ancient Onkalots to humanoid jaguars, the Kiritian ancestors called us Anunnaki, Kandrok, whom you will soon meet," Nanawak smiled sardonically, "associated us with their ancient monotheistic deity, the Lightbringer. For the inhabitants of Karikon, we were Great Mages. And so on and so forth."

"Toniatuh helped me many times after I prayed to him."

"Maybe these were all coincidences? It happened what was supposed to happen? Placebo effect when you motivated yourself?"

"I heard his words. I felt in my heart a blessing flowing on me."

"Your imagination prompted you the words, and into the state of euphoria, you got yourself."

Aggro smiled.

"I don't belive you anyway. I know otherwise."

"So, what are you asking for?" Nanawak reciprocated by the same. It was not, however, a malicious smile, but an indulgent and serene one. "Think what you want. Hear you are, it's yours. The guard found it in the mine." He handed him the obsidian dagger. Aggro realized that the lance wasn't nearby. Probably the guards had carried it out when he had lain, dying. "It's been a long time since I had so much fun. You accidentally orchestrated the slave rebellion and organized the workout for the guards, and this attack in a frenzy of yours ..." He chuckled. "You gave me a lot of entertainment with this. In return I will help you, my gesture will have no effect on Nimja's authority anyway."

"I need to contact Paul. He may attack the fortress if he discovers that something has happened to me."

Nanawak's soft smile grew sneering.

"Come to the window."

Aggro approached the stained glass with curiosity and anxiety, looked out through the transparent element. Once again on that fateful day, he felt terrified. The blue lights seen earlier turned out to be a form of an energetic cage binding the entire Perfarius. Tilted to one side, it rested on a plain at the foot of a mountain. From the tiny object, impossible to see due to the distance, came a multitude of light rays that ended at many points of the armor of the ship's landing gear.

"What have you done?!" Q'ualel couldn't take his eyes off the terrible but also fascinating sight.

"Paul attacked my house as promised to you. However, your electronic toys are nothing compared to what Nimja has at its disposal. For example, now a small orb fired from concealment by a guard was enough to deactivate the entire ship, including the androids. I've known for a long time that you were getting closer. However, I was curious how the situation would develop when you met my subordinates, so I didn't react, knowing that you didn't pose any threat to me."

Q'ualel turned slowly from the stained glass and gave Nanawak a dry look. He would have most willingly showed him open hostility, but he didn't want to risk that the Nimja member would change his plans and give up the graciously offered help. For a moment he was under the illusion that the members of the Great Family had some goodness in them, since Nanawak had saved him from death. Perhaps the others presented themselves better, but not Nanawak corrupt to the bone, who, for pure entertainment, was ready to sacrifice even loyal subordinates and defenseless slaves. Nonetheless, Aggro considered that he might have not understood the nature of the beings living for eons and having other priorities. Would have Onkalots also become like that, if they had developed equally with Nimja? Did he have the right to judge Nanawak's species, since factions of his own, like Jun Kame, were famous for their cruelty? He thought of Chimalmat. The female, doomed to centuries of solitude, had also become insane, but didn't have the powers worthy of gods, which could cause great harm.

Meanwhile, an upset Nimja member, it is unknown what they were capable of, perhaps even destroying the ancient civilization of Tamasul. Kiret told Q'ualel that many Kiritians didn't withstand the test of immortality and lost their minds over time, even though they were positively selected for an achij. Did the distortion and madness affect every long-lived creature?

"Will they be okay?" He asked hesitantly, looking towards the ship.

"Yes, it is enough to turn off the orb. Now come with me."

VIII. In the shadow of Kandrok

A heavily unshaven man hadn't spoken to his companion sitting in the adjoining pilot's seat for the second hour. They both had sullen expressions, each was immersed in dark thoughts about the past and the difficult times that were to come. The future wasn't optimistic, so it was wiser not to dwell on past events, but to focus on the task awaiting both achijes. The bearded man hoped that a hiding place he had chosen for Forkis' body would be the best option, he would only have to somehow placate a mad guardswoman who might cause problems.

"Kiret?" Captain Victor Shane broke the neurotic, almost void silence, slightly disturbed by the subtle work of the devemer's cockpit devices.

The neighbor looked at him indignantly.

"Don't call me that," he hissed. "Call me Matthew Rain, I asked you. We have no guarantee that they don't eavesdrop on us. We have to cover even greater distances."

"It's impossible, sir. Kandrok has not reached this zone, perhaps it will never come here. Without our maps, it is not easy to find inhabited planets, especially since we destroyed or took away the documentation before escaping. Kandrok has amazing technology, but I don't think they have light years sensitive biological scanners."

Kiret shifted his gaze to the canopy and stared at the brighter group of stars.

"Do you think that's a problem for them? Remember how Erceses found us. Rather, Kandrok has its own reasons why it hasn't taken everything from us yet."

"Erceses were sent to terrestrial-type planets in general, they didn't know they would find life on any of them."

"These are still conjectures, not facts. Oh, 'sir' let it go too. Your habits can lead us to death."

"With all due respect, but I'm fed up with these shitty restrictions, si ... Rain. I feel like puking from this."

"Like all of us, Victor. As a nation that has been successful for centuries, we are not used to such a situation. I'm sorry that since your promotion you haven't had the opportunity to show that you really deserve this promotion."

"You think so, sir ..."

This time, Kiret got really angry.

"Call me, the collapsed star, by my first name. For a long time ago, I have not been your emperor, but a frigging scrap metal dealer dressed in rags!" Kiret refrained from mentioning that achijes caused him pain every time they referred to him with the title that he had lost and never deserved.

The captain noticed Necron's hand, sunken in a wide sleeve, tighten into a fist. He didn't stall the conversation, they flew in silence again, staring out into the cold and black expanse encrusted with points of light. The light that was the only source of true faith for the Kandrok people. Viktor finally turned his attention to the digital image of the devemer, their small, black Ordovician cephalopod-shaped transporter, adapted to carry valuable cargo, and therefore equipped with the best Kiritian camouflage technology.

Necron was going to apologize to his neighbor in plain clothes, he opened slightly his mouth, but closed it immediately. Words only have power when they are not empty and are not spoken to temporarily ease the situation. Although the anger had passed, probably from the sight of the cosmos cold as ice, yet soothing the nerves, soon he would probably again feel an impossible desire to lace into someone because of his own powerlessness. Kiret worked on himself, tried to be fair to the people he had left, and he indeed did it better and better, but anger like magma crammed in the bowels of the earth has to find an outlet from time to time. Anger at himself, at his weaknesses and failures, although friends stubbornly repeated that it was not his fault that the Kandrok people had turned out to be better and pushed the Kiritians off the pedestal just as they had once the opposition led by Commander Aveo Lacetti. Necron knew the history of mankind and that no empire lasted forever, even if one managed to survive for millennia with a powerful army, strong currency, dominant religion, and an economy knocking other nations into a cocked hat. Everything passed, finally receded into darkness. Each new mighty ruler secretly dreamed that he might have been able to create something permanent that would be cherished by countless generations. However, his descendants had their own plans and ideas, believing that their ancestors' designs were not theirs, since they were gone. The difference, however, was that past rulers were not immortal like Kiritians. So, would Forkis have had a chance to create an eternal empire if he had not died at the hands of Drunkenstein? Being a synthesis of an immortal human and Onkalot with psionic abilities, would he have been able to resist Kandrok?

Kandrok.

The memory of the beginning of the end made Kiret feel ashamed and painful, and these often resulted in irritability ending up with lacing into his surroundings. This time suffered innocent Viktor, which, however, was patient and understanding.

The conflict began with the departure of Aggroteh and the arrival of the next alleged refugees from the RC Galaxy. Erceses turned out to be pseudo-humans at the stage of development of the Earthlings from the first half of the twentieth century, they couldn't even fly into space, therefore they inhabited one planet and not several, as they skillfully lied during interrogations. It couldn't be verified with equipment and specifics due to biological convergence - the chemistry and structure of their bodies only visually resembled human. On the subject of Kandrok members, the Kiritian intelligence determined that they were probably travelers, they were classified as three-coma-five on Kardashov's scale, so without firing a shot, they took over Erceses' globe and made them their puppets. Kandrok soon discovered the existence of Kiritians. The inhabitants of RC were given the technology and resources to be able, as alleged war refugees, to settle the planets of the Zodiac Universum and be infiltrators of their masters who wanted to know the level of development of the Immortals. The plan was successful, for years thousands of spies lived like a Trojan horse in Kiritians' sphere of influence - until it was attacked. Just like that. Without negotiation, without a reason. The aggressors didn't want new planets, habitats, raw materials (they only mined heavy metals from time to time) or food, and their motives had remained unknown to this day, though some believed that Kandrok was a militant nation of cyborgs, attacking only for the pleasure of fighting. It occupied the conquered area of space, learned from the defeated new things, and then the stronger and wiser migrated further in search of the next victim.

Kiret wished terribly that he had listened to General Velkee Warfighter at the ill-fated Council meeting and had thrown the Erceses from the empire. Then Kandrok might not have established the degree of development of the Immortals to this day.

After examining the sparse cyborg bodies captured during the fighting, the Kiritians found that the people came from a virus-free environment that was the primary medical unit of achijes. Meanwhile, Kandrok achieved eternal life quite brutally - with age they changed their worn organs to metal parts until only the brain tissue survived, according to their religion, the carrier of Light and soul (they called it orhada). They mutilated themselves willingly and with fanatical joy. Stuffed with chemicals and drugs, the brain functioned for centuries, but it too was eventually replaced with a component, making the cyborg a complete machine. Kandrok's cyborgization was not only about health and life extension, but also improved the body of a healthy and young person, but you had to deserve it. Kiret tried to understand the religion and mentality of aliens, and concluded that the cult of the brain around which

Kandrok's medicine practically oscillated might have been the cause of their belligerent designs, since the body was irrelevant and could be replaced. But what happened to consciousness and orhada when, after brain death, it was also changed to metal? Kandrok believed (uncertain findings of Kiritian intelligence) that after long cooperation of the brain with the artificial body, the orhada switched to the latter, and the metal individual felt the same as with the biological organism. For Biffter, who had been brought up in a different culture, this manner of acting and belief was inconceivable, just as he couldn't imagine that there were infinitely many universes, or that one could be stuffed to the size of a pinhead.

Kandrok plunged into the Kiritian life like a Liphyr brassolis larva into an anthill, rushing forward and freely destroying everything in their path. The Immortals fell in battle after battle, they lost more than half of their planets, including they were pushed out of the capital. The council, except for imprisoned Anna Sandstorm and escaped General Velkee Warfighter, was killed. And the former First Galactic Dignitary blamed the catastrophe solely on himself - for not being strong enough like Forkis to defeat the enemy.

The nail in the coffin for Necron was the battle for the capital, or more precisely - the K'otz'ib'aja massacre. The Kiritians found out too late about the huge, hostile armada that traveled through space, because the enemy had destroyed the reconnaissance squad even before recognizing the threat, and the electronics, it had easily blocked. Utilizing elevator drives, the Kandrok fleet appeared as if out of nowhere into the Capricorn Universe, leaving the Kiritians seven hours to organize their defense. Morascrik didn't have an air-orbital defense, because what would have the nation that the entire Zodiac Universum had feared for centuries needed it for? An attack from unexplored galaxies was considered completely unrealistic and unfounded. It was recognized an ancient rule, supported by extrapolation research, that if a civilization developed somewhere, it was at a level no higher than Erceses'. This was a huge mistake that cost the lives of millions of people. Kandrok suffered almost zero casualties first in space battle, then in air and ground ones. The biggest problem turned out to be entrasers, once invented by the rebels, then modified and improved by Kiritians. During the fighting, some of the achijes had older versions in their heads, which, after information was transferred to the brain, didn't flow out with the urine or dissolve. Kandrok easily reprogrammed them and made the enslaved Kiritians lung at their companions like incapacitated machines controlled by the enemy. Seeing no chance of keeping the capital, Necron and his commanders decided to retreat, ordering the army of the Immortals to scatter across space to reduce the radiation and heat signatures as much as possible.

Seized by despair, Kiret tried to take his own life in the Utza'm Achij cave, to drown with his ship. Anna found him in time and brought him to his senses.

Soon after, Kandrok took her away.

They must have had specific plans for her as a national dignitary, unless she became an accidental victim of a roundup. But for what purpose they kidnapped her, where they held her, and whether she was still alive, Biffter had no idea. Any attempt to rescue Anna was as sensible as boiling the ocean. He himself, with Shane's help, barely managed to escape from the planet.

Since that battle, Kiret had to hide in zones unexplored by the enemy, and as if that were not enough, the lively opposition considered taking advantage of the confusion introduced by Kandrok and overthrowing the remnants of the Kiritians. Necron assumed a second identity, he ordered the achijes scattered across space to camouflage. He himself put on an idiotic outfit of a poor scrap collector, who could have been attacked only by bandits wanting used metals. And such, Kiret could easily take care of. The imperfection of the entire plan was that he was flying the Kiritian devemer, but that too could always be explained, or he could constantly use masking. The lack of heavy, safe armor, he could get over, but his long hair, beard, and mustache drove him crazy. He had served as an oders in the New Order Army, and perhaps the only good thing he had gotten out of it was shaving his head.

An unknown remained Aggroteh's mission, who was too far away to be contacted. As long as he was still alive.

"We're almost there, sir."

Viktor's voice reached Kiret as if from another dimension. A short while passed before he got rid of his gloomy thoughts. He saw H14 in front of him with a ribbon of greenery around the equator.

"Try not to be conspicuous as we agreed," he suggested, disregarding the captain's mistake with the title of honor. He looked around the orbit for a lit shopping station, then searched the space with a scanner from the instrument console. "No contact with objects or indigenous people. When we get into the atmosphere, we will fly through the wildest area. And what are you laughing at, heavy cannon?" He grunted as Viktor started to chuckle at his laborious attempts to take out his chin tangled up in the clasps of his cloak.

He laughed too; he couldn't remember how long it had been.

***

While the invaders scattered throughout the Scorpio Universe, Leo seemed to remain outside their area of interest. Kiret hoped it would last as long as possible, as part of the dispersed Kiritian army found a hiding place in the Cargoo and Mezzo nether regions. He also considered H14 as a shelter option, but eventually gave up on this idea. There were monuments of Onkalots on the planet, many of which had been destroyed during the colonization times, so they would have been poor hiding places. He also didn't want to bring a possible enemy to the apolitical inhabitants of the planet. The third thing is a unique ecosystem. Nature regained what had been taken from it by the aggressive colonists, then killed by the Kiritians. The mountains and steppes of the far north and south were again bound with permafrost, while the equator and tropical zone were covered with jungle. "If nothing has changed since my last visit a few years ago," Necron thought, "the planet's only inconvenience are lycans."

The devemer stuck like an invisible arrow into successive layers of the atmosphere. Over the tops of the jungle, it left nosediving, changed the type of propulsion from space to planetary one, and leveled his flight, losing speed at the same time. Shane scanned the area but found nothing suspicious. Of noteworthy things, he tracked down several farms within a two hundred kilometer and a small machine traversing the forest that could be destroyed by a shot from the worst devemer's weapon. He turned off masking.

They wanted to land in the same place near Tz'aqol's Temple as seven years earlier during a research expedition, but the vegetation had managed to recapture the cleared area. The small devemer fit in the square by a building, crushing skeletons and brush with the undercarriage.

"Today we will finish this whole show. I've had enough after all these years."

Necron left the cockpit and walked into the cramped orlop. Having checked the safety of the precious cargo, he shaved his head with relief. Touching his smooth chin with satisfaction, he stepped off the board. He went to a wide stream, where he examined the water for toxins and pathogens. Satisfied with the analysis, he stripped naked and took a bath.

As he returned to the devemer, he found the captain already clad in Kiritian armor wandering around the area, trying to target Chimalmat with the nucloindector he was holding.

"She may not be here," Biffter said a few minutes later, also having donned his armor. "The female was the guardian of this temple, so if nothing has changed, she should find us herself. Maybe she is just sitting somewhere watching us from hiding."

"We would detect her then." Kiret nodded at the nucloindector.

"Not if she hid in the temple vaults. Do you remember what was with the lycans? Some of the pyramids seem to be like insulators when it comes to detecting life, although I bet more on Nimja jammers that work even after millennia. As if they wanted to mask their presence in the past."

Viktor's amused expression suggested that he wasn't taking his own words very seriously. However, this was the only reasonable theory so far as to why the Kiritians failed to detect lycans at that massacre, with their equipment in working order.

"I don't know. Let's go now." Necron checked the combat plasma rifle and moved. The captain stood for a moment with his foot on a human skull, looked carefully around the area, then followed Biffter's footsteps.

"Is it really a good idea?" He asked, catching up with Kiret. "She's insane."

"If you have a better one, Captain, I'm listening. Ultimately, if something happened to the body, it can be recreated."

"Soon we may not have the conditions for it."

Before entering the building, they put on their helmets and switched to night vision, additionally they turned on flashlights integrated with the weapons. Necron led the way, illuminating the corridor and remnants lying at their feet.

"The last time we were here, there were probably less bones?"

"I don't remember, Rain."

"Now you can call me Kiret."

Viktor smiled.

"I know, sir. Actually, I should apologize because I just wanted to check your reaction."

Biffter didn't share his serenity, which was an enviable trait of Shane in the current situation of the Kiritians.

"Can you finally end up with these sirs and gentlemen? I screwed up completely, and the titles must be earned."

"Can I be honest? I swear this conversation will stay only between us."

"Go ahead."

"With all due respect, you are not a god, but a man, and man is not almighty, he makes mistakes."

Nervous, Kiret stopped and turned away.

"Do you even hear yourself, Captain? You can make a mistake pouring too much beer, pouring it onto your hand, not when you are responsible for the lives of millions!"

Shane did a successful combination of swallowing and a sigh before he said honestly what he had long intended to say:

"I know how much respect you have for Forkis, but you are not, and never will be him. You want to shoulder a weight that you cannot bear."

"Are you trying to point out my indolence?"

"I haven't said that."

"Be quiet."

"Have I pissed you off so much? You yourself gave me permission to be honest ..."

"Viktor, damn it ... Hush, there's something in there."

They stopped in the sarcophagus chamber, sweeping it with circles of white light. Had it not been for the hum of breathing and the clank of armor, there would have been deathly silence around it, "perfect for such surroundings," Necron thought.

He froze like a stone carving, hearing a faint murmur behind him and somewhere above that could be made by, for example, a man descending a rope. Remembering his previous adventure in the temple, he took the disturbing sound as a harbinger of approaching lycans. It was, however, the Onkalotian female, which fell behind Viktor's back and put the blade of a stone dagger to his throat. The captain didn't react, knowing that she didn't endanger him.

Necron smiled under his helmet, then slipped it off, which was accompanied by a warning hiss of the female.

"Chimalmat."

Amazed, the Onkalotian female sprang, pointing to Biffter with the dagger. Several pebbles rose as she nervously used telekinesis.

"I know you, I remember! You've been here before." She narrowed her eyes shining in the flashlight, tilted her head. "What did you come back for?"

"Easy, my friend." Necron attached the weapon to the magnetic buckle on his belt. "That's right, I'm Kiret Biffter and I was here once. Then you helped us. You probably remember Victor Shane too."

"Hello, Chimalmat." The captain also slipped off his headwear. The female hid the dagger in the cover, the pebbles fell.

"Is Q'ualel with you?" She asked hopefully.

"He's not." Necron couldn't not smile again. "He flew far away, wanting his friend's life back."

"Oh yes, I know, I remember. He flew to Nimja's Great Ancestors!"

"That's right. He will be gone for a long time, but he will return." Biffter lied, contradicting the Kiritian idea of truthfulness, which had practically collapsed with the nation's defeat anyway. He had no guarantee that Aggro would ever return from the trip. "And I have to ask you again, unfortunately, for help."

"Why unfortunately? Is it wrong? Did you do something bad?"

"We didn't. However, the place where we held Xajb'a Kej's body is no longer under our control. Hostile tribes have flown there and we must move it to a safe hideout. We thought of you, Chimalmat, because you are a great guardian and a wise Onkalotian woman."

The female began pacing the tomb, scratching her nose thoughtfully with her claw.

Shane took up the Necron game:

"You care about Q'ualel, don't you?" He surprised Chimalmat with it, who stopped, straightened and raised her previously lowered ears high.

"Not at all!" She flatly denied. A half smile appeared on Viktor's face.

"It would be nice if you helped us. We need to give Q'ualel some more time, a few more years, to complete the task. Then he will fly over here and you will meet. He will be grateful for your help."

"And what do you, mighty demons from the stars, require of the weak guardian of the Ik'ib'akam people?" She asked distrustfully.

"Keeping Xajb'a Kej's body safely in the temple vaults," said Kiret. "You won't have to do anything but make sure that no outsiders get to him. Xajb'a Kej is lying ... in a machine powered by a helion battery." He had no idea how to translate it for the Onkalotian female. "And this machine will keep the body alive until we come back with Q'ualel."

"An artifact will protect him," prompted the captain.

"I remember, you said," the female whispered as she stood in front of them, "that my distant brother lost his atole. But without atole there is no life, the body is dead!" She finished, showing clenched teeth.

Viktor didn't want her to start talking about the spiritual realm of Onkalots, the more he saw no point in explaining to her what Kiritian medicine was. He decided that the trick of influencing the ambition, coupled with arousing the guilt, would be the best here.

"The body must remain in a safe hiding place until Q'ualel returns with Xajb'a Kej's atole," he said. "And the person most trustworthy is you, Chimalmat. So, will you help us? Will you do this for Q'ualel and his friend whom you will meet when he comes back to life? Please."

The female started pacing the room again, mumbling to herself and thinking. Finally, determined, she stopped in front of Kiret.

"Yes. I will help."

"You don't even know how grateful we are," Necron said sincerely, smiling broadly. "Is there a safe hiding place in the temple that only you know exists?"

"I know such places," she replied in a venomous whisper. Viktor pulled on his helmet. "Before we get to work, please kindly light a torch. We're going to need a lot of light."

***

Forkis's body lay in an airtight cryo-chamber topped with a clear puronax carapace. It was bare, only a strip of cloth covered the hip area. Only three people had access to the container after the DNA scanning - Sandstorm, Biffter and Shane.

With the help of stone mechanisms, Chimalmat opened a hidden, completely empty room the size of the living room of an average house, the purpose of which she had long forgotten. After examining and scanning the room, it turned out that it was safe.

The Kiritians took the 'sarcophagus' on the anti-gravity plate out of the devemer board. Following the cryo-chamber hovering above the ground, Kiret kept his hand on the carapace. The organism beneath it was visually and genetically identical to the original - the effect of Dr. Maksimus Figam's work was perfect. However, the knowledge of one of the best modern scientists ended on creating an exact copy of the deceased. The Kiritians achieved immortality by contracting the most powerful virus ever created, but they still failed, despite their scientific breakthroughs, to bring the dead back to life. Knowledge in the field of necromedicine still oscillated within the boundaries of philosophy, theory and assumptions. Kiret had one more worry beyond the uncertainty of whether he would ever regain his friend: if Forkis' return would change anything in the present crisis. Figam had recreated the body before the Kandrok attack, when the political situation was manageable, and the mere return of Xajb'a Kej would have been enough for the Immortals to be reunited with the idea and charisma of the emperor. Now the nation was defeated and even Forkis, a combination of two intelligent species, could do little. "But now that we have started," Necron reflected, "we must complete the task, even if the result is the still-dead emperor." Nothing better occured neither to him, nor to the achijes who remained with him. The thought that they were bringing Forkis back to life only to burden him with such a heavy weight seemed to Biffter very embarrassing. He promised himself that if Forkis was revived, he would do everything in his power to help him get rid of Kandrok.

After checking the parameters of the cryo-chamber, the men left it in the room. A slab of dressed rock, weighing several tons, moved with a creak behind them. Lit by torches, they stood for a moment in silence.

"He'll be safe here," Viktor said.

After a few minutes, he and Chimalmat left Tz'aqol's Temple. The K'ajolom star was slowly setting, dragging the mantle of red and yellow sky behind it.

A skulak flew out of the jungle. Kiret glanced briefly at Viktor, but the latter was already keeping his hand on the weapon, watching the machine land in the courtyard. A tall, slim dark-haired man, dressed in a dark green jumpsuit, muddy and torn here and there, threw his leg over the wide seat. The young man's face, dirty with soil, looked no better; there was clotted blood in the place of scratches. At his belt there was a Kiritian X17A4 pistol, behind his back stuck out a rifle of unspecified type, and a third weapon, a drill machine, whose ammunition exploded, plunging into the body, was placed by the skulak.

Before anyone spoke, Chimalmat, surprised, gave the identity of the man approaching the group:

"Darius? What are you doing here?"

Something dawned on Kiret. He remembered the boy of the same name from the Schindlers' farm who had once been raving about the Kiritians and their equipment.

"Darius Schindler?" He asked when the newcomer stopped. Viktor was still holding his hand at the gun, ready to shoot dead the intruder in a second if he violated Biffter's safety.

The tanned boy looked at Necron searchingly. His green eyes nearly popped out of his skull; he staggered with the impression.

"Impossible, Mr. Kiret Necron Biffter!" He pointed somewhere between the sky and the jungle. "I recognized the Kiritian unit, but I didn't think ... that ..."

With a wave of his hand, Necron motioned for Viktor to withdraw his from his hip.

Chimalmat looked alternately from the Kiritian to Darius, then began to back away.

"I'll go away, and you two talk. If needed, Chimalmat would be nearby."

Necron folded his arms into the basket.

"You're lucky, son. Emperor, I don't believe ..." The young man still couldn't come to himself.

"So, you're the one from the Schindlers, right?"

"That's right, sir. My name is Darius Schindler.

"And I am no longer the emperor," muttered Kiret. "It's a past."

"I've heard the rumors at the shopping station," Darius said sadly. "But you are still emperor to me, sir. I hate the Kandrok people. May all of them evanesce!" There was a clear hate on the young man's face.

Viktor nodded towards the skulak.

"Can I know, young, what are you doing alone in the jungle before sunset? Your weapon is too strong to hunt animals, there would be nothing left of them."

"No, Mr. ... Corporal Shane? I also remember you."

"You almost guessed it, I'm the captain now."

"I'm very sorry. I couldn't know what your rank was at the moment. What are you guys doing here?"

"My captain asked you the question first," Kiret replied in a relaxed but firm tone.

"So sorry one more time. I'm still in shock."

"Alright, maybe before we start talking, let's get comfortable, because we won't be loitering here like three pegs." Necron pointed to a fallen trunk. "Maybe there. Unless you're in a hurry, Darius. If you're going somewhere far away, we can drop you off."

"It will be unnecessary," the boy droned, looking down at the ground.

Soon they were sitting by the fire, which Schindler had eagerly lit, starting with gathering wood. Viktor brought condensed food portions, plates and cups from the devemer. They took fresh water from the stream and boiled it over the flames in a metal container.

"I don't have a home anymore," Darius began to narrate, having tossed a stick into the fire. "We were attacked by lycans. We thought they might never show up in the area because we hadn't seen any of these suckers in a few years. But they came. They came to kill. I was not on the farm then, because I went with Eredal to the Rafens to take some stuff needed for work and that saved our skin. Lycans ransacked our home, stole the crops and destroyed what they couldn't take, killed our parents. Ever since then, Eredal has lived with the Rafens, because she couldn't stay at the crime scene, but I had nothing to do with this land anymore. I became an adult and was able to decide my own fate. So, I left, I live like a hermit. I had had a gun before, since the attack on the farm I have hunted scoundrels. I've already killed dozens. Chimalmat that I sometimes meet in the forest helps me in this. However, I haven't seen any lycan for a month, maybe we've already killed them all."

Kiret and Viktor watched as a fist and face muscles of the boy staring at the flames twitched. Sometimes he was nodding unconsciously.

"We're sorry about what happened to you," Biffter said sympathetically. He raised a cup of water to his mouth.

"It may sound strange, but I had a feeling that I would see you again," Darius said softly. "That we would meet again. I was expecting you. And here you are back, although I don't know why. And why the emperor himself and the high-ranking achijes travel in the little devemer. But I guess you guys are hiding and you came here for a specific purpose that I won't ask about."

"Good thinking," Necron said. "But as you've yourself said, our affairs will remain ours. Why were you waiting for us?"

The boy got up and straightened.

"I want to be one of you," he said seriously. "I'm an adult and I know my goals and needs. I have not dreamed of anything else in the seven years that I saw you. I realized that this was the only thing I wanted in my life - to be a Kiritian." Necron raised his eyebrows as Darius fell to his knee. "If you think I qualify to be an Immortal, please don't reject me, but take me with you. It is no coincidence that we are meeting now."

The achijes looked at each other. Necron made a 'number' face, then rose from the trunk.

"Get up," he ordered Darius.

The boy obeyed right away, stiffened as if at a military roll-call. Biffter started to survey him.

"How old are you?"

"Nineteen."

"The height and weight?"

"One hundred and eighty-six centimeters, when I last weighed myself, it was seventy-eight kilograms."

"Well, well, we are the same height, although I'm a little heavier. Are you healthy?"

"Totally. Not counting the little wounds I got in the jungle, of course."

"And the Kiritian weapon, where did you get it?"

Darius got a little confused, put his hand on the X17A4 pistol as if to cover it.

"I think you know the Kiritian domain has always been truthfulness," the captain announced. "This is one of the reasons why we have become the most powerful nation - no one deceived anyone. So how was it?"

"I got the gun from Corporal Tsar Seymour. He gave it to me when I was visiting your ship."

"Great. That's all Tsar." Kiret smiled. "I'm glad you're honest with us. Can you fight? Overall, I mean physical fitness."

"Of course. I grew up in dangerous areas and have recently been hunting for lycans. You can try me, sir."

"So hit me in the face."

The boy was amazed, even scared.

"I can't ... You are ... the emperor."

"Just hit me. Go ahead, come on. Do you want to be with us or not? Won't you obey the first order in your life? Damn it, hit me finally!"

Encouraged by the sharper tone, and not wanting to come over as a coward, Darius swung his fist with all his strength, clenching his teeth. Kiret effortlessly parried the lightning blow with the bracer, counterattacked, and with a few careless movements of his hands, painfully sent the boy to the ground. Darius balanced on all fours for a moment, with his head lowered, and waited for his weakness to pass. He got up and dusted himself off.

"Hope you know what you want to get yourself into. What will happen to your body when you are infected with the super virus. Not to mention the fact that you can die in the first encounter with Kandrok, if such takes place. The times of safety are over for us."

Schindler's eyes twinkled.

"I realize everything, sir. And I'm ready for any sacrifices and circumstances. I also know that I don't need to have the virus given right away."

"It's nice that you know our affairs." Necron glanced at Viktor sitting next to him, the latter nodded slightly. "We practically need as many dedicated people as possible right now, so you are lucky, Darius, to meet us. Of course, you will be tested and then observed before we finally decide your fate."

The boy was speechless with amazement.

"Welcome aboard, son." The former First Galactic Dignitary winked at him with a smile. "We'll see the Rafens and your sister first, and then you'll go on a journey with us, and Captain Shane will assign you to someone."

"Tha... thank you very much, gentlemen."

IX. Matthew Rain and Jenny Bidwell

Kiret didn't plan a joint flight to Cargoo. He was going to split up from Viktor and Darius in H14 orbit and go to Jenny towards Atla in the Pisces Universe. He hadn't seen his daughter Sandstorm in a long time, and he wanted to make sure she was okay.

The three landed at a neutral trading station, where anyone could do business, as long as they obeyed the rules, guarded by androids or mercenaries paid by the owners of the facilities. Many goods were traded, mainly food, gardening and household equipment, but also a civilian ship could be purchased. For security reasons, Viktor persuaded Necron - although after a heated discussion - to stay on board the devemer, while he himself went with Darius to the other end of the station to buy the machine. Taking the boy with him turned out to be a good idea, he was well known here, and his story was believed that Captain Shane in plain clothes was his wealthy uncle from Nephrida, who wanted to buy a new ship. What he came in, fortunately, no one was interested in.

Viktor was disappointed to see a dozen inferior according to Kiritian standards Oderses' machines, but having no choice he bought for gold the best option - a twenty-meter-long ship for carrying a small number of passengers, seven times slower than the devemer.

After determining the next place and date of the meeting, the men separated: Viktor and Darius headed for Cargoo, while the former emperor waited for them to depart, and began his journey to Atla in the devemer.

As Cargoo orbited in the same star system as H14, after positioning the anti-g and anti-radiation shields, Viktor made only one subspace jump towards the target planet. The maneuver reduced the journey time from a few weeks during which the ship would have traveled with a plasma drive to three days. It was a long time anyway - Oderses' subspace drive was much worse than Alcubierre's version used by the Immortals.

Although the journey was peaceful and monotone, it turned out to be a great experience for Darius. The boy had never flown further than to the H14 orbital station. He tried to act as a serious and emotional person in front of the captain, but the scenery behind the canopy made him watch everything with the eagerness of a child. The sight of the brown and red Cargoo geoid made him speechless. The young man's delight had a relaxing effect on Viktor, he often summed up his behavior with a smile, even with a chuckle, and then he described to Schindler the objects of his interest.

Cargoo hadn't changed much since it was discovered and recognized as a terrestrial planet for terraforming. Apart from setting up atmosphere synthesizers on its surface and planting several species of unattractive agricultural plants, mainly shrubs, it had lost nothing of its original appearance. It wasn't inhabited, except for a dozen or so operating mines on the surface, drawing groundwater for the needs of machines and workers. The damaged surface, usually flat areas left by weathered rocks, gusty winds and hard, barren soil didn't make the globe a prime candidate for farmers or lovers of premises under palm trees. During the Kiritian-rebel wars, opposition troops were sometimes stationed here, but after the victory of the Immortals, the latter took over Cargoo to establish military bases. Eventually they returned to the capital, and plans to build the installation were put off. When Kandrok attacked Morascrik, part of the Kiritians returned indirectly to Cargoo to seek shelter. In order to remain invisible from orbit, building anything was abandoned and underground mines were seized. They were transformed into bases and laboratories developing new technologies against the enemy. The Kiritians managed to bring in several mobile base-shuttles from space, which after landing covered themselves with a mountain-like coating.

Before the ship could reach the exosphere, two small luminous balls flew towards it and immediately receded.

"What is this?" Darius asked worriedly.

"Orbs," said Viktor calmly. "Spy and combat objects. The Kiritians already know we're here."

"And what now?"

"Nothing. We're just landing."

A few minutes later the ship settled in a small cave, through the opening you could see uneven terrain littered with boulders.

The largest of them were the size of a multi-story house. The horizon was guarded by low, jagged rocks.

"Our stop, young," Shane announced amused, glancing at disappointed Darius, who hoped to see a military base and machines stationed everywhere.

"It looks a bit like Precambrian Earth, except without lava. You can breathe normally here, gravity and pressure also won't be alien to you."

Viktor changed his civilian clothes for Kiritian armor and left the ship with Darius accoutered in a flight suit. Accustomed to the tropics of H14, the boy began to grind his teeth from the cold and rub his shoulders, but he stopped when Viktor looked back.

"Hurry up. There are three kilometers of walk ahead of us."

"I expected that we would land at the airport next to the base entrance." Darius caught up with the guide.

"Before we settle down with machines in front of the descent to the nether regions, we have to observe the orbit for months. We don't want to be visible to anyone at this stage. Neither to Kandrok nor its spies. Even though we are safe here, you can never be too careful. The masking of ships and naval craft cannot be turned on all the time, because it consumes a tremendous amount of energy. We have a lot to do, learn and understand before we decide to attack the enemy."

"So, there will be a war?" Schindler asked with poorly hidden enthusiasm. Brought up on the boring planet, he had dreamed many times of getting away from this hole and taking part in a real fight.

"I suppose so, but many years will pass before that happens. It all depends on the expansion of Kandrok and technological advances in the military field of our scientists. It would also be good to find the enemy's weak points."

Darius saw a flash on the rock wall. He didn't care about it, taking it for the reflex of K'ajolom's rays, which for a moment peeked through the gap in the dense clouds. But when the reflection repeated on the other side of the low ravine they were walking, and he additionally registered the movement, concerned, he approached the captain.

"There's someone there."

Shane surveyed the sky, then moved his gaze over dark rocks. "This is what we have become," he thought with melancholy. "We have turned from a proud predator into an animal hiding in a hole. We surrendered the worlds we had managed for centuries, almost without a fight."

"They're just my people. They have been following us for some time. You must have aroused their curiosity."

"Why won't they join us?"

"It's too steep."

The achijes descended the rocks a half kilometer farther as the terrain grew milder. K'ajolom disappeared behind the clouds for good. It started to snow slightly - something that cold Schindler had never seen. Contrary to the windy nature of the planet, even the faintest gusts died out, causing the flakes to fall vertically.

The newcomers slid opened the strobilis of their helmets. A freckled achij with red hair cut into several strands, walked over to the captain, drew himself to his full height and saluted.

"Welcome to Cargoo, sir."

"Rest, Corporal Darkoris. It's nice to see you again." Viktor smiled politely.

Darius had the man in front of him whom he also remembered well from his childhood. In seven years, Rasmus Darkoris hadn't changed even a bit, like Shane or Biffter. Schindler had just begun to realize that the Kiritians really were immortal, something he hadn't bothered about before, though he'd known it for a long time.

Shane looked at Private Shimizu, Private Walker, and Senior Private Bradshaw, who were famous for beating Erces asylum seekers on Morascrik. The fourth Kiritian, unceremoniously holding his weapon on his shoulder, wasn't from Darkoris' squad.

Darius groaned inwardly.

"Good morning, Captain." Corporal Tsar Seymour looked at Schindler with the eye of an amused hunter, certain that awaits him delightful play with his prey. "I met Darkoris' team by accident, so I went with them."

Viktor's mood improved more than once when he dealt with this specific achij loving stimulants, who got away with everything, especially non-statutory behavior. Despite these and several other variations, Tsar was considered a great achij. Now, surprisingly, he was sober.

"What's the situation?" Viktor asked.

"It's boring as hell, sir," Tsar replied cheerfully.

"Great. The emperor has made it to Atla, sent me a message that he was fine as well. He will contact us if he needs an escort. He preferred to fly alone so as not to attract unwanted glances."

"And who is this princess? You bombed the castle on your way to Cargoo, sir?" Seymour gestured with his chin to Darius, who withstood the insult and didn't show that he was nervous.

The captain put his hand firmly on the boy's shoulder for a moment.

"May I present Darius Schindler from H14. He has decided to join us. I spent some time in his company and found him to be up to our standards. He is recommended also by the emperor. He could be temporary assigned while he gets tested."

Seymour slung the strap of the weapon over his torso, stepped close to Darius, and began examining him.

"Wait ... Don't we know each other?" He got the flash. He backed away. "It's you!" He pointed his finger at him. "That kid from the field! You tricked me, you little shit!"

Viktor raised his eyebrows. The other achijes, amused, waited for the situation to unfold.

It turned out that the cosmos was an absurdly small place, such a meeting Darius hadn't expected. He wanted to laugh and hide somewhere under stones at the same time. He had intended to achieve a flattering reputation among the Kiritians from the outset, being polite and cooperative, but he didn't want to avoid a bit of feistiness or strong language, lest he come over as a pushover or wimp. Now he didn't know how to act.

"Yyyh, I didn't mean it," he managed to say. Was he supposed to address these achijes by their ranks? After all, he was not yet a Kiritian.

"I didn't mean it? That's all you have to say to me?! In addition, you escaped somewhere into the bushes like a terrified virgin at the sight of a bird, to avoid complaints!"

Kiritian or not, Darius wouldn't let him pan him.

"Because you were treating me like a kid."

"Because you were a kid. And you still are."

"Is it so? Now I'm looking at you from above."

"You must have grown so fast that you hit your thatch against the barn roof and your mind flew to your heels. Cheeky little shit."

"Lightweight junkie. And that would be it for a good first impression."

"Lightweight, you think?" Tsar smiled slyly. He wasn't angry, he was having a great time.

"Sir?" Corporal Darkoris looked at Viktor walking away.

"I'm going to cry over the future of our nation," replied the captain. "I also want to see my wife. Let me know when you're done."

Darius and Tsar glanced at the officer, then at each other.

"You like to mess, huh? So, tell us what a badass you are." Seymour playfully slapped the boy on the forehead. He liked his courage; it was possible to control youthful anger with time. It was nice to see recruits on Cargoo who didn't let anyone push them around. They needed such people. "I understand that you know how to pilot ships and have several years of experience in using various types of weapons. Or at least you can fly on a barn door."

"Not yet when it comes to piloting, but I already have experience in killing with firearms," Schindler replied proudly. Seymour gave him a look of the 'I'm all ears.' kind. "I spent some time in H14 forests, all alone, hunting for lycans. The wounds on my body can confirm this, though not Mr. Shane, because he only listened to my story."

"And I can see you still have my gun. Seymour pointed to the X17A4 at his belt, which the boy covered with his hand. "So, you're saying that you can chase savages in the woods and swing on a branch. How many skulls do you have on your account?"

"What, damn?" Darius naturally misunderstood Tsar's black humor, who began to laugh at his expression.

"Never mind. So, let's see what clay they made you from." Seymour put an arm around Schindler's neck, patted his shoulder. Then glanced at Darkoris.

"I'm taking the kid to my squad. Working, he will compensate for that number with the devil's weed from seven years ago."

The corporal was stunned.

"Tsar, are you crazy? Did you trade our weapons for drugs? With the child?!"

***

The star approaching the zenith reigned in the clear sky, and intense light reached even the lowest parts of the forest. Breaking through the thickets, Jenny Bidwell could clearly see the obstacles in her way. She knew the area beyond the gates of the estate anyway, so that even being nervous, as now, she knew where and how to put her foot in order not to fall into a hole, not to get stuck in a rotten trunk or smash a mound of red ants. As usual, her foster parents ran after her and called, but gave up at the yard fence. Firstly, because they couldn't leave their sons at home alone, secondly - Jenny, despite being eight, was one of the faster people in the colony of 40,000. She could easily escape adults, especially the unfit Bidwells. Kindra worked behind a desk at the Colonial Resources Section, like her husband Abraham, and didn't have the time or a particular desire, to exercise outdoors. Jenny, on the other hand, had loved movement from an early age. She ran through fields, forests, even climbed - without the care of her guardians, of course - smaller rocks. She achieved a good condition which she liked to enjoy away from people.

The need for isolation stemmed from the fact that the Bidwells, for reasons unknown to Jenny, were guarding her as if she were some king's daughter living in a slum. They kept her at home, didn't even allow her to go out to the yard alone, while her peers could wander kilometers away from the borders of the colony. An extremely safe colony, because the worst thing that could happen to a child here was a sprained ankle. Everyone had everything, so no one attacked anyone. Jenny turned from a sulky girl into a little rebel and started sneaking out of the house. She was familiar with all the safeguards; she knew how to sabotage or bypass them. They had been bought and installed by the mysterious, unshaven man called Matthew Rain, who came and visited the Bidwells on Atla from time to time. Jenny didn't want to worry anyone, so she just sneaked out to feel a little free. She always came back before dusk, often bruised and scratched, but content.

That the Bidwells weren't her real parents and the three-year-old and six-year-old boys weren't her brothers, she discovered some time ago. Also, the fact that Rain's name was different from that with which he introduced himself. Jenny had a casual conversation about crossbreeding in school, and that was where it all started. Among the Bidwells, everyone had blonde or white hair, an olive complexion, and blue or green eyes, also thick bones. Jenny wore pitch-black hair that was trimmed to her shoulders, her eyes were hazel, her skin was light, and her bones were small although strong. Sitting on the roof under the stars in the evenings, she wondered if handsome Matthew was her father. Otherwise, why would have he come and see how she grows and pay for her maintenance?

Soon she got to know the rest of the facts.

At the same time something very strange happened.

Sometimes she 'heard' people's thoughts. By the time she was six, she had experienced this phenomenon several times. She understood the simplest messages: someone wants to eat, someone wants to sleep, someone wants to drink. She couldn't control it, and 'reading' people appeared without visible signs, spontaneously. Kind of a vision of clairvoyants who were still popular. The mysterious skill that the girl didn't tell even her best friends about, apparently had grown up with her, because when she turned eight, she voluntarily saw human thoughts for the first time. She started experimenting with Martin called Badass, a class group boy she didn't like - she wanted to find out why he teased her. The attempt was successful. Jenny found that the spoiled rascal of rich parents, used to always getting what he wanted, took it out on her because she had a character and condition that he himself would have liked to have.

The second attempt regarded Abraham. He had just completed his interplanetary holo connection with Rain in his office, and Jenny, who was passing by, didn't manage to eavesdrop on what it was about. Reading the man's mind was successful, but she regretted wanting to spy on the adults. She found out who her real mother and father were - and the man Abraham had just spoken to.

When, outraged, she told her 'parents' off at breakfast, they were sitting in their chairs speechless and stiff like great columns of salt. Jenny thought she would be screamed at and sent back to the room for talking stupid things, but Kindra's reaction was summoning a god and putting her hand over her mouth, while a bead of sweat appeared on the temple of her husband staring at her. Then there was indeed a brawl. The caretakers told her not to mention everything, and Jenny, who had been lying to all her life, shouted in anger that she would spread the news to her friends. Since summer vacation had recently started, she was banned from leaving the house. Abraham even secured the door with a code that Jenny got to know when she burst into his mind once more.

It was realized that she had fled the house when she was already at the fence. It was the last time they saw her.

She was furious. She concluded that her real parents had abandoned her. She also kept thinking about Rain.

She let her feet lead her through the endless thicket of forest. She ran to a clearing with a lake, where in time she hid behind a tree among reeds. The shore was occupied by fat, pimply and generally ugly Badass with a group of friends. There was a girl on the branch above them that Jenny didn't know. Boys in soaked clothes jumped on lines into the water.

She waited a moment for her heart to stop pounding after the long run, then turned back and walked slowly towards the woods. She wanted to go unnoticed, but of course she had to step on a dry twig hidden under the leaves.

"Jenny Bidwell!" Martin's smiling voice acted like an invisible wall. Grasping her elbow nervously, the girl turned towards him with an expressionless face. "Have you come to play with me?"

She shook her head, turned and started walking.

"Wait!" There was little of a request in Badass' tone. "I'm talking to you!"

Jenny didn't bother about the spoken words, she strode, loudly rustling the grass of the clearing. She naively hoped that if she ignored Martin, he would leave her alone.

The boy ran up and took the girl painfully by the arm, jerked her and turned towards him.

Jenny gritted her teeth more with anger than pain. Taking advantage of the fact that she was standing on an embankment of sand, she easily pushed the stalker away.

"Leave me alone!"

Badass had nothing to grab except the leaves of the tall grass, so he collapsed into a stinking, stagnant puddle.

His friends, laughing, ran out of the water, one of them helped Badass up. The boy angrily jerked his hand out of his grip, rubbed his muddy lips with his hand, and looked with his narrowed eyes at the buffer zone behind which Jenny was disappearing.

"I'm gonna kill that stupid cow." He started running towards the trees. His buddies and the female friend rushed overjoyed in droves behind their leader, confident that Martin would get whacked Jenny and kick her. They couldn't miss such a spectacle.

***

Jenny sped up, hearing the screams behind her back, and when the patter of many pairs of shoes reached it, she rushed. Running home meant she would have had to make a right sharply and go back a bit, which was tantamount to falling into the hands of the gang chasing her.

After a dozen or so minutes of intense running through dense bushes, she shook them off, she assumed that maybe she had even been left alone. She stopped; her head was pounding; blood was throbbing in her ears. She was so exhausted that she had to hold on to a low branch to keep from falling to the ground.

Catching her breath, she noticed that she had reached a strange place. It was not even a tiny clearing, but an enclave among trees covered with engraved mossy boulders forming a circle about seven meters in diameter. In the center there was a stone slab with a skull with beads or a cat's head carved into it. Burnt branches were scattered around, as if from a bonfire smashed in haste. Jenny felt peculiar as she stared at the partially starlit disk - scared, fascinated, and sad at the same time, as if these feelings hadn't been coming from her. What if this place had been haunted and there were ghosts?!

She shuddered as a black shape appeared out of nowhere in the sky. It flew towards an estate.

Something rustled in the woods, and soon sweaty, panting Badass rolled out into the enclave. He didn't let go. Jenny was one of the few children who could ignore him, even oppose him, so now she would probably get hit.

"There you are." He immediately attacked her with his fists. Jenny grabbed his hands and tried to twist them. If Badass hadn't gasped like a strangled pig and swayed with fatigue on his legs, he would have already knocked her down with his fatness.

"Get lost!"

She managed to push his hands away from her. She tried to escape, but the hooligan grabbed her waist and they both fell to the ground.

From the forest came the exhortations of Martin's friends who had lost their way in the unknown territory.

The girl started to thrash; she kicked the attacker away from her. They stood up simultaneously, facing each other. The boy's nose was bleeding from being smashed by the shoe; he looked at Bidwell with eyes full of hatred. Initially he had just wanted to scare her and make fun of her, but now he wouldn't forgive Jenny for overtaking him first and then hurting him.

"I'll kill you for this, you larva." He leaned down and wanted to charge like a bull.

But something puzzled him so that he froze.

"You all are to get off me!" Jenny raised her hand high and spread her fingers, then hit Martin's face as if to vent all the anger of the universe on him.

She managed to register five streams of blood leaking from his cheek. Badass turned one hundred and eighty degrees and fell to the stone as if he had been knocked out by a bull, he himself had resembled before. Jenny looked horrified at her fingers, they looked ordinary, except the ones of the right hand were stained red. Unknowingly she started to back away and shook her head in disbelief. The hooligan lay on the stone slab and didn't move. I don't think he was alive! She just waved her hand!

The voices coming from the woods calling the boy were right there. Plants being pushed aside rustled and crackled.

Jenny did the only thing her brain prompted her - she fled, haring off before Badass' friends got into the circle.

***

Jenny had exhausted all her energy for that day. That's why she didn't even fight when she ran into a man in plain clothes who grabbed her wrist.

"Finally, you are here, we're going home," he turned to the girl first, then he said through the communicator, "Everything is alright, I have her. We'll be right back."

It was too much. First, the quarrel with her parents, who were not parents at all, then the moron Badass and his dull friends and ... and the corpse! Jenny couldn't stand it and she started crying like a baby. The man took pity on her and picked her up.

"Kiret," she sniveled, cuddling against his neck. "What a baldy you are."

"I already know about everything. The Bidwells told me you found out the truth. It's good morning, firstly, Jenny ... Sandstorm." Necron was surprised that she recognized him with the changed haircut, or rather the complete lack of it, although the face in earlier meetings had been hidden by stubble or even a helmet. "Hush now."

"I killed him ... I killed him." She couldn't calm down.

"What are you talking about? Who did you kill?"

"Badass ... I mean Martin. A boy from class. I wanted to hit him, and I hurt his head like I had blades stuck to my fingers. Like these of Kiritians wearing gloves." She imagined the body sliced and break down even more.

They reached the Bidwells' yard, where the little girl was taken over by the concerned caretakers. They all entered the mansion. Necron made himself comfortable in the living room. He could still believe the mind-reading story, though it seemed absurd, but hurting the boy ... Was it genetically and physically possible? Forkis had been a human during an affair with Anna, so Onkalotian traits couldn't have passed on to the girl. On the other hand, what could Kiret know of the alien artifact, an extremely advanced technology that had transmuted their former emperor twice? Although Xajb'a Kej had gotten the human body, he had retained some of the features of a humanoid jaguar: a kinetic skull, a very stretchy digestive system and bones around it, a capacious stomach, infravision, telepathy, fangs large for a human. And the possibility of the occasional change of the nails into claws. The incident with Jenny made Kiret put in order in his head puzzling elements from his past and get his answer as to why Forkis sometimes had had scratches deep enough on his body that he had to go to the medical center to seal them. He had gotten pissed every time Necron had asked him for details. The achijes had explained all this to themselves with the advanced transhumanism accomplished by Figam, especially when it comes to the telepathy intended only for the ruler. Kiret was going to honestly talk to Jenny as soon as she calmed down, because she could just invent.

"I think we'll have a problem." The living room where he was sitting and sipping beer was entered by worried Abraham. "I just had a call from Martin's parents."

Necron got up.

"Is he alive?"

"Yes, but his face is savaged and they went with him to regenerate the tissue. His father claims that Jenny cut his son's face with a knife in cold blood and ran away. This is confirmed by all his friends and female pal who found Martin in the forest. The boy himself swears it's true. The parents will be here soon."

***

Kiret was sure he would have settled the matter in a jiffy if he had changed in the devemer his civilian clothes to heavy armor. The sight of the Kiritian still aroused respect and fear on many planets, especially those which cut themselves off from political issues like Atla and H14. However, he had to think of something regarding his face so that the escaped emperor wasn't recognized in him. He chose to use the helmet cover mode, which made his face invisible; the voice, he distorted by the messenger filter. The armor plus moving the devemer from the garage in front of the house were enough to make Martin's parents' visit lasting ten quiet minutes, instead of an hour of arguing and threatening each other with court. Necron, as an anonymous Kiritian, apologized on behalf of the Bidwells and personally paid for the boy's medical expenses with platinum as the uinala currency had weakened because of Kandrok.

By dusk the Bidwells had already peace, but Necron knew that it didn't have to mean the end of trouble. If Martin's parents proved to be pedantic and asked for a forensic medical examination of the wounds, it would be revealed that Jenny hadn't had any knife and that the scratches had been caused by an animal that no one had seen. At the time of the incident, the boy had been shocked and could forget the details, and his story wasn't taken seriously, since he first claimed that Jenny had scratched him with her bare hand, and then, under the influence of his friends' testimony, miraculously knuckle duster with blades found itself in her hand, which eventually turned into a knife. Nevertheless, hospital equipment would immediately detect a wound inflicted by an animal and start investigating why only human DNA was there.

On top of that, there was one more serious matter.

After an hour of discussion with the caretakers, Kiret decided to go upstairs and talk to the girl as well. By this time, she should have calmed down. Meanwhile Kindra and Abraham went to put their sons to sleep.

The man became concerned as he noticed that the attic room was dark, and drapes were twitching at a slightly ajar balcony door. He went outside and looked over the railing, but saw no ladder or anything like that. The height was too large for a person to jump down without injuring themselves. He glanced at thick, intertwined vines growing out of pots on a terrace and ending somewhere on the roof.

"Jenny, are you upstairs?" He asked gently. There was no answer. "Jenny?"

He tried to climb, but he didn't do well with the armor. Leaves were falling densely, the natural rope creaked under his weight.

"Jenny, if you're there, go down right now. I weigh about a hundred and ten kilos with the armor and I will destroy your plants."

"Then get naked," replied a grumpy little voice.

"Come here now!"

"In your dreams!"

"It is you who should be dreaming at this time. The stars are already shining."

"Get lost."

"Who taught you to talk so arrogantly? For sure not Kindra and Abraham."

"Barikon."

"What Barikon?"

"A unicorn."

"Enough of this nonsense, chit, or I'll be there soon!"

"There you go."

Necron sighed, shook his head nervously. At times like this, he was glad that Kiritians hardly ever had children.

In the room, he disposed of the breastplate and other heavier parts of the armor. He managed to climb onto the flat roof without destroying the vines, although he impoverished them a bit, pulling their leaves and flowers. He stood in front of Jenny, looking scoldingly at her, and began shaking off the green chunks. The little smiling girl sat cross-legged away from the edge of the roof.

"Hi, baldy," she said.

"This is my new identity?"

"Yeah. You have an awful lot of them."

"We should just talk about it. Why are you knocking on your head?"

"Because you have a flower on your glowing baldhead."

He did have a blue bellflower on his head, lying like a hat, he took it off and handed it to Jenny.

"You're a Kiritian, aren't you?" She asked. She pointed to the next seat. "Sit down, baldy."

"Thank you, Your Majesty." Necron sat down with the clank of the armor he had left on. "Why did you get on the roof?"

"Why did you cut your hair?"

"I asked the question first."

"So, you answer first."

"Oh yes, you like when others do what you tell them to do?" Kiret feigned anger. Jenny laughed at that.

"Yeah." She stuck the flower in her hair. "All right, but you're ordering me one last time." He admonishingly waved a finger in front of her nose.

"Okay."

"I'm a fairly important Kiritian, at least I was." Necron grew serious, looked at the sky. "How many moons does Atla have? I already don't remember."

"Three, but they suck."

"Jenny!"

"What?"

"How can a moon suck? And why do you use dirty words?" He felt frustrated. He was completely unable to deal with children. He once had a son, but he felt that this distant past belonged to someone else. In a way, it was just like that.

"Because you seem a cool guy. I feel relaxed with you. The Bidwells smartened me up all my life, still only prohibitions and orders."

"They just took care of you at my request, because you are not just anybody."

"Who am I?"

"So, you learned little by reading the minds of your guardians?"

"Only that the real mom's name is Anna Sandstorm and dad's is Forkis, but I don't know his surname, or maybe it is the surname. And they are extremely important." Jenny lay down on her stomach, propped her head on her elbows, and began swinging her legs.

"And we should stop there. For your own good, you shouldn't know any more. You're smart and eloquent, also old enough that I won't lie to you. The names Sandstorm and Forkis alone are enough for you to be sentenced to death. Anyway, the bombers tried to kill you once, but they failed."

"Brave Necron saved me?"

"You think this is funny?"

The girl shrugged as best she could in her position.

"And stop waving those feet because it irritates me."

Jenny, sulky, looked at Biffter, but lowered her legs.

"So, what about my parents? Why did they leave me?"

"It's not like that. Your father had died before you were born. The world you come from is no longer safe and stable, so Anna decided to send you to the safe place. However, she couldn't visit you, because she was captured by the enemy." He added in a lower voice, "We don't know if she's still alive."

"You left my real mother in need?! What kind of Kiritian are you?!"

"You are too young to understand war and politics. Neither I nor my achijes were able to do anything. I was also sentenced to death, so I grew my hair, beard and mustache. That's why I had to hide like a frigging coward!" Necron clenched his hand. He forgot that he was talking to the child, brilliant but still the child. "The Scorpio Universe was taken from us. We lost the war with the enemy, but we will return there and take back what is ours. As soon as we develop technology, strategy and gather destroyed divisions, as well as create new ones."

Speaking into the void, Kiret realized that Jenny had her hand on his bracer and was looking into his face sympathetically.

"Sorry for being rude."

He stroked her head, watching the flower.

"It's okay."

"Will you take me from this place? I don't want to be here."

Kiret felt relieved. The problem he had discussed with the Bidwells in the living room seemed to be going to solve itself.

"You don't like Kindra and Abraham? And your brothers?"

"The caretakers are fine. The brothers so-so, scream terribly. Since I started school, I don't have time for them, and then I prefer to go outside. Anyway, they always seemed strange to me, the whole family. I thought it was because they look different to me and have different tastes. But now I know the cause." Jenny bit her lip and stared at Kiret's shoe for a moment before asking, "Is my mind-reading bad?"

"No. It's probably a psionic gift from your father. But I'll tell you about the details when you are older. Alright?"

"Okay."

"Tell me, can you use this skill whenever you want?"

"Unfortunately, not. This year I only managed it a few times out of hundreds of attempts. But I think if I practice it will be better. It used to be even worse."

"It's probably because you are growing and your skill gets stronger. Could I check something else?"

"Why?"

"I can't tell you, really, and I don't want to flip the script. It is unbecoming of a Kiritian. Then you would worry about it and you would definitely confide in someone. Often ignorance is a blessing."

The girl liked this honest answer, she felt important. She let Kiret survey herself.

Necron didn't notice anything unusual at the junction of the jaw and the skull, in the gums or on the girl's hands. He pressed lightly on the knuckles of her fingers, but they felt ordinary to the touch.

"It's time to go." He got up when he finished.

Jenny rose and took Kiret's hand as if they had been going for a walk.

"Am I fine?"

"Every bit of it. Just tell me one more thing girl. Have you told anyone about what you found out by digging through the Bidwells' minds?"

"No," she replied exceptionally eagerly.

Kiret looked at her askance and raised an eyebrow.

"Certainly not?"

"Well ... only my friend Nebula, but she promised not to tell anyone. I mean, already not my friend, and not even my pal, because we had an argument over the unicorn Barikon. Nebula only told Katarina, Maria and Joe, I talked to them and they swore they would keep the secret. I trusted them, but ... someone blurted out and after an hour half of the class knew it, in the sense of some of the people with whom I went to school before summer holidays. But I'm sure no one else will know about it, I swear! What?"

Necron stood motionless and stared at the girl in amazement.

"That's great ..."

The parents might have taken their kids' stories as inventions, but the tales, combined with the facts that Jenny was very similar to Forkis and raised by the parents with the completely different appearance, could have a chastening effect on people. In addition, Martin's parents saw in the Bidwells' house the unknown Kiritian in war armor.

Jenny waggled her finger, motioning for him to bend down.

"And one more thing," she whispered in Kiret's ear. "It's very important."

"What?"

"You are not to tell the mom and dad that I got onto the roof by climbing the vines."

***

They left the Bidwells' house at dawn. Kindra and Abraham, from the day of entrusting Jenny to their care, knew that the Kiritians could ask for her at any moment, but the farewell to the little girl, with whom they became close as if she had been their daughter, was difficult for them anyway. Necron said he wasn't taking her forever - if circumstances allowed, Jenny would visit them, maybe live with them again.

Despite her earlier sulks, the girl also felt sad about the separation, she was afraid of the change of scene. She had been silent since boarding the devemer.

"It won't be that bad." Kiret looked at her and smiled. "You're flying merely to the other hemisphere of the planet."

"What's it like?" She asked, looking through the canopy at landscapes blurred by the speed.

"Even cooler than here. You're gonna like that place. My property is remote from others, so you will study at home after the vacation. Anyway, it will be safer that way."

"And I'll be alone?"

"Staff live there, ready for my return at any moment. Humans and androids. They will be at your command." Kiret winked at her.

"And children will be there too? I mean, not at my command, but for fun."

"We'll organize it somehow. But in the beginning, you will have to learn a few rules that you must not break under any circumstances."

"Okay, I'll do it for you."

Kiret reached out and stroked Jenny's hair too much as her hair fall down over her face.

"Hey, come on!" She quickly restored her previous hairstyle. "Why can't we see the shadow of the ship on the ground?"

"Because we are scannerly and optically invisible, it is about stealth, and in its subset, it is about bending light over the entire surface of the fuselage. You can't hear us from the outside either, we had to enrich the machine with this modification to reduce the risk of being detected by Kandrok. The devemer is one of the best passenger transporters."

They flew at breakneck speed, averagely two hundred meters above the ground. Jenny would have liked to rest her hands on the canopy fairing and her chin on them for a more comfortable and better view, but she was held in place by the belts.

Until the end of the relatively short journey, they spoke and remained silent alternately.

The girl's despond passed instantly, replaced by curiosity and delight, when the three-story mansion grew in a little valley surrounded by a forest and crossed by a river string. It had a yard, a pool, a small landing strip, even an interplanetary communications tower.

X. Nimja's artifacts

"This way." Nanawak, walking ahead, showed Aggroteh a spiral staircase leading to the nether regions. At the top of his staff, a yellow light flared automatically, diffusing the darkness.

The descent took little time. They walked through a short corridor and stood in front of a gate made of metal unknown to the Onkalot, fitted into stone. Behind them was an elevator cabin manned by a guard dog. It went down lazily, rumbling and echoing in a vast shaft, but for creatures like Nimja members, rush was an alien concept. The gray walls turned the color of burnt brick as they ventured into the ground. At some point, the sounds of the mine could be heard clearly. Distorted, reminiscent of ghouls trying to break into the shaft, they caused goose bumps. Aggro thought that their journey would end in Xibalba itself, the realm of beasts, evil spirits, and death.

The elevator stopped at the lowest level. Having let the passengers through, the guard folded his paws over its chest and stayed by the cabin. Nanawak walked with the Onkalot along the main corridor and a few side ones lit by lamps integrated into the niches of the walls. Unlike the upper floors made of blocks of rock, the nether regions proved to be a kingdom of hardened metal alloy that, according to Nanawak, looked freshly laid even thousands of years later. To say that the sector resembled Kiritian space stations would be highly exaggerated, as the Immortals' objects near the Nimja dungeons looked primitive.

Nanawak led Q'ualel through the gate to a seemingly borderless hall, full of devices and objects unknown to him, of which he only recognized small, golden animals turned into artifacts. Also, this time they scattered around the nooks and crannies as he tried to get closer to one. The ceiling drowned in the darkness, and the walls were lost behind the cascade of aquamarine lights and working machines. Aggro couldn't smell any scents in the cool air, but he noticed fumes in a chasm behind a railing, where shoals of glowing navicular maintenance machines were flying, taking care of all processes and machinery. The sight of hundreds of slowly levitating drones (the humanoid jaguar didn't know any other word that he could use here) acted relaxing. Following Nanawak, dumbfounded, he examined devices and artifacts accumulated on shelves and racks, dead, half-alive and alive. None of them reminded him of anything, just as he couldn't define their use or name the material from which they were made. And each looked fantastic: lights shifting forms and colors, transforming figures, fractal structures, powerful objects locked in artificially made gemstones, and hundreds of other curiosities. They were a bit like the ruler of a fortress - beautiful, but probably very dangerous. Aggro could have bet that a small pebble was able to destroy an entire planet.

Nanawak searched for something on the glyph-marked shelves (Aggro noticed the resemblance to the symbols of the ancient Onkalots), but when he didn't find it, they moved to another sector. They walked over a scaffold set high above the floor, then around a lava-colored icicle generator that powered areas of the fortress that needed energy to function.

They entered another chamber.

"I haven't used them for so long that I don't remember where I put them." Nimja resumed his search. He soon smiled triumphantly as he lifted the find. "There it is. Here is the karitan."

It was a transparent, faceted ball that could fit easily in the palm of your hand, a fire was burning inside. When Aggro looked at it closely, he found that the inside wasn't being consumed by fire - which, after all, had no right to burn in the tight, hermetically sealed sphere - but by ajalmes itself locked inside the object! Among humanoid jaguars considered to be the primary substance of the universe, the energetic progenitor of matter. A thing divine, inaccessible to mortals, and destructive, constantly evolving. People in some mythologies called it chaos. Aggro was terrified when Nanawak pressed the object unexpectedly into his paws, and it couldn't have ended otherwise than in dropping it. After hitting the ground, it turned into a transparent, orange jelly.

"It's just your imagination," the Nimja member whispered with a smile. "The artifact is rational, though dead, and has decided to play a trick on you. You have been right to think that the contents have a lot to do with the substance of the universe that existed before the primeval explosion of the universe in which you lived, if I were to illustrate it somehow simply."

"It was rational. I've destroyed it ..."

"Take a look." Nanawak pointed to the metal floor with a finger. Something started to happen. The semi-liquid slush turned into liquid, which in turn changed its state of matter again and took the original form of a sphere. "No force known to you except the star's fusion energy, that is, extremely high temperature, can destroy karitan. However, once you use it, it will self-destruct without harming your surroundings. As if you were melting ice." Using telekinesis like Chimalmat, Nanawak picked up the sphere, rested the staff on the pillar, and with his other hand, summoned a twin object from the shelf. It looked exactly like karitan except that it glowed turquoise inside. "It in turn is kariban. Karitan will take you that way, kariban will bring you to the place from where you set off."

The Onkalot stared confusedly at Nanawak.

"I don't understand. I've thought you can tell me how to get Forkis' atole back."

The Nimja member's face was serious this time.

"And that's what I'm doing. To return atole to Forkis, you will have to go somewhere to find it. In Terrenic units of time, atole is recoverable up to fifty years or so after the death of its former host. It's a physical constant, part of the cosmic code," he tried to explain it as simply as possible. "After this time, it goes into a different form of energy and gets another owner, alive or dead. And that owner can be literally anything that has a periodic power supply: plant, animal, wire, part of a planet's core."

"What place are you talking about?"

The Nimja member handed him both items, this time the Onkalot didn't drop anything.

"About Amyrade Anfraktoris."

"Is that a planet?" Aggro began to stare at the mesmerizing aquamarine heart of kariban.

"Even I don't know it. But I know that Amyrade Anfraktoris is a location to which you can't fly in any way. Where there is no concept of the constant laws of physics. Where everything is constantly changing. Where time and space don't exist." He added more forcefully and menacingly, lowering his ears, "Where the living cannot enter."

The Onkalot shifted to him a searching look.

"Like Xibalba. The Underworld."

"Amyrade Anfraktoris means the Creators' Dumpster or the Processing Plant, because this place resembles a trial version of the created world, completely unsuccessful. A collection of everything that will someday be logical and arranged. Part of atole also goes to the Processing Plant before it changes its form. We discovered Amyrade Anfraktoris a long time ago, completely by accident, during a portation attempt, but abandoned the research because several of us fell victim to this terrifying plane. We knew that we broke the law that had never been written and that we ended up in the forbidden place. However, after several centuries of work, we managed to create artifacts that can be moved there and returned from there." He pointed at kariban and karitan.

"I've never heard of such a place."

"Because apart from Nimja, nobody knows about it. Similar locations appear in the myths of rational species, but their image always coincides with what they see in their own surroundings. If you are reasonable, you and those who will go to Amyrade with you will not tell anyone about the Processing

Plant. Though, even if you blurted out, you wouldn't be able to go back there unless you reached the level of Nimja knowledge. Your presence there will be as harmful as the march of a few ants through a forest. I won't give you any more artifacts."

Aggro stared at the spheres, holding them close to him. The insides shone intensively and brightly now, and the surfaces became warm. His mind, stimulated by the story, began to imagine the sights he might have seen on the surface of the dangerous, yet intriguing place. All the imaginations could be described as empty, sad and repulsive. Q'ualel noticed that, from the moment the subject of Amyrade was brought up, Nanawak hadn't smiled or mocked. The case must have been serious indeed.

"You can all die there," added the Nimja member. "You're going to the Creators' Dumpster at your own risk. And I won't give you any hints, because I don't know much myself. A person who is familiar with paranormal phenomena would be useful for you during the journey, it would be a little easier then. For example, someone from Karikon, the world that was our testing ground. We tried to make a copy of Amyrade there, but ended up abandoning the planet like so many others. Kiret will know what it is about. Nevertheless, consider whether the trouble is worth the dead emperor that you may not get back."

Q'ualel was surprised to learn that the Nimja member knew so much about Kiritians. Nanawak once again answered his unspoken question, "I watched the Immortals visit Karikon from time to time, but a handful of people know about X4, as they marked it." He put his fingers on the artifacts. "I'll explain how they work shortly. But now," he paused for a moment, raised his ears high, which almost touched with their tips, "it is time to present the key subject."

***

The last of the given artifacts, the humanoid jaguar couldn't see. The device merged with the first genetic material detected and would have become useless if he had touched it. Therefore, the Nimja member, having created the artifact in sterile conditions, had placed it in a container shaped like a small rugby ball. The unknown material making up the reservoir resembled metal and was decorated with patterns impossible for Aggro to decipher.

Several hours had passed since Nanawak cleared his blood of toxins. He began to have trouble breathing again and felt worse and worse, but the Nimja member was reluctant to help him again. To a smilodon caught with a rope and tied to the rock in front of the fortress, Q'ualel got almost bent. Several guards waited near the cat that was in good shape. Two bore bloody traces of struggle.

Aggro placed the bag of artifacts on his back. After calming down and freeing the smilodon, he climbed on its back and headed towards 'Perfarius', freed from the energetic snare.

The ship soon took off. The three passengers quickly left the zone of densely falling gray snow.

After decontaminating himself and the smilodon in a hermetic cabin, Q'ualel escorted it to the hold. Together with silent Paul, brooding over the impotence to which Nimja had subjected him and Kate, they put the animal to sleep for many years. The Onkalot for several minutes breathed a mixture of air from Chulimal, compressed in a cylinder, to feel good again.

When the two reached the cockpit, Tamasul seen from the side porthole was the size of an apple. Aggro slid the bag off his shoulders and released the artifacts that wandered to the center of the cabin, close to each other like polystyrene balls in water. Karitan and kariban shone brightest in the surroundings, emitting colors of amber and turquoise. The third artifact, xik'iri called the Collector, was as dark as a black hole, the wrapper even seemed to absorb the neighbors' light.

From the take-off, the travelers were silent, tense and depressed. The neurotic silence was broken by Kate.

"What is he like? The inhabitant of this fortress?" She nudged kariban gently with her fingernail. The ball moved several centimeters.

Aggro described Nanawak, hammering him.

"So Nimja are people to the nth degree, with more powerful toys," Paul concluded.

"What scared me the most was that they supposedly supported the development of intelligent species only to make them confront with each other sometime. On a whim, giving Onkalots the worst start, Kiritians' ancestors better, and Kandrok best."

"Kandrok?" Kate asked. "Who is this?"

"Tell me one by one," Paul said, running around the cabin and pushing the artifacts so that they bounced off each other and the devices. "And explain how these wonders work." He took karitan in his hands. The android's smile widened. "So we managed to ..."

Q'ualel reported on everything from loss of communication, crossing the caves and the mine, to the descent to Nanawak's Science Complex. He focused on what had stunned him the most - a monumental pole full of devices, the top of which drowned in darkness, as if there had been nothingness there, not the underbrush of the fortress. Surrounded by a swarm of platforms, the observatory consisted of centillions of small-sized beads, each was apparently a window facing some area of space; Paul made the assumption that it might have been the cause of the disruption to their electronics. Overall, the knowledge of the Great Family seemed incomprehensible to Aggroteh, and too frightening for his weak mind. Nanawak showed him his might in every aspect. He must have known that Q'ualel would tell his companions, and therefore tried to intimidate him as much as possible so that no more expedition would be organized to Tamasul.

When Aggro finished his story, the crew members congratulated themselves on their success. Paul put the artifacts in the bag, floated to the porthole, and put the precious cargo in the compartment.

"Well done," he said to the Onkalot waiting in the corridor.

"We all deserve applause. But there is still a lot ahead of us, the most difficult is yet to come. You think it's true about those Kandrok members and the war?"

"If everything was ever planned, it would mean that whatever we did, it wouldn't matter in the slightest, because we are doomed to fail in advance. However, we cannot think that way and we should just do our own thing. As for Kandrok, there is nothing to worry about beforehand, as we don't have a way to check it at the moment. You were incredibly lucky, although I also bet on your brilliant mind that Nanawak gave you so much information. This Amyrade Anfraktoris to me as an android is also incomprehensible. We don't know so much yet. Now that it is over, I can admit that I estimated the chances of success for our trip at four percent." Paul smiled apologetically. "Time for kriosen, Aggro. The way back should be easier."

"You really won't feel anything, sitting for years in one place?"

"Yes. I don't have to worry about the energy I use, because it will be a minimum, I also have universal access to it." Paul nodded to the void behind the side porthole. "The Space Dream company has equipped me with excellent batteries. Get ready. I'll send Kate to sleep in a moment too."

XI. A Deadly Virus

Anna Sandstorm awoke in the same circumstances as one hundred and forty-seven times before. As if she had been getting through the same day over and over again. Having opened her eyelids, she saw first the bright red of the sky behind a lattice, then the contact point of the wall with the ceiling, calendar notches on the granite on the left, the floor littered with sawdust and rags, three buckets, and Kandrok's energy barrage that didn't match the rest of the surroundings. Crime among the Kiritians was almost zero, so in the past primitive cells had been built mostly around the gladiators' arena to serve animals and enemies as a last harbor before entering the forum. They were rectangular rooms of reinforced granite, a rock quite common on seismically active Morascrik. The builders hadn't even bothered to bring energy or electricity there, since the fighters stayed there for a short time. Fire in the corridors or Kiritian generators had been sufficient for lighting.

After the expulsion of the Immortals from the capital, Kandrok filled all the cells with prisoners and replaced the bars with energy barriers of their own technology. It was a wall made of densely concentrated luminous particles that couldn't be destroyed in any way. At least with the means at the disposal of the prisoners. Through the window opening, protected by dhurnsteel grates, it was also impossible to get out, but even if someone had managed to escape, they would have been killed by Kandrok soldiers or by heavy infantry robots guarding the streets. A few days after the imprisonment of the Kiritians caught in the battle, someone managed to escape and run several dozen meters. In front of Sandstorm, they were turned into a skeleton by a cyborg ranger which sent a projectile melting soft tissue at them. The bones literally took two more steps before they fell with a clack to the ground. The cruel enemy had known human anatomy very well, so it was no surprise that it had constructed such a macabrely working weapon.

Sandstorm drew another white line on the wall with a pebble. One hundred and forty-eight days of captivity, and she knew as much as the day she had been thrown into the cell. Kandrok members didn't talk to the captured, perhaps they didn't even bother to learn the language of their victims. Every now and then, they came, opened the cell and took more prisoners, no one knew why, no one knew where. People who were led out didn't come back any more. The rest they brought food and water, every day took under arms to a prison yard which was the remains of the destroyed arena, changed the bucket with waste, and brought a change of clothes once a week.

They did all this as if under duress, only to keep the prisoners from dying prematurely.

Of the more than three hundred imprisoned in the sector, remained six, including Anna. She wondered if Kandrok had any idea how high her position was in the Kiritian people. If they knew why they kept her in the shabby cell like a simple achij, why they didn't murder or move her to a place more suited to her dignity? Someone had already tried to assassinate her once, unless it was all about poor Jenny, whose fate was unknown to Anna. In fact, there was no point in considering the problem. Kandrok came from faraway space, and its thinking could be very different from the norms of the Zodiac Universum.

Every day, Anna saw the enemy in the corridor or behind the window opening. She noticed that to the tasks with the prisoners were sent people who were completely organic, at least they looked like that visually. The cyborgs didn't go down to the seclusion room, and if they did, it was to scold hacks and give orders. She didn't understand their language, but the hostile growl was very telling, not to mention the semi-organic faces expressing anger. Security guards with a low degree of cyborgization guarded the grounds outside. They, in turn, were controlled by complete robots, rarely seen. They looked different, from ones massive, crude, larded with weapons and tools useful both at work and in beastly murder, to such resembling Kiritian androids. On duty were also ordinary humanoid or animal machines, factory-made as working tools, which, after weeks of observation, could be distinguished from high-ranking Kandrok members. Sandstorm concluded that the invaders belonged to a hierarchical, perhaps caste society, where the highest ranks were held by individuals with the least amount of organic body. Unless she confused the robots with armor protecting the organism.

The Kandrok members she saw up close had eyes ranging in color from white to red. In the case of the lightest color, the white and iris blend together, making the eye appear to have only the pupil. The hair, in turn, ranged from white to black. Their complexion was very pale, as if their home world had been poor in starlight, they had been avoiding it or living underground. Only robots or cyborgs wore dark built-in elements, sometimes multi-colored, which made them stand out sharply from the organic ones, like birds of paradise amid the gray mass. In terms of height and stature, Anna had never seen an organic Kandrok member taller than one meter and eighty centimeters, and they also had a weaker build and less developed muscles than the people of the Zodiac University. This didn't mean, however, that they were physically weak. There were fights in prison several times, and the hacks without using any weapons easily pacified the rebels by laying them on the ground. Only cyborgs could afford to enlarge their body and add mass and shape to it at will (unless they had some social norms). Undoubtedly, Kandrok was associated with the war, maybe even cultivated it. And was unquestionably technologically ahead of Kiritians. Although the main cause of the defeat, the Immortals held in the capital considered their own short-sightedness: the invader had probably been watching them for a long time, either personally or through Erceses, had learned about their military structure, so it was prepared for a blitzkrieg.

Six out of three hundred prisoners remained.

Still, no one knew why Kandrok members led them out. And what happened to the rest of the Kiritians from the capital. The neurotic silence lingering in the city and in the sky didn't fill with optimism. Sometimes Kandrok sounded an alarm from the city loudspeakers, as during an air raid, but rather as a joke or they liked the sound, because nothing happened afterwards. The melody that heralded the doom, consisting of long, alternating high and low tones, aroused universal horror and fascination. Perhaps that is why it had survived unchanged for centuries.

As the eye of the red supergiant Betelgeuse descended from its zenith, two Kandrok members came for Gareth. Before the attack, he had been a batab in the capital - the commander of the city guard. Months of waiting, it is not known for what, with an extinguished hope of salvation, broke a handful of prisoners, so he let himself be led meekly like a beaten dog. His gaze was lowered, his hands chained in front of him. He walked with the guards at his sides, the artificial fire from the generators caught out the details of their deep blue armor. Only Anna went to the barrage and watched her companion of misery until he disappeared on the stairs leading up. Corporal Zira Aytar, sitting opposite her cell, didn't react in any way. Indifferent to everything, the woman of thirty at the time of kiritianization was sitting by the wall, casually moving pebbles on the ground. She was thinking of nothing. Once a proud achij with an eternally cold face, before joining the Immortals, she had earned her living as one of the best thieves and assassins on Calvary. She had mastered the art of ruthlessly removing the threat on her way. When Forkis had found Aytar and decided to incorporate her to the nation as an achij obeying orders and the law above all, she had modified her armor to store killer gadgets necessary in the previous profession as well as useful in the new one. The removal of her weapon by Kandrok broke Aytar more than sitting in the cell. Previously, she had worn a cropped, dark blue like eyes mohawk on top of her skull, and she had always kept the tattooed sides shaved. After months of captivity, her hair began to grow back into a red-blue composition, which Anna associated with fire trying to defeat water.

The corporal felt her eyes on herself. She glanced at the prisoners on the opposite side - the four of them sitting in twin cells. To the left of Anna, had been flung geneticist Alejandro Cortez, who had become famous for the fact that when drunk he had contributed to the restoration of fertility to Forkis, which had resulted in the conception of Jenny. To the right of Sandstorm sat Aytars not belonging to the company, nineteen-year-old Privateer Carbon and foreman Stellar, who had used to deal with the urbanization of the capital.

"So, there are five of us left," said Cortez, who was lying on the bunk, wanting to somehow start the discussion. However, time passed, and the comrades remained silent. "As you like."

Anna lay down as well, rested her head on her clasped hands. She was lying so until the evening, changing position when something was numb, or she felt uncomfortable. She hadn't even been able to nap. For the first time since the beginning of their sentence, Kandrok didn't take them to the yard, which they had always done in the early evening hours.

"It's already past the time of going out." Carbon clearly thought the same.

"Strange indeed," Aytar confirmed.

Sandstorm threw off the rag used as a quilt, got up from the bunk and walked to the window opening. She stood on tiptoe. It was a moment when the indefinitely summoned cyborg (she didn't notice the communicator anywhere) broke into a run, with a weapon in hand, leaving the post. The depressive city silence was interrupted by distant screams muffled by the buildings. Anna frowned; her heart pounded. She thought maybe Gareth had freed himself and caused a commotion, though the voice of reason clearly contradicted it. In mysterious circumstances, even the most valiant and intelligent of the prisoners disappeared, and sometimes whole groups were taken, so why would have the batab been an exception and been able to cope on his own?

The screams soon subsided.

Another hours passed. Nobody came with food and water, nor to empty the buckets. The cyborg didn't return to its post, even though there had always been someone there or at least a shapeshifting drone had been flying.

The next day looked as if Kandrok had only turned out to be an extremely long nightmare. A gusty wind blew through the cracks, tossing the sand of the arena, creating high vortices. Over the pyramid, which was a plant processing energy constantly being supplied by collectors from above the clouds, a modificant inhabiting the nearby hills, called the volcanic phoenix, flew around. Sandstorm noticed it when she looked through the bars for what seemed like the fiftieth time this morning. She knew for sure that something must have happened, because Kandrok had come every day, for reasons known only to them, wanting to keep the prisoners in good condition. She even thought that Kiritians had come from outer space, broken into K'otz'ibaja and neutralized the enemy. But if that had been the case, they would have checked the prisons immediately. And the diversion wouldn't have taken place in complete silence.

Also, the next day no one came to see them.

Anna had only leftover water, and the food ran out in the morning. Carbon had run out of supplies earlier and was already complaining about being thirsty. Stellar tried to give him water in his clasped hands through the hole between the barrage and the granite.

Everyone stood up, stunned when the power barriers shut down an hour before dusk.

Moments later, Gareth ran casually down the stairs, leaned heavily against the wall just around the corner. He was shaking like a delicate creature in the cold, gasped for breath. In his right hand he held the lowered pulse rifle, and he had on light armor. Also, a bloody face and a wild look.

"Quickly, let's get out," he hissed urgently. He pointed the rifle at the top of the stairs. "Come on, it's safe for now."

"What's going on here, a heavy cannon?!" Carbon was the first to leave the cell.

"Garet, what happened?" Aytar asked. "How did you escape from Kandrok?"

Soon the five of them surrounded the batab in a semicircle.

The man wiped the blood from his face with a glove, or rather smeared it. Alejandro noticed that it was barely flowing from his cut forehead because a clot was already forming.

"I didn't escape," replied Gareth. "I mean, I fought for two days with the couch to which they attached me, naked and weakened by some filth. It was only recently that my strength returned, I fell over with the day bed and managed to free myself. I thought I would freeze there or die of thirst sooner."

"Did they experiment on you?" Stellar growled in bewilderment.

"They left you alone for two days?" Anna glanced nervously up the stairs.

"They didn't, damn it," replied the batab, not caring that he was talking to the former Council member. He started to laugh stupidly or cry, but Anna fully understood his reaction when he added, "All the organic Kandrok members are dead."

"They are dead?!" Aytar blurted out.

"Normally. Everyone is lying where it caught them. They fell like flies sprinkled with acid. Two died before my eyes. Only robots and a few more mechanical than biological cyborgs remained, but I escaped them because they had more urgent matters on their mind."

Sandstorm sighed.

"But what killed them?"

Leaning his head against the wall, Gareth laughed before answering.

"A plague."

Five of them looked at each other, understanding nothing. Having heard the word 'plague', Carbon looked at the batab's blood and took a step back. The hand he wanted to press against his nose and mouth twitched.

"You don't get it?" Gareth grinned. "Our super virus killed them! It changes us, it kills them!"

"Oh, crap ..." commented Stellar.

"So, what do we do now?" Private Carbon looked at Aytar, who had the corporal rank. The former assassin looked at Sandstorm in turn.

"You are older than me and have more experience, Aytar," said Anna. "Bring us out with Gareth. Take charge."

The batab and the corporal looked at each other, the man nodded briefly. Sandstorm was the captain of the now defunct Kiritian company, experienced in space and air combat, not infantry. Moreover, everyone knew, including herself, that Necron had given her such a military position to make her deviate too much with her prerogatives from her political position on the Council.

"How's your health?" Stellar asked the batab.

"I feel good now. I was on brief recon outside, there was no enemy in sight. We need to take advantage of this and get to the armory quickly." Gareth raised the rifle to a combat position and moved up the stairs, the others rushed after him.

They ran through the corridor and passed the empty gatehouse where Gareth had previously figured out how to disable cell security.

"Why are the robots and cyborgs all right when the rest of Kandrok are dead?" The foreman asked.

"Probably because they are more machines than living things," Andro replied, gasping, "especially the robots are fully mechanized. I absolutely must see these bodies."

"What for? What if Gareth is wrong and something else killed them?" Carbon glanced at the batab running ahead.

"They got to the medical center where we store the super viruses," the batab said. "They discovered our greatest secret, wanted to understand it and paid for it with their lives."

"Why didn't they take the serum?" Asked the senior private.

"They are a people from another world." Andro looked nervously from side to side. "They look like us but are probably built differently. The antidote may not work for them. Although I have some suspicions, but I would have to examine a body, preferably several."

"Excellent, but shut up now," Aytar demanded dryly. They left the arena outhouse and went out under the red sky. They clung to the wall of the nearest building. They listened and looked around. Gareth surveyed carefully the area behind the coign.

"It's clear. We're going."

They were a mile away from the armory. They decided to walk the distance so that the radiation and heat of the vehicle didn't lure the robots like an emitter. "Unless we have already been noticed," Gareth thought grimly.

They held on to the wall surrounding the generator pyramid, then stuck to the foot of the next building, avoiding open space.

When they reached the square and noticed several bodies of Kandrok members lying on the granite slabs, Andro, hungry for knowledge, decided to examine them closely. He judged by the condition of the closest one that the pale deceased with collapsing skin must have died the previous day - in agony, losing blood and dissolved organs through the body's openings.

Anna grimaced and put her hand to her nose.

"Disgusting."

"Idiot." Stellar mispronounced a harsher curse, staying many yards from the dead. "What if they didn't die from our super virus? We can also get infected with some filth and pop off!"

"Gareth witnessed Kandrok members' death in the medical center," replied Cortez, who pored over the corpse, pressing a piece of junk on its tissue. "Everything happened meters from him, they looked exactly like this one. The work of Maksimus Figam finished them one hundred percent, otherwise the batab would have also gotten sick."

"Cortez is probably right," Gareth confirmed. "The Kandrok members died literally several minutes after opening the container with the super virus, their health deteriorated almost immediately. They had no security, as if they had been viewing a collection of stones. They clearly didn't understand what they were dealing with. They got to examining our greatest discovery wrong."

"Why do they look like this?" Carbon nodded toward the corpse.

"This is how their bodies reacted to the super virus." Cortez moved the dead Kandrok member from belly to back. Anna looked away. "As you know, Maksimus Figam created it using the genetic materials of the most virulent viruses, and the worst of the whole bunch was the Martian Ebola, also artificially created by the way. It can kill in several minutes. In turn, a variant of the coronavirus spreads rapidly in the air, hence the rapid and great contagiousness among enemies, although it doesn't matter to Kiritians, because we cannot infect. Kandrok's environment lacks such pathogens, so they all died without being immune to them. And this means that we must have common genes with Kandrok, because the super virus would be indifferent to alien genotypes from space." He turned to face his impatient companions. "Damn ... It should be investigated, according to Ponomarjov's theory, pathogens from a given planet only harm developed creatures on the same planet, because they are evolutionarily related to them." He stroked his chin. "It seems we have a common ancestry with Kandrok, so distant that our genes have changed, but still, something remains ..."

"Cool, doc." Aytar grabbed the man's arm and pulled him so forcefully that he staggered. "We don't have time for lectures on astro-evolution. All the saved Kandrok members from the city have already probably traced us."

After a few steps, Cortez broke free from her.

"You don't understand anything!"

"Shut up, you're making too much noise." She looked at him with an icy glare. "You came out onto this square like a mouse into the middle of a room to cheese in a trap."

"If I'm right, here we have gotten the powerful weapon in the fight against Kandrok!"

"And this knowledge is about to die with us."

A hunch was right to order Gareth to look to the left. He noticed a combat robot far away in the block, which had come around the corner. The colossus was turned sideways to them.

"All to the gate," he hissed, pointing with his finger at the hiding place.

Aytar and Alejandro immediately stopped the quarrel. The group hurriedly entered the partially demolished staircase of a residential building. They froze in silence. Cortez was afraid to breathe. They heard the machine heading down the street towards them. The metal was hitting the ground louder and louder to the rhythm of the steps being taken heavily, the moving joints were hissing mechanically.

The guard stopped right outside their edifice, began to speak in a metallic bass that sounded like a report. Through a tiny hole in the wall, Anna could see its bowed back, on which were stuck six containers, three on each side. They could have been accumulators for weapons attached to the right arm, as they were connected to it by some wires.

"You think it has tracked us?" Carbon asked in a whisper as the sounds outside died away and the robot vanished. "If it had been so, it would have reacted violently," replied Gareth. "Maybe they are not interested in us, having bigger worries. Let's get out of here."

They decided to go down to the basements and move along their net. Forkis had ordered to build K'otz'ib'aja on the model of the ancient cities of techno lithic Onkalots, where all the dimensions of the objects, counted in meters, were a multiple of the number four. The buildings of the Immortals were impressive, monumental and durable thanks to the use of the toughest rocks and modern construction techniques. Therefore, the capital had been slightly damaged by the shelling of Kandrok's ships, and the heavy infantry transferred to the surface, but the nether regions, created with carving machines in solid rock, remained intact.

In the basement, they found the several-day remains of the corporal. He had a hole in the armor, savaged ribs and insides. Anna felt a sickening tightness in her stomach, even the toughest of them, Aytar, inhaled loudly. No one had had time to watch the damage during the attack. Then some of the

Immortals had fled into space, and the rest had been killed or caught. Sandstorm only now had a chance to see how powerful weapon the enemy had possessed; how easily it had coped with the biometal of Kiritian armor, which few small arms from the Zodiac Universum could have pierced. It was said that enemy weapons had been specially prepared against the Kiritians after the Erceses' reports.

Aytar closed the man's eyelids.

"We have to go." Gareth grabbed depressed Anna by the shoulders and gently pulled her away from the corpse.

"I have never even dreamed that one day I would hide in the basement of my own backyard," Carbon muttered walking at the end.

"What did you think that we would rule forever?" Stellar said. "Nobody has achieved it yet. Sooner or later, everything passes. Or changes."

"Which side are you on, philosopher?"

"Ours, but I'm saying what the situation is."

"Kandrok will beg us for mercy, you will see." They came to the surface after walking several hundred meters. The batab left first, keeping a finger on the trigger guard, and the stock at his hip. Using a gun scanner, he checked the intersection of the streets. He summoned the rest, waiting by the shaded wall.

If they had decided to walk across the great empty square, they would have gone straight to the arsenal, but Aytar, trusting the alleys and narrow streets, easily persuaded her companions to slip that way. They made the right choice, as some disturbing noise began to come from the side of the square. Again, they had to wait nervously and in hiding until the blissful silence returned.

They made it safely to the weapons warehouse. The dilapidated main gate led out into an open space and, according to Gareth, it was certainly being watched, so he directed the group towards the poorest of the entrances where waste had once been taken. It was shielded by extensive beeches.

Gareth went in first. As he led the group, he showed it another safe corridor. The lights came on automatically as they passed the threshold of the depot. The armory had been almost completely emptied, first by the Immortals, and later by Kandrok, which, after taking control of the capital, had readily reviewed the enemy's arsenal, but each of the refugees, apart from already armed Gareth, found something for themselves.

After what Anna had seen in the basement and through the bars of the prison, she had doubts about taking any weapon or armor.

"We could run to the hangar right away," she said. "If we meet Kandrok members, we'll be dead no matter what we put on. They pierce our biometal like a knife paper." Despite it, she was putting on armor elements.

Gareth, guarding the entrance, smiled slightly.

"It's always a good idea to have a weapon and something to protect your body with. Even with a stone and naked, you can knock down an enemy armored to the teeth.

"Right, weapons are essential," Andro confirmed. "But more important is the brain."

"I think I've heard that story somewhere," said Stellar, having almost completed the armament.

"David and Goliath, the Bible," suggested the batab.

Carbon snorted.

"And we're supposed to be naked, David? Really, the guy was fighting with the dick out?"

"Nudity is a metaphor," Gareth explained. "I've meant that we are weaker."

"What about food and water?" Aytar asked flatly, wanting to end the pointless chatter.

"Maybe we'll find something along the way, but every ship should have survivals on board." Gareth meant enteral energy pills that crew members used on long space travels in the event of food exhaustion or cryochamber failure.

"If we even find a working machine in the hangar," Anna muttered glumly.

They put biometal armor on their tightened uniforms, everywhere but the joints and neck. They put on shoes. Their heads were left without headwear because the helmet covers were nowhere to be found. Finally, they picked up their weapons: Stellar took the drilling gun, Sandstorm the Kalashnikov, Andro the plasma gun, Carbon was the only one who didn't want an energy weapon and settled for an old-fashioned bullet rifle and two sets of ammunition, which he hung on his torso. Aytar hoped to find her own personal armor, but when she found out that it was gone, she put together a new one without compartments for additional weapons.

Zira was the last to go to the side door. Gareth was surprised to see that she was carrying a bag full of weapons and ammunition on her back. He had ordered to put on light armor

- there was no heavier one anyway - so that they could move quickly.

"I know what I'm doing," she said coldly, as she passed the batab that was to guard the rear from now on.

They agreed that, if circumstances allowed, they would call by a barter grocery store they were supposed to pass along the way.

Gareth's weapon detector tracked down moving objects, and soon they heard conversations coming from behind the coign. When the batab glanced at the block, he saw three cyborgs discussing, each holding a gun. The immortals withdrew carefully and took a roundabout route to their chosen store. The door was locked. Aytar took an energy lancet from her bag and began to burn a circle in it while the others watched the area. A few minutes later they rifled the interior of the facility, drank water greedily, then gathered supplies in backpacks they found, also powdered food and the one in ampoules.

Going to the hangar, they moved along side streets according to the plan set in the store. On the way they passed the bodies of Kandrok members, eerily blending in with the backdrop of the sky red from Betelgeuse rays, the dead city, and distant volcanoes completing the image of a dystopia. From one of them after years of being dormant seeped smoke. Kandrok members hadn't turned off the air filtration systems in the capital, but carbon dioxide was above the norm, regardless.

The end of the route turned out to be the most difficult, because they had to walk through the open space, first in front of Utza'm Achij cave, then past scaffolding and collectors drawing energy from above the clouds. The group had to wait a quarter of an hour, lying next to a barricade created during the fights, because cyborgs together with a large robot were walking around the landing field and the boulevard and checking the dead. When they decided that nothing could be done, they left the bodies and moved on.

"I suggest walking along the outer wall of Utza'm Achij, up to the guardhouse surrounded by the barracks," Gareth announced as the boulevard was deserted. "Then we'll improvise. However, we still have to cross the square. In our position, it is the only way."

Nobody had a better idea, so the plan was accepted. To be sure, they waited a few minutes before moving on.

Snaking, they ran along the wall of Utza'm Achij. The moment they reached the guardhouse where the batab had once resided, his pulse rifle scanner detected several Kandrok members. The red dots on the mini screen stopped, then began to move quickly. And disappeared.

The Kiritians shifted questioning, concerned glances from the screen at each other.

"They know we're here," Aytar snapped.

"No shit," Alejandro interjected. He didn't add anything more when Zira gave him a dry look.

"Why can't we see them?" Anna asked Gareth.

"Maybe they turned on masking."

"But why? What can we do to them?"

"For example ..."

The cyborgs appeared from a completely different side - they cut off their access to the area with collectors.

The fugitives ran around the corner moments before a beam of unknown energy swept a part of the guardhouse wall.

"... to surprise a detected intruder."

"So, what do we do now?!" Cortez shouted.

"That's water under the bridge now. Carbon, Aytar, come on." Gareth sped up and jumped the two meters from the corner of the building to the broken granite block. The rubble touched a monument to an anonymous, armed achij. After making a quick roll, the batab knelt behind the pedestal and opened fire.

Each of the three cyborgs instantly activated the form of an energy shield in front of them, behind which they crouched.

"So much for the discreet crossing," Stellar said sarcastically. He, Anna and Cortez kept their weapons at the ready in the event of an attack from across the street.

"That's the best you can do, you canned asholes?!" Carbon began to shoot his rifle at the enemy from behind the rubble at the corner of the building, hoping that he would weaken their shields with an aggressive salvo. Shell-cases clattered around him.

Aytar rolled behind the rubble, taking the third position. She loaded the chamber of a small rocket launcher with an automatically guided missile, which, after being indicated the target, flew to it and caused an explosion within a radius of several meters. However, the Kandrok members being machine-gunned, safe behind their shields, retreated behind the two barracks, leaving the crossroads empty.

"Cease fire! Bullets and miglight don't do shit to them," chirped annoyed Gareth, in the second case talking about energy impulse rifle ammunition. "We have to break their shields somehow."

Something robotic, large and four-legged with the appearance of a bear, appeared at the end of the street overlooking the square with collectors. The creature directed its muzzle at the cyborg giving the command, got motionless briefly, snarled, then moved away, jumping. It vanished from sight of the Immortals.

From the side of the Kandrok members, who took advantage of the break in fire and leaned out from behind the coigns, a volley flew. Carbon, crawling, retreated around the corner, and Gareth with Aytar huddled as shards of the monument and wall began flying among the dust.

The woman grimaced, gritted her teeth with pain, and gripped the bottom of her calf with both hands. Gareth used the embankment of the newly formed rubble to crawl to her. Thanks to this, he avoided being crushed by the monument, which collapsed on the ground with a crash. Aytar was hit by a piece of rock in a place not protected by the armor plates; therefore, the Kiritians wore full heavy armament for an infantry battle.

Batab hovered over Aytar and covered her with his back to protect her from the rain of debris. Kandrok stopped firing, not seeing the target or considering it dead - the Kiritians had no opportunity to study the enemy's war technology, so they didn't know the power of their scanners.

"The artery is intact, it's a superficial wound," Gareth announced, having examined Zira's bruised, heavily bloodied leg with his hand. The sharpened boulder had torn the entire biometal plate off the calf. "Can you run?"

"I don't know, I'd have to get back on my feet."

"Carbon, barrage fire. We're leaving!"

The adrenaline-fueled senior private was very eager to resume the continuous fire as he outthrusted his rifle from around the corner. Forced to reactivate the shields, the cyborgs didn't attack the two, which this time had to cover the unprotected stretch to the building - the previous barrage ceased to exist. Once the companions were safe, Carbon retracted the barrel and leaned his back against the wall.

"Everybody's okay?" Gareth asked. Alejandro nodded slightly, mutely answering for the group. Aytar took a few lame steps, leaving droplets of blood behind her.

"It hurts when I touch the ground with my foot, but I will make it."

"Okay, we gotta beat our way somehow among a few buildings. Then we will use the collector base as a cover, running across the square from one building to the other. There is no other way. Kandrok cut us off from this side, and we won't be able to kill them."

"They certainly know that we are heading to the hangars," announced Anna.

Carbon wanted to comment, he opened his mouth slightly as he heard a clatter and scuffling coming from the end of the alley. The Kiritians looked in that direction. The creature sent around by Kandrok did resemble a giant bear, but it was not known whether it was an animal clad in armor, or an at least eight hundred-kilo robot was growling at them. Its body occupied almost the entire width of the street bordered by buildings.

The beast with completely white eyes opened its mouth, displaying silver tusks, each tapered like a fish's. It started running, lopsidedly at first, but as it picked up speed it became obvious that it intended to sweep the Kiritians out into the open, directly under the cyborg fire.

"Everyone, fire!" Gareth shouted.

Energy mixed with the spheres. Both ricocheted off the creature's armor or did minimal damage to it.

The enraged robot bear was rushing tirelessly ahead. Even exploding Aytar's grenades, which did more damage to the walls of the buildings, didn't stop it. Relentless heavy fire managed to at least tear the casing off the machine, but it kept closing the distance to the Kiritians.

Fifty meters.

Forty.

They didn't have much choice: either they would retreat and be swept away by the cyborgs who might have called for backup in the meantime, or the combat machine would get them before they could smash it.

Aytar threw away the grenade launcher and crouched next to the lying bag. She reached for the earlier rocket launcher and fired several loaded missiles, crouching.

The robot was making a long jump when it was hit by mini rockets. It was now a skeleton coated with sheets of molten metal, still rushing and dangerous. It got escaping Stellar that was closest to it and crushed him with its mass. The man didn't even feel any pain as he died. The rest of the retreating refugees were still shooting. The remains of the Kiritian and the robot that rolled over him like a tank mixed, falling to the ground in a bloody, glistening mass. Andro and Carbon were knocked off their feet, but only got battered.

Behind the coign, footsteps could be heard.

"There is nothing we can do anymore." Gareth stopped terrified Anna with a jerk of her free hand as she tried to help Stellar. The geneticist and the senior private got up from the street.

"Now we have a chance," Aytar announced.

"Come on." Alejandro pulled Anna with him. The corporal followed, having put the bag on her shoulder. She limped but gritted her teeth and kept pace with the others. Carbon and the batab ran at the end.

Kandrok went to see what happened to the robot. Meanwhile, the Kiritians encircled the guardhouse from the other side, left the barracks behind them, and fled, running out onto a square on three sides surrounded by the waters of a great lake. When they passed the first of the collectors with a diameter of fifty meters, they tried to run so that the colossus's foundation was behind them and protected from the city's Kandrok.

At the base of the second collector there was a control room, a combat robot emerged from it, from which the Immortals had previously escaped to the nether regions.

Carbon had been agitated as if on drugs since the shooting, and Stellar's death shocked him even more. Instinctively, without an order, he opened fire on the robot. The latter immediately activated the energy shield with a mechanism attached to its forearm. All the bullets ricocheted.

Aytar brutally dragged the senior private with her. Out of breath from running, the Immortals hid on the other side of the collector's base.

The Kandrok member deactivated the shield, raised its right arm partially transformed into a rotating mitrailleuse, straddled for better stability, and launched a volley hitting the collector. Although the targets were hidden, the intensity of the fire continued, the energy bit into the protective wrapper, straining it more and more.

There was a rumble in the light of the collector as if hundreds of dung chen trumpets sounded loudly along the entire length. The pipe, weakened by the air ride of Kandrok from a few months earlier, groaned spookily, the screeching noise seemed to drill the skull. The earth shook.

"Come on ..." Gareth and the rest of his companions looked skyward, from where the collector emerged like a giant lamprey.

"We're getting the hell out of here!" Cortez's scream turned out to be unnecessary, as he was the last person to detach from the wrapper.

The colossal pipe began to bop like a whirlwind, then its base broke, destabilizing the entire structure. The upper parts of the collector collapsed, crushing the lower ones. Fragments of the spans and flexible metal flew down.

The Kiritians were running towards the pier.

The noise was unbearable as the collector began to tilt. Several seconds later it hit the pavement, breaking the sidewalk slabs, creating a deep ditch. Visibility decreased as if volcanic ash had spread above the ground.

The escaping fell over near the fountain, got behind the casing and, huddled, waited out the raid of flying debris.

The fallen pipe separated the robot from them, but the machine, blackened with dust, passed to the other side, using one of the many cracks. The poor fountain was no obstacle to the re-raised mitrailleuse.

The ancient capital of Kiritians was pierced by the sound of a siren. The robot lowered the barrel, and raised its head, looked around the sky. It growled dissatisfied and quickly backed away.

The Kiritians rose from their crouch. Puzzled, Anna looked at Gareth, but he just shrugged, shaking his head. He flexed his muscles and raised his weapon, seeing far away a group of Kandroks running - not towards them, but towards the city.

"Anyone understand any of this?" Carbon brushed off his armor. "What are they playing that sound for?"

"It's rather nothing good," Aytar said sharply. "We were sitting ducks and they let it go."

Alejandro stopped fighting the particles in his eyes and began to lead them over the gaps between the clouds. The sky some time earlier turned black-blue and was crisscrossed by red streaks, as if it had been scratched by a heavenly being.

"Something is flying there." Anna drew the attention of the rest to the point moving above the clouds. "Falling star?"

Gareth, with a slight thrust, directed Cortez towards the pier.

"It doesn't matter. We have the chance. Quickly!"

They bypassed the temple of all gods, decorated in an austere, monumental techno lithic style, where once every Kiritian could contemplate any faith, using gardens, gazebos, and caves. Behind the wall separating the facility from the military area, they crossed an open space. The gate to the hangar turned out to be ajar. In the middle of the dark hall, they noticed a Kandrok member fighting the pathogen. The not-robotic man was on his knees, doubled up, vomiting blood and semi-liquid flesh. Aytar in no time cut short his suffering by piercing his throat with a knife taken from the top of her shoe.

"Let's look for a transportation, something fast and with thick armor," Sandstorm gave the guidelines. She ran to the control room, where she switched on most of the lights and opened the bulkhead in the ceiling.

As in the arsenal, also in the hangar little of its former contents remained. The best ships and naval craft were missing. There were a few light fighters with places for one or two pilots, transporters with disassembled weapons, a damaged corvette, also a defective gunboat and an armored recycler commonly known as a garbage truck. Sandstorm searched in vain for her White, a white fighter with the designation XRS-14 Ghost, endowed with the AI, first in a digital directory of the control room, then scouring the hall by herself.

From the outside, a monotonous siren whine was coming incessantly. Through a gap in the ceiling, the Kiritians saw an object oblong like a cigar move across the sky, illuminating the early night with increasing intensity. They looked at each other meaningfully, with gloomy expressions.

"We'd better hurry up," Aytar ground out.

With little choice, they decided to take the best option available: the recycler hauling garbage from outer space. It lacked combat weapons, but it fired powerful neutron beams that could break the toughest materials, and it was also equipped with the thickest armor used in space aviation, right behind astro-carriers[10] and delegate ships. Anna activated the

[10] A space transport unit for smaller ships and naval craft, and at the same time an independent combat unit with a huge firepower.

cockpit control panel, bringing it to life with a blaze of yellow, blue and green lights, then diagnosed the machine. The problem may have been the low fuel and low energy levels in the batteries, enough to jump from the planet in the first case, and then barely one subspace jump on the energy vapors. But if they could get far enough from the Morascrik, they would in peace extend the panels and absorb any scattered cosmic energy to power the batteries for the next jumps.

The batab entered the cockpit, stopped behind the chair's headrest, and leaned his hands on it.

"We checked several machines. There are empty fuel tanks and uncharged batteries everywhere. We'll have to take the recycler into the orbit with what we have."

"It should work," Sandstorm replied without turning around.

"Can you fly this?"

"Sure." She turned on the scanners. She froze, as did Gareth, seeing several Kandrok members leaving the planet in a hurry. Their machines had a simple, geometric shape. They were ugly, angular and irregular, basically looking like pieces of battered brick or badly mined, dressed rock.

Sandstorm located a 'comet' in orbit. As expected, it turned out to be interplanetary missile, perhaps launched from an enemy ship. It crossed her mind that Kandrok had apparently learned to use the siren's signal for its intended purpose. Now it became obvious why they hadn't killed them in the square then - obeying the orders of their commanders, they retreated to hasten the evacuation.

"Not good. Start the engines, be ready to take off." Gareth exited the cockpit, running.

Over the lowered gangway, Aytar and Carbon were hurriedly loading the cryogenic chambers placed on technical carts. Gareth rushed to their aid.

"They're shooting at us from space," he said, struggling to control his nerves.

"A hundred years we'll be flying anywhere in this garbage truck," Carbon grunted as they dragged the last cargo aboard. "It's subspace drive is an old and poor version. It is not suitable for fast, long flights."

"If you have a better idea, I'm listening," Aytar said dryly.

"We have damn thick armor," the batab eased the situation. "It's not that bad with drives, you can chase space debris with the recycler."

"And what good would that do if we don't know where to go and what's going on outside of Morascrik?" Carbon continued. "Not to mention the fact that Kandrok can wipe us out with merely a shot."

"You really are not helping us by airing your bitter grievances," the woman replied. "Even Cortez could shut up."

She looked for him. The three eloquent glances met.

"Where is he?" Gareth asked.

"He was standing outside by the chambers!" Carbon stepped onto the gangplank. He noticed the geneticist's plasma gun on the floor.

The batab sighed briefly.

"Earlier, Andro said something about taking Kandrok members' bodies. I hope he didn't ..."

"God, protect such people from me, or they will suffer, and I will be responsible for criminal acts." Aytar wanted to leave the machine in a hurry but cringed and grunted in pain.

A shock of unknown origin, as if the rest of the sky-high collectors had collapsed at once, rolled through the hangar. Almost all the lights went out, part of the structure collapsed, banging away terribly at the recycler's armor. The Kiritians lost their balance and fell down. Aytar groaned as she overloaded her injured leg. Gareth wrapped his arms around her waist and helped her to her feet.

"Carbon, can you go for that asshole?" He said. "Just be careful."

The private nodded and ran down the gangplank, holding his rifle with its flashlight on.

As he passed the pyramid of crates, it seemed to him that he heard steps being taken lightly. Soon he noticed Cortez pushing in front of him a levitating anti-gravity disk with a capacity of up to half a ton. With its sides glowing blue, it resembled a deep-sea jellyfish.

"Look what I found!" Andro exclaimed happily.

Carbon tapped his fingers against his forehead.

"What are you doing, dumbhead? We're flying away! The hangar is collapsing!"

"I have to take the killed Kandrok member. It may prove to be very important."

The private didn't have time to protest, as Cortez immediately trotted towards the body, pushing in front of him a conveyor hovering one meter above the ground. Binding under his breath, Carbon raced after him. He decided to help him, because that's the only way they would get out of here the fastest.

They loaded the body onto the disk, then headed for the recycler.

In front of them, an organic, unarmored Kandrok member grew up in a deplorable, pre-mortem condition. The robotic companions fleeing the planet had left him to be lost. He had chemical weapons whose macabre property of turning a human into a skeleton the Kiritians had experienced several times before.

Kandrok aimed at Carbon holding the rifle first, considering the unarmed geneticist to be less of a threat.

They fired simultaneously. And they killed each other at the same time. The lightly armored skeleton fell on one side, and the bullet-riddled body on the other. Cortez was stunned. He stood paralyzed, fearing that he would be the next target of another enemy lurking somewhere nearby. He jumped up and groaned as he felt Anna's hand on his shoulder, and on the other - Gareth's.

The three of them in a hurry got on board the recycler. Aytar, sitting in the cockpit, with her leg already covered, hid the gangway and slammed the airlock. Sandstorm immediately rushed to the bridge to ignite the faintly panting drives.

Gritting her teeth in barely controlled anger, Zira walked stiffly down the corridor from the cockpit to the hangar, where she got Cortez. She slammed him against the wall and held the knife to his throat.

"Aytar, stop it. He is not our enemy!" Gareth thundered. "This is not our enemy," he added more calmly, articulating the last two words. He put a hand on the shoulder of the former assassin. He was a batab, once a city warden, not a soldier like Aytar, so he couldn't give her the order.

"Calm down, it's okay. Alejandro acted stupid ..."

"Stupid? Because of that fool, the young man is dead," she ground out. "It is I who sent Carbon to Andro. So, I am to blame for his death."

"No." Zira shook her head, staring at the panting and sweating geneticist. "We wouldn't have lost another human if that jerk hadn't gone there. Frigging scientists ..."

"And now we'll lose one more if you don't let go. Kandrok will turn out to be unnecessary." Gareth gently grasped her forearm, began to slide his hand down until he touched the knife. "Give it to me. Enough."

The woman spread her fingers and Gareth took the knife from her. Instead of venting her gall on Cortez, she pushed the disc with the Kandrok member's body and passed through the bulkhead to the second deck.

Looking at the blade in the batab's hand, Alejandro rubbed his grazed throat and moved away from the wall.

"Thanks, man," he whispered, looking at the smudged blood on the pads.

Gareth punched him in the face, so strongly that more blood was shed, this time from his nose.

"You're welcome."

***

Aytar hurriedly took her seat next to Anna as co-pilot, while Gareth and Andro, fighting gravity, secured the enemy's body in a cryogenic chamber intended for Carbon.

With rocket propulsion, they pulled the garbage truck out of the thick atmosphere, using up all the fuel. As they reached its outer layer, slowly turning on the subspace drive, a supernova of Kandrok kinetic attack exploded.

The Kiritians managed to escape at the last moment.

Nevertheless, the shockwave broke into the generated tunnel and swept away the recycler like a hurricane a butterfly.

XII. Journey to the B9

Seven warriors accoutered in purple robes surrounded Corporal Tsar Seymour and his charge, Senior Private Darius Schindler. The former stood still, alert and ready, holding curved sabers in front of them. The desert wind tossed the fragments of fabric sticking out of their black tagelmusts. The dark eyes - only so much of the body the desert warriors revealed to their opponents - were filled with a lust for murder. Two had fallen dead under the Kiritian blades a moment earlier. Their robes and arterial blood merged coloristically, which gave the effect of huge red puddles lingering on the sand.

Seymour was panting and dripping with sweat that soaked into the fabric of his flexible combat uniform. Unlike Darius trying to focus, waiting for his opponent to move, the corporal's face was twisted by an amused smile. He waved his saber obstreperously. The Kiritians had shortness of breath less from the fight than from the fire raging a few paces behind the warriors' backs. These two circles of obstacles seemed difficult to overcome.

"Which one now?" The corporal asked with amusement. He started swinging his weapon, making weird figures and whistling.

"It's not funny, Tsar." Even though the two achijes were separated by age and experience among the Kiritians, sometimes they treated themselves as friends gibing each other, even brothers. Darius grimaced in pain, but he didn't dare to bend down and focus on his cut, bloody calf, then he would certainly have been attacked.

"Of course, it is. It's all for fun. Cheer up."

One of the warriors let himself be provoked by Seymour and lunged forward with a fighting cry. Driven by aggression and hatred, he put a lot of effort into a cut made in an arc from behind his back, but it was performed sluggishly. Prepared Tsar easily countered it, he rushed himself forward, switching from defense to attack, and after a short exchange of blows he beheaded the exposed opponent.

"You've screwed it more than God a snail," he said cheerfully to the falling corpse.

Six yelling warriors threw themselves on the Kiritians. Tsar and Darius stood back-to-back.

Five years had passed since Viktor Shane gave Darius to the corporal for training, so there had been enough time for the achijes to trust each other and learn to act as one organism without uttering words. Especially since they became friends.

"If it were for real it wouldn't be that easy for you." Schindler, with a clatter of steel, parried the first strike, then the second and third, each made at a different height, at a different angle. In a way, with these words, he wanted to validate himself, seeing that, unlike him, Tsar hadn't been hurt. Darius was doing a little worse, he was ashamed of it.

"But it's not happening," Seymour laughed, defensively fending off his opponents. The latter were conveniently fighting, using the 'worker's' method: while one was hitting, the rest was watching how he was doing. "Just have fun."

"You can't do otherwise. You treat everything as fun."

"You are absolutely right. On this occasion you won parsley. Are you proud of yourself?"

"You cannot dream of a better reward!"

The blades danced, fire reflections flashed on the metal, sand slipped from under their boots. The desert warriors outnumbered the Kiritians but were inferior in skill to them. They reacted with rage to Seymour's laughter, his provocative words, or other forms of taunts, thus reducing the quality of the fight.

After a few minutes, all the warriors lay gutted or decapitated.

The corporal was panting, wiped the sweat from his brow, leaned over, and rested his hands on his knees. With eyes with dilated pupils, he looked at his macabre work.

"I have that black belt in Kama Sutra." He plunged the blade into the sand.

Tsar came out of the fight without a scratch, the senior private had a lot of cuts, a long scar on his wrist and was stubbed in the shoulder.

"Why don't you go to the doctor?" Seymour suggested.

"I will endure," Darius replied boldly, amped with adrenaline. "I don't feel pain."

Tsar grinned at him.

"So, what did you say at the beginning? That the 20D medium mode is for suckers? Then watch this."

Schindler suppressed a moan. The corporal made a few quick movements with his fingers at the controller attached to his belt. The fire was gone, only the corpses were disrupting the monotony of the endless desert and the dark gray evening sky.

A hill materialized in front of them, which got filled with dozens of black and purple-clad soldiers.

Darius eyed up his new foe with apparent indifference.

"I think you tripped out a bit. Show off that black belt of yours then."

"Don't choke. Here you are, for encouragement." Tsar grabbed Darius' hand and poured a pinch of white powder on it from a miniature tube. When Schindler had joined Kiritians, he had been hostile to drugs and anything that blunted the mind, but years with Seymour had crushed his stone code of rules, developed on the wild planet H14, where vigilance had been constantly required. Tsar had laughed at the boy for being boring and sanctimonious like Zira Aytar, one of their missing achijes. It had turned out that Seymour had not only consumed high-end drugs but had also selected those that hadn't damaged the body, and even supported the work of the brain. At least that was the case with Seymour himself, who could make endless combinations of natural and synthetic substances. Being in his company had changed Darius. After the death of his parents, he had been often tense, aggressive and rebellious about everything, under the influence of Tsar he had become more relaxed and detached from many things, although he still hadn't been able to control his anger.

They both took the drug.

In the accompaniment of the collective "Aaaaaah!" warriors began to run down the hill, dragging a sandstorm with them. They waved their sabers or held them over their heads, preparing in advance to kill the enemy.

Tsar pulled his cold steel from the sand, spun it.

"It was a really bad idea," said Schindler, commenting both on the raising of the sparring level and his own thoughtless words at the beginning that training would be boring and easy. The powder was starting to work because the boy's insecurity was fading away, and the sight of enemies rushing at them became more and more amusing.

"Relax, they are not strong enough to get our economy out of the crisis."

They stood and waited impatiently as the enemy sped on. It was getting closer. The first warriors reached them. Each attacked differently to confuse the Kiritians. The pounding of his heart and the hum of blood in Darius' ears drowned out the tumult of his surroundings. And suddenly everything was gone, including the weapons of both achijes. Just when Seymour was about to cut his opponent with the saber held with both hands after a counterattack.

They stood in a large, sterile underground hall of the Cargoo complex, illuminated by bright lights. Deactivated atoplaxal particles scattered over it like real sand. It was they which a moment earlier had created the desert environment and warriors from two thousand years earlier. They gave the holographic projections a physical form, so session participants could be injured or even killed, depending on the training or entertainment program turned on. The particles were completely unlike their other form - hyper-heavy flecks, which in the form of a sphere wrapped in a separate, autonomous environmental bubble were used during space travel to generate artificial gravity on large ships and naval craft.

The door to the hall crack opened and the figure of the technician Corporal Rasmus Darkoris appeared.

"You've ruined all our fun," Seymour said with a mock reproach as he raised and lowered his hands.

"Your communicators are turned off. General Biffter wants to see you," the technician said seriously, then withdrew.

A few years after the Kandrok attack, the Immortals had decided not to use political titles, groundless and useless for a nation deprived of its home planet, so Necron used the military rank. Although the achijes had long persuaded him to at least take the position of chief general, it hadn't been easy for him. Out of habit, as well as believing in the return of the old power of Kititians, his subordinates had often called him emperor, much to Biffter's irritation, which he had eventually ceased to show, knowing that admonishing those who believed in him was like talking to a brick wall. Anyway, they had been right - he had been responsible for them.

Seymour and Darius looked at each other, then headed for the exit of the room.

In the corridor, Darkoris barred Schindler's path and firmly pointed to the right-hand embranchment.

"Go and patch yourself in the medical center."

"The general wants to see both of us."

"I'll explain your delay. Now get out."

Schindler didn't object, he really couldn't go and show himself to the commander-in-chief in his bleeding-limping state. So, he moved in the direction indicated; molecular glue would quickly close the wounds formed during training.

Seymour followed Darkoris down the underground corridor to the command center.

On the spot Rasmus left him, Tsar entered the room in a shape like a half of an egg cut lengthwise. Rebuilding mine complexes and abandoned opposition installations for the Kiritians resulted in still unremoved rock and earth piles by the walls. Seymour noticed them first.

"Hello, emperor." As usual, good humor didn't leave him.

Kiret turned away from the group of achijes sitting and working at kapripods. It didn't surprise him that the corporal standing in front of him looked at the world as usual with dilated pupils. Currently, the general didn't care about it, in the past he would have accused him of breaking the regulations as well as health and safety rules, and then he would have imposed a penalty for taking drugs on duty. Apart from his stupid lines and his sometimes-irritating body language, Seymour didn't hurt anyone in any way. Being on drugs, he functioned like any other achij, even better. You just had to get used to his way of being.

"Where's Schindler?" Necron glanced at the door.

"He's patching himself in the stretcher-bearers' facility. He should be here soon."

"Corporal, go to the auditorium next door and take your seat there."

"What's going on, sir?"

"There will be an expedition. You will find out everything in the room."

Seymour didn't have to go far. In the past, the room had belonged to the rebels, trainings had taken place there, so it had the appearance of a classic lecture hall, with the half-rings of the chairs pointing towards a rostrum located at the lowest point. Presentations or three-dimensional projections had been displayed next to it. There was no point in rebuilding the facility that fulfilled its function, so new users had only replaced the lighting with more convenient one.

Tsar started to descend to the front row where four people were seated. He recognized pale, beefy Private Kazuo Shimizu and Private Nexon Walker with those blonde braids on his chin. Both achijes belonged to Corporal Darkoris' team. He didn't know the other two. Recently, the Kiritians had adopted a strategy of mixing their people. It consisted in the fact that when the mission was nearing, achijes from various units who were not currently burdened with work were gathered for the task. In this way, the squad commander could get Kiritians he hadn't dealt with before. After Kandrok's attack, with many standing units decimated or completely destroyed, the formation of mixed troops became common. And a squad would be formed, Seymour had no doubts, since Kiret had mentioned some expedition.

"Hi, guys," he said, raising his hand. The three men with the lower ranks greeted him, using the title 'Corporal'. However, they didn't get up or salute. The fourth said a casual "good morning". The military standards of the Kiritians remained unchanged and were still based on friendship and trust, and each achij could talk to the other without fear of breaking any point of the rules. Centuries ago, the orthodox regime on the commander-subordinate line was abandoned, the ranks were only supposed to work during the action, when orders were flowing, and every Immortal was required to know the place and role in the row. The subordination applied only when achijes with low and high ranks met officially.

Seymour sat down next to the rest. Before he could ask if they knew anything about the task, the door opened and Captain Victor Shane and General Kiret Biffter entered.

"Oh, it's going to be something damn important," whispered Tsar.

"Don't get up," said Kiret as he descended, and made a sweeping gesture with his hand, as if chasing away a fly. A moment later, he took his place in the chair behind the projection table.

Shane stopped beside him, slightly straddling, folded his hands on the seat, and turned to the Kiritians:

"Welcome, gentlemen, to the briefing. There were supposed to be eight of us in the room, but I received information from the medical center," here he glanced scoldingly at Seymour, who pouted, lifted and lowered his shoulders helplessly," that Private Darius Schindler had to wait sometime after the regeneration procedure, so the recording of the meeting will be sent to his PDA."

Viktor moved a bit aside, dimmed the lights, and turned on the projector. Above the tabletop appeared a three-dimensional steel-brown planet with a diameter of one meter, and two moons, white and red, orbiting it.

"Our destination is the terraformed planet B9 from the Pisces Universe. Naturally terrestrial, like all colonized by humanity. The snag was that B9 needed to be treated twice as it became depopulated after the global catastrophe involving the asteroid. Fortunately, no one was killed because the exodus had taken place long before the collision. Earlier, scientific institutions of various specializations had operated there. Later, some people returned to it, but the globe didn't regain its former glory. The target of our mission is Dr. Maksimus Figam, who settled on B9 after the planetary catastrophe. As you probably know, he voluntarily ceased to be a Kiritian because he was no longer mentally coping with the burden of immortality. At the beginning, when he left us, he stayed on Calcaris in the Libra Universe, then flew to B9 to be part of the scientists' resettlement campaign. We'll try to get the doctor to join us again, at least for a while. His skills and knowledge could prove invaluable to the Kiritians in such difficult times. Unfortunately, we haven't had contact with the planet B9 since Kandrok's attack, and flights into those sectors became dangerous. Now, however, the situation has changed a bit, because, according to intelligence reports, enemy units have shifted to our advantage." The holographic image of the planet was replaced by the images of two machines: grayish, angular, in the shape of broken rectangular blocks.

Seymour leaned forward.

"And what are these monsters?"

"Hybrid test ships Aural 1 and Aural 2, Corporal," Viktor explained, pointing to the projection. "So far without artificial intelligence but equipped with an autopilot in case of a crew indisposition. They were built, as you can see, to resemble Kandrok's flying machines, but from Kiritian materials. They have basic drives, but masking and weapons are completely new. This technology has been developed by our scientists in recent years, during intensive research, which, for obvious reasons, required acceleration. The large concentration of atoplaxal particles in the chamber above the engine room forms a hyper-heavy mass with a circumference of just a fist, which creates artificial gravity on board. Of course, the molecules traditionally find themselves in a bubble of an extra-dimensional nature, otherwise the machines would have to be as massive as some moon. The objectives of the upcoming mission will be basically two: find and bring Figam to Cargoo and see how Kandrok will react to the presence of ships nearby, and it shouldn't react. We recently released unmanned aerial vehicles into areas of enemy activity and, undetected, they returned safely to the place of departure. This would prove that Kandrok is unable to spot our new inventions, in this case a form of masking based on cutting edge technology. This flight is to prove the truth of the theory floated."

"Is it possible, Captain," Walker took the floor, "that the enemy saw the probes, took it for its, and therefore didn't react? As long as they were modeled on their infiltrators."

"Yes, they were modeled," Shane replied. "But I don't suppose they were detected. Kandrok members certainly, like us, use passwords, call signs, or access codes, so they would have been immediately interested in supposedly their machines that were flying and not responding. In our case, as we don't mark with numbers or names hulls of ships and naval craft, there are also specifiers installed under the armor, thanks to which we know the identity of the unit and the personal details of the pilot who flies it. Kandrok apparently doesn't use such a method. The manned mission with humans is to confirm that our reasoning is correct." The captain turned to Necron, the latter nodded.

"Just in case," Viktor continued the briefing, "two machines will be sent, but not more, so as not to incur possible losses in people, materials and gold."

Tsar briefly spread his arms in frustration.

"Thanks!"

"The team will look like this." The captain gestured to a Kiritian unknown to Seymour, with his arms folded across his chest. "The pilot of smaller Aural 1 will be Lieutenant Aurelius, with the team on board: Corporal Seymour and Senior Private Schindler. Aural 2 will be flown by me, with the team on board: Private Shimizu, Private Walker and Private Evasiv." Finally, Shane nodded to another person the corporal didn't associate.

"Quite a strange crew," commented Tsar, with absolute honesty typical of him. "A statutory squad dead straight."

"I chose the available achijes, Corporal. If the information from our informants is still up to date, we will pass Kandrok on the way to B9, thus inertly completing half of the task. We'll pass them unnoticed, at least I hope so. After landing on planet B9, Lieutenant Aurelius and I will remain on board, as trained to fly the new machines we must not put ourselves at risk. You, Corporal Seymour, take the rest of the achijes, pick up Figam, come back and we leave."

"What if the doc doesn't want to come with us?" Tsar muttered.

"I believe in your ability to persuade." Viktor smiled slightly.

"And if we don't catch him in?"

"Then we come back without him. We could live with that. Our young scientist Sariel Jelinek, a rising star, may be able to come up with something effective to fight Kandrok."

Seated with his arms resting on the armrests of the chair, Necron said:

"You are to do nothing else. No poking around on the planet. No playing heroes or provoking Kandrok. The target is solely Figam's mansion. Nevertheless, I count on your flexibility in case things get complicated."

Shimizu became concerned, he shifted his gaze from the former emperor to Viktor. "For example, sir?"

"For example," Seymour grinned at him, "that our friends making bumpkinish ships are having a party on B9. If they see us, they'll thump us like a storm a little tree." He began to whistle and move his hands, simulating two trunks being tossed by the wind.

"Seymour, can you shut up kindly?" Aurelius growled.

The corporal put his hands down on his belly and whispered under his breath:

"I have a feeling that we probably won't like each other."

"Are you done girls?" Viktor interrupted the exchange of views. "Corporal Seymour is quite right. Kandrok may have occupied planet B9 or cause disturbance in its vicinity, hence the communication vacuum. They have recently started mining heavy metals on rocky globes as if they were gearing up for something serious. The informants are unable to fly beyond the enemy's activity area. We must be ready for anything, even to interrupt the mission, so as not to endanger the crew. But if we can get Dr. Figam back, he will surely help us invent some clever biological weapon. He is an amazing man. He gave us immortality, so if we help him with his work and provide the necessary resources, we will sort out also with Kandrok. They would be useful for examining their bodies, but mostly they take or destroy their fallen." Shane turned off the projector and turned on the lights. "That's it for now, you'll get the details soon. We're departing tomorrow evening. You can scatter."

***

Contrary to Shane's fears that the enemy would track them down, the journey to B9 turned out to be monotonous and boring. The flight was supposed to last two weeks, so cryosn was abandoned, and the captain also forbidden the use of sleeping pills and tranquilizers. No more than one person could rest on the ship at any given time. Despite the relative calmness, the commander of the expedition required vigilance so that in the event of an emergency the crew was fully operational and aware.

"Fat chance." Lying on a sliding bed, Tsar flicked a fly, which he had been watching for several minutes as it was tramping on his arm resting on his knee. Well, he almost flicked. The annoying insect, no matter how quickly the person reacted, always managed to spread its wings and escape from the huge, killer hand. Usually, it then sat back on the victim's body, in the exact same place, as if amused by the awkwardness of this supposedly intelligent being.

His sleep time had just run out, and Seymour left the porthole and headed for Aural 1's bridge. The cockpit cover was constructed in accordance with the Kandrok standard so that it was possible to freely see the surroundings, while the outside observer saw an armored facet similar to sanded rock. Lieutenant Aurelius was at the controls. Darius sat next to him learning to fly.

"Look, asteroids!" He said delightedly. He had spent several years on Cargoo, training to be achij with the Kiritians. So, he enjoyed everything that was ignored by his long-lived companions, who repeatedly made interplanetary journeys.

Seymour stepped between the men and rested his arms on the headrests. He looked out into space but found the same colorless sight as usual. Some of the celestial bodies seen earlier had disappeared, and others had taken their place.

"And officer?"

"No outgoing or incoming signals. Complete silence," replied the lieutenant matter-of-factly. You will replace Schindler right away. At present speed, we should see the planet in seven Terran hours ..." He choked on air. Disturbing readings appeared before him. Amazed, Darius unbuckled his seat belt and leaned out of his chair to see the details better.

The crew heard the sharp voice of Captain Shane flying with the three crewmen several kilometers away on board Aural 2:

"Lieutenant Aurelius, can you see this in front of us?"

"Yes. I was hoping it was a measurement error," the officer replied grimly. He turned to Darius without taking his eyes off the screen, "They're not asteroids, young Schindler. If we encountered their belt, they would be hundreds of kilometers away from each other, or else the rocks would be drawn together by gravity."

Seymour removed his hands from the seats and slowly straightened, peering through the canopy.

"Kandrok," he ground out that awful word first.

"We're cutting off contact until we're safe," Viktor announced through the communicator. "We're keeping all covers one hundred percent as before. Turn off Aural 1's engines, we're shifting to the drift. Shane, over and out."

Darius, with his heart pounding hard, slumped into the armchair, fastened his seatbelt with trembling hands. Aurelius obeyed the captain's orders and deactivated the impulse drive, which was still operating at ten percent of maximum power - after setting Aural 1 in motion with an impulse, undisturbed by any external force, it could fly indefinitely.

The first Kandrok's machines the size of Egyptian pyramids emerged from the darkness. The Kiritians couldn't tell what genus they belonged to, because they were crude lumps made up of hundreds of smaller ones. The crew froze as more giants began to emerge from the blackness. Even Seymour looked silently through the ceiling porthole as they passed over Aurals like whales over krill. Soon an armada of gigantic, large, medium, and small lumps flew over them, tugging the braids of drives mostly of red colors. In terms of shape, rarely any machine was like any other, just like fragments of shattered rock seen in the mountains. Despite the captain's order to minimize the activity, both hybrid ships had to slightly deviate from their course to avoid colliding with one of the objects. Seymour counted over two hundred hostile units. Each was lightly lit, for what would have such a flotilla feared in space? He also noticed markings made of variously painted or cut lines on the metal.

"They can't see us," Darius whispered.

"It seems so," replied the lieutenant.

"I wonder where the bastards are going so slowly." Tsar continued to stare at the ceiling.

Aurelius took a risk and calculated the flotilla's trajectory by touching the screen in front of him.

"I don't know. But if they don't stray from their course, they would not reach any orbit of the colonized planet."

"Is it possible that they are leaving the Zodiac Universum?" Schindler asked hopefully.

"I would really, honestly like this, boy."

"Darn, look at their armor." Tsar laughed nervously. "No wonder we couldn't do anything to them during the Battle of Morascrik."

"And we still haven't invented a weapon to crush it," the lieutenant remarked.

The last Kandrok machine vanished from their sight a board hour later. Viktor waited another quarter of an hour and resumed communication.

"For security reasons, we have to choose a different return route," he announced. "We will fly along a parabola with respect to the current one, after jumping from the B9 atmosphere."

"Reasonable move," agreed the lieutenant. "I thought about it myself. It will be longer but safer."

Shane smiled.

"Looks like half the mission is over. Successful: Kandrok didn't detect our 'Aurals'."

"So, what now? Mass production and going to war?" Seymour said carelessly, once again standing between the pilots' seats. The lieutenant gave him an oblique look, and Darius a cheerful smile.

***

Thino'pai was almost motionless in his command post, from time to time he moved his hand or head, contemplating the cosmos. He fell into a slight lethargy, had long not seen the strong source of cosmic light which the religion and philosophy of his people orbited. No pulsar flashed in sight, no star exploded, and Betelgeuse illuminating the planet that had been overrun by devoka in the past was too small and had too low power by the standards of Kandrok, who worshiped powerful, pure and all-encompassing light. At least the size of the star VY Canis Majoris, as devoka called the hyper-giant discovered by Kandrok.

The invaders named devoka people from the Zodiac Universum and the RC Galaxy, the latter, still using as puppets. Among the soldiers of Kandrok, there was a division into combat ranks, like military ranks among achijes. Thino'pai was a xepo, meaning a high commander, a fighter of level eight of ten. He had power over several squadrons or a battalion in space if he were on the surface of the planet with conditions suitable for hostilities. Above xepo was troh, the commander of the fleet. Lyyh was the highest, just below the king or queen (that position was called gerha), for absolute power always belonged to the unit controlling the semi-autonomous super-collectivity Kandrok. Lyyh had commanders of all fleets in his unit, coordinated the war. Thino'pai dreamed that he would get this rank someday. Kandrok was already over eight hundred years old, according to the calendar of the royal planet Asephor 'Cerotis, and long ago he had gotten rid of the body, even the longest-lasting brain, to become the Liberated. A complete machine, but with orhada received from the Lightbringer at birth. Thino'pai had become resistant to adverse factors, which would have been unthinkable in an organic form. For example, now, for many nirs corresponding to human hours, he had stayed at the post feeling no fatigue and no pain.

To stop meditating, prompted him one of the bridge crew members, a young and organic Kandrok, a fourth degree umen.

"I have very strange readings," he told his commander. "Recently, undefined turbulence has passed under our afferis, as if there was a small object or a group of objects there."

Thino'pai turned the metal face towards the umen.

"Is that something worth your attention?"

"I don't know. However, it is certain that it has already moved away. Maybe it escaped from our afferis. It was heading very slowly towards planet B9, as devoka call it."

Xepo tapped a finger on a diarduk mask that hid his face from chin to eyes.

"There is nothing of value on B9 anymore," he said. "We took the necessary elements and metals from there, killed all the devok members we met so that their processed blood and bodies powered our demo. In such a case, who would like to go to the exploited planet?"

"Maybe it's a devoka-scout from outside?"

"Can I say something, xepo?" Another umen broke in, with a cybernetic right hand.

"Speak," Thino'pai ordered.

"If it was devoka, we would spot it easily. They use very primitive equipment. Maybe it's space rock or the remains of a machine?"

"What's the harm to check it, dear varoth?" Thino'pai asked, making a mighty hand gesture towards the breastbone plate of his armor. "We're not in a hurry to get anywhere. Send out a small but quick demo for scouting so that it can easily catch up with our affairs afterwards. Let's explore these unruly rocks of yours."

XIII. Maksimus Figam

The B9 consisted of barren landscapes, mostly rocky-steppe landscapes interspersed with salty seas and lakes. The crew of Aural, flying one kilometer above the ground, was surprised by the enormity of the damage to the landscape. It had been caused by an unknown, great physical force acting in many parts of the planet. The Kiritians quickly recognized the hand of civilization in it: heavy soil exploitation, gigantic pits, dents from spacecraft weighing hundreds of thousands of tons, explosives, industrial dumpsters. The colonists' agglomerations and research centers that the planet had once been famous for had also been destroyed and abandoned. There were traces of melting on the buildings. The synthesizers of the atmosphere were destroyed the most, so that the once poor B9's biosphere now practically didn't exist.

Aurals flew past one of these colossi, resembling three-kilometer-high chimneys, when Private Shimizu commented on readings regarding the air on the shared channel:

"There is too little oxygen and nitrogen, you can't breathe here. We won't come to the surface without the masks."

"Are we gonna need the suits?" Darius looked at Lieutenant Aurelius.

"It won't be necessary." The commander of the ship kept a finger to his mouth and analyzed the readings visible in both machines. "The air is not toxic to the skin, only unbreathable. Cosmic radiation is within the tolerance range for the human body - the ozonosphere has not been damaged."

"But who made such mess and what for?" Seymour muttered. The ships had an active general channel, so Shane replied:

"I think ... no, I'm sure it's Kandrok's doing. Can you see the breach in that synthesizer next to us? Only the Kiritians have such firepower, but we don't use melting weapons, and this wall has been eaten away to the core. As if someone had poured caustic acid on their hand. Besides, our members haven't been here for a long time, and the damage looks fresh. Do you remember the dump of metal you passed, which probably came from used mining machines? We also don't use such metal."

"Why would have Kandrok members destroyed everything around when they could take advantage of it?" Private Walker asked.

Tsar shrugged.

"The devil knows. You can't even communicate with them. At least we know they didn't come to us just to destroy," he nodded toward a kilometer-wide niche visible behind the ship's cover, "but they're looking for something in the ground. Probably ore. They take what they want, because they are strong and can, and they don't bother to cooperate or ask for permission. They also blasted the little bit of civilization that had been reborn after the fall of the asteroid."

"You think someone survived?" Darius surveyed the devastation anxiously.

"You wanted to ask about Figam?" Tsar smiled. "In his place I would run for the hills."

"Where?"

"You're asking stupid questions, Thomas. And look for a specific grain of sand on the shoreline of a sea. Especially since the doctor could hide and disguise somewhere."

"What Thomas? I'm Darius." It wasn't the first time Seymour called him by that name. Schindler decided that he would ask the corporal why he was doing so.

"Tsar, if you took a line before the mission, I'll arrest you and lock you in the engine room until our return to Cargoo," Aurelius growled, showing Seymour a stern face. "We must not screw up this task! And I certainly won't let anything get messed up because of you."

"I didn't take anything." Tsar waved his hands. "And it won't work anyway. Just look at this mess. Probably even cockroaches were exterminated on B9, and they are more immortal than us."

"Shut up, Seymour."

"Gentlemen ..." Shane sighed. "We are about three hundred kilometers away from the point the Emperor marked for us on the map. In order not to wait idly in the ship after dropping you off, I will fly and check the adjacent synthesizer on the interior to see if it is also damaged. Thanks to this, we will know whether Kandrok destroyed all of them on purpose, or the first was hit by a ricochet during the exploitation of the ground."

"With all due respect, Captain," Aurelius replied, "but General Biffter gave us one specific task: find the scientist and return. I've always found you a competent officer ..."

"I'm well aware of the danger, Lieutenant. However, if the planet is depopulated, then we are safe. Kandrok flew away, and there is no trace of the indigenous people. It will take me a moment to assess the losses. And it will not hurt us in any way, we can only gain additional information thanks to it. I must be sure of the enemy's intentions, especially since the next atmosphere synthesizer is not far from Figam's residence."

***

Flying at low altitude, they saw single or grouped human skeletons. Soft tissues were melted together with clothing, making it impossible to estimate which social group their owners had belonged to. The arrangement of the bodies indicated that they had been escaping or trying to fight.

Silent, the Immortals reached Figam's mansion, alert and tense, as if Kandrok had been about to appear on the horizon. According to the information provided after the briefing, the scientist's property consisted of three domed laboratories connected by corridors and a little house nearby. Indeed, the arrangement of the objects huddled against the rock massif was correct, except that the domes had collapsed, and resembled eggs butchered after hatching of the chicks, and the house had been razed to the ground. The skeletons and mummified bodies knocked around the yard.

"And you've set a stone rolling," Aurelius snorted at Tsar. "Happy?"

The corporal didn't answer, just looked at the destruction with despondency untypical of him. He hoped to see the famous scientist who had made him immortal, regardless. Alive.

Before Viktor ordered to land, they scanned the area twice to make sure they were absolutely alone. He dropped Shimizu, Walker and Evasiv off Aural 2, then flew away as announced to inspect the synthesizer. Dissatisfied with this, Lieutenant Aurelius also released his crew of two. He himself stayed on board to coordinate the operation and stay in touch with Viktor.

"So, we're going, guys," Tsar said in a robotic voice because of the helmet cover connected to the breathing container on his back.

The five of them set off with their weapons in their hands. The pink and indigo evening sky grew darker and darker. From Aural 1 to the first laboratory, the section was separated by two hundred and fifty meters of rock facet adapted to driving heavy machinery. Before reaching the nearest building, they examined the lying and sitting skeletons.

"They are strange," Evasiv pointed out.

Apart from dirt superimposed by wind, the bones were perfectly clean, with no sign of dried soft tissue, as if someone had prepared remnants and then left it as a warning. As during the air reconnaissance, also in this case the clothing was not conducive to identification. The dirty clothes were in no less deplorable condition than the deceased, they might as well have been a sheet, a uniform or a smock.

"What mess." Seymour got up from his crouch. He looked around slowly and carefully.

"Do you think Maksimus is among the dead?" Darius asked him.

"Walker, give me the nucleo-inductor. Is it calibrated?"

"Yes." The private handed the section commander the small scanning device which, having access to the central database, could use a sample of proteins and DNA to determine the identity of the owner.

Seymour examined all the corpses in sight, seven in total.

"Figam is not among them," he said, returning the nucleo-inductor to Walker. "But crap was displayed. Only three deceased could be identified, they were civilians, residents of B9. At the rest, no data popped up, as if the bodies had been composed of proteins unknown to us."

"The rest may not be in base," Lieutenant Aurelius, who had wiretapped the section members and had seen the images from the recorders in their helmets, told from Aural 1. "I don't think I need to tell you how difficult it is to control the populations of colonized planets, especially now that there is communication broken because of Kandrok and we have problems updating the information."

"Or it was Kandrok," suggested Evasiv. "After all, those uncyborgiz ... uncyborgz ... well, those organic, look almost like us."

"Probably not," Seymour replied. "Kandrok take their dead bodies or destroy them if they don't have the first option. Let's go. Damn it!" He almost fell on his back as his leg sank knee-deep into the ground. Swearing, he pulled it out of the hole and vigorously brushed sand off it.

At the laboratories, they found three more skeletons, this time in uniform and armed, if that can be told about the dead. They managed to establish that it was the complex security. To the laboratories, the Kiritians got through gaps in the walls, the armored synthetic fibers of which wasn't an obstacle for Kandrok's weapons from the ships. After a short examination, it was known that the enemy had been flying over the surface of the planet and destroying everything human. The equipment inside didn't work due to damage or power failure, only the lunar and solar panels on the roofs were functional, at least some of them survived. However, the poor energy processed by them didn't power anything in the buildings, so in dark rooms the section had to use flashlights on weapons or sight amplifiers. They found no more bodies. There was disorder everywhere, pollution from outside had been blown in; Aurelius estimated the damage at hundreds of thousands of uinals. Figam's house couldn't be seen because it had turned into a mound of metal, armored glass and rubble.

Searching the debris, Darius noticed a plain, wooden tablet on the ground with creatures painted on it. He picked it up, cleaned it with blows and a hand. The characters were arranged in two rows separated by a line. Those above looked like devils surrounded by fire or demons from ancient Earthlings beliefs, underneath there were probably angels and a man with gray hair and a beard. Although Darius had grown up in the quiet, hardworking farming family, where Christian traditions had been practiced, they hadn't paid attention to symbolism, but rather to faithful relationships with another human being and belief in God in general. The demons and angels made of a piece of wood seemed to suit the symbols of the Christian religion.

"What is it?" Darius didn't realize he had Seymour behind his back. The corporal took the plaque from his hand and examined it. "Probably some trinket from the cottage." He threw the object on the ground. "Come on, man. The task is complete. We'll wait for Viktor and get out of this mess."

Schindler stared at the plaque for a moment before following Seymour and Evasiv. Shimizu and Walker returned from their tour of the terrain behind the mutilated fence and joined the rest.

"Hey, look what a jigamaree!" Walker showed a tablet like the one Schindler was looking at. "My girlfriend likes such crap on wood, I think I'll take it with me.

"May I?" Evasiv took the find from him. He examined it. He was also a Christian like Schindler, but more closely related to the sphere of the sacred, so he easily recognized the symbolism. "It's heaven and hell, but upside down. Hell is up here when it should be down. The old man symbolizes God and his hosts. They hide from Hell."

"I just found the same thing," said Darius.

"I saw something like that in the beginning, too," added Shimizu. "At one of the skeletons."

Darius and Seymour's eyes met.

"What if it's not some kind of ornament from the house?" Schindler frowned. "Why would have someone scattered religious pictures all over the place?"

"For example, as a guideline for the sussed," suggested Shimizu.

"And if you are right and this is actually a clue for the savvy?" Tsar turned his head towards the ruins of the house. "The greatest trick is to go through hell and not become a devil. That would mean that your section commander is a complete idiot."

"This is nothing new to us," Aurelius replied from the ship in a tone in which it was impossible to recognize whether it was a statement or a joke.

"Lieutenant, what do you think?"

"Something might be up," Aurelius said after a moment, which was followed by a long sigh. "Private Shimizu is thinking well."

Darius hurried away, returned soon with the tablet that Seymour had thrown away. He compared it to the one from Walker. They turned out to be similar, but not identical, indicating manual work and not mass production. Schindler began to circle and think.

"What can you say about Hell and Heaven?" he asked Evasiv, ashamed to have such failings in his own faith.

"Hell means bad and heaven means good. The latter was presented as the first, supreme, dominant force, and was in the heavens inaccessible to mortals, that is, up, above the human world. Hell was the opposite of Heaven: chaos, disorder, despair and fear, filled with the damned and rabble offspring. Satan wanted the same power as God and tried to get people to his side. The struggle between God and Satan lasted from the beginning of the creation of the world."

Darius's eyes lit up as something occurred to him.

"Heaven dominated, just like the Kiritians. Then Kandrok appeared and pushed us underground, taking our place on the pedestal."

"Did you swipe my weed, buddy?" Seymour said, amused.

"Think, boss, it makes sense! This is evidently information for us! Kandrok is technologically ahead of us, so anyone who wanted to send us a message would not use the technology for fear of interception or decryption. So, they referred to the primitive symbolism, known only to the inhabitants of the Zodiac Universum, additionally, to be sure, they messed with it. So that we come to the truth, but not Kandrok members. Even if they know our beliefs, they don't attach much importance to them because they probably think they are heresy, just as they hate us all."

"So what?" Increasingly impatient Tsar raised his eyebrows.

"Namely the old man on the board is not God, but Maksimus Figam, the angels can be his employees, the B9 surface is a hell dominated by Kandrok, which is a bad force for us." Enthusiastic, Darius looked at the corporal's leg, grains of sand were still visible in the slits of his armor. "Simply put, Figam dug a shelter underground and hid there. Just look, boss! Look at this board and the angels! As you look at the picture in general, you can see the figures, but if you look closely, you will see black markings on the legs of the angels, barely visible. Same as on the uniforms of security guards at the laboratories!"

Seymour grabbed the item from Darius.

"You know you might be right?"

"Figam might have scattered these plaques around, hoping we'd figure out how to get to him if we landed on B9. Since he did it, his communication broke down completely."

"Or he barricaded himself so that no signal could penetrate the underground barrier. That's why we couldn't track him electronically," added Shimizu.

"Well done, Dar." Evasiv put a hand on his shoulder and shook him.

"It could still be a theory," said Schindler modestly. "And I wouldn't have thought of anything without you. Thanks."

"You are to search the area thoroughly," the lieutenant said. "If there is an underground complex, find and penetrate it, unless it endangers your life."

Tsar walked over to Schindler.

"Did you really come to this, sober?" He asked in a whisper.

***

The easiest way to get to the nether regions was shooting the ground from the ship, which, however, risked collapsing possible tunnels. The Kiritians inspected the destroyed buildings once more but found nothing that resembled a basement entrance or a hidden door activator. So, they went to inspect the pit where Seymour had put his leg. After the excavation, it turned out that there was indeed a tunnel underground, though primitive - square in cross-section, with bare walls hardened with clay, reinforced with stanchions and beams made of items available in the estate. Someone had used everything that was suitable for fortifying the shelter.

Darius slid into the widened hole first and landed on firm ground. Shimizu followed him, then Walker jumped. Seymour and Evasiv were supposed to guard the entrance. The tunnel was lit by spheres attached to the ceiling at equal intervals. The type of power supply, the Kiritians didn't recognize, but the yellow light could be permanent, because the solid was a hermetically sealed system. Darius realized this as he stepped onto one of the boulders knocking around the corridor and looked at the lamp closely. Excluding boulders, the passage was neat and tidy. The reader indicated that breathable air was flowing through it, but the men took no chances and remained in their helmets, especially since they could depressurize the complex with a hole.

They walked a short distance and found a bent steel door, bunglingly integrated into the doorframe. A stream of air hissed in the gap. Darius reached out to push the door as it cracked open with a creak from the inside. Illuminated by the intense light, the achij jumped back. Like the companions behind his back, he aimed the gun at the stunned figure which was also armed and ready to fire a Kalashnikov at anything that was dangerous and dared to enter their place.

In front of Schindler stood an older man of medium height, with a completely gray hair, but voluminous and comically protruding hair in all directions and a long beard. He had worn pants and a shabby sand-colored sweatshirt on his lean body. He was probably holding a gun pointed at Darius' chest, which might have been a sign of his military past. The boy immediately associated the man with the image on the wooden plate, he slid open the helmet cover, seeing that the man was walking without a breathing apparatus. In the ensuing situation, Schindler was even less concerned with maintaining anonymity. He pointed the barrel to the ground and asked in surprise:

"Doctor Maksimus Figam?"

The man, poorly hiding his fear beneath the mask of mock indifference, also shifted his weapon toward the ceiling. After a moment he was standing as surprised as Darius.

"Kiritians?" He put back the Kalashnikov and started laughing. "I can see that you understood my scribbles. Because you understood, didn't you? Or you got here by accident?"

"So, you are the famous doctor Maksimus Figam, right?"

"So famous that I've been staying like a mole underground for years, afraid to stick my nose out."

Shimizu and Walker attached the gun to their belt and back, also exposed their faces.

"We got here completely by accident," Darius said, unable to contain a smile. "Corporal Tsar Seymour, who is waiting outside, stuck his foot in a hole in the ground, then we found broken tablets. We figured they meant something, so we started looking. We deepened the hole and discovered the tunnel."

Figam ran his fingers through his matted hair.

"I was afraid that these tablets were infantile, and I lost all hope that anyone except Kandrok would come here. I associate Corporal Seymour, are you on his team?"

"More like a section, hastily put together. We are a rescue group for you. We could only come to B9 after the Kandrok flotilla had shifted, but we risked anyway. I am Senior Private Darius Schindler."

"And I am Private Kazuo Shimizu."

"Private Nexon Walker is bowing."

Figam shook hands with everyone.

"What the hell are you doing in there?" Seymour said over the communicator. "Did you discover a brothel? Report, you slobs!"

"Dr. Figam is here!" Darius replied happily. "In one piece!"

"This is very good news! Take him and go up. Viktor is about to fly over to us, and Aurelius is on a hedgehog and picking on me constantly. He disconnected for a moment, and of course he can't hear it. Are there any problems? Should I send Evasiv?"

"None," said Schindler. "We'll be up soon. Because there aren't any, right?" He asked the scientist.

"You don't even know how glad I am to finally get out of this hole! I have long tried to get out of here, but that would have been certain death at the hands of Kandrok. Until you told me, I had had no way of finding out that they had moved."

"Not that I'm questioning your cleverness and your survival skills, but what problem would it have been for Kandrok to find out what was going on underground? They would probably detect people hiding at the very core of the planet."

"Probably so. But maybe they didn't feel like looking for, or it wasn't their primary task to exterminate. They did it along the way."

Figam shook his head despondently. "It was horrible. Even though I live in the hole, I have conducted my own garage research on this people. I would like to take the notes with me."

"We'll help you."

"Come on then." The scientist waved at them.

They made their way briskly to the laboratory behind a warped door, which was nothing more than a dry, underground cave lined with metal sheets, which, together with inhibition paint, formed an improvised Faraday cage. Figam had saved some of the equipment from the surface, and thanks to his knowledge of physics and chemistry, he had access to water, heat and electricity. The accumulated condensed food and pills would have allowed him to survive in the nether regions for the next years.

"Connectivity, however, I didn't manage to achieve," he said, looking for a suitably large bag between the cabinets. When he found it, he put it on the counter. He picked up a small black disk from the shelf and held it up with two fingers. "These are data carriers made by me, I have my research saved on them. Put every you find in the bag. Handy notes too. Where are you taking me, anyway?"

"On Cargoo. We have a refuge there now." Darius and his companions searched for media and carried them into a bag.

"So Morascrik is still in enemy hands?" Figam asked sadly, bustling from cupboard to cupboard. "You absolutely have to tell me everything afterwards, because I am completely cut off from information."

"Are you here alone?" Shimizu asked.

"Yes, only I survived." The doctor threw a small box into the bag from three meters away. He winced as he missed. Walker picked it up and put it inside. "Thanks, son. I was at home when Kandrok started firing. Blessing in disguise, it was all so collapsed that I was stuck in a niche formed in the rubble and the enemy didn't know about me. However, three of my bodyguard assistants died."

"There are more remnants outside," Walker said.

"These are artificial skeletons made of organic matter. Support models that I had in the labs. I set them up to make the area look like a bigger mess and make Kandrok not care about it. As you can see, it worked. So, the planet is safe since you came."

"Yes, Kandrok isn't here at the moment," Darius confirmed. "It is going somewhere with a whole fleet. We flew in with prototypes of brand-new machines, with the best masking technology, and we hope they didn't notice us."

Figam sighed and leaned his hands on the headrest of the blackened chair. "I was afraid that you guys xed me out for good. That the Kiritians would forget me," he said softly, closing his eyes for a moment.

"What are you talking about, doctor?" Darius paused his work and walked over to Figam.

"I helped Aggroteh reconstruct the living artifact that led to Forkis' fall. I also gave Beliar Drunkenstein the gun, believing in his story about mining problems on Cargoo and blowing up rocks. I've always been too good and naive; everyone took advantage of it." He moved away from the chair. "I live with a terrible burden that it was my fault that my best friend died, who allowed me to taste eternal life for several centuries, and the fall of the empire began."

"Even though I have been with the Immortals for several years," Schindler said, "I know their history perfectly well. It's absolutely not your fault with this artifact and Beliar's assassination. You can't read minds like Forkis, so you couldn't know the true intentions of Aggro and Drunkenstein. In addition, you are used to living in the nation that doesn't lie.

With the goodness of your heart, you wanted to help one who was in need at work, and another to recover his dead pet. As the ancient saying goes: a knife is neutral and harmless until it is grabbed by a madman. Or something like that. You only made the knife and nothing else."

"Just Figam. Or Maks. Call me like that."

"If it's not a very personal question..., may I know why you left the Kiritian?" Shimizu asked carefully. "There are rumors that you argued with Forkis about your worldviews."

The doctor managed to put the last old papers into the stuffed bag. The achijes finished collecting the data media from the laboratory, so they allowed themselves a moment of break, sat on the table or leaned against it and stared expectantly at Figam who was full of seriousness.

"That too, we argued more than once, but the main reason lies elsewhere," said Maksimus. "I was, dear children, a Kiritian for several hundred years. But I could no longer bear the yoke of immortality. It turned out not to be for me. Even though I reached the pinnacle of people's dreams, I became apathetic and unhappy. Every day I felt boredom and nonsense of existence, it got worse and worse, and I didn't let anyone to root in my head. Nature has programmed us to do something different, to be born, multiply and die, which is why so few Kiritians were created, just a few million. Although almost everyone dreams of eternity, only one person in several hundred is able to lift its weight mentally and organically. And yet, from among the kiritianized people, I was asked every now and then to selectively clear someone's memory. After being given the serum, after the infection was over, I came back to life and felt kind of a fulfillment, even though my time had become limited again, as it was naturally given to everyone." In Figam's faded blue eyes flashed sparkles of peace, he smiled sadly. "It was like going from a cicada larva to an imago. Do you know what a cicada is?"

"Some animals?" Shimizu suggested.

"An insect that comes from Earth and can make very loud noises. Cicada species can be found on several colonized planets, especially those with a tropical jungle. Some spend decades underground to pupate and then live only for three weeks. But to live, not to vegetate. By looking at your ranks, I estimate that you are young, so these are rather things that are difficult for you to understand."

"I think I understand," Walker said after a moment's pause. "Thank you for sharing this with us, doctor.

"Schindler, go up! Something strange is happening with the air ..." Darius was concerned by a note of uncertainty in the voice of fearless Seymour, who spoke loud enough to make the senior private's ears buzz. "WHAT THE ..." the corporal shouted the last words.

Darius thought his head was going to burst when his ears at which he had the built-in communicators were bombarded by the nightmarish sound of an explosion. Immediately after that, there was a series of thuds. In the first flash of thought the boy imagined that an asteroid had hit B9 again. In his mind's eye, he saw Figam's hideout collapsing, and he was terrified that they would be buried alive.

Shimizu and Walker fell on the shaking ground. Streams of sand mixed with dust flew from the ceiling, obstructing visibility. Part of the lighting went out.

"Corporal Seymour?" Darius coughed, getting to his feet. Tsar didn't respond to the summons or the next few. The lieutenant and captain also gave no sign of life.

Confused, Schindler ran out of the room, reached through the smoky tunnel under the hole through which they had descended to the shelter. There was a burning smell at the outlet. He could hear the sizzling fire from above, but nothing else. Walker and Shimizu soon arrived, Figam was cradling his bag like a child.

Climbing Walker's shoulders, Darius got outside. The heat and the stench almost physically hit him in the face, so as soon as he slid his helmet shield over his face, he raised the weapon to a combat position.

He was dumbfounded. Only the subordination instilled by the Kiritians kept him from fleeing to the nether regions as his heart leapt into his throat and his stomach got clenched by panic pincers.

Aural 1 didn't exist. Its remains were scattered all over Figam's estate. Aural 2 lay with its flaming drives, buried partially in the ground behind the fence.

Kandrok's flying machine, large and dead as a piece of a rocky mountain, was stationed nearby.

Darius noticed Tsar lying on the sand, he might have been unconscious or dead. Because the senior private Evasiv was definitely dead - a multi-ton fragment of "Aural 1" had crushed him like a monolith that fell on a tourist.

The shaken boy didn't answer the calls of the companions left below, nor gave them any order, so Walker, Shimizu and Figam decided to take a risk and left the tunnel.

"Tsar!"

Schindler moved towards the motionless corporal. Behind the quivering curtain of smoke and incandescent dust, he saw a figure move, but instead of expected Shane or Aurelius, a Kandrok member merged from it.

Darius opened his mouth, but was unable to roar with hatred, much less puncture the enemy into a sieve, for some force, which took the form of an electrified spider's web, turned him into a puppet that could only breathe and move his eyes.

XIV. Happy ship

Everything happened lightning fast. As Seymour waited at the descent into the tunnel, he heard a humming noise above his head that he associated with the engines of 'Aural 2' preparing to land. However, instead of Viktor's ship, Kandrok's machine materialized in the air and spread Aural 1 over the entire area with a few shots, as if the target had been a wooden house. Lieutenant Aurelius had no chance of surviving this.

Thrown back by the shock wave, Tsar flew several meters. He felt as if the two hundred and six bones of the skeleton had turned into a few thousand when he painfully hit the ground. Metal rain rushed through the curtains of fire and smoke. Blood was dripping from the corporal's nose. The fall stunned him, he couldn't take deeper breaths because a stabbing pain in his ribs griped him.

He barely managed to think that both Kiritian prototypes sucked along with their shoddy cover when Aural 2 appeared behind the enemy ship. Captain Shane tested the state-of-the-art cannons on Kandrok's machine before the latter was able to turn it properly towards the ship.

A brief firefight ended with flaming Aural 2 crashing to the ground along with Kandrok's machine. Then Tsar passed out.

***

He emerged with his cheek pressed against the cold metal floor. His skin itched under the clotted blood on his face, the iron taste of which he felt in his mouth, and a dull, sweet smell in his nostrils. He didn't have a helmet. Tsar imagined that one of the achijes had taken him unconscious aboard extant Aural 2, but the alien surroundings firmly denied this association. And his own comrades wouldn't have immobilized his hands with something rough behind his back. Not to mention that everyone wouldn't have been lying unconscious or dead next to him, including the scientist, Maksimus Figam. Seymour didn't see Evasiv and Shane among them, and even gloomier thoughts came to him.

He looked around at his surroundings. Glass-smooth floor in feldgrau color. Bead-shaped lamps built into the walls, or whatever it was, gave a hazy, milky light. Around it, there were pattern steel engravings like on a child's scribbles, numerous fractal details. Some form of energy flowing in transparent wrappers like blood in an artery. Everything except for the ground was raw, sharp and angular, just like the shells of Kandrok's ships. And a lot of light, as if someone had been crazy about it or pissed in fear at the sight of shadow, but at least it didn't hurt the eyes. Tsar couldn't tell if the room was warm or cold. And whether he felt anything more than the blood and the stench of burning from his armor. He had slight breathing problems, as if there had been too much carbon dioxide in the surroundings for human lungs. The weapon had been taken from him, of course.

The corporal got rid of his doubts - he had been taken to an alien ship.

"Hey, Darius. Walker. Shimizu. Doctor?"

He bent back, wanting to see his companions as best as possible. But he quickly returned to his original position, wincing as the hard struck of his back against the ground was still taking its toll. It was only movement that made him realize how sore he was. The immobilized Kiritians and the doctor didn't respond to the whispers, and nudging Schindler with a shoe had no effect either. Figam lay on his side as if deprived of his soul.

Seymour tried to free himself, but all he achieved was rolling from belly to back, groaning.

A Kandrok soldier passed through a door shaped like a casket lid. Seymour determined it by his navy-colored armor with black trim and a weapon held with both hands. He was shorter than the average Kiritian, also of smaller build, considering the size of the armor. The only part of the body that was exposed was the head topped with a ribbon of white hair stretching backwards from the center of the forehead. As the Kandrok member circled Seymour, he saw that it was waist high. The stranger's skin was as colored as his hair, his irises were yellow like a cold reptile's, slightly like amber, and his pupils were as small as a pin prick. The newcomer stood over the prisoner, pressed the barrel to his temple and brutally tilted his head to the side.

"Ow," Seymour protested.

The stranger eyed him up, withdrew his weapon, knelt. He spun Tsar without finesse and, also without finesse, freed him from the cold thing that painfully hamstrung his hands. As soon as the limiter fell off, pain started to leave corporal's body, excluding that resulting from the fall.

"Nuberoh ro meka, devoka," Kandrok said sharply and firmly, he had harsh voice, medium in pitch. He waved the gun at the door.

"I don't understand shit," Seymour growled. The soldier hit him in the face with the barrel. Tsar felt a warm, iron liquid running down his right nostril. "Ow ..."

"Rivak, devoka!"

"Alright, alright! I think I know what you mean. Just don't hit me anymore, or I'm gonna be ugly."

The corporal stood up, with his hands slightly raised. A trickle of blood traveled from the nose to the chin, a few drops were drizzled on the armor. Seymour felt faint for a moment, but he stayed on his feet. He wasn't going to pull a stunt, remembering that Kandrok's chemical weapons turned living people into skeletons, and there were still a few suitable to be questioned on the floor if the aliens had failed with Tsar.

Kandrok moved behind his back and pushed him with the barrel towards the exit from the room.

They walked through a corridor bordered by symmetrically spaced doors, entered a spherical hall with pillars and energy matrices of various colors, and then got into the corridor again. They turned and reached the cockpit - a chamfered room with three sides. There were two armchairs, the left one was occupied by a bald albino who was fumbling at the instrument console. A several-meter-long control desk was threaded with hundreds of microscopic switches or some sensors. The whole thing reminded Tsar of a lot of pieces of black glass, sticks and conical stones nailed into a soft asphalt patch. In the center hovered a ball of shifting filaments of light, as if diplopod, driven to a thermal fever, had been wandering inside. Behind the canopy, the corporal saw Figam's destroyed laboratories and dead Aural 2.

The Kandrok members began talking to each other. First matter-of-factly, then more and more nervously. It was no different from the dialogue of people at the Zodiac Universum who had different opinions. Soon Tsar's Cerberus was almost shouting at his companion, and the latter repaid him the same, and in the finale, he desperately slammed his fist on the control desk and shook his bowed head.

Seymour, who was forced to sit in a vacant chair, naturally didn't understand a word, but after a brief observation he noticed that the Kandrok members were using gestures familiar to him. Their emotions were also close to people's, maybe they were even more aggressive than the average person. The soldier sitting next to him stared blankly at the empty space between the protruding teeth of the communication frame, repeated the same phrases over and over, and moved the same switches. Seymour thought that he would have done the same if he had tried to call his supervisor. He easily guessed the merits of the conversation, the smile appeared on his lips by itself.

"Oh, is the communication broken, gentlemen?" He grinned. The Kandrok members looked at him with disgust but also with curiosity, the former was much stronger than the latter. "So, we won't boast the new prisoner to the commander, will we?"

The white-haired man hit him in the face, this time with an armored hand.

"Ow ..."

"Nu, heroko," he growled. He leaned his back against the headrest of his companion's chair, sighed, looked at the ceiling and remained so for a while.

Tsar looked alternately at the white-haired man and the bald one, who continued to try to establish a connection. They were both broken, they also made their movements casually.

"I understand you guys, I would be angry too if I had to do overtime, especially if I had interesting plans after work." The corporal couldn't refrain from making another mocking comment, but this time they didn't react. Unexpectedly, a very crazy thought came to him, close to idiocy. But if the idea works, it may be possible to save the skin of both him and his companions.

"I think I have an effective solution to your performance," he said again after a few minutes. The Kandrok member seeking inspiration on the ceiling, gave him a hostile look. "You look tired, hungry, and pissed off, and I can fix these problems in no time. We've developed in different parts of the cosmos, but we're very much alike, biological convergence or whatever the eggheads call it, so maybe the method will work. It seems we even breathe similar air, except you like more carbon dioxide."

The aliens aimed their weapons at him as he reached into one of several small armor compartments. He carefully took out a little bag. Inside was the herb of fire reptile from Nephrida which Seymour had visited after suppressing the opposition of Commander Aveo Lacetti. The stuff was weak, at least for the corporal's body hardened in drug addiction, but when given to a layman it was conducive to relaxing the atmosphere and making friends.

"See? It's nothing bad, just some plants." Kandrok flinched as Seymour opened the bag, took a deep, theatrical breath. "A wonder! Look, it's not poison." He took a pinch of dried leaves with his fingers and snorted it. He also put a little on the tongue.

The white-haired man lowered his weapon, looked sheepishly at his seated companion, who shrugged his shoulders. Tsar lifted the bag slightly, shook it.

"A plant. A wonderful herb."

"Plavnat," the bald man repeated, pointing his finger at the bag.

"P l a n t," spelled the Kiritian clearly.

"Plant!" The white-haired man said sharply and fully correctly, like someone who knows Kiritian fluently. He glared at his companion, who put his hand to his forehead and made a face as if he had realized something disturbing. The white-haired man sighed. Tsar didn't understand any of this.

"Plemt," said the hairless man.

"Almost." Seymour extended his arm. "Here you are. Give it a try. Don't be afraid. I took it and I'm alive. I wish I had something to kill you, intergalactic assholes, like you killed my lieutenant, but there still will be time for that, right?" He smiled warmly.

The bald man looked at the white-haired man. The latter shook his head, frowned, and said something in a warning tone. The bald man shrugged again, answered gently, hopefully. He ripped the wrapping away from Seymour and looked inside.

"Plant," he said correctly this time. "Niguh."

"Sure, niguh, niguh!" Seymour indicated the bag.

"Ager o mahum, likera ti mu sarre!" Cerberus waved his weapon menacingly, having looked into Tsar's eyes.

"Blow off steam from your testicles, or your penis will knock out your eye," replied the Kiritian. "If you have anything more than three centimeters in action. It's possible, otherwise you wouldn't be flying around the galaxies with huge guns to make up for that divine joke. By the way, your hair is nice, you could wave it at the howling alarm on board. Ha, ha, and what do you say? It's fun to listen if you don't understand anything?"

The bald man sniffed the contents of the bag and took a little bit of it on his tongue.

"Niguh," he said with a smile to the white-haired man, having clearly relaxed. "Domo?" Cerberus refused with a wave of his hand. The bald man tried again and snorted the part with his nose. And he started laughing.

After a few moments of observing the companion, who was okay, the white-haired man put the gun down on the console and took the bag from the other man.

"Bika tira!" He said enthusiastically, swallowing some dried leaves.

Soon both Kandrok members were cackling, looking at their surroundings from under half-closed, bloodshot eyes. The bald man threw his gun on the other end of the cockpit, and it amused him so much that he lay down on the floor and grabbed his belly with laughter. The white-haired man knelt beside Seymour and, mumbling in Kandrok, happily patted him on the shoulder. With the other hand he grabbed his ponytail and began to twirl it.

Tsar stared at them in amazement.

"Damn, such a strong and fast effect, I haven't expected ... The gentlemen will have to practice hard."

***

When Seymour returned to his companions, Figam, Darius, and Walker were already awake. Shimizu was still paralyzed and not moving, like a corpse.

Schindler froze and widened his eyes as he saw the corporal entering the room and the Kandrok member hanging from him, as if Tsar had been supporting a wounded man.

"Boss, you traitor," he hissed, thinking the matter was obvious. Astonished, Walker said nothing, just as stunned Figam.

Seymour stood near the men and smiled amused.

"Sonny, it's not what you think. Here I have made new friends for our cause."

Raising his head and torso like a seal, Darius looked at the white-haired Kandrok, who, exhilarated, began to babble and point to the ceiling. Anger gave way to surprise.

"Tsar ... what did you do to him? The guy is completely stoned!"

"I showed him what it means to relax in our standards. There are two Kandrok members on this ship, the other one fell in love with the cockpit floor and is probably hugging it now."

Darius understood immediately.

"Which herb did you give them, boss?"

"They got reptile."

"After reptile, even an eight-year-old would act as if he ate too much sugar. These here are completely deprived of their memory and mind!"

Tsar placed the Kandrok member on the floor.

"Exactly, young. Weird. Maybe they don't take drugs at all? They are not allowed, or they don't have anything like that?"

"Come on, boss. Everyone takes them."

"Maybe in our civilization, Kandrok is governed by different norms. You should be happy, not philosophize, because they are so high and stupid right now that I have full control over them. Oh look." Seymour knelt. He shook the white-haired man, and when the latter managed to focus his attention on him, the Kiritian crossed his arms at the back, then moved them forward and waved his palms. "Will you free my friends? Yes, yes, hands. Remove the safeguards. F r e e."

The Kandrok member's mind, dazed by the drug, encompassed little, and the stranger didn't understand what Tsar was saying to him. Only after a few gestures and pointing to the lying Kiritians and the doctor, he nodded with enthusiasm and an exhilarated smile. Staggering, he went on all fours to Darius, put a wallet-like device to his hand, which was attached to his wide belt. The rough protection fell to the ground like a dead, dried snake. The same action, the Kandrok member repeated in front of the doctor, Walker as well as Shimizu, who began to recover.

"My notes," said Figam. "The bag's left somewhere outside, I need to get it back."

"Where's Lieutenant Aurelius?" Darius sat up, began rubbing his wrists.

"He's dead," Tsar said.

Schindler pounded the ground, then sighed and rested his forehead on his knee.

"I was hoping the lieutenant had saved himself somehow. Private Evasiv had also fallen, crushed by scrap iron."

"I was afraid of this when I didn't notice him with you."

Shimizu, Walker and Schindler fixed their worried eyes on the corporal.

"And the captain?" Darius asked.

"I don't know," Tsar replied. "Kandrok destroyed 'Aural 1' and seriously damaged 'Aural 2'. However, Shane gave as good as one gets response, and fired on them, which caused them to lose communication and be cut off from their comrades, it is also possible that they have temporary problems with taking off. I suppose that then in space Kandrok's fleet noticed us and sent a single scouting ship to the B9. Probably the command of the aliens took us for harmless suckers, and therefore didn't transfer more units, better armed. Otherwise, we would have become a pulp."

Walker wanted to twist the neck of the Kandrok member, who sat down next to him and, with a blissful smile on his lips, put his arm around his shoulders like a bum another bum. He wasn't going to complicate the situation, however, as he was beginning to understand that stoned enemies could prove to be extremely useful in the circumstances.

"Now that they are in such a state," Tsar nodded to the white-haired man, "we can check Aural 2."

"We'd better do it quickly, because Viktor may be dying." Darius got up and found himself fully recovered. Helped groaning Shimizu to his feet. Walker also regained full fitness.

"I'm so sorry that so much bad happened because of me," said Figam, despondent, trying to order his lush gray mop.

"Nonsense," commented Walker. "Kandrok could have beaten us if not in such a situation, then in another."

"I will go with you to find your things, doctor. Private Shimizu," as Tsar had now the highest rank, he set about organizing, "stay on the ship and keep an eye on the Kandrok members. Don't hurt them. Remember, these are the same mediocre soldiers for a dirty job as we are. We'll try to come back as soon as possible. The rest with me."

***

Figam regained his notes and was the first to return to Kandrok's ship. Tsar, Darius and Walker boarded Aural 2, found Shane in the cockpit who, with blood clotted on his head, was lying unconscious in the pilot's seat. Seymour found a medical device called a neuromogram, he scanned the captain's nervous system and the general condition of his body with it. Viktor had suffered a concussion, but luckily there were no hematomas, no clots or strokes. It was much worse with the ship. The drives were damaged to such an extent that without the help of a workshop with the use of professional and heavy equipment, it was impossible to repair them. Interstellar-range communication also didn't work, only close-range one, covering the distance of several astronomical units.

"Then we're screwed up," Tsar summed up their situation.

Resigned, Darius looked at him.

"And the support?"

"Support? You must be kidding."

"What are we gonna do now?"

The corporal thought for a moment, looked at Walker wandering around the cockpit, smiled and replied:

"We will take, my friends, Kandrok's ship."

"What?" Nexon sank into the chair next to the unconscious captain.

"Our drives are broken, and their communication as well. But we have an autonomous short-range communication module with a battery that can work for another month. It is enough to transfer it to Kandrok's ship."

"Pretty bold idea, boss," Schindler replied. "But you didn't take a few things into account. If I can?"

"Go ahead." Darius began to count on his fingers:

"A: Kandrok's fleet is not led by morons, because morons wouldn't have defeated us, so their command knows where its unit is. It probably also knows that it is damaged, and someone will come for it right away.

"B: 'Our new 'friends' will rather not want to pilot for us.

"C: We don't know Kandrok's identification system or the forms of communication, so it is rather certain that we will bring the enemy's armada straight to Cargoo.

D: if we meet Kiritians by chance in space, they will take the opportunity and start shooting at us, seeing the lonely enemy ship."

The corporal replied without hesitation:

"A: that's why we have to get the hell out of here.

" B: there will be enough drugs for the return journey, we only need to give them to the Kandrok members from time to time, and they will obey us. Unless they pop off because of them sooner.

" C: The ship could be wrecked on the way if we could transfer, although General Kiret Biffter would gladly deliver it to his specialists.

" D: that's why we have the working module - we will shout on the air: 'Our comrades are flying here!' on frequencies unavailable to Kandrok."

"How do you know that unavailable? Although we don't like to talk about it out loud, Kandrok is better than us. It is said that on the Kardashev scale it is almost a degree higher than we are. As for the herb, boss. We can kill these two by accident, as you just summed up. Their bodies appear more sensitive to drugs than ours. Who will lead the ship then?"

Tsar's amused expression was the perfect contrast to the serious face of Darius. The corporal walked over to him and patted him on the shoulder.

"More optimism, sonny. If you have a better idea, I'm listening." He smiled even wider, indicated the boy sighing nervously with his finger. "Aaaaah, you see?"

"What about the captain?" Walker was using a damp bandage to wipe the blood off his head.

"We're taking him to Kandrok's ship. We also take all the necessary things from Figam's ship and dungeons. Let 'Aural 2' lie and please the enemy's eye. If more Kandrok members come here, they should think that their ship damaged our ship and that the Kiritian crew had been abducted or fled. And they will wonder what happened to their unit."

Darius picked up unconscious Wiktor by the arms, Nexon took his legs.

"You have a head, boss," said Schindler, encouraged.

***

Shane regained consciousness several dozen minutes after he was transferred to the ship, but he didn't remember anything that had happened on B9, and he had a terrible headache. The alien unit was used for short-term actions, the soldiers experienced comfort only on the counterparts of astro-carriers, so in order to provide the captain and themselves with rest, the Kiritians carried sleeping capsules from Aural 2 and foldout bunks from the doctor's hideout with Figam's rovers. After receiving restorative medication and a painkiller, Wiktor went to bed and fell asleep.

Seymour tried to convince the Kandrok members to take off and go in the direction he had set. Another dose of the drug helped a little bit in the conversation. Words naturally failed, but gestures and associations proved helpful. Eventually, the slightly irritated corporal drew with soot on the floor in front of the Kandrok members the planetary system in which Cargoo and H14 circulated and tried to imply that they had to go there. He was glad to hear that they didn't know the system, which meant the Kiritian base was still safe.

After two Terran hours, some consensus was reached. Tsar and the Kandrok members fair to middling agreed on the first half of the route.

The machine went up. And quite differently from the way Kiritians were used to, who took off with an anti-gravity propulsion, less archaic, but still effective, rocket. It made a short jump from the surface of the planet, which was still unattainable for the Immortal technology, because the energy produced during the take-off could obliterate many square kilometers of the area, or the naval craft or ship itself. Therefore, achijes made subspace jumps deeper in space.

Only the stars and no sign of B9 were visible after exiting the jump. The second phenomenon turned out to be the fact that the mass of the vessel was too small to generate artificial gravity, and atopaxial particles, Kandrok rather didn't have, and yet Seymour and the rest could walk on board like on the surface of Morascrik or Cargoo. They also didn't feel they were flying at all - the ship's shields, producing an autonomous environmental bubble, Kandrok had more advanced than the Kiritians. Even Figam had no idea how it could all work.

Seymour spent the next hours learning to pilot under the tutelage of cheerful pilots, whom he often had to put in a vertical position as they slid off their seats without bothering to strap themselves on. And even when he secured them, they laughed in his face and unbuckle again like children spiting their father. Nevertheless, thanks to their blissful eloquence, he learned many phrases in their language, and got to know many useful things that no faithful sober Kandrok member would have ever revealed to their enemies. For example, the fact that the extremely durable ship armor was made of an alloy called diarduk, which was also used in cyborgization or the production of armor. The white-haired man even started listing the composition of this mixture, but Tsar didn't understand much. It also turned out that all Kandrok's - just like Kiritians' - machines had a combat value, but much more. The line between what could be a ship and what a naval craft was very blurred.

"Umen Rei'thannnnnnnnn." The white-haired man pointed to the torso with both hands.

"Is that your first and last name?" Seymour placed himself on a chest filled with equipment, medicines and food, a few of which had been taken from the doctor's hideout. He smoked a marijuana joint, the only consequence of which was a delightful relaxation. With the highly developed medicine of the Immortals, the health consequences of taking drugs could be easily eliminated. Tsar, however, didn't use detoxicants, his body became extremely resistant to the harmful effects of many types of stimulants.

"Rei'than!" The white-haired hit his chest.

"Umen Ly!" The Second Kandrok member didn't want to be worse.

"Ly." Tsar exhaled a large dose of smoke through his nose and mouth.

"So, your names are Rejtan and Li in our language, and umen is some rank? What's further? Do you have names?"

The Kandrok members looked at each other seriously, then burst out laughing.

"Alright ... I'm Tsar Seymour. Tsar Seymour," he repeated more slowly, touching his finger to his chest.

"Devoka Tsar Seymour!" Rei'than leaned over and prodded the Kiritian with his fist in a friendly manner. If the corporal hadn't pushed him backwards in time, he would have fallen, face down to the floor. Darius entered the cockpit.

"How's the pilot course ... Damn, boss, how much smoke!"

"Sit down, Dar." Tsar managed to settle down on the three joined crates, he crossed his legs, clasped his hands behind his head.

"Make yourself comfortable. See, nothing is happening at all, no one is attacking us, no one is chasing us, the company is nice. Life could not be any better."

"As long as this company remains mind mush." Schindler sat down on an empty box. "Boss ... will you give a joint?"

Seymour handed Darius a joint he had made of the paper Figam had used on B9.

"I've taken a break and I'm learning the language now. How's the captain doing?"

"Better. Shimizu and Walker are with him, we told him everything he had missed while he had been unconscious. He's gonna come over here and eat us out for this shit. The whole ship reeks of weed!" The boy fanned himself ostentatiously with his hand.

"It has been consistently the best drug in thousands of years." Relaxed, Seymour exhaled another portion of smoke, after him, Darius his first.

"Can I also learn the language?"

"Go ahead." The corporal gestured with the joint to the Kandrok members, engrossed in mumbling conversation. "The one with the lock of white hair introduced himself as Rei'than. The second is Ly."

"Will they understand anything I say?"

"The basics, they have already encompassed. Especially Rei'than remembers incredibly quickly and easily, even in his condition. You only need to say something to him once. If there's such a need, you can gesticulate, their gestures are similar to ours."

"Er, hello," the senior private began, catching the attention of both umens. "So how do you say, for example ... a large ship?" He made the outline of a space machine with his hand with the joint.

Rei'than associated, Tsar had recently asked him with gestures about something similar.

"Gefombe demo." He raised his clasped arms and began to slowly unfold them to the sides.

"This is surely a great ship?" Darius's voice was skeptical. "And not by any chance sunrise, or the devil knows what else? Tsar, what if they're kidding us?"

The corporal rested his feet on the control panel and shrugged, busy smoking the joint. Rei'than addressed his question to Schindler, pointing his hand at his and his own mouth. Darius looked at Seymour.

"I think he wants to know how we say hello," Tsar said. "So, you haven't learned the basics yet?"

"Of course, we did weapons, ships, war, vodka, drugs, sex, tits."

A satanic smile appeared on Schindler's face. He remembered Tsar's first conversation with the Kandrok members, which the corporal had related to them. He got up, parodied a bow and said:

"My penis is three centimeters long. This is what the greeting sounds like."

"My penis is three centimeters long," Rei'than repeated after Darius quite correctly and solemnly, although it was extremely difficult for him to stay on his feet.

Seymour rested his arm on his forehead and laughed uncontrollably, so that tears flowed. Darius began to laugh as well, feeling the effects of marijuana mixed with the fire reptilian that the Kandrok members had recently stopped smoking. Rei'than and Ly joined the Kiritian with their outburst of merriment. The room was getting grayer with the lazily swirling smoke. The stars behind the canopy looked so beautiful.

When Shane, Shimizu, Walker, and Figam entered the cockpit, Darius was on all fours and still couldn't calm down while the Kandrok members held each other and sang. Tsar looked at the puzzled achijes and the doctor and shrugged from his position on the crates with a pitying smile.

"My penis is three centimeters long." Rei'than greeted Shane, bowing slightly, struggling to keep his balance, and flew at Darius.

"Corporal Seymour ..." Viktor growled furiously. The expression on his face tensed by anger changed very rapidly. "You saved our asses."

***

Having noticed that Seymour was doing quite well, albeit in a rather controversial way, the captain retired to one of the rooms. He tried to determine what type of unit they were dealing with. The presence of starkly decorated orlops indicated that they were flying in some sort of short reconnaissance machine. Wiktor wasn't feeling well, his head hurt, he had blood in his sputum, so he decided to rest for a while. He was relieved that Seymour had taken over his duties. He had long ago concluded that Tsar's way of being achij left much to be desired, but the corporal rarely made mistakes and almost always surprised with spectacular victories. So far, he had basically screwed up only one mission - on planet Aj, during a storm involving carbodur, a highly ferromagnetic compound, he hadn't noticed Emperor Forkis which had crashed there with Anna Sandstorm. Luck apparently clung to him, as in the discovery of the precious nether regions on H14, and now Figam's shelter.

The doctor was wandering around the board, interested in the operation of the ship. More than once he got motionless for many minutes, watching in devout concentration the machinery free of the wrapper at work. At least in this way he could keep his mind off the next deaths and misfortunes he had witnessed. Schindler, Walker and Shimizu were in the cockpit with Tsar, curious about Kandrok and the instrument console.

Seymour already had some grasp of the ship's navigation and speed indicators. He knew where the Kiritian VMO[11], DI[12], ACS[13] counterpart, early and long warning ones, energy level

---

[11] Maximum allowable operating speed.

[12] Course indicator.

index, pressure, temperature and air mixture bioregulator were. And the most important now - AHRS[14]. He had learned how to switch from automatic to manual control and vice versa, how to increase and decrease the power of the engines. He was surprised that despite the technological advantage, Kandrok didn't use AI in their space machines - at least in the ones he had had contact with so far, which were a small sample. He wondered if, with the present knowledge, he would have been able to steer the ship himself, using polygonal or virtual knobs and switches, or more precisely, if he could have altered the course taken by Kandrok.

Narcotic vapors filled the cockpit, lazily swirling as thick gray clouds. Soon they took over the whole ship, so that even the doctor and the captain felt somehow nice, even though they were pondering the loss of two achijes. The jokes in the cockpit - especially teaching the Kandrok members profanity by Darius - continued until Ly, unaccustomed to the stimulants, collapsed. Walker and Shimizu dragged him like a staggering drunk to the farthest orlop, where the air was still reasonably clean. Ly slept for several hours, and when he woke up, the narcotic thoughtless gaiety passed, and the hatred of the Immortals instilled in him by the leaders of Kandrok returned. Seymour had him tied up, he didn't want to drug Ly again, because his body might have not been able to withstand another confrontation with a foreign, toxic substance and possibly he would have died before landing on Cargoo. The inmate had a fit of thirst and hunger, Walker gave him the water he had taken

---

[13] Position control in space.

[14] Position and course information system.

from Aural 2, and as food, the Kandrok pilots used jelly-like, transparent pulp.

Seymour took care of the autonomous short-range communication module, switching to various frequencies agreed on Cargoo - which were constantly changing for security reasons - to catch anything on the air. Even though their course led beyond the boundaries of the Zodiac Universum, in the total air void, Tsar preferred not to be ignorant and meticulously monitored his surroundings. Especially since Kandrok's ship's warning system reached farther than the module's communication range.

Seymour was accompanied in the cockpit by Darius, sitting silently on the console next to the canopy and staring at the stars. The men put out their joints the moment Ly passed out. Attached Rei'than slept almost silently in his armchair.

Suddenly, Tsar picked up the signal. Faint, repeating at ten-second intervals. Surprised, he looked at Darius, who copied his expression. The usage of this frequency had been discontinued several years earlier.

Someone was sending an incredibly weak S.O.S. signal into the air, as if their power source had been running on a vapor of energy, making it short-range.

"What is it?" Schindler staring at the screen, hung at the corporal's side.

"I have no idea. According to the module, it's awfully close, barely two AU from here."

He switched the ship's drives and activated the braking procedure. Rei'than had previously shown him which switches to use for both activities, although the process itself, the corporal didn't understand. The Kiritians used the calculation of long flights when braking, as well as the gravity of celestial bodies or objects of considerable mass. Seymour felt as if they had hit a monstrous, flexible tank filled with water - something must have been created in front of the ship's nose. And they braked, the machine began to drift slowly. They passed a mysterious object somewhere on the starboard side.

"I have to inform Wiktor." Seymour stood up.

"We should probably do this before we take any action," Darius muttered.

When Tsar entered the captain's orlop, Shane was already awake and arguing with Figam. Soon all the achijes and the doctor were stuck in front of the communication module screen.

"Could this be an ambush?" Shimizu asked.

The captain took a deep breath and let the air out loudly.

"Hard to say. This part of the cosmos is alien to us, there is nothing of value in it. But why would someone lure us with our own signal that has not been used for several years?"

"I think I associate it," Tsar said, staring at the screen. "Didn't we use one in the capital before the alien attack?"

The captain glanced at the sleeping Kandrok member.

"Seymour, do you know how to shoot this?"

"You mean the ship's cannons?"

"Exactly."

"In theory. A lick and a promise."

"So, I understand that if there's such a need, you can do it."

"Let's say yes."

"Let's fly over and check the source of the signal. I have some assumptions."

"Captain?" Darius looked at Shane's focused face, who frowned. "If this information is not intended solely for senior officers ..."

"What do you mean?"

"I've heard unofficially that General Velkee Warfighter escaped into this sector, outside the Universum."

"Take it easy, boy. It's nothing secret. I thought the same. General Warfighter, a member of the Council that no longer exists, has never been found or contacted. You're right, while leaving Morascrik, he probably flew into this area with a handful of men from the destroyed regiment accompanying him."

"You think the signal is from the missing?"

"If we fly to check, we'll find out. There will be no answer without risk." The commander looked at the Kiritians and Figam. "You all agree? Anyone against?"

Nobody said anything.

XV. Seymour's Story

In order to get near the unidentified object, a slight impulse of propulsion that sent the ship into the air was enough. Pleased with himself that he no longer needed the Kandrok members to pilot, he slowed down like the last time, but in this case the deceleration distance was nine kilometers before the ship switched to free drifting. Four metal-melting chemical cannons protruded from the cavities of the armor.

S.O.S. signal sounded continuously on the reader of the Kiritian module. The corporal followed it making course corrections. The Kandrok alert system was constantly rumbling and irritating, but Tsar was unable to decode alien handwriting, thus to turn off the annoying device. However, he suspected that the caught object was considered rather harmless, since the colors marking it didn't differ from the flight parameters, which remained within the normal range.

The distance to the mysterious object had been decreased to tens of meters, yet through the canopy it looked like a small black hole absorbing light. Seymour would have turned on the outside lights if he had been able do so, and he didn't want to refer to trial and error.

"Hey." He prodded sleeping Rei'than. Only when he pounded him harder in the face did the Kandrok member open his eyes. He was still muddled and completely unable to grasp what was happening around him.

"Rivak, Rei'than," said the corporal. "Likum." He indicated a few points behind cover where the ugly armor of their ship began.

"Likum?"

"Yes, likum. Turn on some lights for us. The Kandrok members began to smile at each one in turn. He raised his hand in the gesture of a beggar.

"Niguh. Niguh."

"You'll get niguh later. First the lights." Seymour grabbed Rei'than's hands and moved them onto the control panel. "I would turn them on myself, but I don't want to accidentally blow up the ship in space and destroy such a treasure as my herb."

Rei'than muttered something under his breath but did as the corporal ordered. As a reward he was given a joint, with which he was busy for the next minutes, looking at it blissfully like at a holy relic.

The red lights flashed from two sources, intense enough to illuminate the sender of the signal accurately.

Surprised, Seymour and Shane looked at each other. Darius grimaced; a comical expression of surprise appeared on his face.

"The garbage trucks? Seriously?" He commented.

They watched the drifting civilian unit used on Morascrik to remove junk and rock from the orbit. One of the sides was dented, as if it had collided with impetus with some space object. At worst, someone had overdone the subspace drive, and in the generated tunnel, the crookedly flying machine was crushed by the pressure at too high a speed.

"Darius, get ready," Wiktor ordered. "We're going outside."

"Are you sure, Captain?" Tsar asked. "I can check it, after all, I will take one of the boys with me."

"Stay, Seymour, as my deputy. Only you can fly this lump and you get along best with Kandrok." Viktor pointed to the recycler. "I need to take a closer look at this."

The corporal didn't argue this time, indeed so far, he hadn't considered the fact that he had become the most important person for the mission and shouldn't have exposed himself hastily.

While still on B9, Tsar had discovered that the last section of the board, with diamond-shaped protrusions on the walls, floor and ceiling, could be hermetically cut off the rest of the ship, and the smaller airlock door could be opened in several ways, including by hand. So, he instructed the captain on how to get out into space. Rei'than turned out to be willing to help, and in his will to do it, he intended to open the main airlock without cutting off any part of the board. Shane stopped him in time from carrying out this idea, ordered him to be taken out of the cockpit and placed in an orlop with the tied companion, which made Rei'than incredibly amused.

The Kandrok members had two suits but turned out to be too small for the Kiritians. The air tanks used in the armor on B9 also worked well in space, but not for long. Nevertheless, the twenty minutes calculated by Figam were to be enough to look inside the recycler, if there were no problems with getting on board. Sealed armor should also work as a temporary protection against vacuum and radiation.

After cutting off the last deck and opening a small maintenance hatch, the captain and senior private bound with ropes made their way into space. They turned on the lights on their helmets. To float into space, the men only had to bounce strongly off the ship's armor with their legs.

Viktor and Darius hit the charred, thick casing of the recycler, but they stabilized quickly, catching the nearest protrusions. They still had more than half the length of the ropes at their disposal. The captain shifted, peering into the cockpit through the cracked cover. He concluded that this probably contributed to the creation of a vacuum that seized the inside of the frosted, dead recycler. By Viktor's order, Darius tried to use a lancet to burn a hole in the side of the damaged airlock, large enough for them to slip through. In vain. The armor of the recycler exposed to the bombardment by space debris was one of the thickest Kiritian materials.

Pulling themselves up gently on the ropes, the Kiritians returned to the board of Kandrok's ship, where they refilled the air and took the Rei'than's chemical rifle before turning back to the garbage truck. They watched in amazement and horror as, after a few moments of work, a narrow passage opened before them. They looked at each other, thinking the same - how easily Kandrok could annihilate everything the Immortals had created.

Inside, they unhooked the ropes and anchored them to the dhurnsteel ribs of the corridor. There was a vacuum around, it was dark and cold. Various objects, smaller and larger, hovered everywhere, tapping the men floating in the hangar. Shane diagnosed the rear of the recycler with the multifunction scanner, found no pathogens or other recognizable hazards, but the monitor clearly showed that there was some life smoldering on board. In fact, a few minutes later they found five cryogenic chambers, sealed off from the surroundings, where people were sleeping. Four alive, and there was a corpse as well, as the readings indicated. Black, frosted carapaces made it impossible to look at the bodies.

The captain floated to the cockpit only to discover that the entire recycler had enough power left to sustain vital functions in the cryochamber, and the dying signal S.O.S. could go into the air. The garbage truck (leaky, by the way) couldn't be refilled with air, pressure and temperature couldn't be changed, and in order to establish the identity of the sleepers, the cryochambers had to be moved to Kandrok's ship.

It took over an hour, with returning for the air several times and the rest of the Kiritians involved. Thanks to Tsar's maneuvers, it was possible to rotate the ship so that the board entrance was located five meters from the hole in the recycler widened by Darius.

When the doctor opened the first cryochamber, everyone watching his treatments was speechless. Under the cover, Gareth, the commander of the city guard in K'otz'ib'aja, was sleeping soundly. But when another carapace was lifted, Tsar was sure he was overdosing and hallucinating because he saw Forkis' ex-wife and a member of the Council of Dignitaries.

"Deus ex machina," he commented. "That's a meeting."

***

Anna Sandstorm, Corporal Zira Aytar, Batab Gareth and Alejandro Cortez could be woken up and put on their feet safe and sound within a few hours. The body of the killed Kandrok member, frozen in a cryo-capsule, was placed in a separate hold, where the items recovered from "Aural 2" and Figam's hideout had been previously brought.

The Morascrik fugitives were more amazed at the unusual encounter with their saviors than they were with them, when they found out that they had drifted asleep in space for several years. It turned out that the shock wave of Kandrok's bomb, dropped on the plague affected K'otz'ib'aja, had broken into the subspace tunnel generated during the jump, and damaged the recycler. Only the thick armor had prevented it from being completely burned. The machine had been thrown into the abyss of space outside the Zodiac Universum, with all energy absorption panels completely destroyed. The remnants of the power, Sandstorm had ordered the cryo-capsules to be fed, and the crew had been to rest for a long time, possibly eternally. Before falling asleep, Gareth had turned on a permanent S.O.S. signal, unfortunately short-range on a cosmic scale.

Survivors were depressed and overwhelmed by the news that the Kandrok problem had not been resolved, even eased, over the years. Seymour, despite Shane's frown, quickly found a solution to their negative emotions, turning them into blissful peace and relaxation. To take the drug, he even persuaded eternally dispassionate, reticent Aytar, who had already in her childhood gotten contempt and caution towards mind-numbing drugs. The deck was again taken over by the gray cheering smoke. Alejandro didn't join the smoking companions, but instead sat down next to Figam and was telling him for a long time about the events in the capital, especially about the doctor's interesting reaction to the super-virus.

"There will be a lot of work waiting for us on Cargoo," said Maksimus, looking at the cryo-capsule with the dead body. "Thanks to this trip, we learned a lot of useful things. I understand that you will want to help me with the research?" He smiled indulgently at Cortez.

"Naturally!"

"I will gather as many scholars as possible. It's time to devise an effective weapon against Kandrok. Expiation should help me a lot. And you also."

"What?"

"You can tell me what you want, but it is I who is indirectly responsible for the death of Forkis and Beliar's attack in the capital." Figam stared at the white face of the dead Kandrok member. "And now I have a chance to compensate you for such enormous damage, at least a little."

***

They arrived at the Cargoo system alarmingly fast. Figam decided that the first thing he would do would be to investigate Kandrok's propulsion as soon as he obtained permission to do so. Viktor told Seymour to purge the air of the smoke, but nothing came of it - the corporal couldn't do it, and Ly and Rei'than regained their senses and were ready to burn everyone with hateful eyes if they could. The captain wondered how to explain to Biffter why, on such an important mission, everyone was either stoned or overjoyed due to the volatile particles wandering around the board. But it wasn't Seymour and his drugs that were the biggest performance. Probably never in the history of mankind had there been such a bizarre return of a unit to its base. Firstly, two had flown away, and one came, and in addition belonging to the enemy. Secondly, stolen Kandrok's ship had 'Aural 2's' communications system, which aroused the suspicions of the Kiritians from Cargoo, who remembered Beliar Drunkenstein's Trojan horse very well. Biffter didn't know what to think of all this, he had the ship temporarily anchored in orbit. Captain Victor Shane's voice sounded very real, but who could know what kind of tricks Kandrok was capable of? They could voice after capturing the crew. The corners of the ex-emperor's mouth rose, however, as Seymour, attached to the rope, stepped off the board and began making vulgar gestures and waving his arms to convince the Cargoo squadron that had been sent into orbit that he was him and no one else.

"Give them permission to land," Necron said to the Kiritians who had a shift in the underground air traffic control room.

There were more quirks as the ship unskillfully landed in front of the onlookers and the cloaked airport staff. The crew sent to B9 multiplied, including the two tied Kandrok members and the corpse. It was unnaturally cheerful, unlike the enraged aliens kept in solitary confinement during the last part of the journey. One, screaming furiously, rushed with the intention of smashing his head against the rock. He was caught in time and overpowered by several Immortals. The second trapped, at the sight of Biffter, began to say something about penises, to which

Darius, stopping a burst of laughter, reacted lowering his head, and Captain Shane looked up at the evening sky. Smoke was coming from the ship, but when the crew moved with the intention to contain the fire, it came to a dead stop at the airlock. Kiret noticed Anna Sandstorm only after a while. He was speechless. He missed the moment when the overjoyed girl reached him and threw herself into his arms. All he was able to do for long moments was to hold her tightly against his mighty chest.

***

Two days later, a roll-call took place on the square, which was simply a smoothed rock with a diameter of almost one hundred meters. A dozen or so Kiritians were promoted to higher positions, including Tsar Seymour. The military ceremony had once been performed by the Council of Five in K'otz'ib'aja, but when it had been destroyed and the number of Kiritians had fallen dramatically due to deaths and disappearances, General Kiret Biffter undertook it on Cargoo. Soon, Anna Sandstorm was also to help him, who after the collapse of the Council, had only the status of captain. Now that their frail population was richer thanks to Dr. Figam and a boost of knowledge about Kandrok, Necron planned to create a more unified structure of his achijes, perhaps a new Council of Dignitaries.

The general standing on the platform began the ceremony by commemorating the fallen, then he passed on to a motivating message to all, then he made a speech to the promoted, congratulating them on their new positions and wishing them success in their professional and private life. He walked from one achij to another, talked to everyone in person, then spoke formally and promoted with a short sword, with which he touched the right shoulder of the kneeling candidate. This eye-pleasing, nostalgic custom had been practiced invariably for centuries.

Kiret was silent for a moment as he faced Seymour, which had his hands clasped behind his back, and was as sober as he was at birth. Or at least that's what the general estimated.

"Corporal Tsar Seymour." The commander of the Kiritians had a severe expression more appropriate for participating in the conviction of a murderer. "You are the craziest and the most incompetent achij I have dealt with, which you have probably heard many times," he began truly according to the regulations. "A junkie, a madman, and a complete freak. I sent you with the task of bringing Dr. Maksimus Figam to the planet Cargoo. And you ..." He smiled indulgently. "You not only located his hiding place. You also obtained the valuable alien ship, prisoners, body for research, and you found the missing Kiritians, including the former council member." He indicated Sandstorm standing at the podium. We have paid tribute to the fallen, but now we must share the new responsibilities that we will face each day. Kneel down." He raised his sword. "So, I'm making you a lieutenant. You will take the place of Lieutenant Aurelius who died in the mission to save Dr. Figam." Kiret retracted the blade, gave as if groggy Tsar his hand when the latter was already standing. "Congratulations, achij, on the officer epaulette. From now on, you have the right to possess your own platoon. We're starting to reorganize soon, the Kiritians will have a constant army again."

The visible symbol was not there, only the entry in the register and the general awareness of the individual changed.

Surprised, Tsar staggered, having stumbled over his foot as he realized the achijes around him were saluting him.

"From a corporal to a lieutenant at once?! Holy cow and a hundred policemen ..."

***

Two hours later, Tsar and Darius roamed the wild foregrounds a few kilometers from the underground base. Seymour knew the rocky landscape very well, he had often gone there for workout and patrols, the latter being more exercise than looking for threats - the Cargoo planet was still safe.

The promoted lieutenant rested his leg on a boulder and pulled at the end of the joint. Contented, he was letting out thick, white smoke for a long time, then flicked the cigarette towards a steep slope stretching for tens of meters. The achijes were silent, each found himself in a different state: the lieutenant was calm and content, while Darius was a big bundle of nerves and panic fear.

Seymour, who watched the valley, began to whistle, amused by the consternation of his companion behind him, which he wanted to extend a little longer. He was hoping that Darius would somehow get a grip and calm down a little before it all started. He took a deep breath of clean air - the synthesizers of the Earth's atmosphere worked flawlessly. The huge setting star K'ajolom flooded the coarse rocks with red and amber colors, which made them seem to burn at the contours. Tsar's modified irises and slicked-back hair also looked like weaved from blood red.

"Cargoo is very similar to Mars, but warmer. Do you know Mars, Darius?"

"No." The boy's thoughts were in a completely different place.

"I've visited it once. Interesting planet. The first of the colonized."

"Maybe I won't be able to visit it," Schindler ground out.

Smiling, Seymour turned away.

"You will. I bet you will see all the colonized planets and moons at the Zodiac Universum. Time will no longer matter to you." He paused for a moment. "I'm used to Cargoo, but I miss my home a lot, I miss Morascrik. Volcanoes, fire, heat and this suggestive twilight."

"Perfect place for evil demons."

Tsar stared at the vanishing quarter of K'ajolom. He wasn't sure if the achij was already raving with emotions, but he replied:

"Demons were not bad in the original beliefs. On the contrary: they looked after rivers, lakes, forests, fields, and so on. Then the human understanding of the world was distorted, and many things changed, both religions and demons. The truth is, nothing is wrong. Evil doesn't exist. Good neither. Everyone has their point of view. In any given civilization, there are adopted norms and laws that must be obeyed. Often unstable and fluid. Sometimes it takes a few decades for good to begin to be perceived as evil, and vice versa."

"Forkis said so ... Can you stop talking at me and prolong?"

"Darius, are you sure of your decision?"

"Yes," Schindler said firmly and nodded.

"Definitely? You're twenty-three, maybe you want to wait a little longer? Most Kiritians choose the time between the ages of twenty-six and forty. You have had the right to contract a super virus for several months. It will not be taken from you because you have shown your loyalty and successfully passed all the trials and tests. It's a certainty."

"I've considered everything, Tsar. I want to do it right here and now, without any public scenes like the one you had with your promotion today. So that no one except you is staring at me." During Forkis' lifetime, kiritianization had been carried out in front of numerous witnesses, for example in the halls of medical centers, but recently a custom had developed that a new achij could get the super virus from their commander, family member or friend in a place of their choice. Without a ceremonial if they didn't wish it. "Anyway, it could be undone, if I wanted to wait it out and take the super virus again."

"But you know, son, that you can even die then?" Seymour straddled a boulder. "It doesn't work like a snap, Kiritian medics will sort it all out. Time is in your favor; the body has to adapt to such drastic changes. Taking the serum shortly after infection is suicide."

Darius paled. Right, he had heard about it this morning from Figam, with whom he talked about kiritianization, but then it had been all in the sphere of imaginations, and now he was standing in front of the unfolding fact and felt its burden. He amazed himself that he was reacting so emotionally as if he had come to his own execution and not for eternal life. The likelihood of an adult post-injection death was as minimal as winning a huge sum of money in a lottery, but it existed. Children and adolescents were worse off because if they had been injected with the super virus - the developing organism could have been smashed by a cytokine storm after its program of action was completely changed, contrary to the laws of nature. The mortality rate in adolescents was fifty percent, so the super virus should have been administered after the age of twenty-one, which was statistically considered by the medics as the safety threshold.

"Could you give me ... some ..." he turned to Tsar.

"No. In this particular case, I have to be consistent. You know you must have clean blood, without any drugs or stimulants, or something may get screwed up. And remember the most important things." Tsar took out of his field uniform pants pocket a container filled with blue liquid, with a secured needle. He leaned forward. "If anything happens, I can't help you. The body has to deal with it itself."

"Will I die?"

"Hey, stop panicking, kid. I can't give you one hundred percent for a successful kiritianization, because nothing in the universe is certain, but considering how strong you are, I know that you can do it. You were tested in this regard. But you remember what Figam told you: the stronger someone is, the more they suffer, because the body struggles more."

"How was it with you?"

Seymour smiled and straightened.

"I was so fucked up I can't remember anything at all. I was the exception to the rule, but I'm alive, talking to you, and I'm normal."

"About the last one, I wouldn't be so sure, boss." Darius expected that, joking, he would somehow relax, but his nerves didn't want to let go.

The lieutenant laughed and stood up vigorously. He grabbed Darius by the arm and put him down on a boulder, with his face to the setting star.

"Okay, we're starting. Don't be so tense, are you afraid of injections too, girl? A little dignity, it is the most important event in your life. Speaking of girls. When it's over, we'll go to the right place and take the best babes. I haven't had a woman in a few weeks."

"I think I will pass. My father taught me to have one for my whole life."

"Then I will show you how bad this approach is and how it interferes with human nature. With all due respect to your dad. Keep your head up, don't stare!"

Schindler flinched as he heard the needle being unlocked. The prick under the occiput, which took place almost immediately, stung a little ... and that's it."

"Already?" The senior private grabbed his neck and instinctively began to massage it.

"Of course, what have you expected?" The lieutenant replied ironically, though he was discreetly watching for the body's reaction.

"And what's next?"

"How should I know? We'll wait and see."

The star was disappearing behind a jagged horizon; tense Darius sat on the cold boulder, Tsar stood beside him, whistling again.

And nothing happened. Minutes passed and the boy felt completely normal. He even felt disappointed because he had prepared for a strong reaction from his body, he was also ashamed before Tsar that he had panicked like a child going to a doctor.

The excruciating pain tugged unexpectedly at Darius' insides, as if a voracious parasite had nested under his ribs, with fangs, spines and claws, and suddenly he felt an uncontrolled hunger coupled with a lust for murder. Schindler groaned, fell off the boulder like flaky. Holding his belly, he curled into a hoop stick.

Tsar stood over him, twisting his lips and frowning.

"What a mother fucker!" Darius rose to all fours, still keeping his hand near his navel. He began to vomit. His lungs ached terribly, he had difficulty breathing, and there was a throbbing in his head as his pressure increased from nerves. "Tsar, you frigging hypocrite! You mistook the vials! You infected me with a fucking Martian Ebola! That's why you had talked about Mars before ..."

"Dude, you're raving. Calm down. Everything is normal."

"This is supposed to be normal?! Fuck, it hurts so much ..."

"Martian Ebola is the most virulent virus ever created. A few minutes after infection, you have pains, then you vomit the contents of your stomach, and forty minutes later you throw up your insides."

"You have comforted me! You have the nerve! Ow..."

"I just wanted to tell you that Figam used Ebola genetic material to create the super virus, but it's not Ebola."

Darius didn't hear it, he didn't even have the strength to swear anymore, he just hissed, groaned, clenched his teeth, tossed his head from side to side and writhed on the ground like a broken worm. He had a seizure. Saliva leaked from his mouth.

Seymour wanted so badly to react, but he couldn't. All he could do was stand like an executioner over his fading victim and watch Darius tire. There was one more thing he could do: take out another joint and light it, which he did with trembling hands.

"Come on ... Endure, Thomas. Don't die. You are fighting, that is, you are strong," he whispered. He had a feeling he hadn't experienced in a very long time, and it gave him the impression that it was something new - fear.

Schindler was so weakened, and the pain and fever so great that his body finally couldn't stand it and he lost consciousness.

***

When he awoke, K'ajolom had already set, giving way to navy-red stripes of clouds in the sky. The world was plunging into darkness. Many stars twinkled in the east. The temperature dropped as if the area had been trying to faithfully reflect what was happening to Darius: he was cold, he felt terribly weak, dizzy, but the most important thing was that all the pain had passed. He realized that he was covered with a blanket.

He was greeted with a look by Seymour slightly smiling, which was sitting on the ground, with a joint in his hand and his back to the boulder. The remnants of blunts were scattered around. Schindler knew that the lieutenant smoked one after the other only when he was nervous, and such situations hardly ever happened. At least his soul was warmed.

"And how are you, man?"

"I'm very faint. I can't get up."

"So, lie a bit, we're in no rush." Seymour grinned. "Congratulations, you are a full Kiritian from now on."

"This is ... already? I'm like you?"

"You will be only deprived of your fertility as the price for your immortality, but this time it will be a simple injection, with no unnecessary entertainment. Horse doctors will turn off your sperm. But you know it, so I'm not going to bore you. Speaking between us, I think Kiret will soon abolish this law so that the Kiritians can reproduce. So many of us died because of Kandrok. In the days of fighting the rebels, sterility made sense, because almost none of us died." The lieutenant released a circle of smoke. "You got an inert form of the super virus that got attuned to your body's proteins. Therefore, Kiritians are not able to infect anyone. I must admit, kid, that at one point I was scared, it looked bad. And the last time I had been so afraid was when my father had forcibly dragged me in front of Forkis. People undergo the change differently. I heard Forkis was puking like a cat." Tsar laughed, but Darius didn't understand the joke. "Anna Sandstorm hallucinated, then fell asleep. Apparently, she tripped so much that she wanted to kiss Kiret. One of my colleagues got up and started running along the wall, with his head scrubbing against it as if he had wanted to crush all the nits or had had a parasite in his brain wanting to take control of his body. But you had a really hard ride."

"Lieutenant, I'm so sorry for my words. I didn't mean to insult you and curse like that."

"You were in a strong affect. It's okay, kid." Tsar leaned over and prodded Darius in the shoulder.

"I think I was hallucinating too; I was hearing strange things. For example, you called me Thomas ... I had heard that before. Why do you call me that?"

The officer took a long drag, staring into the distance, before answering:

"Sorry, I forget myself sometimes, especially when herbs or emotions go to my head."

"Who's Thomas?"

Seymour spat the joint, stood up, slipped his hands into the pockets of his pants.

"He was my brother. He died when he was around your age."

"I'm sorry. Can you tell me what happened? You talk so little about yourself, Lieutenant." Schindler was genuinely interested in the subject, and he would have also liked to distract himself from worrying about his own state.

Tsar grew serious. He stared at lying Darius for a long time, until Darius gave up hope that the lieutenant would speak an explanation.

"Alright, at least talking, I will take your recovery time. I don't talk to anyone about it, so feel special. It might surprise you a lot, but when I was little, I was the exact opposite of who I am now. I was born in 2911, I come from Calvary, colloquially known as the planet of criminals. My family lived in poverty, near a slum. I was a skinny, sickly bastard, spending my days in a decaying neighborhood where pity was considered the domain of the weak. I was constantly hit in the trap by someone because of my small stature and low height, I was bullied and teased because I could not return, my blows were as strong as of a stick insect. I ran with a complaint to my brother, who was a few years older, and he always stood up for me. I admired and trusted him, he never closed his ears to my request, never refused to help. You know, it's a classic scheme: the older brother pastes those who tease younger siblings. However, as he grew older, he changed completely. I don't know the reason for this change, maybe it was a girl, maybe some coaching fool that told him balderdash about broad horizons and unlimited perspectives, or some gear shifted in his head. It doesn't matter, anyway. Thomas got smart; he became a go-getter. He decided that he wouldn't end up poor like our resigned parents. He wanted his own family, which he planned to start, to live in peace and prosperity, to have the best medical care and decent neighbors. However, he didn't want to pursue his dreams of wealth, as many did around him: trade in everything that was prohibited by law, steal or murder on commission. He was disgusted with this world, he wanted to have knowledge and education, to get a good job. Fly to another planet where he could realize himself. However, as a poor fifteen-year-old, he had to start with small steps. Neither he, I, nor our two younger sisters went to school. Our parents taught us to write and read as well as the basics of politics and astro-geography, because education was too expensive and optional in a district like ours. Besides, the government didn't know how many unregistered kids lived there. In addition, the gendarmerie taking minors to school wasn't in the habit of visiting the ghetto, having the strength of a dozen or so of their own officers against several thousand local thugs. I'm not droning on?"

"Speak, Lieutenant. It calms me down." Darius did indeed get absorbed in the story. He started to feel better and better, he was no longer cold.

"Thomas got a job in an inventor's workshop on the outskirts of the estate, he spent the earned money on textbooks, receivers and data carriers. He worked during the day and sacrificed his evenings to study. I was very proud of my brother, as was my mother, crying over her own helplessness. She said something like that, 'Thomas lives surrounded by weeds and grows like a strong tree, resistant to blows from everywhere.' Wise, good, hard-working, sensitive to human harm. My father couldn't help us because his health was fragile, so Thomas decided to get himself and the whole family out of this fix. He was interested in metallurgy, he wanted to go to Mezzo, where he planned to become a director of a factory producing covers for spacecraft. He didn't take drugs, he didn't smoke anything, he limited alcohol, he wanted to have only one woman in his life. In a word: conservative, exemplary man. It was hard to believe that someone like him had been born in the slums, had perfected himself on his own, with no role models around, and little support. He impressed me. I caught the bug from him, I wanted to be like him someday. Achieve something, although as a punk I didn't know yet what. I fantasized that I would have the fastest flying machine on Calvary, expensive clothes and my own home, to which I would take my younger sisters. Soon the lives of Tom and my family started to fall apart. It turned out that my mother had cheated on my father, they broke up after a juicy brawl, she took my sisters with her and left. Why she didn't visit us later, and why the parents divided the children that way, I never found out. The three just disappeared from my life like stones thrown into a sea. And that was all what was left of my sister-care plans. I also received the first lesson, namely erudition from my father, that a man is not a monogamist, so most of such relationships go haywire. Life began to ridicule Tom perfidiously. For faithfulness to friends and boundless trust, fate repaid him with their falsehood. With failures for diligence. Illness for taking care of health. When I watched my brother and his setbacks, my worldview completely collapsed, everything became a chaos, it didn't make sense, because until then I had thought that there was justice, that for work you got fruit adequate to it. This is what Thomas had taught me.

One fall evening he was killed on his way home from work. He just died. So suddenly. Violently. Everything he loved, what he had painstakingly built over the years, had gone out just like that. Like a blown-out candle. It didn't matter anymore. They mistook him in the dark for someone else and shot him dead. And when the gangsters realized there had been the mistake, they were concerned about it as if they had accidentally trampled on a cockroach. Since Tom was the most important person in my life, probably the only one I loved, because I was only attached to my father, I felt as if I had also died in part." It seemed to Darius that Tsar's eyes were moist. "I fell into apathy for many weeks. And when I started to recover, after long reflection, I finally learned the lesson from life. And I wanted to test my theory in practice. I started fussing, taking drugs, hitting, drinking, and when I got older, going to whores. I didn't care at all about anything. I became a slacker, lived off benefit and theft. And you know what, Darius? And everything, the heavy guns, started to fall into place! For evil, life paid me back with prizes. When I swiped someone's money, the gendarmerie didn't catch me. I had little or no ailments after the drugs, but I suppose I was naturally immune to them. Laughing, I could dance on the stimulant on which someone else would have popped off. I stopped drinking quickly; I wasn't into it. The girls came to me by themselves. I had a lot of friends. When we organized a robbery, one covered for the other, no one turned on anyone. So, I was lucky in this area as well. I moved out from my father because I was able to get money for a new apartment and my own maintenance without unnecessary effort. I started traveling around the planet, I joined various criminal groups, getting to know their habits and skills. The most memorable is the Headhunters, one of Calvary's terrorist organizations fighting against expansive refugees. They used to behead captured enemies and use their skulls to build additional walls in their bases. I liked it, taking such a macabre trophy. As you know, there are thousands of religions and worldviews in the universe, but the oldest and largest ones, such as Islam, Christianity and Buddhism, still dominate. Mostly Headhunters were Satanists whose doctrine said, 'do what you want and be happy'. This means there are no restrictions, nothing is real, everything is allowed. Within reason, of course. I found it to be the most normal and healthiest approach to life, subconsciously I felt that it was something for me. Satanism is not a religion, as many believe, but an ideology, and it has a multitude of varieties, both primitive factions, such as lycans, and such requiring wisdom and enormous knowledge. And this is how I lived for several years, carelessly, without worries, without effort, and I still managed to do everything. It became second nature to me, and I became who I am also now.

However, the idyll lasted until the age of 27. My father condemned my life, he scraped by and drank, but he wasn't a criminal. Once upon a time Kiritians stopped on Calvary and he trickily gave me up into their hands. He said it was for my own good, that a soldier's rigor would make me a man. They recruited me, I was physically and mentally fit. At first, I was scared as hell, especially of Forkis, from whom there was no way to hide any thought. And then, as the months passed and I got used to my new life, filled with practice, discipline, conquest, and brotherhood, I thanked my father mentally for the decision he had made for me. Because nothing better can happen to a man than getting endowed with immortality and unlimited personal freedom. Forkis accepted me as I was, aware that an achij's performance diminishes when they are changed forcibly. It was worse with the acceptance among his subordinates, but over time they also understood what the essence of Calvary's ward was. Decades passed and I met you." Tsar paused to catch a long breath and swallow as his throat got dry. "You are so similar in appearance to Thomas, and your character is identical to him in his youth, when he defended me from my persecutors. Also, in you I saw myself when I was younger, when you leeched me on H14 at our first meeting." They both burst out laughing. "Probably not many people will believe it, but even I have deeper thoughts sometimes." He smiled without merriment. "I was wondering if it was a coincidence that I met you on my way. I don't believe in reincarnation, but does it really not exist?"

Grimacing, Darius slipped off his cover and rose to his knees.

"That would explain why you favor me so much, Lieutenant. Thank you for this story and for the person you turned me into. And for the blanket. I'm almost okay now."

"Can you go?" Schindler got up, walked to the edge of the escarpment. He stared where the K'ajolom star had vanished.

"I'm immortal," he whispered. The meaning of the word slowly began to come to him. "I will live forever. I will never die. I will not die ..." He held out his arms. Tossed by wind, he smiled wildly and dementedly. "I'm immortal, yeaaaaahhh!" He screamed into the young night. He reached for a handful of pebbles and threw them in front of him. One time, second, third. He howled, danced.

"Come on, kid." Passing by and smiling like a wolf, Tsar put a hand on Schindler's shoulder. He picked up the blanket and rolled it up. "Now I will show you how really is celebrated receiving a promotion as an officer and the gift of eternal life."

XVI. Aggroteh's Return

Paul had already made many jumps with the Perfarius elevator drive, but he still marveled at this alien invention and couldn't get used to the form of travel so different from that used at the Zodiac Universum. The ship's automatic control system searched for the nearest nodes in space, then asked the pilot which point he wanted to go to. After the selection, a portation occurred that looked as if the machine had disappeared in one place and then appeared in another. As an android, Paul didn't feel the effects of such an escapade, he wondered how Kate or fully organic Aggro would have reacted to that, but both were still asleep. After the portation, there had to be a break, even several months long, for the ship to accumulate energy for the next jump.

Perfarius finally emerged at the Zodiac Universum, near the outer, ice dwarf planet of the Aries Universe.

"October 17, 2974," the android sitting in the pilot's seat read aloud the date in front of his knee. "Seventeen years, two months, three days, twenty-one hours, two minutes, and at that moment fifty-six seconds is the journey in total. Right now, too, the dwarf planet VX09 should be nearby, in its two thousand six hundred and three-year orbital cycle. Barely fifty-four kilometers in diameter at the equator. But I can't see you, a huge chunk of ice. And what's this?"

Instead of the ice dwarf, Paul saw on the scanner tens of thousands of rock fragments.

"It looks bad."

The fragments were very distant from each other, sometimes they formed clusters, being pulled by gravity, so the android could fly between them without any problem. He began to awaken the crew of two sooner than planned. Kate was up a few minutes after the lid lifted, but it took Aggro two hours to recover, which was faster than last time. He also felt much better. Taking advantage of weightlessness, Aggro floated to the cockpit.

"Is this the end of the journey?" He asked excitedly, having greeted Paul and Kate. "Where are we?"

"The return journey from Tamasul took ten years, I had minor problems with a few nodes and therefore everything dragged on. We recently passed the planet XV09, which doesn't exist," the android reported with a mockery.

"In the sense that it is in a different part of this star system?"

"See those rocks on the scanner?" Kate pointed at the objects with her finger. "This is our planet. Destroyed."

"That's why I woke you up earlier," Paul said. "I cannot establish a connection with the Council, Kiret Biffter or Viktor Shane, according to the guidelines I had to contact only them. I should get feedback in a few hours at the latest. I fucking don't like all this."

"Maybe you need to wait longer," suggested androlak. "The called may be temporarily busy."

"All at the same time? Would they downplay such an important mission?"

"Are you broadcasting on the right frequency?"

"As you probably know, I'm an android," Paul replied, too seriously to find it a joke, "and I don't make such mistakes. If there is an error in this case, the other party is solely to blame. The ship's communication works 100% smoothly, there are no disruptions on the way to the source. I did exactly what I had agreed with the emperor before the departure. I used pre-arranged coding and frequency separated for Perfarius' communication only with target people."

"Well, then we have to keep trying," Kate sighed. They fell silent. Aggro stared at the remnants of the planet on the scanner for a while - the cosmos visible through the canopy was a solid black speckled with glittering dots of stars.

"You think he was right?" He asked finally. Kate looked at him. "I mean Nanawak. Could someone really attack our Universum, which results in fights? This planet ..." He sighed, shook his head. "How could he know all this? He called himself the Observer. Maybe there was something in it, that he compared himself to a god."

"Regardless," answered the androlak, "how negative he was in our opinion, Nanawak is smarter than us. We don't understand the methods of his conduct just like an insect doesn't understand the methods of human conduct. Of course, I've chosen the comparison at random. I also have a feeling that the planet was destroyed by someone intelligent, and it didn't collapse as a result of a cosmic catastrophe. Our universe is too mature and orderly for such drastic natural episodes to occur."

"Wait, I think I have something," Paul announced. Aggro floated to him and peered over his shoulder. "Something is moving in our direction. Two or three objects."

"More rocks?"

"More like machines that use drives, but they do look like rocks." The android rubbed his chin. "Very strange. I have not seen such ships yet. They head straight for the Perfarius, but have not yet made contact."

"Maybe they can't see us," suggested the humanoid jaguar. "Are we flying with masking?"

"All the time. According to Emperor Biffter's guidelines." Gessner pressed her hair with her hand.

"So, I think we have the answer. Their course accidentally crossed with ours."

"Just take into account, Kate," Paul replied, "that absolutely no one flies in such a dark nook of the Universum."

"Didn't fly seventeen years ago. A lot could change during this time."

The android pointed to the scanner screen.

"There you go. They have disappeared ..."

Accustomed to the onboard deafness, Aggro flinched as the communicator buzzed unexpectedly. The resounded voice belonged to Kiret, he was surprised, overjoyed and scared at the same time:

"This is General Kiret Biffter. Aggro? Paul? Kate? Is that really you?! Unbelievable ... You are finally there! Hello! I thought something bad happened to you. I expected the journey to take so long, but ... Sorry for my skepticism. I know your location. Listen very carefully now. Don't communicate with me anymore, just flee from where you are! You hear me? You are to get out now! As far as possible from the remains of XV09. Head to the Fish Universe. You are in danger ..."

"It promises to be nice, just great." Paul crossed his arms over his chest. "They greet us finely after seventeen years of work."

"Fly to Chulimal," continued Kiret. "Don't use the official name of the planet aloud under any circumstances, because Kandrok can hear it. I will meet you there and explain everything. We may be eavesdropped on, it's unlikely, but be extremely careful. Good luck. Over and out."

The three looked at each other in silence: Kate worriedly, Paul assumed an angry face and frowned, Aggro was stuck behind his chair in amazement, trying to catch sense in the emperor's chaotic utterance.

"Looks like our bossy dog from Tamasul knew what was up." Paul increased the power of the plasma motor to give Perfarius the speed it needed to make the jump with the subspace drive. "Let's do better what Mr Biffter says, since we don't know the situation at all. Buckle up properly."

Kate mentally agreed with him, she shifted to next chair.

"Where are you planning to emerge out?" She asked.

"A couple of light years away. We will land on the outskirts of the Fish Universe, and from there to Chulimal we will only have two days of fli..."

The shock was as strong as if Perfarius had fallen from a great height onto rocks. However, it was not the head bump on the control panel that turned the android off on the spot, but a bright energy discharge that filled the entire cockpit. Aggroteh passed out after hitting a wall. He hung in the cabin like a corpse in the water. Only Kate was fine, because she managed to secure herself, grabbing the back of the chair.

The previous two ships appeared on the map of the surroundings, several kilometers from Perfarius. They were so ugly and misshapen they looked like asteroids with drives.

"Paul! They're shooting at us! Wake up!" The desperate androlak shook her companion, but quickly noticed the futility of this action. She didn't know what the impulse from the alien ship was or how it affected Paul. She supposed it had something to do with the fact that, unlike her, the android was a hundred percent machine, and he reacted much like the ship's hardware. She tried to revive the Onkalot, but also to no avail.

She was left alone. The fate of Nimja's companions and the artifacts being carried now depended on her. She hastily attached Aggroteh to the rear cockpit seat and sat down at the machinery. In human life, she had known geology and had a gift for attracting bad people to herself, but over the hundreds of years with Paul, she had mastered many useful skills, including piloting. Thanks to this, the couple 'lived', traveling and accepting contracts. Kate knew that she would never be as perfect as the android series Liquid 5, but she had to do her best.

Another shock ensued. Almost all the lights went out. The androlak cursed. She tried to contact the aggressor, but the impulse damaged or blocked the communicator.

Ships of unknown origin flew over the roof of the ship, disappeared into the depths of space, but soon began to turn back.

Before the woman continued the activity abandoned by Paul, she out-thrusted the cannons from the armor and responded with fire to the enemy. The rock-shaped machines easily bypassed the combat plasma fire and disappeared from the scanner again. That's exactly what Kate wanted - a moment of peace. She had no intention of starting a battle. If the enemy was playing with her, trying to destabilize the whole Perfarius piece by piece, they made the mistake of moving away with a too wide angle.

The androlak quickly accelerated the ship, switched from one propulsion to another - and 'Perfarius' made a jump. Time and space broke down, were no longer measurable in any way. The cosmic objects took on brightness and moved like glowworms passed by a skulak flying through a jungle at night.

And then everything went back to normal. The red-hot 'Perfarius' ended up in the Pisces Universe, but the temperature of the armor, which was harmless to the crew, was rapidly dropping. Kate switched the subspace drive to the plasma one with the touch of a finger; thanks to the artificial body, she didn't feel the jump in any way. Nervous, she looked at her companions. Paul was still turned off, and the Onkalot unconscious.

In turn, on the tail of Perfarius there were two enemy units.

"What the hell?! How?!"

She couldn't have known that Kandrok's machines could use the newly generated subspace tunnel. Over a distance of several light years, they easily got to the same point as the victim they were pursuing, as if they had been chasing them through an ordinary underground tunnel. Perfarius might have escaped if it had jumped with the elevator drive into a random node, even one of the closest, but it would be a long time before the ship built by Kiritians regenerated energy from its previous portation. Kandrok had long since solved the energy problems associated with jumping with elevator propulsions. The Immortals had barely stolen the technology, but Kate hadn't had time to consider it. She was forced to make a quick decision to escape.

The ships barely made it out of the subspace tunnel and began the fire again. Accurate. Hyper-resistant by Kiritian standards, the dhurnsteel armor weakened with each hit. And the enemy used the minimum power of their weapons for entertainment. "If it continues, they will break through and cause decompression," Gessner got scared. "As long as everything doesn't explode sooner."

Even more machines of unknown type appeared on the scanner. They flew at Perfarius from the front.

"So, it's over now."

Kate sighed resignedly, feeling very sorry. She had failed Paul and Aggroteh. She would lose the artifacts and Forkis would never be reborn. She would disappoint the Kiritians and give satisfaction to the enemy with unknown intentions.

Dozens of ships approached. The attack began ... not aimed at Perfarius.

"What's going on?" Paul moved. Kate grabbed his suite and started shaking him.

"Paul! What's wrong with you? Are you alright?"

"If you don't stop tugging at me, I won't be." He looked around the cockpit semi-consciously. Behind the canopy he saw ephemeral flashes. "What's happening?"

"I don't know. They're fighting."

"Who's fighting?

The androlak withdrew her arms, nestled against the back of the armchair and briefly summarized what had happened.

"Well done, Kate, with that subspace leap. Now go help Aggroteh." As he spoke, Paul kept his eyes on the spectacle unfolding in outer space. He was as confused as his girlfriend when he saw naval craft of an unknown type firing at ships of an unknown type. The squadrons that attacked the aggressor consisted of machines similar to those used by the Kiritians, with the organic nature of the hulls resembling ciliates. Paul considered that during their expedition to Tamasul, the Immortals might have created new series of ships and naval crafts. He didn't see his role in this conflict. Distracting the fighters with messages could prove fatal, and the communication of 'Perfarius' didn't work anyway. The android felt as useless as an ant, above which wolves are fighting. He decided it would be best to wait at a safe distance, so he directed the ship out of the fighting area.

Paul's battle and doubts didn't drag on endlessly. Two aggressor units, even with their technological superiority, stood no chance against dozens of ships and eventually became stardust. But they held out for a surprisingly long time anyway.

The android calculated that they would have had a chance to win in a twenty-to-two skirmish.

Soon the communication blockage was over, and the winner of the skirmish contacted 'Perfarius'. In the man's harsh voice there was an obvious threat:

"This is General Velkee Warfighter. You've gotten five seconds to identify yourself, or you'll end up like those Kandrok carcasses."

"I'm the android Paul, Perfarius' pilot hired by Emperor Kiret Biffter. The mission code is 92351825. My companion Kate Gessner and the Onkalot Q'ualel known as Aggroteh are also on board."

"Wait, I have to get a confirmation. Don't take any steps, Mr. Paul without last name, until I give you an order."

Aggro began to recover; he massaged his bruised neck and a growing lump on his head. Seeing that nothing serious had happened to him, Gessner floated to the android and looked at him expectantly.

"I know, Kate," Paul said. "Quite a mess formed during our absence."

"So, it's indeed a war."

"We'll probably find out soon. I know this general, he's one of the members of the Council of Five of the Immortals. The battle must therefore be on a large scale."

Surrounded by Kiritian units, they waited half an hour before Warfighter set the ball rolling again. This time he had a nicer, calmer timbre of voice:

"General Kiret Biffter confirmed your words, android. He asked you go to Chulimal. I'm taking my fleet to the Cargoo base, so we are going in a similar direction. The sector you're in is safe, you must have brought the enemy with you from subspace. However, they have been liquidated and are no longer able to inform Kandrok of the situation. I understand that you would like to accompany us?"

Kate smiled and nodded at the irrecusable proposition.

"Yes, we will," the android replied matter-of-factly. "And thank you for saving us." He still didn't know what was happening at the Zodiac Universum, but the Kiritian fleet accompanying them should have still aroused public fear. "So, our job is done," he said to Aggroteh.

"Hope it's not a ruse," Kate remarked. "Mr. Biffter should contact us himself, not through General Warfighter."

"Apparently something is restricting him, since he avoids contact," the android said grimly.

***

Jenny Sandstorm had been staring with slight curiosity at her father's body for some time. She glanced twice at Aggroteh standing at the entrance to the chamber, looking for similarities between him and the contents of the cryo-biochamber. She had gotten to know the detailed story of Anna, Forkis and Onkalots, as well as the problem of Kandrok, a year earlier when in her youthful verve she had kicked up a row with Kiret that he had treated her like an egg and ignored difficult questions. After making arrangements with Anna, Necron had agreed to tell the seventeen-year-old girl about everything. It had been a while before she could fully safely see the hidden body in Tz'aqol's

Temple. She supposed she would experience the event, but after the fait accompli, she felt absolutely nothing, as if she had been looking at any of display cases in a museum. She had never dealt with Forkis, so she wasn't emotionally attached to him, therefore she only eyed up the clone and compared him to herself. The case was different with Anna standing next to her, constantly recollecting the events from the time when Forkis had still been alive, especially the adventures on the planet Aj, where two deadly enemies had gotten up close and personal with each other.

With his arms folded across his chest, Necron was leaning against the corridor wall facing an open room. He stared blankly at the back of the women talking in low voices, thinking himself about the inconceivable things Aggro had told him in front of the temple the day earlier evening.

From the moment of his arrival in Perfarius, the humanoid jaguar had been constantly accompanied by Chimalmat. She had hugged him warmly as if they had been old acquaintances, intimidating him. Aggro had stayed with people for a long time and managed to forget what Onkalotian honesty and kindness was. Despite the presence of carefree, though slightly insane Chimalmat, he himself was unmerry and in a gloomy mood. For he had learned from Darius, who had come to Chulimal with Necron and the Kiritian team, about the fate of his parents. He felt responsible for their deaths as he had chosen to go on the trip rather than stay with and protect them. He was afraid to visit the Rafens, where Eredal now lived as a mature woman. He was afraid of the changes that had taken place in her, more mental than physical. He was constantly tormented by Nanawak's words, advising him to leave her forever.

"I've preferred to meet on Chulimal. It's a safe planet right now, good for thinking out," Necron said to get his attention. Aggro nodded, casually wrapping an arm around Chimalmat clinging to his side. "Anyway, I've been planning to show Jenny her father for a long time, so your return and our flight synchronized. After everything you've told me about Tamasul and Nanawak, I got confused. I'm even shocked. I thought there was nothing worse than Kandrok. Soon I will officially announce everything on Cargoo regarding the Tamasul mission and my plans. I thanked you yesterday as well as Kate and Paul who left us after receiving their salary, but I will do it again. I'm grateful to you for everything. You refused to take financial prize, but if I could do something for you ..."

"You really don't have to," replied the Onkalot, smiling politely.

"If there's such need, we're your debtors. I will always help you."

"Can you explain to me, Kiret, what's going on? Yesterday we focused mainly on my relationship. What is the current situation?"

"As you already know, four years after your departure, we were attacked by Kandrok. For a long time, we were only victims furious at our own powerlessness, but much changed when Ly and Rei'than, whom we are keeping alive, fell into our hands, and Dr. Figam and the promising scientist Alejandro Cortez returned. Hidden, we develop new technologies and perfect inventions, acceleration of development is in full swing. We also captured several Kandrok's ships and bodies, which expanded our knowledge of it. We copied some of their technology, adding our own elements, for example the elevator drive went to conveyor belt production. I was hoping your trip would give us a chance to get Forkis back, but at least we're on the right track, as long as Nanawak didn't trick us. Contrary to his words that everything was planned long ago, we will fight. With the former emperor at the helm and the innovative military base, we could declare hot war on Kandrok. Two years ago, we found General Velkee Warfighter and part of the missing Morascrik fleet, which added to our main force on Cargoo. But it is still not enough. We need more people." Kiret sighed, looked up at the ceiling, and saw an old, matted cobweb. "I never thought it would come to this, but the only way out of this situation is to ask the opposition for help. I considered this move for a long time, I searched for arguments to dismiss the idea as ineffective, but I lack such. I'm afraid the rebels, while still under our tutelage, will take advantage of our weakness to finish off the lying."

"I don't think that's possible." Chimalmat, Aggro and Necron turned their eyes to Anna, who left the room with her daughter. The Onkalotian effortlessly slid the heavy stone door closed with a technolytic mechanism that was still working. "There is a distance, cultural and also biological gulf between the people of Zodiac Universum and Kandrok. The latter is not colossal, because, according to Figam, we share eighty-nine percent of genes with them, but it does exist, although no one knows how it is possible. Moreover, the enemy doesn't want to communicate with us, and their actions in our territories don't make any sense, they are chaotic. Even Lieutenant Tsar Seymour, who was the only one to get some information from Rei'than and Ly after applying ... his methods of persuasion, failed to get the answer what Kandrok is looking for in this part of the cosmos. It looks like they have some kind of brain blockade that prevents them from giving certain information even under the influence of drugs and medication, or they just don't know a lot as lower rank soldiers. For now, we only know that Kandrok flies wherever it wants, conquers what it wants, mines only heavy metals and sometimes round up people to get from their bodies," Anna grimaced in disgust, "the foundations for the production of fuels. However, the lieutenant learned many other useful things."

Jenny looked at Necron and kept her eyes on him. Kiret returned the look, absorbed in wondering about his numerous problems, then glanced at Anna again.

"So, as you can see, Kiret, the rebels will not join our enemy," added the captain. "Let's not get hysterical."

"You know the opposition, Anna. You grew up among these people. Do you think they would cooperate with us?"

"I don't know what their mentality looks like after a dozen years of illusory freedom, but if you want to be sure we can pay them an official visit on Nephrida. They have to be convinced that Kandrok is also a threat to them, which is rather truthful. Perhaps they believe that when the strongest dies, the enemy will not be interested in the weaker ones."

"The visit is probably the best solution; we will finally be able to use the rebels for something. When we get back to Cargoo, I'll organize a delegation to Nephrida. It is possible that they will have to be bribed with something to prevent them from stabbing us in the back, and certainly be offered something that they need. But we'll discuss everything in detail at the Cargoo briefing, together with General Velkee Wharfinger."

"I understand that I'm also going to Cargoo?" Jenny having tilted up her chin a little, said in an official tone. Also offended, as Necron paid attention only to her mother. She had to let him know that she was there, too, and that she was no longer a few years old to be ignored in conversations.

"No, you're going to Atla," he replied immediately. "To my mansion."

Jenny spat ostentatiously. This time she embraced Necron with a gaze as cool as the nether regions of that temple, brushed his mind telepathically.

"Because I'm a stupid chit? That's what you think of me right now."

"How do you address the general?" Anna scolded her. "Mr. Biffter has achieved a lot in his life, he doesn't deserve such treatment."

"We're going to eat outside," Aggro said, dragging Chimalmat with him. He didn't see his role in this conversation, and he wasn't going to experience another nerve-racking situation, looking at the whims of the teenager.

Embarrassed, Kiret scratched his head as he accompanied the Onkalots with his look. Though Jenny had claimed in interplanetary conversations that she had learned to read minds almost as well as Forkis, at first, he had thought she had exaggerated to attract attention. It had turned out that she sometimes did it flawlessly, as now. Necron spoke to Aggroteh about the phenomenon. He learned that among humanoid jaguars psionic abilities were sometimes passed down hereditarily, although they were usually directed by the environment. He couldn't understand, however, how they could have passed over to Jenny since she was conceived when Forkis had the body of a human.

"Sorry, Jenny," he replied calmly. "But that's exactly how you've been acting lately. What's going on with you?"

"You know what? Better give me a break," the girl said sharply, then turned on her heel and walked away into the temple lit by torches and Kiritian fire. Necron put his hands on the hips, shook his head, exhaling loudly. Anna looked into his eyes, made a move with her eyeballs towards Jenny, then returned to him with her look.

"I don't have the strength anymore. I give up. Maybe you will achieve something, Necron."

"Okay, I'll take care of it," he panted.

"Thanks. And sorry for her."

"Why don't you go and see what about Darius and the guys, if they're back from the trip?"

Kiret followed the teenager who had already disappeared from sight. When Anna was found in space, she moved to Cargoo. Due to the numerous responsibilities and the threat of being targeted by Kandrok, both she and Necron rarely visited Jenny, still officially using the surname Bidwell. Anna didn't want to involve her in military and political issues and bring her from safe Atla, moreover, the sight of her daughter reminded her of lost Forkis. Both had never built healthy family relationships with each other. Jenny was an oders, and it seemed strange to her that her mother looked several years older than her. To that day, Anna had remained more alien to her than Kindra Bidwell, she trusted more Necron, whom she saw more than her mother. She knew he existed, he was real, flesh and blood. Recently, however, she had developed a tendency to give him layers of rage, especially after seeing him with Anna. Kiret and Jenny had gotten along very well until the day he first met the missing captain after she was found by Shane's crew. Then the sulks began, with more intensity from month to month. The man explained it to himself thinking that Jenny was just growing up.

He found her sitting on an empty pedestal.

"Alright," he set the ball rolling as gently and as calmly as he could. "Tell old Necron what happened this time."

He noticed that Bidwell, sitting sideways to him, was twirling with her fingers something she quickly put in her pocket, like Tsar Seymour drugs at the beginning of his tenure.

"You're not that old at all," she replied. She turned around. "How old are you, biologically? Thirty-four?" She asked the unnecessary question: she knew almost everything about Necron. The age at which he had become a Kiritian was the first thing she had remembered. But she liked to hear him talk about it. "Hey, why can't I read your mind right now?"

Kiret smiled, slightly showing his well-groomed teeth.

"Your father taught me this private thought-blocking trick. It is simple, at least for someone who has practiced for hundreds of years in the presence of the telepath emperor. You just need to express yourself automatically, without using your imagination. Simply put, keep your head empty when you talk. Of course, I have to focus on this, which I didn't do before when you got to know my thoughts." He sat down on a corner of the plinth. "So, you tell me, frog, what are you mad about?"

"Mistake!" He bit his tongue almost immediately. He remembered the explosions of the teenager when he addressed her as in childhood, with all sorts of 'frogs', 'suns' or 'hearts'.

Jenny stood up, staring at him with bulging eyes like of a crushed bird.

"Guess. And don't talk to me as to a child that I have not been for a long time!"

"Sorry about that frog," he replied agreeably. If Forkis had been in his place, for such a sign of arrogance and disrespect for the elders, Jenny would have landed on the wall much earlier. Meanwhile, he patiently took all her verbal hits, which annoyed her even more, as she expected a sharper reaction. "But I didn't mean anything pejorative. 'Frog' is a nice and warm term."

"It is as if I called you an old, slow fool. Nice?" She sat down heavily, more like collapsed on the plinth. And with this action, the collected air went out of her lungs.

"You said yourself a moment ago that you don't think I'm old. So, enlighten me, who annoyed you today? Darius Schindler again?"

"Guess."

Necron slapped his hands on his knees.

"Come on, girl. Darius, right? Because he wanted to make friends, but you didn't?" As he looked at her, the resemblance to Forkis was immediately apparent: the same black hair, but tied up into a high ponytail, big brown eyes, fair skin. But her character was almost like Anna's, at least her crude version from the rebel period. The difference was that Jenny used a whole range of emotions unscrupulously, sometimes ostentatiously, while Anna never cried. It is said that Forkis was the first to reduce her to tears.

"You lead the interesting life." Jenny replied calmer. "You travel, you are surrounded by your happy soldiers while I'm stuck as if under house arrest at your Atla estate," she counted on her fingers, "with the bodyguards, gardener, cyber-nannies, steward and two cooks. Don't count the gardener anyway, because he had to quit his job for private reasons."

"It's strange that he didn't report it to me himself, neither the manager. I'll scold them."

"There's no need to. I told him not to inform you because you still had your important matters. I will find someone suitable for the position myself."

"No irony, okay? Because I won't talk like that. I would like to inform you that these 'important matters' are a fight for the safety of the entire Zodiac University. In addition, I have to approve the production of new machines, analyze reports from many planets and moons, suppress revolts, lead the army, participate in roll-calls, make speeches, attend briefings, monitor the rebels and do many other boring things for you. Jenny." Kiret put his arm around her in a friendly way. "When Anna was your age, she didn't have such blessings as you have now. She couldn't stay on the peaceful planet, in the beautiful mansion, where the greatest concern are school exams. Please think about it and appreciate what fate has given you. Anna would love to take you to Cargoo, believe me. She's troubled by your separation. However, this planet has become a military facility, where you will find neither respite nor peers. It is not safe, because we have developed a metal infrastructure in the nether regions, and Kandrok is able to find places rich in metal. We are ready to evacuate at any time. We thought several times that we had been detected, fortunately they were false alarms. We even keep Forkis' body on Chulimal."

Though Jenny was delighted to be wrapped with his arm, she slipped showily from his embrace, wincing.

"Only during exams do I have a chance to meet my peers. And normally I'm constantly alone, sometimes I feel like talking to the trees. Home learning takes place either remotely or by tutors. I'd rather get some entraser knowledge and do something specific. You made my life like that. I'm far from home, my whole world is virtual. I don't even have a boyfriend. No friend. It's not as good as you think. But you don't have children and you don't know ..."

Necron waited for a moment, thoughtful, before answering:

"The situation is not normal, we need restrictions. I think you will appreciate it someday if you don't look at life through the prism of youthful emotions. If we manage to get Kandrok out of the Zodiac Universum, of course. We are keeping a stranger named Rei'than in prison, we learned from him that in their community the highest position is held by someone like a king, they call him gerha. Sometimes it happens that the opponent wants to throw a gerha from the throne, first murders his offspring, then he takes care of his dignitaries, and finally the ruler himself, although not always. Sometimes the coup ends with a life imprisonment of the overthrown ruler. Kandrok applies its customs to other species, doesn't tolerate or recognize otherness, which is why it still hunts for my head and that of General Velkee. Once upon a time, like you, I had to hide under a false surname. I even grew the long hair and beard that you loved so much as a kid."

Jenny smiled against her resolve to keep her face offended throughout the entire conversation. She imagined Kiret with spiky hair like Dr. Figam's, and that amused her.

"If we were captured," continued Necron, "they could imprison and torture us, but they would kill you one hundred percent as the Emperor's daughter. According to Kandrok's thinking, you could be my and Forkis' successor, since you have the gerha's blood in you. It looks a bit like in ancient human families, as long as Rei'than didn't make fun of us."

"Nonsense. I will never lead anyone. I don't like it, it's not my style."

"But Kandrok doesn't think so. I promise that when we hopefully throw them out of both of our galaxies, you'll cease to be sheltered. I will organize a tour of the coolest planets for you." Necron's mouth corners lifted.

Jenny folded her hands on her thighs, tilted her head and looked at the sand-strewn floor.

"It's also about my mother." She looked at her neighbor with her left eye. She felt a hint of anger again and wanted to lace into the man when she saw him and Anna in her mind's eye. "You lech after her, don't you? More than once I saw you hugging or whatever else you were doing. You know you're acting like a complete punk? Anna has a husband who is helpless and unaware of the existence, he has no way to hit you in the face. Respect that. Respect what Aggro did for you! He was risking his life to get those idiot artifacts. He lost his family and friend as a result!"

Necron covered his face with his hands in an attempt to suppress his anger, which Jenny interpreted with satisfaction as bitterness and an admission of guilt. He withdrew his hands and stood up.

"You have gone too far, young lady," he growled. "Know that I don't lech after the captain, I only offer her support. I haven't touched her even once!"

Jenny got up too, moved her hands with clenched palms backwards, as if she had been going to jump into the water.

"So? Will you lock me up somewhere in the temple like my mother once in the K'otz'ib'aja chamber? Damn, you're so blind ..."

Kiret approached the girl, who didn't move even a centimeter, towering over her. In terms of height, she took after Anna, not Forkis.

"And that's what saved her from dying in the arena. That is why you are here now, dear child."

Jenny grew angry, hearing the gently, yet coldly spoken words. Her mood changed a hundred and eighty degrees again. Surprising herself, she hugged Kiret like the aforementioned child. He returned the hug, stroked her back as he had done when she had been little and for any reason, she had run to him crying.

She lingered to free herself from his arms, but finally moved away from Biffter, holding his wrists for a moment.

"You really don't understand," she whispered sadly. "You are an obvious proof that even hundreds of years of life will not give a guy a little bit of sense."

She withdrew into the corridor.

"Women. And how to be wise ..." Necron didn't care about her sulks. "Just an explosive, raving kid," he thought. Just like Darius, who a few years earlier, in the same place, had wanted to save Chulimal from evil like a book hero.

***

Corporal Darius Schindler returned from patrol in the afternoon as announced. Together with the three privates, they did their rounds in skulaks on the planet, on the way Darius visited his sister Eredal. He was satisfied that he hadn't found a single lycan anywhere.

As he descended from the antigravity machine, he noticed depressed Jenny leaving the temple corridor. He had met her on that trip to Chulimal and at once he had made a hit with her. He had been captivated by her delicate beauty and fragile figure, which, with an explosive character, constituted an interesting, bipolar mixture. Big deer eyes too, though with sparks of sadness and anger that often vied for dominance. Schindler had been literally struck like a tree by lightning, and from the moment he saw Jenny, it hadn't wanted to pass, he had thought about her incessantly. It was the first time he had experienced such a feeling. Tsar had forced into his head for years that this was something bad and it would eventually destroy any man, he recommended stifling any blind infatuation, but this time Darius was somehow dealing with it poorly. He tried timidly to pick up the girl, but she ruthlessly put him off.

But he kept trying.

He made one of his learned, disarming smiles and said a neutral, "Hello." Jenny, however, passed by indifferently in a direction known only to her, maybe not having the destination. She showed Darius her interest as intense as in a stone in grass, though at least the stone could be kicked if it irritated.

"Not your league, sir. She's the boss' daughter," said some achij amusedly, but Schindler, whom Seymour had taught to conquer all the maids of the universe, wasn't interested in jokes about himself.

"You are dismissed till the evening," he said to his subordinates. "Then we're leaving the H14."

He accompanied Jenny with his look until she went over the gangplank to the ship and disappeared into the depths of the hangar. Moments later, Aggro was approached by Darius.

"Where's Chimalmat?" Schindler asked.

"I sent her to the woods. You asked yourself yesterday to gather some rare weed."

"Oh yes. Lieutenant Seymour asked me." Darius smiled meaningly.

"At least I could keep her busy for a long time. I'm going to see Eredal."

The Kiritian grew serious.

"You said you didn't want to. Why did you change your mind? I can assure you that she is fine."

"I thought it over again. I need to see her."

"It's a long way from here. I understand you want me to take you there."

Aggro pointed to Perfarius stationed not far from the Kiritian ship.

"I have a smilodon, it is awake. It would be nice if you accompanied me."

The boy shrugged.

"If that's better for you. I'll just ask the general if he needs me for something. Keep in mind that once we're on the spot ... you may not like certain things."

After a quarter of an hour, they were both on the road: Aggro was rushing on the back of the huge cat, while Darius was flying in the skulak several dozen centimeters above the ground. The animal with winter fur, not adapted to tropical conditions, tired quickly and overheated, so they chose a route through the lower parts of the mountains, where the wind was stronger, it was cooler and thinned vegetation grew. They took breaks while the smilodon wallowed in streams and caught fish. The eclipse brought much relief when one of the two moons of H14 obscured almost the entire shield of the K'ajolom. The condition lasted a long time. The temperature dropped slightly, and the less light revived the smilodon.

After a few hours they were on the spot. They left the animal and the skulak on the edge of the forest, and they themselves covered on foot a little distance in an open, hilly area. While on the Shindlers' decommissioned farm mainly grew bulbous onions with a high content of nutrients, on the Rafens' one dominated bananas, carambolas and kakis, growing separately on large plantations. The buildings that made up the farm and the hotels for workers were located in a shallow valley, so Aggro and Darius could stop on its edge and watch the work of the people below. It was the idea of the humanoid jaguar who at first had intended to go to the Rafens' house and ask for a conversation with Eredal, but he refrained and decided to take a look. Again, he remembered Nanawak's words that he should have left the girl alone. The unexpected visit after several years of absence would surely disturb the peace of his old friend.

Darius felt stupid spying on his own sister, whom he had recently visited, but he had promised Q'ualel that he would accompany him.

Aggro saw her quickly and felt a nasty pressure in his heart. She had changed. Thanks to the achievements of medicine, oderses could live up to one hundred and fifty years, and eighty-year-olds could resemble thirty-year-olds with verve and appearance. H14 farmers, however, preferred to live in accordance with the cycles of nature, therefore they didn't artificially extend their lives or modify their appearance. Eredal was about forty now, and thanks to Aggro's good eyesight, he could see her hair shorter than before, a little faded from the sun. She wore a summer dress and a large, braided hat. She had taken shape. The smile and warmth in her eyes remained the same. She was crouched by the steps of the house, showing something to a ten-year-old girl with red hair like in all the Rafens. Soon a skinny teenager ran up to Eredal, who in turn wore golden hair just like that she had had in her youth. They exchanged a few sentences, then the woman pointed her finger at a banana field, to which the boy went, having taken a wicker basket. A man came out of the house, Aggro recognized him as an adult Anton Rafen. He kissed Eredal, put his arms around her waist, gave his other hand to the girl, and the three disappeared into the hallway.

Aggro lowered his head, stared for a long time at the ground next to his forepaw.

"Let's go," he muttered.

"But you wanted to ..."

"No matter what I wanted. I should listen to you. Eredal's life is arranged. Nothing here for me."

Darius sighed.

"Alright, as you wish."

He descended the gentle slope towards the forest. Crouching Aggro straightened and looked proudly at the farm in the valley.

Eredal went out onto the porch. Subconsciously, something made her glance towards the hill. She saw the humanoid jaguar looking at her. She clenched her hand and brought it to the lips parted due to the surprise, stood there for a moment, then lowered her fist towards her heart. She looked at Q'ualel sadly, with pity and disbelief. She made no gesture or step, just stood and looked, and the wind moved her hair.

Aggro turned and simply followed Darius down the hill.

***

They returned to the square of Tz'aqol's Temple late in the evening, when the sky was of various shades of red, orange, and pink, and the two moons were shining brightly in different phases. Chimalmat expecting Aggro, brought him a sack filled with plants. The Onkalot asked her to take the smilodon onto the board of Perfarius and feed it, while he himself went to Kiret.

He found him sitting with his achijes by a large fire. There was also Anna with her daughter.

"Mr. Biffter, a quick word?" He whispered to Necron.

"Oh, hello Aggro. I'm coming." Necron stood up. They walked away a bit, out of earshot. "And how was your meeting with Eredal?"

Q'ualel, who was not in his best mood, ignored the question.

"You mentioned earlier that you were organizing an expedition to Amyrade Anfraktoris, a secret place that Nimja showed me. Can I volunteer?"

"So, I understand that the conversation went wrong." The man gave him a sympathetic look.

"There was no conversation, Mr. Biffter. Eredal has a family and children. I just walked away."

"I'm sorry."

"I want to fly with you, to Cargoo."

"Aggro ..." Necron began seriously, he had worried expression. He put a hand on his shoulder. "You are doing again the same as before the expedition to Tamasul. You're nervous, cool down a little. I will not let you risk your life a second time, especially since now it will be much worse than before. And no, no high-flown arguments that you're doing this for Forkis!" He said sharply when Aggro was about to speak. "Look, I was his friend too, even greater than you, I spent many centuries as his right hand faithfully following Forkis' orders. I'd love to go to Amyrade myself, but I can't. I'm the chief general of achijes, the supreme authority among them. Kiritians need a leader, I cannot be selfish, nor leave them when the war with Kandrok is approaching. In turn you are needed by Chimalmat." Necron nodded to the Onkalot female, who had already returned from the ship, sitting on the trunk and looking at them. The man lowered his voice. "Don't leave her alone, Aggro. Nobody knows better than you what true loneliness is. You don't have to do anything for Kiritians, I will find the right people for this mission. Why do you want to expose yourself again?"

"I'm going to see everything through. Since I was on Tamasul and survived, why wouldn't I go to Amyrade?"

"Maybe because there's someone who needs you now? Maybe because there are so few of you now?"

"And your immortal people, you can put them at risk?"

"Unlike you, we are soldiers. And every soldier, immortal or not, who voluntarily joins the army, agrees to place his fate in the hands of the White Lady, even if the juxtaposition of the gift of immortality and death in battle seems absurd. We've talked enough about it. My decision will remain the same. Sorry, Q'ualel. This time I will not budge. Stay on H14, the planet is big, so there's room for you and Eredal." He poked him comfortingly in a shoulder with his fist. "Guard with Chimalmat Tz'aqol's Temple and Forkis' body."

Whatever Aggro wanted to say, the words got stuck in his throat. Walking away, he let out a short sigh.

The female smiled broadly and carelessly, wiggling her tail slightly as he walked toward her. Aggro also bestowed a smile on her, a small but spontaneous one that he hadn't had on his face for a long time.

XVII. Rebels

Kiret studied the three items brought from the Jaguar Galaxy, sipping wine from his goblet, standing. Captain Anna Sandstorm and General Velkee Warfighter were also present in the small conference room on Cargoo. They both sat in armchairs at a transparent projection table supported by black metal brackets. Nimja's artifacts lay on the top. The room was sparingly lit, adapted to the late evening hours - Kiritians had in mind that strong, artificial light disrupted the functioning of the body after dark. The hall was located in the building of sector A of the military-research complex, which was then the only object protruding above the surface, but it blended in with the surrounding rocks on the principle of pareidolia. It was considered an achievement of human civilization only when the flaked ceiling was cracked open to observe the sky.

The trio had been discussing for three hours, a cloudy night fell. Kiret spoke the most, recounting the events of the Tamasul expedition. The wine he drank in sparing sips turned a peculiar red under the influence of the xik'iri's casing, known as the

Collector. Sandstorm tried to understand the phenomenon of the object that, unlike kariban and karitan, which had the same matrix taints, sometimes changed colors. Regardless of humidity, temperature, pressure or lighting. However, she didn't come to any conclusions. Dr. Figam was particularly interested in the items Aggroteh had brought, and he was disappointed when Biffter forbade him to study them in depth. However, as an outstanding scientist, he understood that it was better not to touch the only copies given to them by the creature reaching six on the Kardashov scale.

Velkee casually rolled karitan with its interior the color of fire. The artifacts made little impression on him, but he was worried about the tactical aspect of the upcoming mission.

"Incredible." Kiret put down the empty glass and filled it to the brim with wine from the decanter, but he grabbed turquoise kariban instead of the drink. He brought it close to his face to see more clearly the tiny ornaments fumbling inside. "Such inconspicuous something that looks like a child's toy can transfer to another dimension and return from there."

"As long as we haven't been fooled." Warfighter held karitan with a finger. "This Nanawak, or whatever that dog is called, didn't specify where that Amyrade Anfraktoris was. So let us not assume that it is beyond the limits of the physical universes."

"True, General, over-interpretation on my part." Kiret put the item back. He took the goblet and drank it down this time.

"I don't like that we are not able to plan the mission in any way. What will we tell the people we select? Do what you think is right? We cannot train them or sensitize them to anything.

Nothing, absolutely!" Velkee slapped his open palm on the tabletop, so strongly that the objects jumped up.

Necron folded his arms over his chest.

"There is someone who could help us."

Velkee looked at him urgently.

"Who? Dr. Figam?"

"Raver Divinus Relagard."

Astonished, Anna almost choked on the fruit juice.

"That killer from Karikon, appointed as an assassin from the name of their Order's founder?"

Karikon, designated X4, was the only planet not marked on official maps, and a very small group of Immortals knew of its existence. The globe of the Aquarius Universe in Andromeda was inhabited by peculiar animals, some as intelligent as humans, and had scientifically inexplicable anomalies that primitive indigenous peoples called magic. Aggroteh's expedition to Tamasul had made clearer this phenomenon - X4 had been in the distant past the experimental arena of Nimja, which would explain the numerous physical aberrations and mutations among fauna and the piety of the society which in terms of development was in the Early Iron Age. At a time when Kiritians hadn't yet conquered the Zodiac Universum, and the exploration of new worlds had taken place through private companies or state institutions, a group of scientists and soldiers had reached Karikon. There had been a conflict between the members of the expedition, some of them had wanted to make the strange globe a strictly protected reserve, while the rest had intended to destabilize the fragile civilization and bring the citizens of the overpopulated Earth in its place.

There had been bloodshed. The notable Karikonian killer from the Order of Assassintiar, Raver Divinus Relagard, had been involved in the conflict, and in order to save his imprisoned friend, Princess Rizlah, he had killed most of the strangers. After negotiations with the assassin, the two survivors had taken to space the news that X4 had been another of the billions of worthless rock planets, which had saved the local community from annihilation. Time had erased the memory of the planet, but the group of Immortals had still remembered it. Centuries later, Kiritian researchers had dealt with the observation of X4 and the phenomena that had taken place there. It had been decided not to interfere with the planet's nature or the life of its inhabitants, completely covering it with a reserve. It now became clear that 'magic' had been Nimja's legacy, an imprint of incomprehensible, highly advanced technology, and that Nimja itself had survived in the myths of Karikon as Great Mages. Divinus, who obtained their infinite life-extending artifact, sometimes collaborated with Kiritians - if collaboration could be called kidnapping, putting to sleep and examining on board a ship. However, as a remedy, he received the weapon from the Immortals, giving him an advantage over all the people of X4. Living in hiding, he didn't show off his asset, and it was usually seen by those who were about to die.

"Div grew up in a world that is different from the planets we know," said Necron. "From Q'ualel's story it appears that Amyrade Anfraktoris may be similar to Karikon, because on the latter Nimja wanted to recreate the experimental conditions prevailing on the former. Therefore, the help of the assassin would prove invaluable."

"Are you going to introduce him to our plans?" Velkee asked. "What exactly would he do?"

"He would go as an adviser."

"And if he refuses?" Anna interjected. "I know this man's story. He belonged to several assassin orders in the past, but now seems to be acting alone. Due to immortality, he isolates himself from the world. He sides only with the werewolf Rizlah, the Wolf Princess, who is also long-lived because of her condition. Div stays everywhere for no more than a dozen years. What is our guarantee that such a loner will decide on team cooperation? What can we offer him?"

"It's easy." Kiret looked up at the sky, having slid open the conical flakes of the ceiling. "Adventure."

"Adventure?"

Biffter folded his arms behind his back and began walking slowly around the room.

"Next to Forkis and Figam, I was the oldest Kiritian. Out of this trio, only I survived, because the doctor split off. Sometimes achijes call me even the Eldest. That's why I understand probably the best of all Zodiac Universum people what immortality is. It's something that eventually becomes irritating because life becomes boring. An ordinary man of forty years old is bored with existence, let alone someone who lives for hundreds. However, we Kiritians have a highly developed neurology, we can completely or selectively reset memory, also interfere with memories, so we don't fall into the madness known as the syndrome of immortality. And this, too, doesn't always work out, as in the case of Dr. Figam. Think about what must experience Div, in whose world medicine is the use of amulets, herbs and sewing up with a needle wound, eliminated with urine. I've seen him and I know what he wants - total change. Introducing him to the world of our technology will certainly be what he has been waiting for a long time. He is a murderer, but extremely loyal one to the current employer. Unless the latter deceives Divinus. But I'm not planning to do it." Necron sat down in the armchair. "I will hire him and drop off on Karikon when it is all over. Everything according to his credo."

"As far as this Amyrade Anfraktoris is not one big spoof." Warfighter regarded Biffter with skepticism. "By the way, what idiotic names that Nimja comes up with."

"Apart from Divinus, who else will we include in the team? Who are we appointing the commander?" Sandstorm asked.

"They can't be big fish, but at the same time no one foolish with a lower rank," said Warfighter.

"I think Captain Victor Shane is the right choice," suggested Biffter.

"Shane's out." Velkee shook his head. "I sent him to the borderlands. The company commander there had a serious accident and until he recovers, he will need a replacement for the platoons patrolling the borders. Kandrok activity in those areas is becoming more and more visible."

"Before we choose the commander, I would like to propose Corporal Zira Aytar as a participant." Anna shifted her look from Kiret to Velkee. "I think she would get along very well with Divinus and help him integrate with the team. On Calvary, she lived a life similar to the assassin, and they both have similar characters."

Velkee smiled, overly merrily.

"Reasonable idea, Captain. A middleman between the Kiritians and Divinus would be useful on the expedition, if he was in no hurry to assimilate with the team."

"Aytar is alright. Spontaneous but right choice." Necron shifted position in the chair. "A person like Relagard would be useful for us. Someone who can look at life abstractly and has an open mind. Who wouldn't go mad after seeing the overturned world of Amyrade. Assuming, of course, that Nanawak didn't deceive us."

Sandstorm and Warfighter looked at each other, smiled simultaneously and said:

"Lieutenant Tsar Seymour."

Necron couldn't not chuckle.

"Well, well, I didn't think about him. Tsar would be thrilled if Amyrade turned out to be a world like from a narcotic dream. And he would surely know how to find himself in one. But if we were to send Seymour, he probably would like to take Corporal Darius Schindler, his favorite achij. These two are like lovebirds."

"I don't associate the guy," muttered the general.

"He's new. He has been with us for several years. Aggroteh's friend from H14, with whom he lived in John Schindler's house. Such a classic hot-tempered soldier like any youngster. But I vouch for him that he will not cause trouble, he will listen to orders and gladly follow them."

"How many people are you planning to send?" Anna asked.

"From a structural point of view, a team won't come out of this, rather a section. I think seven or eight people will be enough. What other suggestions do you have? Who are we appointing the commander of the expedition? Because probably not Seymour."

"All devils forbid!" Velkee shouted immediately. Anna crossed her legs, leaned back comfortably in the seat, and of the drinks on the table, this time she reached for wine.

"Figam bothered me that he wanted to investigate Amyrade Anfraktoris. I perfectly understand his thirst for knowledge as a scientist. He would be as delighted as Tsar."

Warfighter objected firmly:

"I refuse! He is the best brain we have on Cargoo. If we lost him, it would cost us a lot. A golden goose is not allowed to go into the unknown."

"Don't forget about Andro Cortez, who will probably match Figam in a few years. He is very timid, but he's a good scientist."

"Cortez has a narrower range of specializations, mainly genetics. Thanks to Figam, we can have a new weapon."

"Then let's send Cortez."

"An even dumber idea, dear Anna." Velkee smiled. He liked to tease her. "I wouldn't send an armaments specialist or a budding scientist to a fairyland."

"I just wish to remind you, General, that Dr. Figam himself asked me to select, and it is not my idea."

"No quarrel, my dear," Necron reminded them of his presence.

"We're just talking." Sandstorm put her glass back.

"I'll send Sariel Jelinek. He is a geneticist, technologist and at the same time physicist of our team, currently reporting to Figam. The guy is pretty good ... but from the replaceable category," Biffter finished glumly, rubbing his temple.

"I understand your dilemma," Velkee replied seriously. "We have to gather decent professionals but take into account that we may lose them."

"Shit, Velkee, it's not like that! Sometimes you could hold back from making judgments."

"It is like that." Warfighter gave Kiret a defiant look. "In such a narrow group, let's call a spade a spade."

Anna began to count:

"Divinus, Seymour, Schindler, Aytar, Jelinek. Who else? Maybe another scientist?"

"We need a technician," said Kiret, "that is able to handle the rovers we are building for this trip. Corporal Rasmus Darkoris is on my mind and let him choose two people. Such a group will be appropriate."

"And the commander?"

"Captain Michael Avadar of the emerging D Company of the 3rd Cargoo Infantry Battalion has come to my mind," Warfighter suggested. "Currently, he has no more important duties than training recruits. He has performed tasks on planets with extreme conditions in the past, so perhaps he will find himself on Amyrade."

Necron pondered the proposal for a moment, analyzing the pros and cons.

"All right. Captain Michael Avadar will lead the team to Amyrade. His deputy will be Lieutenant Seymour. Do you have any suggestions for the composition of the team?"

After a moment's thought, Anna shook her head.

"No," Warfighter shared her opinion.

"That's great." Kiret got up to walk past the table and restore circulation to his right leg, which had gone numb. "Although the Council doesn't exist officially, we still reach consensual agreements. It is thanks to this that Kiritians have achieved so much. So, the case of Amyrade Anfraktoris is settled. The code name of the operation is 'Revival'. The mission will begin in a month when the new rovers are ready and we bring assassin Divinus to Cargoo. It is not too late yet, so I suggest discussing the departure to Nephrida. Anna, Velkee, it would be good if the three of us went there. Our former enemies will understand that the Kandrok affair is serious when they see the Kiritian command instead of the ordinary envoys. General Warfighter," Necron looked at Velkee, "will provide us with sufficient protection. If only ..."

Kiret paused as the room door opened slightly. In the aisle stood a corporal, whose name he didn't remember, being on duty in the communications center.

"Mr. Biffter. Interplanetary conversation, priority," he announced.

"I'll be there in a moment." As the corporal was gone, Kiret turned to the two, "I suggest ending the meeting, because I don't know how long this conversation will take me. We will resume it at nine o'clock in the morning, in the same place. Anna, put the artifacts in the locker. I wish you a good night."

Necron immediately went to the Communications Center, where it turned out that the sender of the holo call was Aveo Lacetti, the president of Nephrida.

Sandstorm picked up one item of each kind and carried them to the armored cupboard. Velkee handed her also kariban, and they secured the door. Anna touched a switch in the wall and watched the ceiling shutters close slowly, like a flower after sunset.

Velkee put a hand on her shoulder which she knocked off.

"Not now. Someone might come again," she bridled.

"Don't panic, Captain. You should chill out a bit." The man stepped behind her and placed his hands on her shoulders, which Sandstorm accepted this time with a soft sigh.

"Before the briefing, I had an argument with Jenny again."

"I noticed that you were nervous all the time."

"Do you know what she did?"

"I'm waiting for enlightenment." The general inhaled the magnolia scent of her hair.

"In not her house, not saying anything to me or Necron, she hired some unknown guy to replace the old gardener."

Warfighter started massaging Annie's shoulders, she closed her eyes with satisfaction.

"She's almost grown-up," he said. "You should give her more freedom. I'm not surprised she rebels, since you treat her like an eight-year-old and keep her in a cage. She will try hard to prove to you that she is no longer a child."

"On H14, she took it out on Necron. Today it was I who had a hard time."

The general smiled. He kissed Sandstorm on the head.

"Relax. It is possible Forkis will come back to us. We will defeat Kandrok. And the family will be together again."

"You don't believe it yourself." Anna didn't recognize whether he was joking or ironizing.

She felt guilty about killing loneliness by flirting with the achij from the base. She admonished herself with exaggerated overzealousness that it was casual and only temporary. Every time during the affair, she imagined Forkis to be with her. For several weeks, she had been hooking up with Warfighter, who had met her needs perfectly, despite the fact that he was biologically more than twice her age, and as a Kiritian he was three centuries old. Anna had waited long enough for Forkis to be revived, she still loved him (at least she tried to believe it), but the needs of the body won over a celibate life. The no-obligation relationship really relaxed her, eliminated unnecessary energy, allowed her to relieve tension, but on the other hand, she felt deeply ashamed. Velkee was only an equivalent. Sandstorm had a soft spot for Necron because he looked like Forkis, but he remained steadfast and culturally rejected her more than once, though she knew he liked her too. It made her feel embarrassed, sometimes he felt even hatred, it is not known whether bigger for herself or Kiret. She envied him that he was emotionally stronger. Maybe he already had a girlfriend. Anna didn't raise the issue, and Necron didn't mention anything about his relationship either. She decided to give up on him.

Even a minute didn't pass, and she was already, partially naked, being caressed and kissed hard by Velkee as he pressed her to the top.

***

Significant changes had taken place on Nephrida since the day the Kiritian fleet defeated the rebels and forced them to demobilize. Though they didn't deprive them of their civil liberties, they exercised tight control over former New Order

Army fighters. After Kandrok's attack, Kiret withdrew the achijes from Nephrida to fight the new enemy. Contrary to appearances, it was not an unreasonable move on his part - the disarmed rebels had no way to harm the Kiritians, and the quarterly control of the planet made it impossible to plot secretly. The opposition had once inhabited other worlds permanently or temporarily, including Cargoo, Mezzo, and Calcaris, but after the Immortals retaliated for the death of Forkis, it was interned on Nephrida. From then on, the former rebels dealt with developing their own society. The Kiritian occupation was gradually dying out, and after a dozen or so years, Nephrida even received permission to create a new army, whose main purpose was to protect against space catastrophes and natural disasters.

Over time, because of Kandrok, the Immortals ceased to exercise power over the rebels.

In 2974, five million citizens lived on Nephrida, both descendants of the former New Order Army and immigrants seeking living space on new planets. This was the average number of people per colonized terrestrial globe. The most inhabited was still the Earth from the Old Zone, because as much as one and a half billion people lived there. New virus outbreaks, asteroid strikes, space migrations, world wars and other armed conflicts, as well as the little ice age that paralyzed large parts of land, especially Europe, left the planet with a scant population of that amounting to nineteen billion in the twenty-second century.

Nephrida in the past was a loose community of cities in the form of polis, towns and villages, where each metropolis organized power as it pleased. If something didn't suit someone, they could move to a more convenient place, even build a house away from civilization and create a micro-state. A few years ago, a great change took place on Nephrida: a planet's president was elected from a dozen candidates, the former commander of the 3rd Rebel Fighter Regiment, Aveo Lacetti. Following the example of the Kiritians, a Council was also created, but with thirty-one members. A parliament and senate, popular in the past, were abandoned, believing that these organs were made up of too many people, and party pluralism always ended in chaos, in turn a few members of the Kiritian Council seemed to the Nephridians a ridiculously small number. The president performed representative and ceremonial functions, approved and validated all decisions of the Council of Thirty-One, he was also a member of the Council and participated in debates and votes. Even though the number of members seemed satisfactory at first, during each debate there were disputes and quarrels anyway, and things could drag on for months.

Kiret was supposed to take part in one of the meetings. He wanted an alliance with the former rebels, because besides Kiritians they had the best experience in space and planetary combat among oderses. Only their military training left much to be desired and was more suited to chaotic, aggressive terrorist battles than to a standing army. Necron mainly needed pilots who could have been trained and equipped with modern weapons, even if a deal had been made with the old enemy. However, he believed that the guarantee of inviolability could have been maintained if both sides had benefited after the campaign was over. He also considered deals with the mercenaries from the Capricorn Universe, but it would have meant spending horrendous sums, and he didn't know what relations existed between Kandrok and the Gangster Zone. He preferred to stick to the strategy of small steps for the time being.

Necron and Warfighter agreed that no more machines than a squadron would fly to Nephrida. The likelihood that Kandrok would appear in the Lion Universe was small, and the view of the large fleet would have been taken by Nephridians as a comic demonstration of the strength of the weakened nation. The astro-carrier and four ships remained in orbit. To the surface, Necron flew in 'Perfarius' accompanied by a representative squadron including Anna, Velkee, Tsar and Darius.

Already on Cargoo, Anna had wondered if she had really wanted to go to Nephrida and meet her old friends, now rather enemies. In the end, she explained to herself that the visit to the planet she hadn't visited since retaliating for Forkis' death was purely official.

While the seat of government was customarily located in the capital, on Nephrida it had been built two hundred kilometers from the larger metropolis in a calm, biodiverse environment. From the outside, the four-story building resembled a white colosseum with large-sized windows. The walls were made of an amalgam of natural materials and synthetics, which gave the building a matt mother-of-pearl appearance. The gate led to a circular square, with a fountain illuminated by plasma humming in the center. Several dozen hectares of gardens stretched around the building, all kinds of modificants grew there, as well as plants genetically untouched by human hands. The once tectonically active Nephrida was not a fertile planet, it was more suitable as a test field for weapons or a mining site, so the soil for the gardens was brought from H14, which was cheaper than fertilizing. Residential buildings for visitors were erected among orangeries, but also near the landing field. They were also used by the rulers and the population of the nearby town of thirty thousand, mainly descendants of former rebels.

Anna felt relieved as they prepared to land in an unfamiliar place. She feared that the sight of her former base would rob her of a bit of courage, which she had painstakingly sustained during her flight to the planet. She wouldn't avoid meetings with people from the past as a representative of the Kiritians. She tried to walk with dignity and cautiously watch the surroundings once they settled down and the gangways fell to the ground. Tsar Seymour unwittingly cheered her up as he and Darius exchanged frivolous comments about the planet's female population a few meters away.

The Kiritians had arrived a few hours before the start of the deliberations. The president Aveo Lacetti - Anna knew it would take her a long time to get used to the new role of the former commander - was waiting for them surrounded by security and a few members of the Council of Thirty-One. They officially exchanged handshakes with Necron. Aveo then greeted Warfighter by shaking his hand as well, and Sandstorm by kissing her hand.

Annie's blood pressure surged. She had psyched herself up for a cold but visible reaction on his part. She even felt disappointed when the sixty-four-year-old man dressed in a suit didn't frown or even hold his breath, with full control enjoying the benefits of convention. She considered that he might have not remembered her anymore, though it was more likely that Aveo was in perfect control of his emotions as a top-notch politician.

The debating duo was walking towards the landing field from the gardens, Sandstorm didn't seem to associate it at first. Almost twenty years meant nothing to a Kiritian, but to an oders it was a long time. The woman's carmine dress contributed to the flash in her memory - a color loved by Julia Croft, Anna's old friend, who had had an affair with Beliar Drunkenstein behind her back. The newcomer had a large, floppy white hat with a magenta flower, lips painted crimson and high heels of a similar color. Her mid-length hair had been dyed from blonde to red. Yes, it was none other than Julia Croft, but thinner, with sharper features and a bigger nose. Anna calculated that she was now forty-five, though she looked to be thirty. In the man accompanying her, she recognized Arkadiusz, her brother a year older than Julia, in her youth called the Splinter. The rebel freelancer had gained weight, his hair was thinned at his temples. The eyes remained the same with regard to the intense blue and keen eyesight, but in the past, there had been no present determination and coldness that the Kiritians' visit might have caused. Or an argument - the siblings quarreled.

Julia stopped short, holding her hat tilted by the wind. Her eyes widened.

"Anna? Anna Sandstorm?!"

The Splinter tore his angry face from his sister, which became even more wolfish when he saw the object of her interest. He clenched his jaws to keep his muscles from twisting more. When he finally evoked official indifference on his face, he and Julia moved closer to Lacetti.

"Here is our councilor, Arkadiusz Croft." Aveo indicated the two to Kiret. " Together with sister Julia Croft-Lewandowska.

There are four more councilors on the way to the government building and we will be at full strength at the meeting. Meanwhile, you probably want to rest after the trip, so I invite you to the guest apartment and to familiarize yourself with our gardens and other recreations."

One of the missing councilors turned out to be Tom Lewandowski, once a cadet trained by Sandstorm. She had remembered him as a having a positive attitude to life, helpful and usually smiling boy, willing to support the aggrieved. He had joined a group of Nephridians and Kiritians on the way; he had grown broader and more handsome in those seventeen years. To Sandstorm's surprise - she missed that Lacetti had introduced Julia with two surnames - Tom took Julia's arm and kissed her warmly in greeting. Anna noticed wedding rings on their fingers. Julia's settling down was the last thing she had expected from the empty-headed, slutty pseudo-friend. Tom wore a sand-colored uniform with markings associated with Nephrida's current army. He smiled cheerfully at Anna, the first sign of sincere sympathy for her on this planet, and knowing Tom's old straightforwardness, Sandstorm suspected that the gesture was not ironic or polite. The case with the Splinter was less pleasing, as he gave her a definite coolness, literally as if he had wanted to ice her with his eyes, when their gazes met on the way to the apartments. Julia would have liked to talk to her, but she was going too far, led by her arm by her husband talking to Necron and Lacetti. So, Anna plodded behind the rest for a while, in silence, until she engaged in a frugal, mundane conversation with Tsar and Darius, who questioned her about the women from her former base.

The apartments looked like giant, elongated egg halves or trapezoidal lumps of gold, and blended in perfectly with the scenery of the garden densely packed with plants. The group stopped; some went towards the government buildings. Necron, Warfighter and Lacetti began a casual conversation about the species of the local trees and the method and cost of importing them, as well as uinals spent annually on maintaining the gardens. The discussion turned to money spent on weapons and fuel for flying machines. Bored Anna, who for the sake of principle sometimes added a few words to the conversation, folded her arms and finally set herself up as an observer. Julia and the Splinter started arguing again, until Tom mitigated them and got into a conversation with Arek; now they were both ignoring the sulky woman. Sandstorm cheered up, as Tsar - who had probably made a bet with Darius - accosted Julia, giving her wide, predatory smiles. Croft-Lewandowska reacted with indignation and ostentatiously turned her head away, but curiosity didn't allow her to disregard charming but simple Tsar for a long time. Finally, she smiled at him, briefly and discreetly, taking advantage of her husband's inattention. Anna snorted silently, refrained from shaking her head. Julia hadn't changed. In some respects, it was a consolation that some element of the past had turned out to be a cosmic constant. A small, solid pillar, though covered with sludge.

Although the comforts and air conditioning in the minimalist apartments left nothing to be desired, Anna preferred to spend her free time strolling alone in the gardens. She wasn't afraid of an attack - every sane inhabitant of the planet knew that the Kiritian astro-carrier in retaliation could obliterate an entire city with an orbital shot. Walking along a path, she looked at organisms in ponds (she recognized a few tropical fish) and plant hybrids, as well as fountains, shaded gazebos and monuments blended in with the scenery of the conservatories and gardens. The most eye-catching were several-meter high statues standing in the central square. One showed a roaring jaguar referring to Kiritians, the other - a maokan, a cross between a seagull and a tern, an old hallmark of rebels associated with aviation and sky. Once associated with the New Order Army militants had used the symbol of a pyramid with the human eye, just like the earth's global government of that time.

The captain hoped she would be able to talk privately with her former friends, but she met only the Splinter. The man seemed to be waiting for her, standing with his hands tucked in his pockets by a several-ton pedestal with a maokan. He gestured with his chin officially and walked towards the shadow cast by a giant philodendron, where fewer eyes peeked.

"You shouldn't be here," he began even in a tone of warning, ignoring the courtesy and status of the interlocutor as they stopped. "You have the nerve to come to Nephrida?" He added hostilely.

The captain was silent, taking the blows bravely and with a hidden sense of guilt, while Croft didn't refrain:

"Know that we find you a traitor. No matter what you have to say to us."

"I don't think you can understand it," she said calmly at last, "since you have the opinion on me."

"What is there to be understood?" The Splinter waved a hand nervously. "You fell in love with the great, mean and rich enemy emperor and joined the stronger as a naive girl! However, a lot has changed. The hatchet was forcibly buried, although Kiritians and the rebels are unlikely to be fond of each other. It is with great difficulty that I'm saying this, but it is even good that one side has finally dominated the other. Thanks to this, after hundreds of years of envy, the guerrilla war was over and we, with the disbanded army, started to develop the community. Paradoxically, war was necessary for peace to come. We understood this only after you defeated us." His own words sounded strange to Arkadiusz. He remembered Anna from when she hated Forkis and Kiritians. The fanatical rebel's turn to the enemy's side had taught him that predictability would never be the domain of any man. His voice lowered, the chill in his eyes remained the same. "I don't know if I'll ever forgive you. Lacetti feels the same, but he has soared very high, much higher than me, and is above showing animosity to anyone. If you're looking for kindness on Nephrida, maybe you can talk to Tom. Overall, I'd be more careful in your position. The achijes will let you out of their sights for a moment and you may have trouble.

Anna had expected this to happen and was not surprised by the Splinter's threat. However, she wasn't in danger of being attacked during this visit. If someone wanted to kill her in the future, he would do so in a typical rebel style: by surprise and possibly anonymously.

"How did Julia get involved with Tom?" She decided to change the subject.

The Splinter shrugged.

"It just happened."

"What do you deal with now, besides being on the Council?"

"I'm a soldier from a volunteer unit, and all I do is protect civilians from the effects of natural disasters. In the case of Nephrida, these are mainly mountain landslides. As you can see, we have relative peace here, and I wish it would stay so long. The seventeen years that have passed since the war with Kiritians is a long time for ordinary people whose radical inclinations have waned. We wouldn't like to have another war on our land, not now that we have created and fixed so much." He pointed to trees behind which the acres of gardens surrounding the buildings began. "Then don't count on Nephridians to show favor to Kiritians." He glanced at a pillar of a quartile clock. "We need to go."

Without waiting for an answer, he turned and walked away resolutely.

Soon Anna was found by Necron, and together with the dignitaries they went to the assembly.

***

The character of the debating chamber had practically not changed for centuries, as its functionality had been well-thought-out. Rows, plowed with passages, had an arched shape and rose from a rostrum that was the lowest. It had nothing to do with the status of the seated, it only served to ensure that everyone in the room could see and hear clearly the person speaking. To the right of the lectern there was a presidential platform, while delegates sat to the left.

Anna looked for familiar faces among the members of the Council of Thirty-One, but only caught Lewandowski and the Splinter, not counting President Lacetti, who sat on his seat. He opened the meeting welcoming everyone, introducing the guests and explaining the nature of the matter.

After his short speech, Biffter took the floor. For several dozen minutes he spoke loudly and clearly about Kandrok and the danger that could fall on the entire Zodiac Universum, if they didn't stop the enemy's expansion. Nothing was left out. He spoke honestly - as Kiritians used to - about every possible threat from the cyber super-collectivity. He finalized the speech with a request for a military alliance and support for Nephrida in the coming war, promising access to the most modern equipment, and the veterans - a salary.

Though initially the Nephridians calmly exchanged arguments for and against, a quarrel quickly ensued that Necron had never experienced at a meeting of the Kiritian Council of Dignitaries. The aggressive quarrel lasted four hours. A group of radicals referred to their former hatred by booing the Kiritians and wishing them the end. Nevertheless, Kiret carefully listened to everyone who spoke and tried to count the votes. The matter wasn't looking good - most of the members of the Council of Thirty-One appeared to be against the alliance, including Tom and Arkadiusz. The main argument was the reluctance to tease the stronger Kandrok, which, since it had dealt with the Kiritians, would likely repeat this feat with the alliance they had formed. Angry, Warfighter argued that the enemy could attack Nephridians anyway, even if they hid and remained neutral. He talked about Dr. Figam and the new Kiritian combat technology that, before the enemy decrypted, would lose the fight against the alliance.

At the end of the deliberations, Necron felt very tired, as if he had had a skirmish with Kandrok. Twice he received a discreet nudge from Anna as his head slipped from an arm supporting it.

"Please, be quiet! I'm suspending the announcement of the verdict until tomorrow," Lacetti said in the finale, silencing the mob with an electronically amplified voice. "At two o'clock, we will take a democratic vote in the Council of Thirty-One, the outcome of which will determine whether Nephrida will consent to the alliance. Please use the time you have received for meditation and analysis in peace," he spoke the last words, looking at Necron. The latter nodded gently to him.

There was nothing else the Kiritians could do. They returned to their assigned apartments with a scowl on their faces.

XVIII. Sex scandal

Velkee took some achijes to the government building as official protection, the remaining Kiritians in security were to be handled by Seymour.

"Come on, guys, let's take a look at the planet," he said eagerly to the five people.

They headed towards the landing field.

"Are we going to walk around and stare so until the deliberations are over?" Darius was surprised.

"Of course not. Warfighter gave me specific guidelines. We will fly to do a reconnaissance."

"For what purpose?" Asked the Kiritian walking beside Schindler.

Seymour stopped, turned to the achijes. He broke off a piece of grass growing by the road and put it in his mouth.

"Think, people ... As you know, they won't let all of us into the government building - it's against the local law. And in order not to wait like clods, we'll fly over the planet and see if the Nerfidians have built something that the Kiritians might not like. To put it bluntly: if any sub-point of the treaty in force after our occupation was broken, and one of them talks about the prohibition of building modern military facilities. Although we left the planet, we can legally move through the entire airspace and search for things that interest us as we used to. Hello, sunshine." Tsar grinned at a young airstrip operator walking in the opposite direction. The girl in drill, with white hair and green eyes, glanced at him as if he had been insane, she tapped her forehead with her finger, and turned away, with her face full of contempt. The subordinates started to chuckle, except for Darius, who smiled demonstrably so as not to stand out from the rest.

Tsar accosted other women. Most of them replied with a smile, there were also words adequate to his taunts.

While Seymour's subordinates were having a good time taking up the commander's game and picking up the girls they encountered, Darius tried not to show his despondency. During the years he had spent under the auspices of Seymour, the latter had presented him his specific way of life, considering it to be correct and the healthiest. Apparently, with it an immortal man couldn't go crazy. Part of Tsar's philosophy was that you shouldn't have a permanent partner, but with gallantness engage in temporary relationships. Darius tried to be like Seymour, a much longer-lived authority, especially since the whole worldview from the corporal's past seemed to have gone with the lost home. When he joined the Kiritians, he realized that John's teachings were not universal, correct, and one-of-a-kind, as his father had assured him. Darius, as a little boy, couldn't follow many models, because his family practically lived in the wild, visiting ranches and farms located far away several times a month, therefore, what his parents passed on to him, he had considered sacred. Thanks to the Kiritians, he realized he had been wrong: there are as many ways to live as people. Although some models prevailed over others, leading a man to success. Such models were used by Tsar. He filled the gap after the death of his parents, suppressed in him the old layers of aggression, which ended in the crusade against lycans.

However, a lot changed when Darius met Jenny. He couldn't get her out of his head. As he watched the lieutenant accosting Nephridian women, he remembered again the rebellious, black-haired teenager with eyes brown like fresh chestnuts taken out of their shell. Seymour's behavior no longer suited him, even discouraged him. He suspected that he would never be like him in male-female matters, though they had already visited together so many brothels and premises with quite a good service. Schindler, that's true, often enjoyed casual meetings, but he never felt complete satisfaction, as if there had been a blockage somewhere in his brain that prevented him from being completely fulfilled. He couldn't decipher whether his personality or the echo of John's teachings was to blame.

They reached the landing field where multi-role Kiritian fighters with the appearance of a common jellyfish waited. From the chassis protruded brackets stabilizing the machine on any ground capable of supporting several dozen tons of weight. The armor looked like a mosaic of mammalian vertebrae - it was common knowledge that Kiritians built machines with inspiration from the organic world, though they were particularly fond of bone and soft tissues patterns.

The achijes started scatter to the cockpits. Darius stayed on the landing pad, following with his distant eyes a girl Seymour was flirting with.

"Forget about her, man." Tsar looked at him with a faint amusement. Leaning his back against a fighter's fuselage, he was smoking a quick joint.

Schindler raised his hand as if to indicate a leaving airstrip worker. Tsar laughed.

"I'm talking about Jenny. I can see that you got high nastily. One doesn't need to have Forkis' ability to know you still think about her. Give up on the girl."

"Why is that? Because it's not my league, as the subordinates said on H14?"

"That's not the point, kid, because every babe can be gotten. You have to bear in mind that Jenny is not a Kiritian woman, and I learned from Kiret that she's unlikely to ever be. She is changeable, not eternal like us, she has a different cellular biology. Remember what I told you about permanent relationships with ... well ... mortals?"

"About permanent relationships by Tsar Seymour." The lieutenant laughed and threw the butt away with a flick.

"I'm telling you you'll regret it, but since you're so stubborn." He spread his hands helplessly. "Now go, achij, to your machine, and when we get back from patrol, Lieutenant Seymour will show you something. I promise it will be fun."

***

They circled the entire planet in four hours. The fighters were traveling in a line, one was flying far away from the other so that the scanning areas didn't overlap. The reconnaissance was monotonous but enjoyable. Darius didn't understand people who hated to fly, and he had met many such persons. Hearing the conversations of his comrades on the air every now and then, he contemplated the passing landscapes and thought of Seymour's surprise.

They didn't come across anything out of the ordinary. They saw standard facilities clustered in and around cities, such as sewage treatment plants, laboratories, water synthesizers at basins, mines, and airports. The military facilities had exactly the same armament and its quantity as provided for in the treaty. It was mainly a defensive weapon to protect the planet from space debris.

They landed just as the deliberations ended.

"So, what have you wanted to show me, boss?" Schindler asked Tsar softly, when they had already left the landing field.

"Go to your quarters." The lieutenant waved his hand at the rest of the achijes. "Oh, look how lucky we are."

Darius glanced where glad Tsar and noticed the same white-haired girl beside a transporter being unloaded, who had looked at Seymour with contempt before the flight. She held a holonot in her hand and made notes on it. Sometimes someone came up to her and they discussed for a while.

"I don't think I get it."

"See that woman?"

"I remember, she laughed at you. So, what do you want to show me?"

"That you can get any fury."

"You failed the first time, boss."

"Because I was playing around. Now sit back, have a beer, relax and learn from the master."

Darius shrugged, at least he wouldn't be bored on this trip. He took a can of alcohol from a vending machine at a bar, sat down on a bench and sipped casually, curious to see what Tsar had come up with this time. Nephrida's yellow dwarf was shining in his back, so he could freely observe the scenery in front of him. As he thought, it was indeed easy for Tsar to pick up, no matter what the type of his female victim was: young or mature, rich or poor, single or married, fighting she-cat or a type of gray mouse. Darius hadn't bothered dating until now, and he and Seymour had gone to brothels where entertainment for money mattered, not deeper partnerships. He considered that perhaps due to the constant suppression of his spontaneous instincts, he completely couldn't assort with women, he was even ashamed to talk to them. The case was different with Tsar. Even though he was shorter, thinner and lighter than him, he had that 'something'. And rather, it was something other than modified red eyes, fiery hair and a cheeky, even chauvinistic smile.

This time the corporal had the opportunity to observe something new and surprising - Seymour completely devoid of crassness and irony, as well as his gallantry. He turned up a hearing amplifier built into a communicator at the auricle, because the dialogue mixed with the sounds of the airport. He tuned the frequency to the nearest human words.

Tsar smiled sympathetically and warmly, walked over to the woman who had stopped working and looked at him reluctantly.

"You again? Do you want something?" She snapped.

"I'm so sorry for the earlier jokes about you. I'm a simple soldier, and I didn't want to pass among my companions for a freak who shows off his erudition and intellect."

The white-haired girl looked at him with ostentatious contempt, but even inexperienced Darius knew that Tsar had aroused her interest. She went back to work on the holonot.

"At least you're honest. But it's probably natural for Kiritians not to lie."

"This was strictly obeyed during Forkis' lifetime. Ideology, propaganda, law, the feeling of being better than Oderses, sometimes fear of power and these matters, but when he died, and with him his cult and mind-reading ability, a little changed with this Kiritian truthfulness. It's a bit as if the power of the house has passed from a strict, respected father to the hands of his gentle and calm son. Of course, I'm not belittling Mr. Biffter's authority here, nothing like that! However, everyone probably noticed that the two emperors' ways of exercising power are very different from each other. Unfortunately, we split into conservatives and progressives, although the latter, I would call a regression. I wouldn't like to obtrude. If I'm disturbing your work, I can humbly ask for a conversation later."

"You're not disturbing. I mean there is no abnormal rigor here, everyone can do whatever they want, as long as the work is done well and on time. But what you want from me, Kiritian, I have no idea."

"Forgive me, madam, I have acted like a simpleton for the second time. I'm Tsar Seymour."

The woman continued to write, staring at the holonot. She shouted to a colleague that was far away and told him to count the contents of one of the crates again. Only then did she say:

"I won't deny."

"You don't like Kiritians, do you?" Tsar was polite and nice all the time.

"Why do you think so?"

"Because you look aloof, and you wouldn't be offended by trivial jokes of soldiers who play around but don't mean anything wrong. Something nice more likely." Seymour grinned wider. "All your - if we can be on a first-name basis - aversion towards me is also not dictated by the fact that I'm disturbing your work, which you yourself mentioned. And I think you did it honestly. So, either you don't like Kiritians or you don't like me and you want to deter me. Option two, however, is out of the question, because you would tell me to get lost, call security or complain to General Warfighter, to whom I report. You look like a doer to me."

A smile appeared on her face, even though she didn't want it there. She lifted her green like shoots eyes to Seymour.

"Oh, what a deduction. Did you memorize this text for half a day? I'm Alice. And you guessed it, I don't like Kiritians. You invaded our planet, which you must have taken into account too, Mr. smart-ass."

"It is a complicated political situation that dragged for hundreds of years. Therefore, it cannot be judged so hastily. Forgive me for telling you it, but from what you are saying, I conclude that you don't know enough about the conflict, since you assume that the attack was solely our fault."

"I didn't say that."

"But you think so."

Alice sighed.

"Did you have Forkis in your family?"

"Simply the art of deduction." Nice smile again. "Nevertheless, it would be nice to be telepathic. No human lie could surprise me anymore."

Darius, who had finished his beer, sat watching but couldn't take his eyes off him. It was as if someone had replaced his lieutenant with a stranger! Politeness, gallantry, the ability to deduce intelligently, staying calm and dignified despite disregard from the other side - that was completely not Seymour's style, who had almost always acted like a complete, stoned idiot. And now? Even though he had known the girl for a few moments, he perfectly tuned his behavior and conversation to her person. To the extent that he droned on with politics, but she listened to him. Even if he had started talking about the weather, he would have probably kept her interest.

"What is this conversation for?" Alice asked.

"Taking advantage of Kiritian honesty: I've liked you very much and I would like to get to know you better."

"So, if you weren't an Infected, you'd be lying to me?"

"Absolutely not." Seymour made a funny face, waved his hands negatively. "I'm truthful by nature, and the nation has nothing to do with it. I'm just myself. One shouldn't judge someone through the prism of their Immortal status and the orders they must follow."

"You decided to be a soldier yourself, so don't make excuses."

"Bad judgment again, Alice." Nice smile. "In this matter, I had no choice. If you feel like it, I can tell you more about the history of Tsar Seymour's joining the Kiritian army. But if you're busy or you have any plans for the evening, I'll walk away immediately and won't tease you anymore."

"You're not teasing. Just tell me why you got interested in me. There are quite a few beautiful women living on Nephrida, although you probably have a better choice among the Kiritian women."

"Why has a man gotten suddenly interested in one of the millions? Science has not yet figured this out. If I strained my brain, maybe I could scientifically present an answer to that question for you, but this time you would definitely escape from me. This is an even more boring topic than politics, so I'll let it go."

"You are really eloquent for a 'simple soldier'." She smiled meaningly. Tsar too. "I thought you would start complimenting me, like my ex at the first meeting." She looked up at the sky. "Asshole. I think I misjudged you. I mean, the latter was an asshole."

"Bad strategy. I won't allow myself to be deterred by the mention of your ex and pretending that you're empty-headed. I'm eager to convince you that Kiritians are not as bad as many people think we are. So, Alice, can I invite you to a cafe or restaurant tonight? Maybe you prefer a walk in the garden?" The girl smiled mysteriously.

"I don't know if the garden will be a good idea."

Tsar took her hand gently and hid it in his own fingerless gloves.

"Then let me lend you my pass if the problem is of this kind."

Alice looked at him obliquely.

"Then let there be a walk in the garden."

"Great. Meet me at the main gate at seven. Does it suit you?"

"It does."

"Goodbye then." Tsar parodied a salute. Alice shook her head and smiled crookedly.

"Goodbye, simple soldier."

Seymour headed for the quarters assigned to the Kiritians. Darius soon caught up with him.

"What was that? Damn, boss, I didn't know you like that!"

"The trick is to choose a right strategy for a right woman."

"But how did you know what suits that Alice?"

"I estimated. It only took a few sentences of conversation, universal chatter with an admixture of balanced complementation for her to present herself. Then I knew what to say and how to behave. That's easy. Don't be so surprised, kid, next move will be yours."

Darius panicked a little.

"What?"

"You're gonna get yourself some local chick. Just for one time. This time, without services and money, it is to be difficult. If you gain experience of this kind, it will be easier for you to get closer to Jenny."

Schindler scratched his neck in embarrassment.

"I'm not sure. I don't like this idea of picking up girls that I don't care about at all."

"It is only supposed to be learning and gathering experience. I can't pick up Bidwell for you."

Darius imagined Tsar hitting on Jenny and her falling in love with him and felt a pang of jealousy. He didn't wish to ever argue with Seymour over a woman.

***

When the deliberation was over, Biffter, Warfighter, and Sandstorm met in a lounge on the first floor of a building made available to them.

"Let devils take these damn larvae!" Irritated, Velkee wandered nervously near a guest table. His anger still didn't pass after the brawl at the meeting. "These idiots think they're safe in this hole, since the enemy is out of sight! We are now to wait for their decision, not the other way around as it should be. We are still better and stronger than them! I wish I hadn't agreed to come here. I'd rather pay the Capricorn mercenaries a lot than make begging dog faces in front of a bunch of lousy rebels!"

"You're exaggerating, Velkee," Anna replied, opening blinds by a window. The travertine floor was flooded by long rays of the setting star. "These are only preliminary stats. If you were Nephridian, you would also like to have time to think. Unfortunately, we must hide our pride deeply. Let me remind you that we had lost our strongest cards before Kandrok attacked us."

She regretted those words immediately. Pensive Kiret, however, didn't seem to hear them, or at least didn't react to the obvious mention of his being in power after Forkis' death.

"Once the opposition has made up their minds," he said, lying with his arms under his head on a leather sofa, "I will fly for Divinus and begin the Rebirth mission. If we could actually get Forkis back ..."

They let the broken sentence hang in the air. Anna sat in an armchair next to Kiret, while Warfighter was still wandering around the living room, now near a fountain spouting from the floor, with a casing made of marble inlaid with silver. The soothing sound of the water falling into the pond slightly cooled his frayed nerves.

"I have a feeling that we will need to hire mercenaries." Kiret took a deep breath. "We cannot force the rebels to obey as we used to."

"You don't have to say the same thing over and over again, as if I suffered from memory loss," the general snapped.

"Do you think that the distribution of votes will change after tomorrow's official vote?" Sandstorm asked.

"It will rather be the same," said Velkee. "To convince them, we would have to send them to Morascrik seized by Kandrok, or hand them over to them. They would see this and that and change their minds out of fear. Because everything we told them at the meeting is pure abstraction for them. As our old saying goes, 'You can't smell blood without blood." He turned to Anna, "It is possible that your old friends deliberately vote against us in retaliation for military actions or for your treason. Maybe they're even glad that someone finally kicked our asses. After all, the Kandrok problem still doesn't concern them."

"I could indeed skip the trip to Nephrida."

"Oh, come on, Velkee." Necron gave the general a tired look. "It's not the captain's fault, so leave her alone. "One vote ..." He clenched his fist. "If only we had one vote more. There is nothing worse than a distribution of votes fifty-fifty."

"Respect." Tsar Seymour entered the lounge, summoned in a moment of landing after the patrol." He stopped slightly astride the table and clasped his hands behind his back.

"Well, well, who's come," Velkee said. "I can see you haven't been in too much of a hurry to report back to your general."

"Something stopped me, sir," Seymour replied with a disarming smile. "A little personal matter. Moreover, Nephrida is in order."

"At least nothing screws up here. You have the evening off. Do what you want." Warfighter waved his hand. "But no brawls and fights. I don't want any more trouble over you, understand?"

"Of course, sir."

"Oh, and you're supposed to be ready for any call, but you probably know that very well, Seymour."

"Of course, sir."

"You can go. Or wait. Such one question. Tell me, what do you think about engaging the rebels in the conflict with Kandrok, as well as other oders nations?"

Tsar only for a moment gazed at the three of them uncertainly looking at him, believing the question had a catch. He quickly guessed that they wanted the spontaneous opinion of a lower-ranking achij. He smiled.

"Well, sir ... Honestly? If there need to be shit, let everyone have an equal part of it. And the sink will spill more anyway."

Anna refrained from laughing with difficulty.

"You can go now," Velkee ordered in amazement, though he could expect Seymour to give such an answer. Walking a moment later down the hall, Tsar was scratching his chin.

"One vote," he repeated what he had heard just before entering the lounge. He shrugged and licked his lip as he fantasized about his upcoming date with Alice.

***

They met at the agreed place, by a high, metal and stone gate, open by day. Tsar arrived a few minutes before Alice, clad as earlier at the airport, in the light biometal armor. Procedures forbade him to put on a more elegant uniform - as an achij commanding the guard, the body among enemies, he had to have secured.

Alice smiled slightly at the sight of him, he replied with a broader smile. She had replaced the grease-stained and worn-out drill she had worn while working with woven sandals and an ashen-white knee-length gown decorated with silver patterns similar to oval leaves. Half of the girl's back and part of the chest were exposed, there were only delicate straps. On her left wrist, she had put on a double, delicate bracelet coupled with little wires.

"You look great," Seymour said sincerely and how originally. He kissed Alice's hand, then raised his arm, which she grasped.

"Thank you, because what else to answer here."

"That's why greetings suck."

"I absolutely agree with you."

Tsar glanced discreetly over her shoulder to see if Darius was standing in a parallel alley, pretending to be enjoying the walk alone, smoking a cigar. Schindler was to observe the couple from hiding and gain experience, apart from the intimate parts of the show, as the lieutenant had stipulated.

"Where do you want to go?" He asked. "The gardens are divided into several parts, depending on plants."

"Oh, you can even rhyme." There was a faint amusement in all of Alice's words, coupled with indulgence.

"The best poetry is created when it's unintended."

"Maybe the antique part, with palm trees and vines? I like it the most. Few people go there at this time."

"I've thought you don't go into the VIP gardens. Unless you have a second job and come here for a different shift."

The girl smiled mysteriously.

"Are you coming or you will question me until dusk?" Tsar showed his teeth again in a broad smile.

"Whatever you order. Madam, miss?"

"Choose the form you see fit. I wouldn't be angry even if you used both alternately. I'm used to different titles."

"Right, beware of monotony, people of the age of cosmic conquests!"

The mention of the titles interested him. So did the behavior of a young watchman standing on the other side of the gate, who seemed confused by the presence of the girl. He blocked their way.

"Are you all right, Miss Lacetti?" He asked, glancing uncertainly at Seymour.

Tsar was also flustered. He blinked and looked at his companion with raised eyebrows.

"I'm going for a walk with this nice Kiritian," she replied. "Is this not allowed?"

"It is, it is!" Said a low, husky voice from the gatehouse nearby, shaded by the long branches of weeping willow. In the field of vision appeared a full-bodied man turning sixty, you could smell alcohol from him.

"Sorry, madam and sir. Alvaro is new and worries about everything," he added hastily, looking at Tsar. All he needed was to insult the Kiritian from the delegation."

"Really, nothing happened," Alice said soothingly. She squeezed Tsar's forearm tighter and they walked down a gravel alley. "See you later, Alvaro and Daniel, have a good shift."

"And you, have a nice evening." The watchman named Daniel waved his khaki cap, then brained Alvaro with it.

"Miss Lacetti?" Tsar asked in surprise as they entered a square bathed in the evening glow of the yellow dwarf. Long shadows were cast by tree trunks and lamps that had not yet functioned.

"You won't tell me that ..."

Alice reacted to his confusion with a crooked smile.

"The president's daughter!" He blurted out. "Oh, great things! Why haven't you told me?"

She withdrew her hand and began walking slowly forward while the Kiritian stood with his hands lowered comically, somewhat like a skinny gorilla.

"For the same reason you didn't tell me you were a lieutenant."

"Huh?"

She stopped and turned.

"As Lacetti's daughter, I know perfectly well what is happening in the areas reserved for officials. It is not my duty, but it behooves to know at least a third of what my father knows. It is not my nature to politicize, but some things are worth knowing. I'm not ignorant."

"It shows."

He approached her. No girl had made such an impression on him as this president's daughter. And it was by no means related to her status. He wondered if her strengths were associated with the position of her father who had taken care of the child's education and urbanity, or she had been born with a sharp mind. In any case, she clearly deserved respect, which Tsar rarely gave to women, because he almost always met vain and empty-headed ones.

"I talk to many people from these areas, from different backgrounds, thanks to which I can look at people's needs and problems from many perspectives. I also observe the surroundings myself. I listen a lot, preferring to remain silent. The intelligence of the interlocutor can be recognized by the fact that they don't boast of wealth, behind-the-scenes dealings or titles. And you passed that test very well, Mr. Seymour."

They walked on, strolling side by side along the alley.

"I was speechless," he admitted jokingly. "The president's daughter became interested in me."

"Don't exaggerate, Mr. Seymour."

"Just Tsar."

"Okay, maybe let's try not to ironize anymore." She smiled.

"But since you are the daughter of the planetary head, why do you have such a down-to-earth job?"

"I like light physical work and being surrounded by ordinary people. In such an environment, it is always fun and something is happening. Sitting at a desk is not good for me, and I could easily get a job like that. Anyway, Aveo Lacetti is the president of just five million Nephrida's population, you could say it's a niche position. For comparison, Forkis ruled the empire of twenty-nine planets."

"Eighteen. Twenty-nine planets in total were colonized by the descendants of Earthlings, not including the moons."

"I'm ashamed that I don't know such an important number."

The lieutenant shrugged.

"Nobody knows everything. Anyway, the numbers change every now and then. We have trillions of rocky planets of the Zodiac Universum at our disposal, maybe it will be profitable to colonize more one day, this would certainly contribute to reducing territorial conflicts. The limitations for the Kiritians are mainly inhuman space conditions near such planets, which even the accumulated wealth cannot solve. Anyway, now our focus is on Kandrok."

Alice nodded.

"Returning to the previous thread. There are no requirements as to the form of officials' work on Nephrida. Anyway, as I already mentioned, the father doesn't fulfill such an important function, because he represents only five million citizens."

"And you think it's little?"

"It depends on the scale adopted. For example, there were a lot of cities on Earth that had more inhabitants than our entire planet. Some giant countries, such as China, boasted billions of inhabitants on the eve of the colonization of space. With such numbers, the president or the chairman mean something."

Seymour rubbed his chin, staring down at the road ahead.

"I believe that every power is important, be it local or galactic, because you have people below you who believe in you and count on your understanding, wisdom and help. So, it doesn't matter if you rule a billion citizens or are responsible for a starving family with a child."

"You're talking wisely for a simple soldier."

"And you for an ordinary girl who is not afraid to walk in gardens visited by strangers."

Amused, Alice nudged Tsar with her elbow, as she would have done it if he hadn't jumped back agilely. He no longer had any doubts about the girl's identity, as successive garden workers and sector wardens greeted her with respect.

Darius followed the couple away, acting like an ordinary stroller. He still had the sound amplifier active, so that even a hundred meters from them, he could hear the conversation as if it had been held nearby. He was surprised not only by the fact that Tsar had picked up the president's daughter, but more by the fact that the lieutenant constantly playing the freewheeler was able to conduct dialogue up to the mark. Schindler's respect for the older officer, hiding his strengths, increased much more. With him he felt his lack of manners, he could also stumble from nerves and talk nonsense. He never would be able to handle Jenny like that. Alice turned back at one point, but only ran her indifferent look over Schindler, as if he had been one of a thousand cornflowers - the couple was now in an artificial meadow, strutting a pink-blue carpet of poppies and cornflowers. Darius had to admit that those responsible for the arrangements had made great use of the once barren lands of the planet.

When Tsar and Alice stopped a quarter of an hour later, Schindler found a comfortable spot on a low, thick olive tree branch, where he could remain invisible and freely observe the surroundings. He would have liked to stay on the ground and act like a human, but walking around aimlessly, he would have quickly attracted attention to himself.

"What am I doing?" He muttered. The couple sat down on a polished boulder by a pond with water lilies. Nearby, there was an incomplete replica of the Parthenon, because there were fewer columns on the stylobate than in the original, and they didn't match the scale of the original. In the center was a sand statue of Athena, now a rarely worshiped goddess. The building was surrounded by lush vegetation dominated by cedars, fig trees and vines; the microclimate maintainers created ideal conditions for terrestrial Mediterranean species.

"Would you mind if I smoke?" The lieutenant asked.

"No, as long as you treat me to it. As a teenager, I wasn't a very polite girl." Alice answered Tsar's silent question.

Looking at rainbow crucians moving drowsily, Seymour took a piece of Chulimal wood paper from the compartment, placed a handful of dried leaves on it, and made a joint. He was breathing smoke with satisfaction as the pipe caught. He handed it over to Alice, who repeated the ritual of inhaling and letting out the smoke. The blunt was a weak drug, it relaxed and calmed down with the power of a dietary supplement.

"It's strange no one comes here," Tsar pointed out. "Pretty nice neighborhood."

"Currently, there are about a hundred people in the gardens, and the Greek sector is on the outskirts. Visitors and locals are usually drawn to tropical regions and flower fields. Enjoy it, otherwise we'd have trouble finding privacy."

"Hope I don't cause you any trouble. People may think different things when they see the president's daughter accompanied by a Kiritian."

Alice stretched her legs out on the boulder.

"There won't be any trouble, and I'll hang out with whoever I want."

"How old are you, if I can know?"

"Twenty-six," she announced without wangling. She handed the joint to Tsar. "And you?"

"A year more."

"Yeah, right." She laughed. "Damn, how this weed relaxes quickly."

Tsar spread his hands.

"That's my biological age."

"And the calendar one? Giving a Kiritian's age in biological years is like measuring an ocean iceberg from its top to the surface of the water."

"Nice comparison. Have you made it up now, or you prepared jokes for our meeting?"

"What do you think?"

They looked at each other askance, then started laughing.

"The age of a Kiritian is correctly given in biological years, specifically the time he took the super virus," Tsar explained more seriously, gesticulating. "The discrepancy is small and is therefore ignored. The biological age changes by only a few years, after which the whole organism regenerates and returns to the state that an achij had at the time of infection. I'm fifty-eight in calendar years, just look at me. You would have felt weird if I had given you that number." He smiled.

"You're probably right. For oderses it is incomprehensible, even a little scary. And what are the mind and mentality like in your place? Do you feel old after the decades and centuries?"

"This is an individual matter. A strong psyche and reluctance to change are one of the many criteria for selecting an Immortal, but they don't guarantee that you will not break down later. Usually achijes do well with time, but it also happens that some go crazy. They can count on medical help, including selective memory deletion, but not everyone agrees to it. I feel like my biological age, but I'm a very young Kiritian. General Biffter is said to have an old man mentality." Seymour pursed his lips and shrugged.

"Tell me more about yourself," Alice encouraged. "I have rarely had the opportunity to be in the company of Kiritians. And I didn't talk to any of them privately."

"What do you want to know?"

"Maybe something about Morascrik. This dark, hot planet is almost inaccessible to oderses, which is why there are legends about it."

"So Morascrik is more interesting than me?" Tsar smiled mischievously.

"I already know one a bit, the other I don't," she replied jokingly. "Let me make a decision later on what is worth paying more attention to. How do you bear the activity of Betelgeuse located several light-years from Morascrik?"

"We have atmospheric filters and heavy overcast. Anyway, when it starts to get really hot, all you have to do is leave the planet and move to another one."

It was already dark before Tsar finished telling, constantly bombarded with questions from the curious girl. It was not without mention of Kandrok and other political issues. He gave Alice an expanded version of what Kiret had officially said at the Council of Thirty-One, except that the lieutenant presented a subjective point of view.

The branch of the nearby olive tree suddenly shook. The leaves, being ripped sharply rustled, broken wood crackled, and the punch line was a curse broken in mid flow. Seymour put his hand to his forehead, but didn't look in the direction of the tree, which was still shaking and making an unstoppable noise. Alice rested her chin on her fists, looked at Tsar expectantly.

"Maybe you deign to finally explain why you took your friend with you and told him to hide in the bushes? What did you bet?"

Seymour looked guilty for seconds.

"Well ... I thought there would be no fatalities."

"Easy, lieutenant." Alice playfully tousled his hairstyle. "I have known for a long time that this young man is following us."

Tsar cleared his throat.

"I can see that nothing can be hidden from you. And since the guy have already fallen from the branch ... My friend," he pointed to the tree, which was now silent and not moving, "has liked a girl, but he has no experience in these matters. So, I made him watch me."

"Great. So, you consider yourself a veteran." Alice smiled mischievously as she slid off the boulder and walked over to the genetically modified palm, which was abundant in apples. She leaned her back against the ring-shaped trunk.

Tsar replied with a slightly predatory smile:

"Do you want to find out?"

"That's why I'm here. And so are you. Although the foreplay has been extremely long."

"Your honesty is terrifying. You said it as if I talked you to death" The Kiritian approached her, rested his hands on the trunk beside her shoulders.

"On the contrary. If I had found you unworthy of conversation, I wouldn't have even said a word to you."

"Back at the airport, you looked at me like I was a moron."

"I was curious if you would fight or let it go. If I found the right person this time."

Seymour moved his head close to her face, felt her warm, rapid breathing against his skin.

"Have your ex, who shouldn't be mentioned on the next date, hurt you?" Am I to find him and cut off his head?"

"We just didn't work out. Julia Croft, now the wife of the councilor, contributed to this. She ruined my two-year relationship and my dreams. A lot of local women hate her."

"What can I say. A woman is an enemy to another woman."

"It may not sound moral, but I liked your reaction to the mention of my ex. That's what the Infected should be like: brutal, ruthless, self-confident, eager to act."

"Seriously, you never considered joining Kiritians? You're damn honest, nothing is taboo for you. As for me, I'm the exception to the rule. My people's family jewels have softened recently, at least of a few people."

"Kiret Biffter?"

He was surprised by her deduction again. He wondered if Alice had figured out his way of thinking after knowing him so briefly. He glanced aside, bit his lip, and made no further comment on the authority's position.

He pressed her against the trunk with his body and kissed her. Alice touched her hands to his face and kissed him back eagerly.

"So, you have to do something about it," she said after a minute.

"About what?"

"The Kiritians, of course. I'll help you."

"You will?" He asked ironically. "What are you going to do? Do you have dealings with Kandrok?"

"I'll show you."

"So, show now."

He kissed her more passionately than before, slid his hands onto her buttocks. Alice cuddled up to him, throwing her arms around his neck.

"What about the young?" He asked. "Shall I send him back to the barracks so that he checks in?"

"Let him stare if he has wanted to."

She pushed the lieutenant away enough to be able to freely slip off her dress and underwear. Tsar raised his eyebrows slightly, extremely pleased with what he was seeing, though he was more surprised by the speed of the unfolding event and Alice's lack of embarrassment. He complimented her naked body only with a short "wow". He didn't undress himself, because she stopped him from doing it. She clung to him, taking blissful pleasure from the touch of the hard, cold biometal of the Kiritian armor.

He didn't remember afterwards whether he had stumbled and dragged the girl with him, or they both had had the same idea of cooling their emotions, because with screaming and laughing they had landed in the pond, driving the crucians in all directions.

***

Darius was really fed up with peeping. Tsar and Alice's tryst was more boring than Maksimus Figam's lecture on new military technologies and the implementation of old projects. In addition, the night was approaching. He fell asleep at one point, lost his balance and slipped off the branch that had rushed up, rustling the leaves loudly. The corporal broke several more before landing hard on the ground, cursing worse than an old lag. He felt like a complete fool. Believing that the lieutenant deserved privacy at this stage of the date, frustrated, he scrambled out of the bushes and headed for the quarters assigned to the Kiritians.

His thoughts went to Julia Croft-Lewandowska, whom Alice briefly mentioned. He knew this woman, he had seen her after landing, flirting with Tsar, or more precisely, it was he who had accosted her. The story of Captain Anna Sandstorm was widely known - it was rare that a former rebel joined Kiritians, previously fully committed to the enemy's cause. Thus, her private life was known. Darius remembered her dating Beliar Drunkenstein before she had gotten involved with Forkis. Julia became the bone of contention in that relationship, and had it not been for her, the further fate of the opposition and the Immortals might have been different. "The woman must have a lot of nerve," Schindler thought as he stepped into a tropical garden where dense vegetation dominated, colorful long-tailed birds minced, and semi parasitic flowers the size of dinner plates stuck to tree trunks. Apparently, Sandstorm had never gotten back at Julia. He would have done so in her place, especially since that woman had humiliated many people. His father had taught him never to let go and to pursue his goal hard, whatever it might have been. Darius himself added a vendetta to the teachings of John. To avenge, he had learned from Tsar, who didn't forgive anyone who humiliated him.

As if his thoughts had taken a material form, he ran straight into the councilor's wife. They collided at the intersection of roads bordered by a wall entwined with vegetation. Julia jumped away from Schindler, raised her hands as if he had poured coffee on her.

"I'm so sorry, ma'am," he said hastily.

"Stupid Kiritian!"

Schindler was disgusted by her reaction. She blamed him, though the wall had obscured the view of both of them.

The woman quickly overcame her anger, even smiled heartily.

"I know you. I saw you in the company of this handsome soldier."

"He's my commander."

"Where is he now?"

"Occupied."

"Pity." Julia was a perfectionist in simulating emotions, now feigning distress. "I've been hoping to see him again." And smile again. "But you can be useful too."

Darius' eyebrows rose slightly. In terms of appearance, Julia was ... well ... a phenomenon whose sensuality was emphasized by the strong red of her dress and painted lips. Despite the fact that her first youth had already passed, she still stunned with beauty and grace: a shapely figure, slightly tanned skin without imperfections, smooth like a child's, hair lush and well-groomed, sharp, predatory features with the most alluring part of them - blue eyes, traps for men. The Kiritian shuddered when he looked at this beautiful woman, a head shorter than him, he stared at her like a hungry person at a cake in a pastry shop. However, a brief appraisal made him realize that Julia had been generously endowed by nature with beauty, but not with reason. He would have liked to know the motive of the councilor, a public figure, who had married such an empty-headed chick, only pretty. Or maybe that was what it was all about - sparkling decoration at banquets, meetings and during the signing of documents.

"Can I help you with something, ma'am?"

"Oh, call me Julia. Because I don't think I look so old in your eyes? With you Kiritians, it may be different."

"You don't, Julia."

"All in all, you could help me. I lost my favorite, very expensive ring and have been looking for it for half an hour. I was just on my way to that lawn, I wanted to make it before dusk. I have no one to help."

"The lights will probably turn on after dusk?"

"Yes, but they're weak."

"Where do you have your husband?" Darius blurted out thoughtlessly, which he immediately regretted. However, Croft-Lewandowska replied to him:

"He's busy as always. He has never time for me. I feel so lonely."

Schindler let loose a vague sound.

"Okay, I'll help you find that ring. I have a night off anyway, no plans unless Tsar calls me." He didn't like the selfishness of the woman thinking only about her lame problem. She hadn't even asked him if he had time now, not to mention that his identity was clearly indifferent to her.

"Thanks! I'll show you where I might have dropped it."

They stepped onto the lawn separating the three types of gardens. The corporal was walking, bent, staring at the watered, trimmed leaves.

"Do you know more or less where you lost it?"

Julia tucked her dangling hair behind her ears.

"I'm not sure, but maybe somewhere in here. Or maybe there." She waved her hand towards a marble and granite bench. "I know for sure that I had it on my finger when I was going for a walk. It is made of rare gemstones, imported from a planet where rain is diamonds. I don't remember its name. Tom bought it for me, and I'm afraid he won't get another one."

"Then, it's actually a catastrophe." Darius said with mock sympathy.

The soon-to-be activated lights were really not conducive to the search for such a trifle as a filigree ring with precious stones. After a quarter of an hour, Schindler was fed up, he said excuse me to Julia and went to his fighter for a universal handheld scanner, one of the functions of which was detecting metals. He quickly tracked down the loss, which was preceded by finding a rusty knife and cartridge cases from the time of fighting with the rebels.

"Oh, thank you so much!" Julia picked up the ring and put it on her finger. For Schindler, the trinket had no value. He knew nothing about jewelry and wasn't interested in it. "I'm in your debt."

"Really, it's not necessary. As I said, I had no plans for the evening anyway."

"So, you have them now." Julia clung to his arm. "I invite you for a drink. Or wine. Or a beer. Or whatever you want. Come on, let's breathe some fresh air, talk a bit."

Schindler refrained from remarking that they had been breathing fresh air for some time.

"Is it really a good idea? You have a husband, there may be a scandal because of it." Although he didn't like the proposal very much (maybe a little), he allowed himself to be led along the lawn, towards an arched, stylized bridge over a reservoir.

"So, what if I have? He is a monstrous bore! We used to be fine together, but then it all burned out. His work and diplomacy over and over again. Frequent trips that he doesn't want to take me on. I fell out with my brother over it today.

And you know what? Arek called me an idiot when I told him that I was already bored with Tom."

"Because you are," the boy thought.

"He told me to stick to him, but I don't want to ..." Julia continued chattering. Darius stared straight ahead and pretended to be listening. Sometimes he glanced at her and nodded with false eagerness, though he didn't know why. He considered letting go. Visually he liked Julia very much, he couldn't deny it, but he perceived her in the same way as pleasing prostitutes - for a one-time adventure, unless he liked one of them, then he visited her more often. He didn't think, however, that he would want to meet with Croft-Lewandowska longer, because her intellectual attributes wore on him. And what the theoretical drink would end in, Darius knew all too well.

"Don't you think I'm too young for you?" He asked, trying somehow ineptly to get out of the situation.

"You absolutely don't look like that. Besides, you can be up to four hundred years old. Don't worry, you will just have a drink, sit down for a while and go. I will feel better when I know that I have repaid you for your help with a nice evening."

"I heard you were looking for my lieutenant."

"Yeah. I wanted to get to know him better. How to put it ... I've never been with a Kiritian. And he had cool red eyes like my dress. When Tom saw us, I had to pretend I despised this lieutenant."

"Oh my God ..."

The boy barely suppressed a rasp.

They came to a small neighborhood where there were little staff houses. The residents were dealing with their own affairs, they were mainly occupying the terraces, laughing, drinking and talking in large company. They were swimming in the pools, played with the animals, someone was trying to outplay an android in basketball, which was being cheered by a group of fans. No attention was paid to Darius and Julia, as if the sight of the councilman's wife accompanied by a stranger hadn't impressed anyone.

"So, Tom doesn't know you're cheating on him?" Darius was surprised by his own directness to delicate private matters. It was part of his father's breeding on Chulimal - not to put your nose in. Unknowingly, he must have picked up the new habit from Tsar.

Julia looked at him with her mouth open.

"Of course not! How do you imagine it? He recently flew to another city and won't be back until the morning. You know, Tom eats out of my hand. He does whatever I wish. It is so easy for me to convince him to do anything. However, we haven't slept together for some time, and I have ... my needs."

"And don't you think that he still loves you, but just works a lot?"

"But I don't love him anymore. Arek, however, told me to get the divorce out of my head, be faithful and think responsibly. He knows about my ... meetings, but for our sake he won't say a word to anyone."

Tired of her blather, Darius soon found out why Arkadiusz Croft had encouraged his sister to stay with her husband. Behind the workers' housing estate, the residences of councilors began, and Julia's house turned out to be one of the most impressive. Off-planet imported volcanic rocks formed a structure like three unsymmetrically adjacent saucers, one on top of the other. The building looked a little like a very small azure-colored spaceship. In fact, it was Tom's estate, for which he had raised funds for many years before he became a politician and started getting a subsistence allowance. Julia had gotten it on the act. When they were passing through a hexagonal gate, she confided in addition that she didn't work because she didn't feel like it.

Schindler genuinely felt sorry for Tom, a brave and courageous patriot from the opposition, who had also taken part in the reconstruction of the rebel society after the end of the war with the Kiritians. He felt a certain unity with him - he had also been betrayed by his girlfriend. He also felt sorry for Annie Sandstorm for having had the stupid and treacherous friend in the past.

Once they were in the garden of the estate, a risky idea occurred to him. For a brief moment his face was lit by the smile of someone who would soon do a memorable number. Julia took it as a sign of delight.

"I see you like my house. Great, right? Wait, I'll go first and turn off the monitoring, it is not in this part of the garden. Tom hardly ever analyzes it, but I want to make sure that he won't look at the archives when he comes back. If there are problems, I will come up with something offhand."

The residence was indeed "great". Neat, shiny, fully interactive, powered by geosolar modules, placed in the form of above-ground columns and ones partially buried in the ground. The porch, guarded by statues of ancient commanders, could be reached walking down an avenue, with a swimming pool on one side and a decorative pond on the other. As a decorative element, clusters of transparent crystals of various heights and shades protruded from the ground. After examining them with his hand, Darius was unable to determine whether they were natural or artificial. Soon Julia summoned him to a vestibule. Everything in the building worked on verbal commands, and for cleaning and preparing meals were responsible robots. "It means," Darius thought, "that Julia does absolutely nothing except wasting time on pleasures and cheating on her husband."

"Wait, I'll choose something to drink in a minute." The woman left the corporal in the lounge.

Darius sat back on a couch and surveyed the surroundings. The entire south wall had been transformed into a window that, apart from the real view, could serve virtual landscapes. Julia chose a panorama of the mountains with the northern lights and a huge orange planet reigning over them. The sterile living room itself, dominated by pink light, could have accommodated up to a hundred people if the movable molecular wall dividing the room equally had been withdrawn. In the transparent floor were laboriously moving shapes chosen by the owner - blue-green tongues simulating water.

Schindler didn't catch the next details, because Julia came back with a robot, who put a decanter and two glasses on the table, then went down the hall. He didn't recognize the nectar he was served to the relaxing music. The cloudy, spicy drink, but with a sweet taste, acted like Tsar's weaker drugs already after a few minutes - it relaxed the muscles and mind, brightened up a day, but didn't cause any strong motor or neurological deviations.

"Come on." Three quarters of an hour later, Julia, smiling flirtatiously, grabbed Darius' hand and pulled him towards the bedroom.

Schindler wasn't embarrassed, he found himself on a well-known ground, where only physicality mattered. He mentally apologized to Tom for his actions but had to continue if his intention was to work out.

They didn't prolong foreplay. They stripped off their clothes as they caressed and kissed, then ended up in a double bed.

After they had an intercourse, Darius decided to implement the previously devised plan. Taking advantage of the moment when the resting woman had her eyes closed, he leaned out quickly and unhooked the military cellula from the armor lying by the bed, then moved it with his leg. After the fourth attempt, interrupted by kisses with Julia, bites and tongue games, he managed to rest the object on the bracer and set it at the right angle. When the woman wasn't looking again, Darius leaned out and activated recording with his foot.

"You're fidgeting so strongly." She looked into his eyes with amusement.

"Are you sure Tom won't suddenly show up?" Darius asked the question deliberately. He hoped to get quite interesting material.

Before the woman lying below him answered, she laughed in his face.

"My boy. This has never happened to me, and I doubt it will ever happen. Calculation plus female intuition. And even if it will, I believe in your reflex and the dexterity of a Kiritian."

"So, of course, the responsibility will fall on him," he huffed in his mind.

"Depends how many you had before me ... such like me." Darius kissed Julia. He turned to a side.

"I'm not even going to count them all."

"So, you're playing hard. You really don't feel sorry for Tom?" She sighed.

"You're asking the same thing again. Don't plague me with him. I already told you; everything is over between us. But I'll keep sticking to him for the money, because where else will I find another sucker like him?"

Darius wasn't going to spend the whole night with her. As - with his twenty-nine calendar years - he felt still very young (apparently, he would stay such forever, because his biological age would be practically constant), and the Kiritian feeling of the passage of time hadn't become his second nature yet, he had some reluctance to intercourse with a much older woman. In addition, Julia was the oldest he had ever had sex with. His father's breeding forbade to go round with a woman who was in a serious relationship. The corporal was disgusted with what he was doing - although he couldn't deny that it was insanely pleasant - but he wanted to see his intention through.

He used a well-known ruse to end the meeting. Once again, taking advantage of her inattention, he activated the communicator on the bracer, switching to the general channel, loudly humming with dialogues. He did it for a moment so that the woman wasn't able to catch the sense of any conversation. He hid the cellula."

"They're calling me." He thought that Forkis wouldn't have been pleased that Kiritian truthfulness began to crumble after his death. He felt ashamed. "Unfortunately, I have to go."

"Oh, that's a pity." Julia sat naked on the rumpled quilt. "Maybe I'll see you again?"

Darius smiled briefly, but not because the prospect of the meeting seemed like a brilliant idea to him - they both knew that they would rather not meet again.

"Maybe." He leaned down and kissed the woman, then began to dress, first in the uniform, then he put on his light armor.

"Then thank you for the nice evening. You were better than I expected," she said sweetly.

Whether it was an insult to crush the male ego or a compliment, Darius didn't know, and he completely didn't care. He had gotten what he wanted, and Julia might as well have drowned now in the garden pond with fish worth thousands of uinals.

***

As he passed the gates of the estate, he checked the material he had obtained. Julia's words were clearly recorded, as was what they were doing in the bedroom. Darius' plan was simple: to discredit this spoiled woman. Process the recording in such a way - fortunately his name was never mentioned during the meeting, so there will be less work - to cover his face and modulate his voice, and then share the material with Tom. Tomorrow, Schindler could deny anything he might have possibly been asked about. If he came across Julia, he would say that he didn't know her. It would have been best if he didn't take his helmet off in public until he left the Nephrida, as he would have looked like anyone from Kiritian security. Monitoring must have been operating everywhere in the gardens, and the witnesses had seen them together, but the matter was not so important to launch a larger investigation. After the romance came out, there was no way Tom wouldn't kick the slutty wife out.

Darius found himself in the gardens. The closer he got to the barracks, the more he doubted. Approaching the matter spontaneously and emotionally, he hadn't considered the further consequences of his act. Tom Croft-Lewandowski (the spouses had the same double surname) would surely find out who was Julia's lover, get upset, and as a member of the Council of Thirty-One, he could lead to a cooling off of Nephridian's relationship with Kiritians, which would result in the failure of Biffter's plan. Nay, Tom could accuse Darius of corruption and an attempt to talk the councilor's wife over. He sat down on a bench and began to consider everything from the beginning, listening to the sounds flowing from a distant banquet, to which no achij of his rank had been invited.

In the end, he decided to humiliate Julia, but by playing with open cards. He would be punished at the most, but he would at least have some entertainment and the memory from Nephrida. Moreover, the satisfaction that he would mess up the woman's life who had humiliated their captain and former councilor. What happens next would depend on whether the opposition still considered Kiritians an honorable and truthful nation.

Schindler pulled out one of the cellula micro memory bones to pass it on directly, but after reflection he put it back in and added to the recording a written message made from sound:

"To Mr. Tom Croft-Lewandowski, a representative of the Council of Thirty-One. My name is Corporal Darius Schindler, I'm an achij of the security of the Kiritian delegation. This recording has been made by me, about its existence, know I and now you. I know the history of the rebel-Kiritian wars well, and your surname, which has appeared many times in it as an excellent freelancer and faithful companion of the opposition regiment. People like you deserve a dignified life, but it shouldn't be passing in the company of false friends and loved ones. That is why I decided to give you this recording from your residence. It is fully authentic, and my questions and actions were a deliberate provocation. I met Mrs. Julia by accident in the gardens and quickly found out what kind of person she was. A war hero doesn't deserve such a wife. I didn't want that at your estate to happen. I just wanted to show the truth. So please acknowledge that I am indifferent to Mrs. Julia and that I have no intention of seeing her again. Please do with the acquired knowledge whatever you want. I would like to emphasize that this is not a trick, conspiracy or any form of deeper plan on the part of Kiritians, for I am the only Immortal involved in this idea. I don't want to harm anyone, neither you, nor General Kiret Biffter, who sincerely cares about making an alliance with Nephrida. I wish you happiness on your further life journey."

After reading and revising the text several times, Darius even felt pleased with himself. It fared infantilely, simply and embarrassingly, which is as it should have been. Now all he had to do was slip the material to Tom or deliver it to him by someone else.

After half an hour of searching, he found Arkadiusz Croft, handed him the recording and asked to deliver it to Tom as soon as he returns. The fact that Schindler didn't intend to wait for his departure from the planet before handing over the proof of infidelity, only increased the credibility of the recording and the author's sincere intentions.

Surprised, Arkadiusz was skeptical about Darius' request, but when he found out using a scanner that the young Kiritian was not trying to smuggle a bomb or a pathogen, he agreed to help.

***

In the evening, an intimate banquet was organized in a building next to an orangery. It was attended by the president of Nephrida, the councilors free from the duties, and the Kiritian elite: Anna, Kiret and Velkee. Both groups were reluctant to be in the same circle, but this type of meeting after the deliberations was a tradition, moreover, after more portions of alcohol, the earlier tension was alleviated.

After three hours of eating, drinking, and especially prolonged conversation, Necron felt weary and wanted a little loneliness. He stepped out onto an empty balcony, rested his hands on the railing, and listened for a while to a concert of cicadas and crickets. He took a deep breath, worried about the next day's vote. The vicinity of the building was well-lit, but not far from the barracks where Seymour and the rest of the lower-ranking achijes were accommodated, there were a few faint lamps functioning by the alleys and water reservoirs. Even though Kiret wasn't carrying a helmet with a vision enhancer, he could see silhouettes flashing like thieves among the trees and plinths. He recognized Alice Lacetti, who had been introduced to him by the president during the day. She was being followed by Lieutenant Tsar Seymour. They both stopped behind the statue, talked for a while, then each went the other way and disappeared from view. Curious, Biffter right after saw Darius Schindler, who sat on the bench, leaned over, tampered with something, and then moved in a direction other than his predecessors.

Necron went back inside. He hoped that whatever Tsar and Darius were up to, it wouldn't lead to an implosion of the cosmos. He knew that Seymour constantly played the fool, but he was an intelligent achij. He gave them both tacit consent to what, perhaps, he himself couldn't settle.

***

The next evening Kiret left the government building as if in a trance. He answered laconically and whatever to the questions asked by his comrades. He couldn't believe that things had taken a positive course for the Immortals. Although President Lacetti had voted against military support for Kiritians last time, he now boldly backed the relief plan. Even more surprising was Tom Croft-Lewandowski, who looked irritated from the beginning of the vote, even the councilors sitting next to him seemed to be settling him down in a whisper. When it was time to make a final decision, Tom declared that he would personally lead the squad to the possible war. And he spoke it in the style of Warfighter: with verve, determination, and a slight aggression, which was completely untypical of the gentle-by-nature, friendly ex-rebel. Even after the sitting was over, the decision makers, immersed in private conversations in the hall, quietly mentioned that they had not seen him so agitated before.

Hours later, as the Kiritians left the apartment in preparation for departure, Necron saw Seymour discussing with Warfighter and he remembered the evening episode he had witnessed on the balcony. The pieces of the puzzle quickly clicked into place, and he felt angry.

When Seymour was alone in the corridor, he followed him, grabbed his arm, and pushed the achij against the wall without finesse, so strongly that his armor rattled.

"Sir?" Tsar was clearly confused by Biffter's behavior.

"You half-assed idiot! Do you realize what you have done?!"

"But what ..."

"I saw you yesterday with the president's daughter. And today suddenly Aveo Lacetti agrees to help us, despite the fact that he was categorically against it, previously. Just like that, he wouldn't have changed his mind in a day. How do you explain that?" Kiret thought that Forkis had treated his achijes brutally more than once. Perhaps there was a method in it, since his empire had lasted so long? He noticed that he was comparing himself to the late emperor again. His self-esteem fell, especially after he realized that the situation had been saved by achijes with ranking much lower than his, to which he had finally given his consent, not reacting at the banquet. In a flash of the moment, Biffter felt anger so untypical of him that he almost punched Tsar on the jaw with the intention of breaking it. He was afraid of his reaction and quickly calmed down. He had no right to baste his subordinates just because he felt defeated and inferior to Forkis. His wounded ego, he wouldn't heal this way either.

"Oh, this." Seymour smiled broadly, but also hesitantly, even though Necron lacked much to be merry.

"Well, it just came out. I laid out my arguments to Alice - we have similar views anyway - and she convinced daddy. She didn't have to do this at all. The wench is wise and bright, has a gift of persuasion, and Aveo often consults her about various matters."

"I know perfectly well what 'your arguments" looked like. This kind of thing is called cheating, you know achij? This time we had almost ninety percent of the votes in favor! As if there had been a thick propaganda of someone influential among the rebels overnight."

"It is possible that the scenario-forming algorithms of the councilors' capripodes, showing the likely effects after entering into an alliance with us, made them change their decisions," added the lieutenant innocently.

"Stop playing the fool, Tsar."

"But it's possible that the favorable agitator was Tom Croft-Lewandowski. I heard that he had a sharp quarrel with his wife in the morning and kicked her to the curb. He was pissed off, and a man's priorities change in emotion. Tom is well-liked and influential, so tell yourself the rest, sir."

Necron remembered the irritation that emanated from the councilman's face during the second deliberations. Indeed, personal trials and tribulations could explain why he was so eager to fight.

"And that's probably your doing, too, Tsar?"

"Of course not." The lieutenant denied with a gesture of his hands and made a prude's face. "I have nothing to do with this, sir. I swear."

"Alright, Seymour." Necron stepped back. He waved his hand towards the exit. "Get out. And I don't want to see you for hours."

Deep down, he approved the lieutenant's deed - he hardly had to admit it to himself - but, of course, he couldn't say it out loud. He chid him on principle, though more so because Tsar, in a way, had turned out to be better than him. Kiret smiled sadly at the back of the man moving away. Either way, Nephrida's army would be ready at call when Kiritians decided to attack Kandrok's troops, for which they had been preparing for years. At least this problem was checked off. Now Biffter would be able to fly with a calmer heart to Karikon to Andromeda, from where he would bring the assassin Divinus. Then awaited them a trip to Amyrade and the awakening of Forkis, of course if the mission 'Revival' didn't turn out to be decanting a lake with a sieve and from the beginning his pipe dream.

Tsar wanted to tell jokingly before leaving the apartment that the incident with Tom and his wife was not his doing, but another achij's who had confided in him, but gave up, seeing the murderous glare of the general, who seemed to want to shoot him right away.

XIX. Eternal Assassin

Raver Divinus Relagard listened reluctantly to his own loud breathing, not much different from the sound of a blacksmith's bellows. It was impossible to avoid this uncomfortable effect in the confined space, the realm of the echo. The assassin had been rushing through the suburban sewers for many minutes, mostly bent over. Though he should have remained safe for a while, he gnashed, hearing the noise whose source was he himself. He was chased through the city of Dadali by a crowd of guards. He lost them in a market square, from where he ran to an empty side street, where he got to the damp nether regions through a sewage hatch.

Divinus had two months to devise and refine the plan for the assassination of the prince, which was commissioned to him. For weeks he watched the heavily guarded castle from hiding, noting the location of the guards and the hours of their work, as well as the servants'. He remembered who, where and when entered and left, along what paths the prince walked, what time the castle went to sleep and got up to do each task, as well as a lot of other details. An assassin dressed appropriately for the vantage points was hard to spot on the roofs of temples, watchtowers, or the adjoining tall city buildings. Even if a passerby had looked up, they would have seen a rag fluttering in the wind, which had caught on something high up. It would have never occurred to them that they saw the cloak of the most famous assassin on Karicon, often considered a figment of the imagination, a pupil of the former Order of Assassintiar who, after centuries of his life, had mastered to remain motionless even for many hours. Div also got a map of the castle. Once, he managed to enter the throne room disguised as an itinerant jewelry dealer. He deliberately inflated prices to make his offers rejected, but even if the king or queen had wanted to buy something in larger quantities, Bearded Joe, the captain of a merchant ship and associate of the assassin, would have taken care of it.

When the plan to kill the prince was tweaked in detail, the assassin set about devising several escape scenarios. The one in which he had to use the sewers proved itself, therefore he preventively broke hydraulic seals of manhole covers for several nights and disassembled trusses in anti-flood tunnels.

The prince died an hour ago, just before dawn. However, not everything went according to plan. Div was supposed to murder him in his sleep, go out the window, climb down the rugged wall of the castle, cross two shaded courtyards, bypassing dogs gotten off with poisoned meat, and finally get beyond the walls, using the calculated inattention of the guards. He knew the perfect plan couldn't succeed and something was going to screw up, as always. This time two things went wrong. The first were the guards on the walls, who stopped and had a chat, which made the 'calculated' cycle go haywire. The second turned out to be the prince's lover - Div didn't know about her. The maid came in a seductive slip through a hidden passage and yelled, having seen the dead heir moments after the murder. The aforementioned guards looked towards the windows of the prince's chambers. Almost immediately they noticed the hooded figure in the garden.

The assassin had no choice but to leave more victims after the operation. He shot both surprised sentries with a miniature folding crossbow attached to his forearm, and immediately began racing up the stairs to a section of the renovated walls, taking advantage of the fact that the other guards were still far away.

The first shots flew as he lowered himself down a crane rope to the pavement outside the castle walls, and as he reached the nearest town houses, the royal gate swung open. Troops of knights and guards poured out into the streets. The bells rang. The townspeople got to the balconies and windows, hungry for spectacles before the start of the next trivial day. Dishwater, potty contents, and food scraps flew down, nearly all of which ended up on cavalry and infantry.

Despite the early hour, the market was blocked by carts and stalls of merchants setting out goods - thanks to them Div managed to lose the pursuit.

Now he was searched on the surface while he made his way through the sewers to the harbor, where Bearded Joe was waiting with his crew and a ship ready to sail. Luckily for Divinus, it had rained many days ago, so in the tunnel maze, he encountered little puddles and narrow streams. The darkness was scattered by the blue light emanating from a sapphire in the hilt of a dagger he held like a torch. The glow was activated with a keyword and extinguished in the same way. Div had once received the dagger from a magician who paid him so for the service performed - the elimination of another wizard. At first, he had thought he had received a cheap trash, barely licked with magic, but after centuries of use, it turned out that he had not been cheated. Some spell must have been cast not only on the sapphire, but also on the metal itself, for after ripping thousands of throats, the dagger still looked like new.

He touched his chest with his free hand, felt a lump of green actinolite hanging on a chain under his coat and sweaty shirt. It was this stone, given to him in the distant past by a werewolf princess, that was the source of his immortality. The girl had put it around his neck when wounded Relagard was dying after fighting the harpy Nyburia, and the actinolite had healed him. He only knew that the stone was a powerful artifact, but how it worked he had no idea. He had always been skeptical about gods and magic, he had despised them, trusting only his own weapons and skills. However, the numerous adventures that had provided him with evidence that supernatural forces did exist and work, had caused Relagard to gain some respect for paranormal matters. He was afraid of actinolite itself, and more precisely what would have happened if he had stopped wearing it. Would have he instantly crumbled to dust as a person who should have died a few centuries earlier, or his time would have begun to pass like of any mortal, starting in his thirties when the Wolf Princess had saved him? That is why he had never removed the stone. Even when he replaced a worn chain, he kept it close to his bare chest.

He quenched the sapphire with the spell. He ran to a loose grate and kicked it outside into a beggars' den with no tenants, then placed the iron circle so that it looked attached to the bricks.

The red eye of the sun began to emerge from the sea, spraying scarlet on dozens of moored boats and ships as Div reached an old, unused cutter where he hid his backpack. He swapped the gray cloak for a deep blue one, which was his favorite color. He walked leisurely along the stone wharf, having not put on his hood. With weaponry hidden under his clothes, except for a short sword, he looked like a poor noble going to the port in the morning to inspect the goods ordered. The bell chime was constantly coming from the city. Div passed an armorer and several fishermen who ignored him, absorbed in conversation about the night stabbing of the prince - rumors in Dadali were faster than assassins.

He descended to a wooden bridge, covered with bird feces, fish scales and algae, passed breeding pools and reached a pier where the three-masted hulk was moored. He got onto the deck over the gangplank without difficulty, giving only a password. The captain of the merchant ship had told the crew about the visitor who would arrive at dawn.

Bearded Joe, a deeply tanned middle-aged man, was waiting for him below the deck with his arms crossed over his chest. With a short nod of his head, he indicated his cabin.

"You broke the contract," he hissed through his teeth as he slammed the door behind the newcomer. "You alarmed the whole city!" He stood close to the assassin and waved a finger in front of him. "I should throw you overboard now, and preferably kill you."

Divinus stared blankly at the weathered face of the hulk owner. Bearded Joe wasn't his principal, the assassin paid him to lead him safely out of the city to the high seas, from where he was to sail to Salvorin's Kingdom, where Caer Sidi was. Therefore, he didn't react to the tirade.

"I hope you are aware, Div, that if I move my ass now, I'll lose the powerful trading partner? Even the greatest cull will associate the immediate departure of the ship with the murder of the crown prince!" Bearded Joe cleared his throat, went to a desk to turn down a kerosene lamp. He began to observe the harbor through the porthole.

"Careful, I might believe you that you will lose a lot of money by doing this." Div smiled slightly, knowing what Bearded Joe dealt with besides trading.

"Oh! You're going to smart off here, you damn landman! Find a loyal, faithful crew and build a special ship yourself from scratch, and don't let yourself be uncloaked for five years, then we'll talk, you sickly hotshot ..."

"You had a stop paid until morning, so why do you think it's weird that you will leave now?" Relagard walked over to the captain, ran his finger over a large white pen in an inkwell. "Do all the sailors now have to delay raising the anchor because the foreign prince has been killed?"

"That's right, assassin," Bearded Joe said, now more calmly. He turned slowly towards the interlocutor, looked him in the eyes, cold as two pieces of ice. "And don't tell me you don't know the customs of Dadali, which have been the same for centuries, since you've been here many times." He frowned, twisting his lips. "You know well what I mean."

The captain eyed Divinus up. Medium height, slim build, narrow face, about thirty years old. An assassin legend, for some reason immortal, which allowed him to refine his treacherous practices to perfection, of which an undeniable proof was his secretly getting into the heart of the royal castle, where even a mouse wouldn't have slipped. True, he had made the mistake and been detected too quickly, but aren't even all-powerful gods infallible? He didn't stay anywhere longer than a decade, tried not to be conspicuous, and mostly faked his death before surreptitiously leaving his place of stay to move to another part of Karikon. He changed identity frequently, but always came back to the real one. However, he didn't take into account folk tales and chronicles in which the suspicious began to look for answers about a man so much like the 'old' Divinus. Several engravings and paintings in honor of Raver Divinus Relagard, disciple of Morion, heir of Assassintiar, who founded the Assassin order in Caer Sidi many centuries earlier, had been preserved. Those who knew that Relagard, who appeared in different ages and parts of the world, was the same person, suspected that he had attained immortality, having killed a powerful arch-mage who had deceived him while paying a bill, and he had seized his power. In another version, Div had fulfilled the commission of the arch-mage so perfectly that he had repaid him by giving him eternal life. Both versions didn't convince Bearded Joe. Why would have the all-powerful wizard asked for help from the assassin who had so much to do with magic that he could only light the stone in the dagger with the spell? The captain didn't find an answer to the question why Div didn't age and die, but the fact was that fate brought the living legend to his ship. He decided not to tell him what he knew about him.

"I just wonder where you have your famous weapon." The captain meant the plasma gun, captured by the assassin at the temple of the earth god Rafidian during his journey with the Wolf Princess to the Skyworld Mountains. Div knew what this weapon was, as he had had the opportunity to meet its creators, but Bearded Joe associated it with a powerful magical gadget.

The assassin saw no reason why he should have made up to the captain who was a cruel man but with principles and keeping secrets. Anyway, time was pressing.

"I lost it a while ago."

"That's not good. But don't be afraid. The news of this won't leave this cabin and reach your enemies."

Divinus nodded briefly, not changing the indifferent expression on his face.

Bearded Joe turned and left the room.

"Crew!" He roared, putting his hands on the hips. "Time to leave this hole!"

"You should have said it at once, Captain," muttered the assassin from the twilight as he approached the exit.

"It doesn't matter now. Since you made a lot of noise throughout the city, we must sail out immediately, before they start searching the ships. And I wouldn't bear that."

The captain walked over to the nearest spar and, with a grunt, checked the tension of the rope, pulling it with both hands. "Come on. Now that you're here, you are supposed to be useful."

***

Bearded Joe supposed it would be hard to assign the right job to Relagard. The captain loved to baste landmen and give them the hardest, filthiest jobs, especially the delicate, powdered swells occupying couches in lounges. Whether he was transporting a poet or a baron, whether they paid him a lot or little, everyone was supposed to work on his ship. However, he liked Divinus and felt respect for him, after all, it was unusual to host an assassin, who, apart from being immortal, was also the best in his profession for an obvious reason. He didn't want to humiliate Div and force him to glance the entire deck or scrape barnacles from the hull, but he couldn't assign him a lighter, professional job that he was completely unfamiliar with.

It turned out, however, that the assassin was not only a perfect killer, but also had mastered many other skills thanks to his long life. He sat down on the planks of the upper deck and, with the three sailors, started braiding the knots and spare lines for the sails, also supporting the barrels and boxes in the hold. The sun was nearing its zenith when he finished. The captain no longer needed his help, he allowed him to roam the ship so that he didn't disturb the crew. Relagard avoided company, anyway. He interposed himself at the end of the bow, standing on a carved bowsprit fourteen cubits beyond the deck. He kept his balance, holding on to a forestay. Above his head, a taut triangular sail called a flying jib fluttered. The assassin liked to make sea voyages this way: to be sprayed with water from breaking waves, staring for hours at a simple landscape of shifting sky and iridescent sea. It was an analogy to his life - people were somewhere in the background, preoccupied with themselves and their affairs, and for Div was allocated loneliness, emptiness and infinity, depressing, and yet soothing. More precisely, he prepared such a fate for himself. More than once he wanted to be normal, to finally bond with a woman, to get rid of that damn stone from his neck, but he was too afraid of death. He didn't understand it. He hadn't trained and perfected himself for his whole life to lose his achievements just like a family its house in a fire, that had been built for a decade with painstaking work and small resources. The consequence of life and death made no sense to Divinus' mind. And he didn't believe in gods and their twisted logic. On the day he met the Heavenly People, newcomers from a region of space known as the Solar System, he found out that the gods were rather figments of the imagination, and that everything could be logically explained, as long as you had the right level of knowledge. Unfortunately, this was missing in his slowly developing world.

The birds that had accompanied them so far disappeared some time ago - the hulk moved far away from the land. Huge fish appeared near the surface of the turquoise water, surrounding the hull like guards of an important person. Div didn't rule out the possibility that they were powerful, shape-shifting mermaids who liked to accompany travelers in seas and oceans. Sometimes one jumped out in the splash of foam, briefly presenting her glistening body, then disappeared beneath the surface, having powerfully waved her tail. The assassin even saw a colony of giant jellyfish with almost transparent organisms, only the tops of the nematocysts and the rims of the bells turned red or orange. The common jellyfish quickly disappeared behind, losing the race with the speeding holk, and these lazy creatures were in no hurry anyway. Behind his back, Div could hear the voices of the crew, which reminded him that he wasn't the only man on the high seas. The observer shouted something from the crows' nest that sounded like another report. The wind favored the journey, pushing the three-masted ship smoothly towards Salvorin's Kingdom, but to the assassin still standing on the bow it seemed that he was heading straight for the sun.

He turned as he heard footsteps on the planks of the deck, which had been damp from the recent mopping. He saw a black crew member with white pants, a headscarf, and a knife strapped to a wide belt. He knew the sailor; Bearded Joe called him Mako.

"The captain is calling you," he said urgently.

Relagard let go of the forestay and walked freely over the bowsprit, then jumped down onto the bow. He noticed that almost all of the crew were focused on the stern and starboard, and looked south to where Dadali was. He strained his eyes; he saw a brown-and-white spot on the horizon line.

One of the sailors handed Bearded Joe a telescope.

"So, bastards have been blown here." He spat over the side, thrust the telescope into Divinus' hand. "Look what you've done."

The assassin put the eyepiece to his eye and adjusted the focus with the knob. He saw the majestic bow of a royal galleon heading straight towards them. A black fish flapped on the sail with a shell in the background, which was the emblem of the coastal city of Dadali.

"The king is not stupid; he quickly sent the chase after us. He even predicted where we're going to head," the captain muttered, rolling the highlights of his beard. "But he thinks he's after a merchant ship. Hence one galleon. He plans to intimidate us into giving up quickly."

Div was silent, aware of his own guilt.

"I should have thrown you overboard or handed you over to them, capping that you secretly sneaked into the superstructure." Bearded Joe pointed to the expanding warship on the horizon. Relagard, looking dryly at him, narrowed his eyes. The captain beamed. "But I won't. Once paid, it must be done. And the boys need some entertainment."

Relagard looked at the dozens of crewmen, now all but the man in the crow's nest, gathered around his captain. Their faces looked anything but ones of surprised traders who didn't want to get into trouble in a battle against the king's army but were ready to make deals. The unshaven, sweaty, tanned mugs were twisted and gleeful, as if, after months of traveling in a men's group, Bearded Joe had told his men to rest in a brothel.

The captain looked at the highest mast where the flag of the merchant ship should have been flying; it had been removed as the last Dadali buildings were out of sight.

"Crew!" He roared happily. He raised a curved saber. "Get ready to attack!"

The deck was boiling as a synchronized scream of excitement answered him. A group of sailors climbed the ropes onto the rails like monkeys to fold some of the sails, the rest fell into the superstructure. The captain himself took the helm and, moving the wheel sharply, began to turn the ship around.

The holk changed significantly in a matter of minutes. What the superintendents in each port had taken to be a deep hold turned out to be a hidden second bottom with a pirate arsenal, that could be accessed through masked hatches. After selling the goods, Bearded Joe had deliberately littered the lower deck with all the foul-smelling debris, from bad fish to rotten fruit and rancid cod-liver oil, to discourage the port janitors from suspecting contraband. So far, the method had worked well. No one was in a hurry to search the smelly, dark hold of the petty trader. From the outside, the lower part of the hull did look additionally strengthened. The captain explained to the curious that he often sailed on the waters armed with coral reefs, fragments of icebergs and protruding rocks.

Now the crew had swept the dirt from the trapdoors efficiently and descended to the lowest deck. Two rows of recesses, associated with specific portholes or cargo improvements, turned out to be gun stations. The bustling people cleaned the barrels and placed bullets in coarse cages attached to the floor. Sabers, crossbows, knives and swords were selected. A box of dynamite was prepared, the inventor of which was the alchemist Quicksand - Divinus had had the opportunity to meet him personally several centuries earlier. Metal-reinforced wooden shields were attached to the side.

The flag with the skull was already fluttering on the mast.

Bearded Joe turned the ship a hundred and seventy degrees and boldly headed for the galleon so that it broke the surface at its starboard side.

The assassin hoped the experienced captain knew what he was doing.

Feeling the steep tilt of the turning hulk and seeing that the galleon was too far away to start firing, Div returned to his position on the bowsprit. There must have been contradictory orders aboard the enemy vessel, or confusion, for the ship seemed to be withdrawing for a moment, but then returned to its old course. The galleon was larger and more massive than the holk, but less maneuverable. The assassin thought that perhaps the first two factors had influenced a decision of the royal captain who calculated that he would simply ram and crush exposed pirates.

The units were sailing almost at each other.

The weather began to change as if in line with the situation. The hitherto clear gold-blue sky was mucked up with the first gray clouds, but it didn't look as though there was going to be a storm.

"Div!" After the captain's shout, he returned to the deck. He noticed that Mako was standing at the mighty steering wheel, gently staying the designated course. Bearded Joe stood next to the assassin. "I think you know what it looks like. You will have to deal on your own. Five hundred sea devils, who am I telling this to!"

"Don't worry, Captain, I won't bother you."

"Need a different weapon?"

"Don't worry about that either." Div grabbed his magic dagger, he revealed his coattail as well, displaying a short sword and a dozen throwing knives stuck in pockets around his belt.

"As you wish. We fight a bit differently, but when it comes to killing quickly, I am a fish, and I will not teach a bird to fly."

The captain turned and, screaming, started setting the crew members on their positions. Div managed to get the telescope, he stood between the bow and starboard where the rigging and the sail cast more shadow and watched the growing galleon. He calculated that if the units maintained their course and didn't change speed, they would be in a good position to fire the guns in a few minutes. The meeting with the king's guard could have ended in three ways: either the Dadalians would board, search the ship and take Divinus with them, or the entire holk would have the assassin back - who had paid a lot for the trip - which would inevitably result in a fight and Bearded Joe might win, or else the holk crew would kill Div, release the body, and maybe offload the blame for complicity in the Prince's murder. This last possibility could prove problematic. Although Relagard had extensive experience in killing, he was not a one-man army with the appearance of a stone golem. However, if the sailors wanted to hand him over by force, he would defend himself and there would be casualties. Bearded Joe realized that if his respect for the assassin wasn't faked, this scenario wouldn't come true. Div hoped that his bad reputation itself would protect him from the fight. The possibility of letting the king's men aboard was also out of the question - passivity was not in the nature of pirates.

So, there would be a battle. And certainly, after the captain's words, talking half to himself, half to Div:

"Well, let Dadali go to the abyss. I was going to let this city go anyway. There, they bone with taxes little sellers like me, whereas big foreign chain stores don't have to pay it. Even if our goods were obtained on seas and islands. Besides, we haven't fought a decent, demanding naval battle in months!"

Relagard could see the figures occupying the bow of the approaching galleon without the telescope, quickly taking the form of soldiers in silver armor and helmets as well as green cloaks of the royal army. Ballistae were also waiting - so the talks were unlikely to take place. There was a slim chance that the guard commander hadn't recognized the holk from the port but had seen random pirates whom he had decided to eliminate.

The ship took on more massive, crude shapes; the broad bow cut the waves hitting the hull.

The holk was still following Mako's course.

Div handed the spyglass to someone and moved away from the side. He began to survey the ship's parts, wondering what would have been the best use of them if he had been forced to fight on board.

The units were within the range of the guns and ballistae, but neither side started firing, and no signals were sent to each other. Bearded Joe's men screamed and howled like a horde of wild beasts, while the guards kept their faces stony, holding back their emotions and sticking to military procedures.

The sailing ships slowed as most of the sails were furled. They positioned themselves parallelly to each other.

The fight started in a flash like an assassin's stab in the victim's body.

The pirates attacked first, trying to force the opponent to defend itself. The guns and bomb throwers were put into motion, that had been constructed in such a way that they exploded when smashed against an object as a result of the contact of gunpowder with oxygen.

The composed guards responded with a volley of ballistae, hurling several meters long iron-hardened bolts, grapeshots, shrapnels or ordinary metal spheres intended to punch holes in the wood.

After a few minutes of firing, the holk lost one of the smaller masts, which broke and collapsed onto the superstructure. The first holes appeared in the deck, but above the waterline. The ballista projectile hit an unfortunate pirate, killed him on the spot, flew through the leaky hull and fell into the sea with the impaled body. The ship shook dangerously - a cannon exploded in the hold, obscuring everything with a black wall of smoke.

Div almost fell over due to crates freed from ropes, although the shock of the explosion itself didn't knock him off his feet.

The galleon fared slightly better after the first encounter: a fire broke out on it, which was quickly extinguished with water from buckets and a wooden cistern, lost a ballista, and the lower topsail was torn.

"Get ready for boarding!" Bearded Joe pointed at the guardsmen with his saber and, screaming, moved forward, encouraging the rest of the crew to attack.

The pirates fired or threw ropes with triple hooks, the guards tried to throw them into the water. Several yokes anchored to the side; the corsairs began to wind the line around the reels.

As the units approached each other within jumping distance, the pirates, screaming, advanced in droves on their opponents.

By order of the galleon commander, a number of soldiers fired crossbows. After releasing the bolts, the front line of the guards crouched to reload their weapons and clear the field of shot for the second rank.

The pirates bursting onto the ship hid behind prepared shields, but a few bolts still hit the targets. Someone was wounded in a foot, other person screamed and grabbed a thigh shot through, one badly hidden corsair died with his breast pierced.

Soon the crossbowmen had no room for maneuver, and drew their swords, defending themselves against the furious blows of knives and sabers.

Div temporarily didn't take part in the battle. He climbed onto the spar and watched the course of events, wondering how he might have reacted. Despite the feistiness and initial offensive of Bearded Joe's men, the disciplined guards began to push them towards the edge of the galleon. However, the pirate captain and his few companions managed to get closer to the guard commander.

Solo and group fights were in full swing. The crews mingled. More fires broke out.

Relagard barely noticed that one of the king's soldiers pointed his finger at him, for his attention was drawn to a loud thunderbolt that rolled across the sky. At first, he mistook the sound for a cannon shot, but even that wouldn't have been as intense. Through the clouds of smoke he caught with his eye a fragment of the skies. If it had looked there was going to be a storm, it would have been a peculiar one, as a thick cloud was forming in the center of the clear sky, literally from nothing, as if a sea battle mage had produced an aberration, but there was no one such on board.

The assassin concentrated on the fight when the bolt of the crossbow whistled near his ear. Another would have killed him on the spot if he hadn't hidden behind the mast.

He drew his short sword and spotted a shooter below. As a foremast rope nearby was burnt and tangled anyway, after grabbing it, he cut it with two blows. He dropped the cut off part on a soldier, and he ran a few steps and jumped from the end of the spar.

Holding the rope tightly with his free hand, he began to fly over the galleon deck. With the blow of the sword, he cut the guardsman's throat before he could take him down with the loaded crossbow. A ribbon of blood several cubits long followed the assassin. Another opponent, he hit in the head with his boot. He managed to kick out the helmet of the next one before he began to rise in an arc. He reached the mainmast, jumped from it, and turned back.

Someone grabbed his leg with both hands and hung like that for a moment, Relagard lost flight stability and began to spin around his own axis. The overloaded arm burned with pain.

Div with impetus bumped into two guards trying to slaughter a pirate lying on planks, defending himself with a saber. He stabbed one of them with the sword in the back. He had to jump back and roll because another soldier swung at him his flaming torch, which he wanted to throw at the part of the holk deck still untouched by fire.

He rolled again, this time barely dodging the sword's stab, but the blade hit a barrel.

The assassin managed to get up in a flash. He wanted to back off, realizing from the screams that he had been identified as the prince's killer, but a few soldiers swiftly surrounded him. He pressed his back against the mainmast. He grabbed his dagger with his other hand. Gritting his teeth in grim anger, he was ready to mow down anyone who attacked him. He could hear his name being called, but he couldn't find the owner of the voice in the clash of weapons, screams, the clatter of boots, the hiss of fire consuming the deck, and the crackle of the rigging and masts of the tilting hulk.

In an instant, all but the most seriously wounded froze. Surprised, the corsairs and guards looked up at the sky. Black, dense clouds began to spread over the pirate banner as if they had been pushed out by an invisible, monumental pipe. It was as if someone with considerable magical powers had wanted to asphyxiate the entire battle area. The phenomenon was accompanied by blue discharges. The cloud quickly grew to the size of a shroud a mile long.

And then such a terrible thunderbolt swept through the world that Div groaned as his ears nearly exploded. All his insides got coiled into seaman's knots. He had rarely felt fear, but now he experienced it with tremendous power that was driven by screaming, bewildered sailors.

"Leviathan!" someone let slip in panic.

"Dragon!" Other person shouted, pointing to the sky with his sword.

Leviathan was a mythical sea creature as big as a city whose existence Div truly doubted. Nature would have had no reason to invent something so gigantic and impractical. Anyway, such a monster would have attacked from the depths. Dragons, on the other hand, really existed because he had seen them. But they were too small to create a smoky phenomenon now unfolding in the sky, from which also fiery dust was falling.

The bloody sword fell from his hand and rattled against the deck. The assassin's blue eyes widened rapidly in surprise. He remembered. He had seen something like this before. Even twice. And then every time ...

Nothing else occurred to him, for he fell unconscious to the planks at the time when a round, silvery shape, as big as a few whales, emerged from the cloud.

***

Necron had made his first trip to Karikon over a century earlier. With the take-off from Morascrik it had lasted five months. Back then, the crew had used a subspace drive, which was the fastest one created by the Immortals. An elevator drive, taken over from Kandrok, made it possible to cover the distance from Cargoo to X4 in a dizzying time of three Terran days, which had taken place luckily during the activity of two favorably formed nodes. For travels with elevator drives didn't have a permanent form.

Now it was the fourth flight to Karikon. The first journey had taken place during the colonization of space, in the twenty-sixth century, when the inhabitants of the solar system had looked for new globes to live on. The visit had ended in a conflict and the death of almost all the quarreling crew. Only two of the participants had survived thanks to Divinus, who had had an entraser implanted in his brain so that he could speak the language of the colonists. The news of the discovery of X4 hadn't spread, and the planet itself had been officially declared unfit for colonization. The next expedition had been of a scientific nature and made by the researchers of Kiritians. They had observed the society and nature of Karikon from hiding, then it had been decided that a small group of people would know about the existence of the phenomenal planet in order to avoid its exploration and destruction. This world had never known higher technology, the primitive society had developed extremely slowly; intelligent beasts had lived on it, and there had been energy dependencies that the locals had associated with magic and divine forces. After Aggroteh's expedition to Tamasul, Kiret had already known that all the peculiarities had been related to Nimja and their past experiments. It was thanks to them that Divinus' artifact had influenced his body, extending its life. During the next visit of the Immortals on X4, the assassin's entraser had been updated and he had been able to speak Kiritian from now on. He had become a kind of intermediary conveying information about his world. The third visit, Kiret had paid with Forkis, and then he had had the opportunity to see Relagard in person.

Necron had never thought that the phenomenon of Karikon could be useful in resurrecting Forkis, and Divinus would be an intermediate link. Besides him and the crew of the small astro-carrier, on the journey went also Anna Sandstorm and captain Michael Avadar, who was appointed the leader of the expedition to Amyrade.

When they reached the planet, one of the probes located Div by a signal from his entraser and protein signature. They couldn't meet him without the participation of witnesses, because he had gotten involved in a sea battle, so Kiret decided to put all the ruffians to sleep so that, as during previous visits, no one saw the newcomers from the stars. After stopping the astro-carrier in orbit, he and Avadar went in Perfarius to the waters where the battle was taking place, and they sprayed a cloud of tranquilizer. After the Karikonians fell on the deck boards, they took Div and returned to space.

When Relagard awoke in the infirmary, his hand wandered instinctively towards his neck. He panicked, and sprang up abruptly from the bed, having realized that he wasn't carrying the actinolite. Sitting, he looked around vigorously at the unusual and strange surroundings. His cleaned clothes and weapon lay on a cupboard beside.

Sandstorm, Necron and Avadar, who had so far been talking to the medical worker on the other side of the room, approached the concerned man.

Having recognized the Immortals, the assassin fell back onto the bed and started chuckling.

"Divinus Raver Relagard." Kiret rested his fists on his hips. "It's been a long time."

"Why is it not surprising that it was you, the iron-body, who kidnapped me again? You're Kikut, if I remember correctly."

Avadar ineptly changed the snicker to a forced cough, putting his fist to his mouth. Anna managed to control her facial expression.

"Kiret Biffter," the general corrected. "For friends, Necron. And it seems to me that I explained to you the previous time that our armor consisted of biometal, an alloy completely friendly to the body, also dhurnsteel, not iron."

"I'm so sorry that it slipped my mind over the last hundred years," Div ironized in his characteristic cold, hissing voice. "There is no such thing on our planet. Primitive steel is the best metal we can produce."

Seeing that he was staring at Anna distrustfully, Necron turned his hand towards her.

"This is Captain Anna Sandstorm, a former member of the Dignitaries' Council which is currently suspended ... Let's say we're in exile."

Div folded his arms on the pillow and rested his head on them.

"And you're telling me so openly that they kicked you out of your homes? I've been living too long not to figure out what it is all about at once. I haven't thought there is a force capable of defeating Kiritians."

Undeterred by the sarcasm of the assassin (deserved, anyway, because they had roused him from his private life), Kiret indicated the other person.

"Captain Michael Avadar, my travel companion and commander of the expedition we will soon organize."

"Nice to meet you. Now give me back my pendant."

Kiret extended his clenched hand in which he held the green actinolite. Div snatched it from him and immediately hung it around his neck.

"Amazing fear of losing your life, given your profession."

"Likewise," Div growled. "You could have killed me. I never part with it, because I don't know how the body will react to the lack of the stone."

"Well, now you know. Its absence, apparently, works like a de-kiritianized Immortal. The body will start working according to nature's normal rhythm from the moment you get rid of the stone."

"And I understand that you all-knowing Kiritians must have checked this by first knocking me out and then ruthlessly taking my property? Didn't you think, Kikut, that I might have died the moment my actinolite was taken from me?"

Necron with dignity and self-control took the anger which the assassin soaked his words with.

"We have professional medical care on board, so you wouldn't have lost your life. At least now we know what it actually is. We have recently learned new information about it." He waved his hand towards the actinolite. "It's an artifact, Div. Very advanced alien technology. We wanted to test it while you were asleep, but it didn't work out, all the measuring devices went crazy. It was as if the stone had treated them with a hyper-powerful electromagnetic field, an impulse of unimaginable polarity."

"You don't have to show off your knowledge. I don't understand what you are saying to me anyway." Relagard sat up in bed. "That this is a kind of artifact, I have known for a long time."

"But you probably associate its properties with magic."

The assassin snorted.

"I'm skeptical about such matters. Although I often see unusual things on Karikon, which the common people interpret in its own way, it is not worth worrying about its conclusions. That is why I'm eager to get to know a reliable explanation of the People of Heaven."

Necron gripped the stone, staring at its smoothed surface. The assassin snatched it from him again.

"As I said, it's high technology, Relagard, which we don't understand. A complicated system closed in something seemingly very simple. This artifact was once created by the people of Nimja."

"Who?"

"Gentlemen, I don't think this is a good topic to start a conversation with representatives of other worlds," said Anna. "Maybe let's move to a more convenient place for such discussions and let our important guest relax."

"Right," admitted Kiret. "So, I invite you to the observation room."

"Can I get my gun back?"

"Naturally, Divinus."

Karikon's best assassin wasn't surprised to be granted permission to carry the weapon around the astro-carrier. It was so packed with this thing called technology that Div would have been put to sleep again before he could think of hurting any of the crew. Walking through the meanders of the metal giant, he wanted to retain dignity and stand back, but he quickly began to look around with almost childlike enthusiasm, and only self-discipline prevented him from touching various elements. The Kiritians who accompanied him couldn't help but smile; the previously nervous atmosphere was over.

"Did I sleep long?" Necron asked.

"About three hours and a bit."

"So how many? We have different concepts of time."

"True. You measure hours with hourglasses[15], if I remember correctly. So, it will be over three and a half cycles."

"It isn't a tragedy."

"This is the first time I see your world live, Necron told me a lot about it." Anna, who had been walking away so far, approached Div from the right side. "You have to forgive us. I know what unconsciousness means to an assassin. However, without the abduction, it wouldn't have been possible to get you on board, too many natives would have seen the 'metal beast', and that might have seriously disturbed the mental balance of Karikon."

"People would have gone crazy," Avadar simplified.

"It's nice that someone has finally deigned to apologize to me. Speaking of which, what about the battle?" Div glanced towards the porthole as if he could see the sea there on which he was sailing.

"It is not known." The captain shrugged. "All of both crews are asleep."

The assassin grinned in a crooked smile.

"And they probably think now that some monster kidnapped me."

"What was it all about in this sea?" Kiret asked. "I iced the prince. And probably half of the kingdom is looking for me right now. So, nothing new. By the way, the man would have grown into a die-hard tyrant, so it's a little loss."

"You must lead an extremely interesting life," commented Sandstorm.

"Nevertheless, the Amyrade campaign promises to be interesting," Avadar muttered. "Lieutenant Junkie. Medieval murderer. Thief. Mischievous peasant. Physicist who specializes in messing and playing with sperm."

"Revision: Forkis' fertility was restored by drunk geneticist Alejandro Cortez, not Sariel Jelinek," corrected Biffter. "I remind you, Captain, that the team selection for Amyrade has been carefully considered. Character traits don't have to go hand in hand with professionalism."

"Forkis will surely be proud of such a rescue team, if it is possible to bring him back to life."

"You don't know the saying that what matters is the effect, not the means?"

"I think the end justifies the means."

"Enough," Anna said sharply.

"Sorry, but I'm here too," Divinus said. "Can I know what trip you are talking about? Because I have a strange impression that it concerns my humble person, and you want to get me into something very unusual."

"And you are right, Mr. Relagard." Avadar entered the observation room first, located on the highest level of the astro-carrier.

***

Divinus felt disappointed as he found himself in the middle of the large room with the encouraging name. Outer blinds had been pulled due to rock debris from the time of the great blast, surrounding with the ring the boundaries of the star system in which Karikon had orbited. Or something like that," Captain Avadar briefly told him about dangerous rocks that were in space the same as stray dogs in a well-kept city.

Necron ordered the return to Cargoo as soon as the assassin was captured, fully convinced that he would agree to participate in Kiritians' case. In addition, they had to hurry - according to Nanawak's instructions, karitan worked more efficiently with the conjunction of specific stars in relation to each other and the center of the Milky Way, and it was certainly approaching. Kiret didn't understand the significance of the celestial system for the mission, but he didn't have the time or the brain to try to grasp even a particle of Nimja's knowledge. The Immortal's brains, including Maksimus Figam himself, stood still when it came to understanding how Nanawak's artifacts worked. Aggro simply told them what he had heard: that it was about some energy channels and a more efficient pulse transfer of the pulsar billions of light-years away from Cargoo, where the mission was scheduled to start. The crew transfer process was to take place with the participation of cosmic energies, well known to Nimja, but not to the more primitive species, so Nanawak conveyed Q'ualel only what the Kiritians could understand and use. Their task was to be the service itself anyway, without going into the way these inconceivable objects worked. Like a pilot who knew how to fly their own ship but didn't have to know its structure down to the smallest screw.

A meal was brought to the observatory, during which Necron briefly told Div about the Immortals' situation and plans, emphasizing that Kandrok's attack would make big waves on Karicon if the invaders discovered this planet. The assassin, hiding his amusement, immediately realized that this intimidation was supposed to have a motivating effect on him, if he had had doubts about the willingness to cooperate with the Kiritians. After lunch, Anna and Avadar resumed their duties, leaving Necron and Div in a monitored room, having drinks mixed with gin. To be precise, only Kiret, sitting in an armchair, was sipping a tangy-bitter drink from a glass. Div limited himself to dipping his mouth politely, having the learned habit of staying sober. Admittedly, Kiret assured him that Kiritians could clear the blood of alcohol in moments, but the assassin didn't want to undergo another incomprehensible trial again.

"So, you want me to be support while traveling through the world that looks like a narcotized version of Karikon?" He asked, standing next to Necron and looking down at his full glass from the depths of his hood. "I am to fly, it is not known where, not known with whom, not known for what purpose, because none of you know it? Did I understand well?"

Necron straightened in his chair. The assassin waited for the display of hilarity on his part, at least he would have had proof that the guy had boldly put him on. Biffter, however, remained serious.

"Narcotized version of Karikon." His lips twitched in a fleeting smile. "That term would fit one of my lieutenants, Tsar Seymour. He is another member of the expedition. You will meet him and the others once we arrive."

"You're saying as if I have already made up my mind." A chill broke into the Div's gaze. "When you didn't even hear what I had to say about it."

"I just know you'll agree," Kiret replied gently.

"Will I? On what basis did you make such a conclusion?"

The Kiritian got up, took a few steps, and stood with his hands entwined at the back in front of the shorter and lighter man who would surely have killed him in seconds if he had a reason, and the room had not been protected.

"I know it because you're just like us." Biffter walked over to the wall, examined the external scan results, then flipped a switch to open the blinds as the space debris was already behind the astro-carrier. The assassin expected to see a fascinating sight that matched his ideas of outer space and was disappointed again to see the blackness and many microscopic bright dots. Immortal and bored. Thirsty for new impressions, even though Karikon abounded in them even too much. But not for someone who had done the same every day for hundreds of years. In the end, you can throw up. Gulping down, he drained the glass and put it back. "That is why nature has decided that a human being should live for several decades, because if they lived longer, they would start to vegetate, think a lot and be terribly bored. Freak out more and more over time. Oderses have reached the life threshold of one hundred and fifty years, they are still coping. Kiritians, on the other hand, are eternal. Many of us don't stand the test of time and want mortality to be restored, as our doctor Figam did.

"I remember. You consciously contracted some changed virus that, instead of killing, prolongs your life indefinitely."

"More or less. But we have it easier than you, Divinus, because our neurology - such a science of the nervous system - has many surprises up its sleeve, like memory cleansing. But not everyone wants such interference. You, on the other hand, must constantly struggle with both your own mind and your social identity. Many of us live like you: think a lot, wonder where the point is in all this, sometimes fall into melancholy, but live on. In our case, medicine has defeated nature. But if it were not for the correction of the mind, many Kiritians would commit suicide. Forkis selected the mentally toughest people for society, but time did its job anyway."

Necron argued, looking at the stars. When he turned to the assassin, certain that he was listening with an indifferent expression, he was surprised to see him pale with vitreous eyes fixed on the wall and floor.

"Div?"

"Sorry." The assassin shook his head barely noticeably. He glanced at the Kiritian. "You're right about everything. As if you were reading my mind. Or maybe you did it while I was asleep?"

Necron smiled sadly.

"I'm not Forkis. And I appreciate the privacy of people as distinguished as you, Relagard."

"So, if I were inferior, for example a peasant, would you do with me what would you like?"

"I will not hide that in the past, when Forkis was still alive, we had such methods. We conquered almost anything that moved and rarely reckoned with someone else's opinion. In the human world, it is probably the norm that any civilized society in its early stages of existence is expansive and cruel. Sometimes it goes on for centuries. Forkis finally came to his senses, he changed for us ordinary achijes who were initially to be puppets fielded as cannon fodder in his ambitious but sick plan." Necron took a short pause. "When he was assassinated, I took over his position. I turned out to be too liberal ... Too tolerant and calm. And that's why we lost our homeland and so many people. I got off the golden center, the pole tilted. And I paid the highest price for it."

They were silent for a moment, Kiret with his back to the listener. The assassin sat down in the general's earlier seat, found the nerve and took a long sip from his full glass. He had needed it for a long time, the utmost vigilance and readiness to fight would have been useless aboard the Kiritian shuttle. He couldn't remember the last time he had felt safe enough to allow himself to deviate from his creed. His mouth stung; his eyes watered as the vapor entered his nostrils. Relagard swallowed the contents of his mouth, spreading the burning across his esophagus and rapidly warming stomach.

"Horrible. No offense, of course."

"I like your directness. As an assassin, you are probably not used to stimulants. It is quite good alcohol. We produced it while still on Morascrik."

"Are you talking about the home you lost?"

The Kiritian nodded.

"Yes." He turned to the assassin. "We built new distilleries on Cargoo, but the taste still reminds us of home. So, what is your decision? In return, you can ask whatever you want."

"Do I have a choice? If I refused, you would make me go on an expedition anyway. You think I don't know we're flying right now? I overheard Mrs. Sandstorm and your captain talking. Although I have no idea how this is possible since the cosmos behind the glass remains motionless.

"It is a cover made of puronax, the most resistant material used to build transparent portholes. Even your steel compared to puronax is brittle like a dry, thin layer of mud. The one above us is a meter thick, even though a few centimeters would already be sufficient cover for interstellar travel without enemy activity. Puronax probably wouldn't resist only Kandrok that we will probably have to fight with. Our scientists are currently working on better protection."

"It's nice to hear such curiosities. They sincerely fascinate me, but you've strayed from the subject, General. Why did you take me so far from the planet? To have a guarantee that I will agree to your request? That as a savage I will panic not seeing my own world? Truly Kiritian methods, even though you mentioned something about the gentleness of mores. You have made Karikon a reserve, and yet we are worms to you. Perhaps you are indeed unfit to be a leader, Mr. Biffter, since you, as head of Kiritians, settle matters this way. And it was enough to just ask."

"I admit, I preponed the take-off, and that's because we only have ten days until karitan is at its optimum of activity. We would wait over twelve thousand years for the next such day. So, I'm not blameless."

The assassin took a long and loud breath and stretched out in his chair. He finished his drink. The warmth spreading through the body turned out to be quite pleasant.

"Forgive my irony. The trip into the unknown might really be of benefit to me." He smiled as pleasantly as he could, although it wasn't easy when you got used to the gloomy face. He couldn't afford friendships, so he preferred to alienate people. "I don't want anything in return. My health is good, I also have a long life, and the money for the orders is enough for everything I need. I would like maybe one."

"Namely?"

The assassin got up.

"Same or similar plasma weapon as you once gave me. Unfortunately, that one was lost."

***

The astro-carrier was not only a shuttle used to transport smaller units for thousands of AU - which meant great savings in energy and fuel - but it also served the comfort of the passengers themselves. After fulfilling Divinus' request and giving him the weapon from the arsenal, Necron had him taken to a shooting range, so that he spent the travel time, training and reading the rules. Relagard, having experience with plasma weapons, quickly encompassed the handling of the rest of the advanced equipment. In this regard, the various rifles, mitrailleuses, shotguns, and pistols were hardly different from each other. Even a Karikonian peasant child could shoot them. All you had to do was find your target and pull the trigger; all the rest was done by automatics. The shooter only had to learn to quickly change the magazine, and in the case of self-renewable energy ammunition - it was enough to wait a while. During the ground combat, such an achij, who was in hiding during the time of combat inability, was replaced by companions. However, the waiting time for the weapon to be reloaded wasn't long. Necron, who came to the shooting range to see the assassin's progress, confided in him that he didn't like equipment doing people's job, because even the best mechanism could fail.

"Well." The general spread his hands. "This is the direction our technology has gone - of the minimalization of everything and creating devices for idiots, so that you don't have to use your brain."

Div was fascinated by the weapon, so he spent half a board day on training. He left the room only before the jump with the elevator drive, because he was curious to see what the space behind the porthole looked like then; The astro-carrier had accumulated enough energy for them to return to the Zodiac Universum. Necron tried to explain to him as simply as possible what speed they would develop but stopped at "monstrously fast".

Also, this time Relagard wasn't satisfied with the show, imagining too much. The astro-carrier was surrounded by a dense field that limited visibility, protecting against radiation and the forces acting in the node. The speed was felt - it was like moving in a deep current of a swift river. That's why Necron had told him earlier to sit in the chair and fasten the seat belts.

The elevator jump to a temporary node didn't last long. After making it, the astro-carrier entered a speed at which the stars were visually barely moving; the end-of-life engines needed time for their next activity. The crew was able to walk freely on the decks thanks to the technology of atoplaxal particles producing artificial gravity.

Div used this time to continue shooting and absorbing Anna's information essential during the travel to Amyrade, as well as facts about Kiritian society. When Necron dealt with his duties and was going to accompany both of them, one of the officers came to notify him that he had a private call.

"It's from Atla," said an achij as Necron moved down the corridor towards the bridge. "From your residence, sir. The sender insists that the conversation be confidential."

"Probably Jenny. Then switch the holo-conversation to my office."

"Of course, sir."

Necron had already learned not to speak to Sandstorm's daughter in front of witnesses. She had a fiery temper after her mother, and for several months she had been unbearable. She often sulked, pouted and screamed, not caring about the position and age of the interlocutors. It didn't surprise him much that she preferred to talk to him than to Anna. The teenager, angry at the whole cosmos, didn't understand that she had had to spend her childhood like an orphan, because only in this way could the Kiritians protect her from another attack.

He was surprised when instead of Jenny's face, he saw on the holo-screen an Erces' face with dark blond hair and yellow irises. He had the feeling that he had already met this skinny, tiny man somewhere, squirming and looking shiftily with frightened eyes at anything but him. He remembered that he was a new employee hired by Jenny.

"Yes?" He asked.

The man on the other side didn't know how to start the conversation, stuttered something. Finally, he managed to focus his look on the interlocutor.

"Mr. Biffter, I really do apologize to you," he was saying in an irritating whisper. "We haven't had a chance to talk so far."

"That's true. Sometimes I saw you in the background talking to Miss Bidwell. She introduced you to me once, but then you bowed your head. What is your name? Because I don't remember."

"I'm Skelver." The man was still scared. "You probably don't remember me, sir, but I'm not surprised. Many people have passed through your incredibly long life."

"What's happening? Why are you acting like you've fled your own execution? Where's Jenny?"

The Erces swallowed nervously.

"You saved my life once, on Morascrik. Corporal Darkoris' men wanted to beat me to death. You stood up for me. Our rules dictate that we pay off our debts, which I have decided to do. For which I can pay with my life ... Life for life. But I can't do otherwise, believe me ..."

"Fuck, man!" Kiret lost his patience. He was alone and could afford to take off the mask of a composed general. Skelver flinched as Necron slammed his fist on the desk, so strongly that smaller objects jumped. "Talk to the point. What are you raving about, man?"

"Miss Jenny. I already know his real name is Sandstorm, not Bidwell. And I know who she is." Skelver spoke faster and faster, grimaced as if he had been about to cry. "I tried to kill her once, but the attack failed. They don't implant us neurocytes, because we're not worthy of them, so we can't interact with leberikses, therefore they gave me an ordinary drone, terrible because without AI. They thought it was enough. I had suspicions about the girl's identity, but I found out the truth today. I had to inform them immediately. They left me no choice. I'm so afraid. Thanks to that, maybe they won't kill my family and I'll survive myself."

"Leberikses? Drones? Neurocytes?" Necron's heart was pounding like after a sprint. He ground out every word. "If you don't speak humanly right now what you did, I will fly to Atla and personally tear your head off and give your skull to Seymour."

Skelver paled.

"They're flying for her! I gave them the location of Atla, which they hadn't known before. Earlier, I had no reason to bother them, because I needed proof. They would have killed me for wasting their time. They don't care about inhabited planets for the time being, they are not their target. They are to wait for the order. But eventually the slaughter will begin. You will all die. I don't know when they'll come to Atla. Whether in a day or a week. I'm only informing you because you saved me. As I said: life for life. My life for Jenny's, maybe yours too ... Mr. Matthew Rain."

Kiret knew who the refugee was talking about. But he asked because he wanted to hear it:

"Who are they?"

"They are Kandrok, sir. All I know is that they have orders to kill or enslave all Immortal dignitaries or those with a chance of future power. What you do next with that information is entirely up to you, Mr. Biffter."

Necron didn't know what to answer or how to react, he was completely stunned. Without a word, he broke the connection and, in the silence of the office, sank heavily into his chair. He stared at the drink mug on the counter. He had screwed up again. This time, due to his stupidity, threatened was the civilian close to him, guilty of nothing. He should have strongly opposed Jenny when, without his knowledge, she brought to the mansion - as it turned out - the terrorist. Instead, he had let her play the adult and responsible person. He remembered Skelver, a fugitive from the RC Galaxy, even though seventeen years had passed since then and the guy had changed a bit. Indeed, Kiret had saved his life. Skelver had been enslaved and trained by Kandrok, who was similar to Kiritians in truthfulness. Besides, Skelver had no reason to lie. His facial expression and behavior seemed natural. Necron could tell a liar from a truth teller, many skills could be brought to perfection over hundreds of years of life.

"I'm useless," he whispered to himself. He was concerned about Jenny's safety. He liked her, though she was moody. She was Forkis' only child, so Kiret, as his former friend and deputy, had made a commitment to do everything to protect her. However, the concept of 'everything' didn't include the immediate flight in the astro-carrier into Atla's orbit - it is not known whether Kandrok had already arrived there. By confronting them directly, he would have sentenced the entire crew of the shuttle to death. Nevertheless, he had to act. Immediately.

He turned on the preview of the shooting range from the cellula and saw Anna discussing with Divinus. He should have kept his conversation with Skelver a secret from her for a while. If she had found out the truth, no one would have stopped her from flying to Atla, which might have been suicidal. Kiret had to take care also of her safety. He looked at the assassin, delighted with the possibility of training with the Kiritian weapons that might appear in his slow-developing world in millennia. Div acted alone and hidden, and Biffter decided to act the same - quickly and quietly. The most sensible thing to do would have been to send a small unit for Jenny so that it didn't put itself in danger. However, he didn't want to make mistakes again and cause other people to suffer because of him. He still remembered Morascrik vividly and the ill-fated verdict he had made at the Council of Five. He should have listened to Warfighter and kept fake immigrants out of the Zodiac Universum, and in case of complications, he should have acted like Forkis and killed them all. Without the Trojans, there would have been no information for the enemy, and neither would there have been the plague of Kandrok, for no developed civilization attacked another blindly. War costs money, the aggressor must be sure that the profits will outweigh the losses.

He shifted his look to the ceiling and closed his eyes. He analyzed further. He was important, but not irreplaceable. If he had gotten hurt, Warfighter would have been great in his role, Captain Victor Shane who would be promoted again soon, would have also been a good commander. "Maybe I should involve Warfighter?" Necron quickly dismissed the idea. Velkee would have flown into Atla's orbit with the entire fleet, and the Immortals were not yet ready for a confrontation with

Kandrok, if they would be at all in the following years. He couldn't say anything to any achij either, because they would have begun to press him to take at least the company with him, although it was more likely that they would have bound him instead, so that he didn't endanger himself.

So, he would fly 'Perfarius' alone. He liked this ship, had made it his private unit, and it wouldn't surprise anyone that he would fly without a word to a safe area of space. Sometimes he had gone on lonely, short flights to relax. He would take off from the hangar when the astro-carrier reached the tranquil Pisces Universe *en route*. Although he was responsible for the movements of space carriers as a general, he wouldn't prepone the journey anyway, because it depended on the efficiency of the shuttle's components, and it had recently left the node.

However, he couldn't leave without saying a word - if he died before reaching the girl, so would she. He supposed Skelver was blocking her communication with space. Anyway, it would have been unwise to connect with Atla from the astro-carrier and make a noise on air. The fewer calls the better. He considered that it would have been a good idea to clue in some civilian from outside the nation to the plan.

And Aggroteh came to mind.

Necron pulled synthetic paper from a drawer and wrote a message using Onkalot glyphs, in which he asked Q'ualel to report anything to Anna Sandstorm or Warfighter if he failed. He mentioned that he would establish contact within two weeks, taking into account possible problems, such as unexpected stellar winds disrupting interplanetary communication. He put the piece of paper in an envelope and sealed it. Kiritians hadn't sent messages this way for a long time.

The rebels had done this during the war against them so that codes, reports or messages were not intercepted and decrypted electronically. A consignment was delivered hidden next to the body or in an inconspicuous looking object.

"The hunter has become the prey," Necron muttered to the porthole overlooking part of the shuttle's hull. "You want my head, then fight for it."

He went down to the engine room, found the youngest achij working there who was from H14, and handed him the letter. He stated laconically that he was unable to meet Aggroteh because of his duties and asked for correspondence to be given. It didn't raise suspicions, because the Onkalot couldn't be contacted electronically.

The conservator was too surprised by the visit of the general himself on the lowest deck, full of grease, stench and hot air, so he decided to fulfill the unusual request without going into details and bragging to his colleagues.

XX. Mission 'Revival'

Although Tsar Seymour, like Divinus, was skeptical of the xik'iri, he watched with slight interest what happened to the mysterious artifact. It was a bit like waiting for a chick about to hatch from an egg. For two hours, the Collector stripped off the metal cover and changed the color of the core. The colors gently blended in each other, having the shades of a circum-horizontal arc. It was impossible to distinguish any pattern in this, the colors seemed to change randomly, with one emitting an intense color for an average of five minutes. One could have the impression that xik'iri would be indefinitely in such a state; it had a calming effect and mesmerized onlookers.

Tsar drew up a chair and straddled it, making the headrest support for his shoulders and head. He figured he would have been pretty high if he had stared at the Collector's core for the next hours, but he might have as well-developed apoplexy or something worse. Even Figam had failed to examine the three items brought from Tamasul - but he had a limited field of action here so as not to damage anything - and no one knew how they affected people. So far, they had seemed neutral to the body like ordinary stones.

In a hermetic, bright room with xik'iri in a container in the center on a landing there were eighteen people. Half were members of the 'Revival' mission: Corporal Zira Aytar, assassin Raver Divinus Relagard, Lieutenant Tsar Seymour, Corporal Darius Schindler, geneticist, technologist and physicist Sariel Jelinek, Corporal Technician Rasmus Darkoris, Senior Private Tau Bradshaw, Private Kazuo Shimizu, and Expedition Commander - Captain Michael Avadar. The rest were former scientists, including Maksimus Figam with his chief assistant, Alejander Cortez, and a few onlookers initiated into the mission, including Aggro from Chimalmat.

The container had been specially designed for the artifact. It looked simple, a clear square box of puronax, with a meter long edge. Scientists had worked on it in sterile conditions, additionally installed inside lamps and devices to kill everything that was organic and microscopic, excluding the basic sample. The Collector itself and the bits of Forkis' biological material - skin, a few hairs, and dried blood - remained safe. Nanawak instructed that at the time of pairing the DNA with the xik'iri nucleus, nothing else organic should have been nearby as this would have disrupted the process.

For the third hour, nothing new had been happening.

Seymour dozed off; he would have started to snore had Aytar not punched him on a shoulder.

"What a boredom." Irritated, Darius waved his hand, got up from the crouch and walked away from the container.

"That's what it was supposed to look like?" Div turned to Figam.

"I honestly have no idea, assassin." The doctor, staring at the artifact, stroked his chin. "Aggro told me everything he knew about xik'iri." He glanced in his direction. The humanoid jaguar, standing with his arms folded across his chest, nodded to him. "Just in case, we talked three times, with a few days' breaks, in case he remembered anything else. The pairing procedure is my idea. And the design of the box was developed by Mr. Cortez."

"The result is a synthesis of the Collector's nucleus with Forkis' DNA, did I get it right?" Avadar asked. "For the artifact to work?"

"Something like that, Captain. But no one knows what it is supposed to look like," the scientist sighed. "Maybe the merge has already happened, and we don't know it." He leaned toward the container. "We can just wait and watch for changes."

"Maybe we shouldn't have put the artifact in the box?" Aytar suggested.

"Hey, folks." Tsar tapped a finger against the wall like an unruly child against a terrarium with an animal. "Looks like something's going on."

They all focused their eyes on the Collector again, sitting, standing, and crouching.

"Look, it has moved!" Darius said.

Seymour strained his eyes. Indeed, the artifact tilted slightly from side to side ... along with the entire box.

"Hey, Doc." Tsar smiled pityingly, waved his hand to Jelinek as if he had been helping to reverse a vehicle.

The young scientist understood immediately, took his hands with which he had unconsciously leaned against the container. The ultra-light structure and its contents returned to their previous position. Aytar looked embarrassedly at Figam's assistant, who gave her an unfriendly look as if she had caused the incident.

"Sorry," he said dryly. By nature, he was repulsive and alienated people.

"The space dog told us a whopper." Shimizu pointed his finger at the container. "How can we be sure that it's not some kind of spy probe? Maybe that Tatarak ..."

"Nanawak," Aytar corrected.

"... is dying of laughter now, staring at the gathering of clowns around the stone that can only shine?"

"All we have to do is be patient," Figam replied gently. He stood bent, with his hands on the thighs and stared at the artifact, but without any prior enthusiasm.

"Maybe Private Shimizu is right," Captain Avadar said seriously, "and we're just wasting our time here."

"Or maybe not, sir?" A smile appeared again on Darius' face. "Now something is really happening!"

This time, no one touched the container.

Xik'iri began to vibrate and make a barely audible noise, similar to that of a spinning brake disc. The organic material incorporated into the process rose - and began to get incinerated as if held over a fire, except that there was no fire. Monitoring parameters also didn't indicate a high temperature in the container. Figam checked the rest of the readings, and nothing changed, except for the slight movements of air and the chemical composition of the separated environment. Whatever the Collector did, it destroyed the biological value of the genetic material.

"Ashes to ashes, dust to dust," Bradshaw blurted out.

Tsar looked at him with disgust.

"Why have people repeated this nonsense for centuries? My parents made me out of germ cells, and I wasn't formed from some burned dirt. And I'll never die and never be dust. Unless I try for it. I mean death."

His argument was ignored. Everyone stared at the container in which successive undefined processes began to take place. Its entire space was filled with a transparent matrix, with thousands of small dots hanging in it, of the colors emanating so far by the artifact's core.

"Amazing ..." Aytar's expression contradicted her words of admiration as she looked at the Collector with full concentration and seriousness. "Is that some kind of map?"

"It actually looks like one," Figam replied, also infatuated with the projection, but smiling unlike eternally serious Zira. "Looks like a piece of space. Tens of thousands of light years on an incredibly small scale."

"Or a nebula," suggested Captain Avadar.

It wasn't without Tsar's comment:

"For me, this is an ephemeral vision of a fucked-up guy."

"Could one of those dots be Amyrade?" Divinus asked. The basics of building the cosmos had been described to him by Anna, absent from the room due to attempts to contact Necron, who had suddenly flown away without a word. He knew the same about Amyrade as the rest of the team did; they had gotten the briefing over.

"I can't answer you, my friend," Figam replied. "If the Collector's core is projecting stars, I don't know any of these constellations." He turned to the assistant, "Alejandro, do the multidimensional scans and then use of Baks' equation. Maybe we'll find something this way."

"Of course, doctor."

The xik'iri projection ended unexpectedly. The artifact turned black and cold like coal long lying in the frost.

And then it exploded like a microscopic universe created in a laboratory. But unlike a daring experiment that would have lasted only a few seconds, xik'iri didn't disappear.

The shockwave resembled a pressure weapon. The densely packed air particles centrifugally dispersed in a ring.

They were all thrown back and thrust against the walls of the room as if during an explosion. The lights flickered, it got dark, but soon the earlier lighting returned, strong and halogen.

The container remained intact in a manner inconceivable to those present.

"What was that?!" Darius jumped to his feet first, grunted due to the bruised spine. Instinctively, he pulled the X17A4 pistol from the cuisse compartment and aimed it toward the center of the room. The artifact was active again, at least visually - something like a multicolored mini-galaxy with a dozen or so arms was spinning in the core, it quickly transformed into a fractal structure to resemble a symmetrical, purple interior of an organism illuminated by bioluminescence a moment later.

Grimacing Tsar got up shortly after Schindler, and he and Jelinek helped stunned, coughing Figam up. The rest also began to scramble off the ground, more or less injured.

"Interesting phenomenon." The doctor looked at the intact box. "The source of the shockwave was certainly the Collector, but it missed the side of the container." He looked at Avadar wiping blood from his lip. "If I could understand the mechanics of this, maybe we could create a new version of pressure weapons that would penetrate the walls of buildings and destroy everything inside. This way, we could neutralize the enemy without damaging key buildings. Maybe the answer is particle size ..."

"Of course, doctor," the captain gently interrupted the discourse. "We also know that the damn thing is dangerous. Is everybody alright?"

He immediately regretted the stupid question, seeing the injured. Tsar smiled at him meaningfully. Before Figam invited the group into the room, Seymour suggested to the captain that instead of the uniforms or regimentals the achijes wore around the Cargoo underground base, they should have come in armor. The suggestion seemed ridiculous to Avadar, but he took into account the argument that the artifact could prove to be dangerous. Now the captain congratulated himself in his mind that he had agreed to his subordinate's idea. The armored people got bruises at best, a few had a temporary breathing problem. The rest ended up with smashed noses and wounds, even a broken arm and concussion. Luckily, Figam, who was wearing a smock, was fine, because he was amortized by Seymour, whom he ran into. Div, who had refused to wear Kiritian armor, preferring his threadbare hooded cape, leather clothes, and high-top moccasins, also survived the incident, standing closest to the wall in the blast. Thanks to his reflex, he turned in time and avoided a collision with Shimizu. Jelinek was trying to stop the nosebleed with his fingers.

The paramedics came into the room immediately. They took the injured out.

Darius holstered the gun. He stared at the artifact as if captivated and walked slowly towards it.

"Damn ... I understand everything ... But how?"

"Schindler, stop," the captain snapped. "You saw for yourself what that crap did. Mr. Figam, it would be best if we all got out of here. We should get some androids into the room."

"That won't be necessary," said Schindler. "It's over now. The stone is loaded and ready to search."

Seymour wasn't the only one to look at him in surprise.

"How do you know that?"

"I just know." Darius got confused, rolled his look over the rest. "You're gonna take me for a moron, but I know everything from this thing." He nodded towards the artifact.

"The stone speaks to you?" Shimizu turned intimately to the higher-ranking person, which was often practiced among the nation in less formal meetings.

The corporal stumbled, thinking about an answer that wouldn't bring him even more disgrace. He sighed, however, and gave up the choice of logical words.

"Rather, it gives me knowledge. And I understand this message. They are not words or sounds. Just knowledge. It appears suddenly. I'm not afraid of it at all." He wrung his hands. "Well, I don't know how to explain it!"

"Great, we just missed the schizophrenic on the mission," Jelinek growled. His nose was all right now, as the paramedic had given him an aerosol that had immediately stopped the bleeding.

"Hey, I don't hear any voices!"

The captain looked sharply at Seymour who spoke, then at Darius, his words sounded similarly:

"It was clearly stated at the briefing that you should not take any psychotropics until the end of the mission."

"But I wasn't taking anything, sir! I swear it!" Schindler solemnly touched his hand to his chest. "Examine me if you don't believe me."

Figam rushed to his aid:

"And what does xik'iri tell ... transmits you?"

"I know it's ready to search. It's enough to take it. You don't need to be afraid of him, because it won't do anything else, at least for the moment. None of us have been irradiated or otherwise damaged directly by the artifact. This was the process of accepting biological data. Do at least you believe me?"

"The explosion could muddle you," Jelinek suggested. "I saw the emperor turning into the cat, and the rodent being transformed into the artifact, and also the planet with dragons, and you ask if I believe you? Why would you make up to us here right now?" The scientist smiled warmly. "I wonder why the Collector speaks only to you."

The question hung in the air; Darius spread his arms in consternation.

"Maybe when the shockwave flew, the artifact chose a guide or something like that. Completely randomly," Seymour suggested ironically. But no one had a better idea.

Darius looked at Avadar.

"May I take xik'iri, captain? I assure you that nothing will happen now, the next explosion will take place only when we are already in the vehicles, but it will not hurt us," he added, seeing that the commander's face was an arrangement of skepticism.

"It could be a ruse," Aytar said coolly, trying to arrange the dark blue hair crushed by the helmet. "A bug. A kind of mind control. We are to believe that Darius became our guide, and it will lead us to our undoing."

Divinus, with his arms folded across his chest, nodded to her. As Anna had predicted, the assassin and the former thief, also a killer, understood each other well, they usually had similar opinions. From the moment Relagard had arrived on Cargoo, they had liked each other and preferred to spend time in their own company, exchanging experiences about their lives in other worlds. Loneliness-loving, taciturn by nature, Aytar was able to say to Div during a day as much as sometimes for a whole month.

Avadar knew that Darius as a low-ranking achij would have been easy to replace if something had happened to him. Like any Kiritian commander, he hated to think in terms of benefit and loss with regard to immortal manpower, but cool calculation was an indispensable element of the work of a good officer. The question was whether the Collector would have forged a bond with someone else if he had caused the boy die. Everything about Nimja was completely beyond the captain's ken. He would have liked to show hypocrisy and drink something strong, though he had chewed Seymour out himself earlier.

"Let it be," he agreed. "Take this artifact, Corporal. But be careful. Let the rest leave the room."

"I'm staying," Figam said emphatically.

"It's unreasonable, doctor. You're not as secured as we are. It is not known what will happen this time." The captain would have liked to say that he didn't want to lose his best scientist at the Zodiac Universum, but it would have sounded bad to Darius' ears.

"I'll take the risk anyway, Captain. I believe Darius that nothing serious will happen again. Anyway, I will stand close to the door and jump behind it if necessary."

"Then I'll wait with you."

Avadar and Figam stayed at the door, the rest left the room, except for Darius. Schindler walked over to the container, stood for a moment, took a deep breath, then opened the box according to the instructions being given by the doctor. Reluctantly as if he had been told to pull a poisonous snake out of a terrarium, he took out the Collector with a trembling hand. Immediately he stopped being nervous. The artifact was pleasant to the touch, neither cold nor warm, smooth as a decade's stone ground by a sea; holding it reassured. In the core shining through the translucent shell, a projection of a strange galaxy was enclosed, off which delighted Darius couldn't take his eyes wide open.

"Everything's all right?" The captain asked.

"Yes, sir."

"Then take the stone and come on. We have to prepare for the next stage of the mission, and time is running out. Though I don't believe this whole pile of pulsar conjunction nonsense or whatever," Avadar added under his breath.

He let Darius go forward through the door.

"The more data we have about the universe, the more we see that we know almost nothing about it," Figam said, looking at the empty container. "But I think it's high time to start using the term multiversum."

***

Necron left the board of the astro-carrier in no hurry, as if he had been going on a few-hour relaxation flight. It was only when he moved in Perfarius two astronomical units from the shuttle, where his scanners didn't reach, that he switched from the plasma drive to the elevator one.

'Perfarius' rushed towards a targeted node and in several seconds moved to the star system with Atla. The general, having switched to the weaker propulsion system, flew for many more hours to his destination - if he had used the elevator propulsion too close to the planet, he could have changed its precession by a fraction of a degree. It's not much from a space perspective, but there would have been geological and weather consequences on the globe itself. Anyway, the jump points were created only in deep space, away from anything material.

After having a brief discussion with Atla's administration, Necron was warmly greeted and immediately allowed to land. He bit into the atmosphere. As he flew over the following cities, he didn't notice anything disturbing. The inhabitants lived their routine, lazy lives, full of leisure and entertainment. The whole planet resembled one big resort or tourist center.

The multi-story mansion, lit by the violet of the setting star and external installations, looked ordinary at first glance. However, it was plunged in suspicious peace. Its steward was silent. Nobody greeted Biffter or exchanged procedural sentences with him, as if the workers had gone on vacation, leaving the automatics doing their job ... or something bad had happened.

Necron thought too late that he might have fallen into a trap. If there was anyone hostile to him, they had long since seen Perfarius hovering above the ground without the cover. He felt weird scanning his own mansion, but at least the parameters he obtained allayed most of his fears: he found no corpses, damage, signs of a fight or a break-in. The population almost matched - Skelver was missing, which was no surprise.

The sight of Jenny, safe and sound, running out of the façade door to the mini-landing pad calmed Kiret down. Earlier, she had probably come back from the stables, or had been going to it, because she was wearing a riding gear: a short, dark pink jacket with a high collar, gloves difficult to distinguish from long sleeves, tight, elastic pants and leather boots almost to the knee. She had tied her hair carelessly at the back of her head, and the blast of the ship additionally did its own thing.

Kiret landed. He eyed Jenny up for a moment, which was standing still as a stalagmite, staring at the cockpit with a mixture of reluctance and relief. He thought that she had grown into a rather attractive woman, perhaps too pale for his taste, which the contrasting jet-black hair certainly didn't improve. Considering her apparition, Jenny would have taken after her mother, if not for her excessively slim build. It was hard to believe that the father of the girl of average height was powerfully built Forkis, over two meters tall.

In an attempt to lull the astro-carrier crew into a false sense of security, Kiret left it clad in light armor. Then he changed it to war. Not because it would have somehow protected him from Kandrok, but more to inspire respect of the locals. Civilians had always been visualizers.

Having folded down his strobilus on the helmet, he descended the gangplank extended through the airlock.

"Hello, Jenny." The greeting came out softly and gloomy, as if he had come to take her to a funeral.

Jenny took it her own way - she treated the lack of verve as Kiret's guilt, who, together with Anna, had cut her off from the universe like a pampered princess. "No," she thought, "even princesses often go out to the people in preparation for their future rulership."

She wanted to keep her face frowned, but emotions quickly took over the plan to pout for a while. The smile appeared by itself, she ran to Necron and hugged him childishly. The general stood for a moment, with his arms comically raised, before he returned the hug.

"Hello, baldie. I thought you would never come again," she said, looking up.

"How are you? Is everything alright?"

"And what is supposed to be wrong?" She moved away from him. "Everything is okay."

"I came to see Skelver."

Jenny darkened.

"Oh, so not with me."

"Of course, with you too." Necron smiled agreeably. "But I haven't seen the gardener you hired too hastily."

"Then you won't talk to him now. He left somewhere in the morning without a word and hasn't come back so far. He didn't even communicate."

"How did he behave? Was he calm, nervous, in a hurry?"

"You know what, in fact, he was kind of in a hurry. He was a little confused, but I didn't ask why. I thought it was his personal matter that he was going to settle. Necron, what's going on? You are looking around nervously. And why did you spruce up as if for war?"

"If anything, one can get dressed as if for war. Pack immediately."

"What's going on, baldie?" A sulk disappeared from the girl's face; the anxiety flowed there naturally.

Necron turned her towards the mansion and pushed her lightly.

"Skelver is a traitor. He wants you dead. Remember when I told you about the attack in which you had been supposed to die as an infant in K'otz'ib'aja? It was Skelver who had sent the payload drone at Kandrok's command. They want to kill both you and me."

"But why?!" She trusted Kiret, so she believed him at once.

"Their ruler is gerha, something like a king or queen, it depends on who they choose in a given period. In the event of a coup, the head of the nation is killed or imprisoned, and the same applies to the successors or claimants to the throne. Kandrok, who attacked the Zodiac Universum for a reason still unknown to us, think naturally in their own categories, not ours." They entered the house. "Skelver found out who we are because you didn't use my other identity in our private conversations."

Jenny stopped abruptly and was hit in the back with the armor before the Kiritian could stop.

"Sorry, I didn't ..."

"It already happened; I can live with that. I also didn't foresee that the attacker from K'otz'ibaja would accidentally find himself in my residence. This is an incredible coincidence and that's it. But even such happen."

She turned to him.

"Not true. It was I who hired him. You understand me! You'll have to move me again, solely because of my fault."

"Jenny, please don't be hysterical now."

"General Biffter."

Necron looked over the girl's head and saw the steward - an older but energetic man with a jovial, sympathetic face. The arrival of Perfarius quickly brought the rest of the home dwellers to the first floor, watching over Jenny and caring for the residence. Soon there were several people standing at the foot of the stairs.

"Good morning, Confucius, as well as all of you," said Kiret. The employees greeted him.

"Good morning, good Morning. It's nice to see you at this abode again. I heard your conversation about Skelver." The steward's thick eyebrows went down. "What a bastard. From the beginning, I had a feeling that something was wrong with him."

Kiret passed the teenager.

"I'm sorry to meet you in such circumstances. Jenny and I are supposedly endangered by strangers, the entire mansion could be in danger. Skelver contacted me and warned me that Kandrok were going to Atla to get the girl. He did it because I had once saved his life. It may be a false alarm, but it's better to be safe than sorry. I'll try to get Skelver later, but first I'll take Jenny out of here, and I'll give you all open-ended paid vacations. You will move out to your families and loved ones immediately. Take care of the animals here. We will see how the situation develops. Wait for contact, I will let you know when you can safely come back."

"Christ," the chubby cook sighed, and put her hands to her chest.

"It's okay, Marcellina." Confucius came down the stairs and embraced the woman's shoulders comfortingly. "I guess we'll all have to go on vacation. Mr. Biffter knows what he is doing."

"What about you, General?" One of the bodyguards asked. They were terribly ashamed that they hadn't recognized Skelver as the enemy's spy. However, it was not a good time to discuss mistakes.

"I'll take Jenny to a safe place," Kiret replied evasively, standing behind the girl and putting his hands on her shoulders. He couldn't trust anyone Skelver had come into contact with. It is possible that he had left a wire or a preview in the residence, or that someone here colluded with him. "Don't worry, I'll take care of her as best I can. Those of you who are believers should pray that everything will turn out to be a mere misunderstanding."

"Is Atla threatened with invasion?" Confucius asked.

"Hard to say. For now, Kandrok is hardly interested in any viable planets. Rather, it uses them as harbors on a journey to an undefined destination or supplement the necessary resources." Kiret ignored the fact that aliens used human tissue to make fuel for their ships and naval craft. He pushed Jenny lightly towards the stairs. "Pack your bags. Jenny, take only the essentials. When we get to safe place, you will get everything you need. I have food and water in Perfarius."

The girl nodded and went to her room upstairs. Less than an hour later, she dragged her bag downstairs. Kiret, who said goodbye to the mansion workers and thanked them for everything, took it from her and carried it to the hold of Perfarius. He ushered Jenny into the cockpit and indicated the co-pilot's seat.

"This is what we'll go in?" She asked, sitting down.

"Well, rather. Do you see that I came to Atla in something else?"

"It's a naval craft, isn't it? Is it that bad?"

Kiret flopped down beside her, caught his breath.

"I don't know, baby." He began to prepare Perfarius for vertical take-off with the anti-gravity propulsion. "I already told you. You weren't listening."

"Don't call me baby."

"Okay, sorry." He smiled.

They took off gently. The machine was rising to the darkening sky; Jenny was looking dolefully at the dwindling house where she had spent many years of boring life. Therefore, she wasn't particularly sad, leaving this place. It was just a little pity to part with the employees she liked. The star's eye, invisible from the ground, glared at them again when they were high. It turned a pulsating purple color in the stratosphere.

"Where are you taking me? Onto Cargoo? Because rather not to Kindra and Abraham. Then we wouldn't go into space."

"That's right..., Jenny. We cannot fly on Cargoo either. If Kandrok is following us, we would lead them along this thread to the planet, and then they would completely annihilate us. I'm aiming for some quiet, safe place whose potential destruction wouldn't sadden me. I think of the planet Proxima Centauri e orbiting the star Proxima Centauri. The place would be perfect, because there are old, abandoned colonies on the planet, but the globe orbits in the Old Zone, that is, close to the motherland - the Earth. If I brought Kandrok to those regions, I could be called the greatest criminal of the human race."

As they passed the last layer of the atmosphere, Necron activated the same masking that shielded 'Aurals' from the Kandrok fleet during the flight for Figam.

Jenny peered into the void through the puronax canopy, so clear and deceptive that it seemed to her that she would have floated into space if she had only unbuckled the belt.

"So where do you want to go?" The Kiritian thought briefly.

"B9. Or Ghost Planet," he replied matter-of-factly. He switched off the anti-gravity drive, useless in space, in favor of the impulse propulsion. One strong recoil from the nozzles pushed the ship into a black depth.

"Ghost Planet?"

"They colloquially call CD4G5 that. In 2770, terrorists pacified its population, took weapons and raw materials to have the means to fight us." Biffter looked at Jenny. "Anna comes from them. Eh, I've blurted out ..."

"I know that. Rebel mother, Kiritian father, and in addition an Onkalot. I'm a very interesting hybrid." The girl managed a slight smile. Kiret returned it, though his was emotionless.

"How's your unilateral telepathy skill?"

"Sometimes it comes out, sometimes it doesn't. In the case of Skelver it didn't work, and I tried to practice on it. My intuition also fell on this point. Otherwise, I would have never let the traitor into your residence."

"That's probably why you failed, because he's an Erces. They share zero percent genes with us, although they look the same, and that could be the reason. Don't worry, it'll be okay." Kiret hoped he would be able to cheer up the grumpy girl by stroking her hair, but he achieved the opposite effect.

"So same old. You still treat me like a baby," she grunted, turning her head away.

He was slightly irritated, used to being treated with respect, but managed to keep his face serene. Living among achijes, he was poor at dealing with Oderses' teenagers.

"How am I supposed to treat you? Maybe I should kiss you for consolation?" He blurted out thoughtlessly.

The girl thanked Atla's black-and-gray striped moon that she could look at it, and the desktop whining with measurement results, that it drowned out her spontaneous sigh. She smiled involuntarily and blushed slightly, imagining herself kissing Kiret. The thought gave her embarrassing pleasure.

Necron returned to the earlier topic:

"I promise that, if time and place permit, I will practice mind-reading with you. It is worth working on this."

"Okay." She was still staring to the side.

"Okay, are you so? Your blood pressure has surged." She looked at the treacherous console and one of its many scanners, indicating the health of the pilots.

"Everything is alright. It's just been a long time since I was flying fucking far and I'm experiencing it a bit." She wanted to mask her condition with anger.

Necron took this as an indictment against him.

"Stop cussing, young lady. Talk to me about your problems, okay? I hate understatement, which creates conflicts and false assumptions."

"Stay away from my affairs, baldie."

Kiret glanced up at the ceiling. He felt as much anger as when he declaimed the tirade to Tsar on Nephrida. He had gotten angry extremely easily lately. He wondered if he was too gentle to the turd who, without feeling that what she did was wrong, undermined his authority over and over again.

"Can you really not withstand even one minute without your sulk? One goddamn fucking minute?!"

She looked at him like a pet under attack.

"Then throw me out into space and it'll be over!"

"Girl, I don't want to throw you out into space. I only expect a normal conversation. I think you can do that much for Kiritians' ex-emperor. Well done," he congratulated himself. Nothing like trying to impress a young 'un with your position. He would surely gain attention now.

"Whose trough was poured by Kandrok."

"Watch your words," he said, cooler than he intended. Sandstorm assumed a rebellious expression.

"Why?"

"For example, I'm a little older."

"I don't give a shit, I'll say what I want!"

"If I had a child like you ... it wouldn't be for a long time. Why are you like that, if you had everything you needed to live and kind people around you?"

"Exactly, around me. And with me no one."

He bit his lips. He felt that now his blood pressure had risen, which, moreover, had been revealed by the insistent medical apparatus of the desktop. He turned it off.

They both fell silent.

A few minutes later, the teenager spoke calmly.

"Kiret?"

"What?" This time he wasn't trying to be nice.

"You told me to talk about everything."

"Yeah, what's up."

She pointed to the top left monitor.

"Should these three dots jump like that? They were not there a moment ago. They grew suddenly."

Looking hard ahead, the Kiritian turned his gaze to the spatial monitor that was picking up a schematic image from across the cosmos behind the tail of the Perfarius. Indeed, a trio of unidentified objects appeared on the periphery of the spherical field.

"They shouldn't ... And why can't I hear the sound? There must be some disturbance." He was looking for a crash on another screen.

"What is this?"

"After all, we're flying masked ..." he growled to himself.

"But you didn't turn on masking on the planet, but barely after we left it. Maybe someone noticed you then, detected the heat or radiation of the ship, and has been monitoring since then?"

"Even if they did, Perfarius should have disappeared from their scanners when the shields were turned on. This prototype model has the best camouflage the Immortals possess."

"Do you know who they are?"

"They're flying two hundred kilometers behind the tail. At this distance, we should have the full specification."

"What do you mean?"

Kiret pointed to another of several dozen screens showing internal and flight parameters.

"This means that models of these machines, obtained from a constantly updated military database, should be displayed. If they had already been cataloged, for example by our intelligence, we would now see their numbers and characteristics."

"Can't we connect with them and humanly ask what they want?"

"No, Jenny. We don't know if they really see us, or they happen to be flying on the same course. If they cannot see us, and they are enemies, we would hang loops around our necks ourselves. As for ..."

The undefined machines disappeared, embarrassing Necron even more and making Jenny stunned.

"Kiritians can disappear like that, don't they," she neither asked, nor said hopefully.

"These aren't our machines, Jenny," Necron muttered dryly.

She bit her lip. She was really scared.

"Come on ... say it finally, Kiret. You know who they are!"

The unidentified objects reappeared - two kilometers behind Perfarius. With such a minimum distance between the machines, its AI found them in the database and displayed the specification.

Kiret quickly understood why the most technologically advanced Kiritian naval ship had difficulty recognizing alien units. This situation happened when data was missing, the instrumentation was out of order, or the enemy had a better one. To his and Sandstorm's misfortune, the third situation occurred.

"Kandrok," he growled. "Those bastards are technologically still three steps ahead of us."

"Jeez," Jenny blurted out as the three machines flew rapidly over the Perfarius' cockpit, though it itself was moving at dizzying speeds. They looked ugly, like monstrous, choppy gaps from a rocky mountain. Had they not shone with the white of a rushing comet, briefly blinding Sandstorm and Necron, the human eye would not have distinguished Kandrok's ships from asteroids or other cosmic debris that had fallen out of their native orbit.

Kiret kept his face stony. In his long life he had experienced a lot of space fights and was able to maintain self-control in a tight corner. At least sometime. Recently, he had been on the verge of a nervous breakdown. But the girl that had been brought up practically without stress got so terrified that she was tongue-tied.

Even though similar attempts had failed in the past, Necron made efforts to contact Kandrok. It turned out as he had expected - he might have as well wanted to find common ground with the asteroids. But at least he didn't stay passive. If the others hadn't understood Kiritian, but wanted understanding, they would have spoken in their own speech. So the problem was not the frequency, which Kandrok had certainly picked up immediately.

The alien machines turned around in a wide, harmonious bend, and easily, as if there had been air in space. Before Perfarius was shaken, Biffter had time to think that Kiritian intelligence should have investigated the phenomenon and delivered records to Cargoo. The mushy bomb smacked like jelly on the cockpit cover and instantly dematerialized - and along with it all Perfarius' covers except anti-g, but it weakened as well.

The Kiritian reacted automatically. He switched off the impulse drive and turned on the plasma one, which allowed for easier maneuvering. The ship quickly dived under enemy machines by space standards. Kiret and Jenny were pushed painfully into their armchairs, blood flowed from their noses, their ears buzzed, and they weakened as if before collapsing.

If the Necron had changed course two seconds later, Perfarius would have ceased to exist. The cosmos behind its tail exploded with red like a microscopic supernova. A wave of undefined radiation deprived the pilot of control over the machine.

So, they found him. Kiret was almost certain that Perfarius had been attacked by Kandrok brought in by Skelver. They used some kind of a bomb deactivating the protective screen to confirm the target's identity.

"Calm down, maybe I'll get us out of this," he said to Jenny that had clenched her teeth, fists, and eyelids. The gravity load turned out to be too great for her, so that she couldn't wipe the blood smeared on her face. Much stronger Necron managed to extend his hand. He had difficulty introducing the coordinates of CD4G5, the Planet of the Spirits, into the system. It was definitely too early for such an energy-consuming jump - Perfarius was not ready, and the node had yet to be found. But Biffter had no choice. If he had fought back, Kandrok would have destroyed them quickly. If he had changed the drive, they would have been caught up. Trying to reconnect was the height of idiocy.

Kandrok slowly followed Perfarius' trail, like predators certain that the wounded victim would bleed out and die.

The scanner paired with the elevator drive searched for bands of information about a possible node in a nearby three-dimensional sector. The general had managed to hate those capricious cosmic creatures which, although wandered like all the elements of the universe, appeared randomly and couldn't be included in any pattern. He didn't reject the hypothesis that the mechanism of their functioning could be like a bubble in a pot of boiling water - it was impossible to calculate mathematically where the bubble would form, only to approximate it. It was known, however, that it would have certainly appeared if the metal had been heated to a high temperature.

Necron risked a lot, trying to make a jump right under the nose of the enemy who could follow them. However, he had no other idea to save them.

"Faster ..." Jenny hissed. Kiret sincerely admired her that she was able to deal with her nerves.

"There it is.

It's found the node!"

He turned on the elevator drive, hitting the control board with his fist rather than pressing it down gradually. He felt no fear, more elation. Scream escaped him itself as the enormous gravity force turned him into a still, hundred-ton statue glued to the chair.

Perfarius entered another dimension. It found itself on the route leading out of the node, jerked by the drive in one direction, and sucked back in the other, as if by a great magnet.

Jenny started screaming too.

The explosion at the back shook the entire machine - Kandrok struck once more.

This time, terminally.

***

"It sucks," Darius muttered.

"Yeah, it's indeed hopeless. I also thought that the party would be more interesting," Seymour echoed. "Flowers, ladies, kisses and all."

The team assigned to the 'Revival' mission stood on a cleared platform in a large underground garage. The lighting dazzled the eyes, and the intrusive echo repeated the words and louder sounds, shortening their original form. But Figam, who prepared the launch of the mission, gave clear instructions: as brightly, little and carefully as possible. So that there was no disturbance, and something didn't explode again. The clearance of space also applied to onlookers who came collectively to watch the moment when the crew was transferred from the Cargoo dungeons to Amyrade Anfraktoris; the mission was no longer secret. The observers were dismissed behind covers, and in the center of the room remained a team, helpers and two multi-purpose vehicles, designed and built specifically for the mission, being the combination of a tank, amphibian, ram and survival unit. Despite the initial plans to equip the crew with flying machines, it was decided to use modified land vehicles. After all, no one knew where they would be thrown out. The probability of breaking through water, magma, or rock was more real than the possibility of flying in air - assuming that the matter found in the Zodiac Universum existed on the surface of Amyrade. In terms of the environment, efforts were made to anticipate as many possibilities as possible, but they still had to extrapolate using known resources. Figam was even intent on - not caring that he laid himself open to ridicule - studying mythologies and scripture, which were full of descriptions of fantastic planes. That is why, even before the organization of the mission, Aggroteh had been invited to Cargoo to add a brick of Onkalotian knowledge. As a result of the brainstorming, two drop-spacers[16] bristling with weapons were created, as vehicles were called with the appearance of twenty-meter fortresses, moving on wheels, tracks or bionic limbs.

Cortez, Figam, and four of his assistants tried in vain to measure within the artifact's field of action. Earlier tests with psychometry and telekinesis of Onkalots had also failed - they hadn't been able to learn anything about the past of the stones, or to lift them psionically. Sandstorm and Warfighter watched everything from a safe distance, standing against the garage wall. And behind the puronax shield, among the onlookers, were Q'ualel with Chimalmat. The female had initially been afraid to leave her home planet, sure that above the sky there were planes of gods where mortals were not allowed to enter. After long persuasion, Aggro managed to take her to the Kiritian shuttle. She panicked, but when she got used to the universe of metal, the noise of devices and the blaze of lights, she made a point of remarking pessimistically. She made the crew laugh with it, and then achijes on Cargoo. She spoke Kiritian thanks to the entraser.

"I see death in this journey," she snarled, pressing her paws to the puronax, scratching her claws on it. "Death and great doom. The gods will take horrible revenge on people who invite themselves to the Highest Houses."

Only Aggro and Anna were disturbed by these words. Q'ualel, despite the theological shock experienced during his encounter with Nanawak, continued to take divine matters seriously. After months spent in the Onkalotian ruins on the dangerous planet Aj, in the company of Forkis, Anna had learned to respect what was enigmatic, though absurd at first glance. Nevertheless, the Onkalotian woman was right about one thing: the expedition certainly carried trouble.

The clock on the wall marked the time until the mission began. The pulsar, unknown to the Kiritians so far, tracked down thanks to Baks' equation and, for lack of an idea for the name called Nanawak's Pulsar, had been sending a powerful, continuous electromagnetic pulse in its galaxy for several minutes. This meant increased activity of karitan. The indicated planets also reached the required alignment. Theoretically, everything was correct.

"Captain, General," Figam turned to the two standing at the edge of the garage. "It's time." Then he said to the helpers, "You go, too. Andro, that applies to you too. Come on, everyone."

The doctor turned Sandstorm and Warfighter around like children staring at candy behind a counter and pushed them towards the door. Cortez and the helpers followed them out. The door slammed shut, hermetically separating the observatory from the garage with the platform.

Nervous, Darius flinched as the metal crackled hollowly.

"Connor's ass, this is really happening ..."

"It's your turn, boy," Captain Avadar told him. Schindler, with his bag held in both hands, stood like a mummy. Seymour rolled his eyes, took three steps, and pushed him.

"Come on, catatonic."

Darius would have fallen had he not moved his leg in time. He took a deep breath.

"Okay ..."

As an undefined bond had developed between him and xik'iri, it was decided that he would carry the remaining artifacts as well. He knelt down, set the bag down, and opened its tails. Yellowish lights burned inside karitan and the Collector, like embers in a dying fire. He took out the stones onto the ground.

Div instinctively reached for the dagger resting in a case under the cloak to feel its soothing coolness and hardness. The assassin was equipped with a Kiritian weapon, but he made a point of taking with him the tools he was used to, including clothes useful in dark kariconian alleys. He was surprised to see that the sapphire in the hilt glowed with a soft light, though he hadn't uttered the keyword. More and more seriously he considered the possibility that the weapon believed to be magical on Karicon might have been created by alien technology, as the Kiritians had assumed.

"Look, it's shining on its own." He demonstrated the discovery to the group.

"What if it disrupts the mission?" asked Technician Corporal Darkoris. "After all, we don't understand how the artifacts interact with each other."

Div looked at him defiantly and pulled his cloak back, muffling the glare.

"Without this gun, I feel like without a hand. If it's a Nimja artifact, it has never hurt me. I slept with it close to my face many times. I've had it with me for hundreds of years and I have not noticed that it has any impact on the environment. Only the sapphire produces light."

"You don't have to worry, you will take it with you," the captain decided. "But we'll keep a close eye on everything. Figam also believes the dagger is not acting as an inhibitor."

"Karitan and the Collector are united, that is probably good." Darius smiled at the stones on the floor, turned and looked at his companions.

"You know this because the artifact 'speaks' to you?" Aytar asked. The boy shrugged.

"So, the absurdities to be continued," commented Jelinek dryly. He irritated every participant of the expedition, but his company as an expert had to be endured.

"Darkoris, check once more that everything is in order," the commander ordered the technician.

The corporal walked across an area marked by red paint. The crew and vehicles were to fit in a square forty meters on a side, which was the area of karitan's operation, although, as was already common in the case of Nimja, no one understood why the field was the square and what would have happened if some part of the vehicle had been centimeters behind the line.

"The scope is correct."

Seymour's smile widened more and more.

"These wonders do work." He pointed to the artifacts. The yellow lights inside slowly turned orange.

Shimizu and Bradshaw stared questioningly at the captain, awaiting further instructions.

"We're waiting," he replied shortly. No orders were needed. Merged with the rest of the artifacts, karitan searched for a node in the Amyrade Anfraktoris environment and was to transfer everything from the separated sphere there, apparently also the air, the floor and the installation underneath it. But how long it would take - nobody knew. Just like no one understood why they should have moved to the node, since they supposedly didn't form near matter. However, the crew was prepared to land in the middle of dark space.

In accordance with the guidelines, a few minutes after activating the second artifact, Darius placed kariban on the ground, forming a triangle out of the stones. He got up and withdrew. The artifact turquoise so far quickly became yellow, then turned orange, and soon the three nuclei burned with a rotten green glow. Apparently, that's how it was supposed to look like. Karitan recognized the essence - Forkis' DNA locked in xik'iri - and set a route to Amyrade, where, according to Nanawak, the emperor's atole was now, transformed into a different kind of cosmic energy, but still able to take its former character. Kariban's job was to reverse the process, so the stone 'remembered' the Cargoo base coordinates in order to bring the team back.

Tsar cast a brief glance at the commander. Avadar, like the others, was completely engrossed in observing the working artifacts. Seymour noiselessly approached Darius and nudged his back.

"Give me your paw," he whispered at his ear. "But discreetly." Darius stiffened as he felt on his skin the touch of numerous little balls, he knew all too well. As his fingers tightened on them, he no longer had any doubts as to the intended use of the molecules.

"Fu... But we mustn't," he whispered back, still looking at the artifacts.

"Shut up, kid. It will turn out that I'm right. It is impossible to go on such a journey sober. Do you know the law of reducing similar words in mathematics? When your mind find itself in a world that looks like a mess, maybe you can view it normally."

"Warfighter forbade."

"Warfighter, Sandstorm and Necron won't be with us. We are going to have to endure all this crap and not go mad."

Tsar's words made sense. Darius was quickly convinced, moreover, he secretly dreamed of easing the fear of the expedition with the lieutenant's method.

"Tsar, do you have any more?"

"I do."

"Where?"

"In the drop chassis." Schindler didn't see it, but he could sense that Seymour was smiling behind his back. "Around a kilo. Several types of drugs, I also took a hummingbird."

"Damn ... You're crazy."

Tsar hit the corporal conspiratorially in a side.

"Be quiet. Hide it in the glove for now and make sure it doesn't get crushed."

"But if they catch us ..."

"Come on, hide it, and don't talk!"

Seymour took two steps back. He smiled goofily and shrugged as the captain glanced at them, having heard the whispers. When he turned his head back, Schindler withdrew his hands from behind his back and hid the drugs in his glove.

"Shit, couldn't you give it to me later, Lieutenant?" He hissed softly.

"Later, there may not be an opportunity."

"Captain Avadar, it's time to take your seats in the vehicles and put on your full armor," Figam said over the intercom. "Don't forget the breathing apparatus."

The initial phase of the mission was scientific; therefore, the doctor coordinated its course and gave orders. According to Nanawak's description, the fully paired artifacts were to merge with the use of beams of white light, having taken on all primary colors. By the time the team split into two teams, the stone cores turned from blue to purple.

Soon the light of the cores transferred to the entire artifacts, it became more intense, displacing the rest of the hangar lighting.

Aggro walked over to Anna standing near Warfighter and Figam.

"Mrs. Sandstorm, I'd like to talk to you."

"Right now?"

"Not necessarily now. A few minutes won't make a difference. And I would prefer it to be in private."

"Alright. In a moment."

The artifacts turned intensely white like miniature stars. Their increasing activity disrupted the operation of all devices in the garage, causing short circuits, overloads, fluctuations or power shortages, and finally turning them off. However, nothing unforeseen happened. The drop spacers weren't turned on, they waited until minute zero.

"Darkness and fear will take possession of everything when the gods depart, taking away from sinners the light once given to them," concluded Chimalmat poetically. Aggro walked over to her and pointed to the platform.

"They're not gods, they're people. They use Great House artifacts because that's the only way to bring Xajb'a Kej back to life. The Kiritian necromedicine has not yet reached the point of resurrecting the dead."

The Onkalotian woman was indignant.

"These people are crazy! They want to go to the Land of the Gods! Mortals are not allowed there!"

"There is no progress without risk." Aggro wondered himself that his time with the Kiritians had so influenced his views. When he had met Biffter on Chulimal seventeen years earlier and been offered cooperation, he had thought the same as Chimalmat. He had been sensitive to the supernatural, had a conservative approach to it, and considered any word that contradicted the law of the gods as sacrilege.

"Heretic!" The female cried. Aggroteh smiled.

"I like you too."

The blast came unexpectedly, like a plasma shot from the sun.

Everything looked similar to the Collector's case, but this explosion turned out to be many times stronger. The hyper-durable puronax cover shattered into hundreds of thousands of pieces as if it had been glass. The onlookers were literally blown away.

Soon the power was back, and with it the incomplete lighting: a few lamps flickered, a few didn't come on at all. The measuring equipment was smoking. Maintenance robots the size and shape of trilobites were released onto the walls to begin repairs. They were scratching, working in the garage. Part of the swarm moved to assemble the puronax shield at the atomic level.

"They killed themselves?" Alejandro Cortez was so stunned that he didn't look where he was walking and stepped on Chimalmat's paw. The female hissed at him, showing her fangs. "I'm very sorry."

Astonished Figam was speechless. He sat grotesquely on the ground, shaking his hair spiked in all directions to get rid of the impurities.

General Warfighter got up from Anna, which he had protected with his body, and helped her up. With his hand, he smeared the blood on his forehead from the wound that had been inflicted by a sliver. He looked around. No one appeared to be injured enough to require immediate medical attention. With severity on his face, he strode bravely toward the garage stairs. He kicked at the broken door, which collapsed in front of him with a crash. The crumbled scrap and shards of puronax crunched under his military boots as intrigued, he made his way toward the center.

In the place of the platform loomed a crater reaching to the bare ground.

The man stopped, leaned over, and rested his hands above his knees, scanning the damage. The onlookers grew up behind him and on his sides like chicks by a mother hen.

Figam was looking down with the general.

"What a clusterfuck," one of the achijes summed up. The solid, sizzling crater looked like after a meteorite impact, it was larger in diameter than the platform, and over twenty meters deep. The ground that mixed with the savaged foundations of the base glowed with red veins similar to lava formations. Rows of smoke rose from the bowl.

Velkee had good eyesight, but he saw no fragments of the platform, vehicles, or bodies.

"Captain Avadar," he tried to call the expedition commander through the communicator. "Captain Michael Avadar, can you hear me? General Warfighter is requesting a connection."

Nothing. Silence. Considering the time it took to respond, the attempt with neither the local link, planetary link, star system nor the sub galactic link was successful.

"Someone gets me the nuclo-indector," demanded the general. Limping from a bruised knee, Cortez brought the device a few minutes later as the blast had thrown it elsewhere.

The nucleo-visor, because such a synonym had the scanner, didn't detect any biological traces in the crater.

The general straightened up, looked at Figam.

"They disappeared. We made it." He handed him the device.

"So, we should probably be happy," said the scientist. "Incredible ..."

"If they survived, they are on their own from now on."

***

"What did he do?!"

It wasn't until two hours after the portation of Avadar's team that Q'ualel and Anna had a chance to talk. She was stopped by Warfighter who had information to tell her about Kandrok's shift, but the formal and boring conversation in Velkee's orderly room ended in a private and very pleasant one in his bedroom. Anna had to somehow work off the fact that the enemy had shifted unexpectedly to the Pisces Universe, where Atla was circling, and the Kiritians had no way of reacting to it. Velkee had been eager to help her with her stress for some time.

She stood in front of the dusty window of her office overlooking the eroded highlands as ugly as Kandrok ships. It was one of the few hidden extensions above the ground.

"What a moron!" Anna raised her voice again.

"I also think that Mr Biffter was unreasonable to decide for himself on such a serious matter."

"No, Aggro." Sandstorm, angry, turned to face him. "You are a moron. No less than Necron. Why didn't you come to me at once, but lingered? Kiret still unofficially remains our emperor!

Our commander! We need him!" She sighed loudly and slowly. She put her fist to her mouth and looked for a moment at a microfauna aquarium. Seeing the orderly, colorful ecosystem at times calmed her down more effectively than anti-stress remedies, and it worked also now. As a member of the Council of Five, she had learned to control her emotions quickly.

"Sorry. I shouldn't have yelled at you."

"It's okay. In the sense that I understand your behavior."

She glared at him accusingly.

"How could you, Aggro. I've thought you are smarter." She lowered her hand. "You guys ... ah! And that damn male solidarity of yours. And density. Regardless of species and age."

"Mr. Biffter feared an armed conflict in case a larger group of Kiritians meet with Kandrok near Atla. That is why he decided to fly alone to minimize the possible number of victims. It is his residence, he knows this planet and its surroundings very well, he trusts himself the most. Hundreds of years of experience speak for him. So, the chances of success are high."

Anna sat down in the armchair and leaned heavily on the headrest as if she had been very tired. She would have liked to run out of the room and start acting right away, but she couldn't show herself to achijes in such a state of agitation. That Anna, who had flown in love into space after the enemy emperor, and then in depression contributed to the attack of her own people, had passed.

"Now there will probably be a war anyway, Aggro."

"How is that?"

"If Biffter doesn't answer in time, his role will be taken over by General Warfighter who may declare himself the new

Emperor. Currently we don't have the right people to recreate the Council, so power will be fully in his hands as the strongest, most experienced, and one of the oldest achijes' commanders. And this is not a good time to reorganize power. Velkee is a conservative full of brutalism, a supporter of order and discipline, a bit impatient, and will probably start a war before Avadar returns from Amyrade and Figam provides our army with new technologies to fight Kandrok. As long as the team comes back at all." Sandstorm got up, headed for the door. "I'm going to the comm center. I need to find out what's going on with Jenny right now."

"You want to go to Atla?"

She stopped, turned.

"Of course. Don't make such a face, Onkalot. I won't act like General Biffter, I will think out carefully this flight and take into account every eventuality. I promise that I will do my best to avoid a fight with Kandrok until we are properly prepared. Of course, I won't fly alone, the achijes and I will disguise ourselves as best as we can. We won't allow ourselves to be caught, much less killed."

"It's unreasonable. Regardless of the safeguards, Kiritians may lose another council member."

The Council is gone, and I am only the captain. Anyway, this position was given to me more due to representation, so that after leaving the opposition, I am associated with the Immortals. There are many Kiritians higher in rank and wiser than me who can support Warfighter." Anna's official tone turned into mild words: "Go to Chimalmat, Aggro. She definitely feels lost in our twisted reality."

After she left, worried Aggro looked for a long time at *Turritopsis nutricula* swimming in the aquarium.

Epilogue

Kiret

"I've never been good at speaking. I preferred to stand in the shadows at the emperor's right hand and listen to his voice, offering advice or an armed arm fully suited me. This arrangement was fine for me. I had no aspirations for power, but being close to Forkis, I was aware that someday I might have to replace him. He believed that as the oldest Kiritian I had a wealth of experience, always being close to matters of the utmost importance. In the end, what I feared happened - I took over from him. And believe me, taking such a monstrously heavy rudder as a succession was the last thing I wanted. I think Warfighter would be a better choice for First Galactic Dignitary, but maybe Forkis had reason not to trust him. He knew people better than I did, and he didn't share many of his secrets.

My laconic nature has not changed, I have always liked specifics. And I was hopeless at keeping a diary, although Anna repeatedly encouraged me to do so. But I don't know why, considering I'm neither an outstanding individual nor a short-lived mortal whose biography can be encompassed.

Therefore, it will be short and specific.

I should focus on events in which Jenny and I participated, but there will be time for everything. Therefore, I will briefly talk about the Earth and my thoughts. Why about it? Because I know you have wondered more than once in the course of this story about what is happening to this planet.

I have betrayed the Earth. This is how I perceive it and I feel terrible about it. Especially now that Kandrok drove me there, one might say. As if fate made me remember a past buried somewhere in the back of my mind. Was it a coincidence? Despite hundreds of years of life and being the Eldest, I will never understand it: Do events happen randomly and there are coincidences, or maybe things that happen to us are influenced by certain forces that assign a specific person to a specific event? Probably one of Nimja members would know how it is with fate. It doesn't matter anyway. I warned there would be gibberish.

I was born and raised in France at a time when the global government was at the height of power and forcibly recruited into the New Order Army healthy young men from ... the European Union? Republic? Confederation? I don't remember anymore. The boundaries of the world and the names of alliances changed like Jenny's moods, so political dementia is no shame for the Immortal who lives hundreds of light years from Earth. Oderses can't be stable, they constantly need these damned, drastic changes. A Kiritian won't understand it. Forkis skillfully separated different individuals from the Earth's population, like errors in the capripod code, creating a nation whose domain was stability.

Meanwhile, human impermanence crippled the planet. Someone always wanted to change something, another person didn't agree to it. More world wars broke out. The third was religious, primitive and inhuman, worthy of medieval ignorance, not of the time Mars was colonized. During the fourth, 1.5 billion people were blown away in a few moments because global nuclear weapon was in motion. More inhabitants died of radiation sickness, but already before the attack, many had flown away to the terraformed planets. The overcrowded Earth caught its breath. World War 5, I don't know why it broke out. I'm already lost in this. I have always wanted to stay away from this filth, to lead a quiet, apolitical life with my wife and children, but the totalitarian global government decided my future for me. I was separated from my family and forced to fight. Thanks to this course of events, for the first time in my life I got angry and rebelled, and in the end, I deserted the army. My fate was intertwined with that of Forkis, but I didn't regain what I had lost. I didn't find my family in the ruins of my hometown and blamed myself for the loss of it. I didn't accept the excuse that it was because of the system that had forcibly pulled me out of my boring but peaceful life. A real man doesn't look for excuses and scapegoats, or at least that's what I think. This is how I had been brought up. Not knowing what to do with myself, I focused completely on Forkis and his serious long-term plans. Figam created the super virus, Forkis created Kiritians. As an Immortal, I left Earth. Over the centuries, I visited it several times for military and economic purposes.

Each visit was short. I felt like a traitor. First, I had left my family, then I left the planet.

And centuries later, I destroyed Forkis' work. I should have never risen to power.

What happened to Earth after my departure - I have no idea. But I knew it had been relieved, which it fully deserved. The air is now clean, the moistened soil looks fertile, the vegetation is regaining the lost lands, and the animals freely roam the land. The glacier that had covered half the planet in the years 2615–2890 retreated.

Now, as I kneel at the famous Freedom Monument, once surrounded by flowers, candles, streets and buildings of the glass-chrome city, I see that the globe evidently caught its breath after the civilization plague that had devoured it for centuries. Sounds scary, but it was enough just to reduce the population of *Homo sapiens*. Nobody cares about the monument anymore, people disappeared along with the cities, and everything will have to be started anew. The most important thing is that events don't turn out the old way. Because although people love change, they also love to make the same mistakes, having self-destruction and aggression written in their genes.

I'll try to catch up and find out what happened in France, where Jenny and I crashed, and in the world in general. I'm taking her and we're setting off on a journey into the unknown."

Acknowledgments

For Marcin Majchrzak for thorough editing, valuable tips and long, helpful talks on physics and astronomy. Ella Raj and Camille Gale for language corrections. Marcin Halski for many motivating conversations, always cheerful :), help with the creation of the poems published at the beginning of the novel and the exchange of promotional and publishing experiences.

Dorota Bożena Foryś for sharing information about advertising, as well as her wonderful, very positive approach to the authors.

Also the supporters from the Polak Potrafi website, who backed my first crowdfunding project, set up to raise funds for the second proofreading of this novel:

Anita Zaustowicz
Camille Gale
Ella Raj
Marcin Halski
Mateusz Osojca

The full list of supporters is available on the Zodiac Universum fanpage (post from February 21, 2021, 1:03 PM).

www.ingramcontent.com/pod-product-compliance
Lightning Source LLC
Chambersburg PA
CBHW031019030726
47497CB00004B/919